# THE OLD CROCODILE MAN THEORY

A Novel of Murder,
Mystery and
Monkey Business

## PHILIP HUNSICKER

Layout and Design by Chip & Jean Borkenhagen
River Place Press, Aitkin, MN


ISBN: 978-1-7347600-6-4


Published by

40274 Diamond Lake Street
Aitkin, MN 56431
218.851.4843
www.riverplacepress.com
chip@riverplacepress.com


philiphunsicker.com

This is a work of fiction. The places are real, but the characters, organizations, and events portrayed in this novel are either products of the author's imagination or are used fictitiously.

This project was made possible by a grant provided by the Five Wings Arts Council with funds from the McKnight Foundation.

FIVE WINGS
ARTS COUNCIL

# Dedication

One might assume, and rightly so, that writers of fiction have fertile imaginations. I like to think I do, but I can't imagine any scenario where this novel would have happened without the support—literally and figuratively—of my wife, Denise.

While I traveled in my mind to exotic faraway lands, she fought rush hour traffic twice a day. While I wrestled with made-up characters that ultimately did what I told them to do, she sat through interminable work meetings with real people who didn't do what she wanted simply because she said so. When I complained that I was having trouble coming up with believable dialogue, she would say, "You wouldn't believe the conversation I had at work today," and then she'd proceed to tell me about it.

Denise is the real hero of this story, and for that, *The Old Crocodile Man Theory* is dedicated to her. Mark Twain wrote, "To get the full value of joy, you must have someone to divide it with." Denise, you are my someone.

## Buy a Book. Change a Life.

By purchasing a copy of this book, and without doing anything more, you have done something good. For every copy sold, a contribution will be made to help the people of the Central African Republic (C.A.R.), a place that has been described as one of the poorest nations in the world. It is also the setting for my story. Two organizations will benefit. The first is Water for Good (www.waterforgood.org), which is an American nonprofit that drills and maintains water wells throughout the C.A.R. to provide whole villages with something most Americans take for granted—clean drinking water. The second organization with which I'd like to share my profits is the World Wildlife Fund (www.worldwildlife.org), an international conservation organization that established a park and reserve in the southwestern corner of the C.A.R. to protect forest wildlife like elephants, gorillas, bongo, and chimpanzees.

So buy a novel, have a good read, learn about a place you've probably never heard of and will probably never visit, and at the same time, help the people who inspired the story.

"Ay, Sir; to be honest, as the world goes, is to be one man picked out of ten thousand."

—William Shakespeare
Hamlet


"Cruelty has a human heart,
And jealousy a human face—
Terror, the human form divine,
And secrecy, the human dress."

—William Blake
A Divine Image

**In the year 1990...**

Nelson Mandela was freed after 27 years in a South African prison.

Exxon Valdez Captain Joseph Hazelwood went on trial for the worst oil spill in U.S. history.

The Simpsons premiered on Fox Television.

The Who and Simon and Garfunkel were inducted into Cleveland's Rock and Roll Hall of Fame.

The Polish Communist Party dissolved, and Lech Walesa was later sworn in as the country's first popularly elected president.

McDonald's opened its first fast-food restaurant in Moscow.

Washington, D.C. Mayor Marion Barry was arrested by the FBI in a drug enforcement sting.

East and West Germany merged to become one united Germany.

The Edmonton Oilers defeated the Boston Bruins four games to one to win the Stanley Cup.

18-year-old hemophiliac Ryan White died of AIDS.

A Chorus Line closed on Broadway after 6,137 performances over 15 years.

The Seinfeld Chronicles—later to be called Seinfeld—debuted on NBC-TV.

Iraq invaded and occupied Kuwait, which led to Operation Desert Storm.

The Hubble Telescope was launched into space.

**And in one of many far-off corners of the Earth, a life was snuffed out way too early, someone saw nothing wrong with that, and someone else decided to do something about it. And that is both the beginning and the end of a story.**

# 1

Despite the tropical heat and humidity, Bolo froze. Sweat ran down his forehead. A single bead continued along to the tip of his nose where it clung to keep from plummeting to the ground. He didn't dare move to wipe it away. Tiny insects buzzed around his eyes, mouth and ears. He ignored them. A pair of ants crawled up his right leg, and as if communicating by telepathy, they bit him at the same instant. He instinctively wanted to obliterate them, but he forced himself to remain still and silent. The muscles and tendons in his right arm strained to hold the long-barreled rifle motionless. He was tempted to ease his discomfort by resting the gun on his hip, but any noise, even the whisper of blue steel brushing up against his shorts, would be disastrous.

He eased his left foot down to the ground, carefully planting it on a soft patch of dirt so as not to make a sound. He sniffed the humid air with his wide nostrils trying to detect any odors in the faint breeze. His eyes darted about, but his head remained immobile. He heard something: a snap of branches off to his right.

It was Vinny. It had to be. Bolo had seen his tracks along the stream bank about a half-mile back. He was headed for the clearing. Bolo needed to catch him before he got that far. The kill had to be made while they were still in the cover of the trees. That way, the body might never be discovered.

Bolo knew these jungle trails well. He had traveled them thousands of times, and often at night when eyes merely took up space in their sockets. Even now, at high noon, he couldn't see much through the thick vegetation. He had to keep his other senses focused on where he had heard the sounds. His life depended on knowing exactly where his adversary was. This wasn't a game.

Bolo stepped off the trail. He climbed over rotting logs and ducked under thick vines. Muscular and built low to the ground, Bolo was designed to move efficiently through this tangle of plant life. He seemed to gain strength from the humidity. Adrenaline coursed through his veins with the realization that he was close...very close.

Out of the corner of his eye, Bolo saw a flash of movement. Vinny was only fifteen feet away, but almost totally hidden behind a massive buttress root. He stepped out from behind the tree and his eyes immediately locked onto Bolo's. Bolo quickly brought the gun to his shoulder and fired. An ear-splitting crack reverberated through the forest. Vinny fell, the earth shook, and the temporary high Bolo felt reminded him once again just how much he liked killing elephants.

# 2

Like all bored students and unfulfilled office workers, Kael Husker stared out a window. Outside was one of those rare colorful mornings in Southeast Alaska when the resident gray rain clouds were vacationing hundreds of miles off the coast and dumping their contents into the Gulf of Alaska instead of into Kael's rubber boots. Chatham Strait, which usually displayed white caps and anger, was now ripple-free, and its blue-green color looked more Caribbean than Alaskan. The sky above was a brilliant blue. Except for a light dusting of snow on the mountain peaks, Kael thought this was what it must be like looking out an office window in Barbados. He couldn't remember a prettier morning in his nine-plus years at the Hidden Cove Salmon Hatchery.

Hidden Cove was located on the remote rocky shore of Baranof Island, one of the thousands of emerald-colored islands hanging on precariously to the lower right-hand corner of an Alaska map. This thin ribbon of land was a gathering of fjords, glaciers, coastal mountains, and conifers. Geography books referred to it as "Alaska's Panhandle." Those who lived there called it "Southeast." Kael called it home.

Road was a four-letter word to most Southeast Alaskans, so the only way to get to Hidden Cove was by boat or floatplane. This inconvenience kept away most of the peccadilloes of civilization. There were no cars, no traffic lights, no rush hour, no fast-food restaurants, no trendy shops, no health clubs. There was only the hatchery. Hidden Cove's nearest neighbors were a colony of belching Steller sea lions living on the exposed rocks in Takatz Bay, about ten miles to the south. They never once stopped by to borrow anything.

A mail plane came in once a week from Sitka, the closest town with a grocery store, a post office, and a plane. The floatplane brought groceries, mail, and a week's collection of newspapers.

The Hidden Cove Hatchery sounded like a turn-of-the-century prison to many, but that was exactly what had attracted Kael. He had come there to escape real-world responsibilities. He shared his self-imposed isolation with three other bachelors, two dogs, and millions of finger-sized salmon.

Kael's co-workers at Hidden Cove—C.B., Sam, and Hector—were an eccentric bunch, but that was the norm in Alaska, rather than the exception. The state seemed to attract the folks who couldn't quite fit in down in the lower forty-eight. Alaska was a haven for the loose screws, the square pegs, the left fielders, the odd ducks, the misfits. Kael theorized that he fit into at least four of those categories.

All four of Hidden Cove's nonconformists were gathered together in Sam's office that morning, just as they were at the start of every other workday. The office was proof that no women worked there. A couple of cheap metal desks cluttered with piles of paper, a few uncomfortable chairs, a dented file cabinet, and nothing hanging on the walls but a dartboard.

Sam didn't seem to be in any hurry to dole out the daily work assignments, so everyone passed the time in their own peculiar way. C.B. fine-tuned his own personals ad that started with "STM (single, tanned male) seeks SBF (single breathing female) for intelligent conversation and stupid jokes." Hector sipped one of his twenty daily cups of coffee while looking as if he hadn't been able to sleep because of yesterday's twenty cups. Kael went back to staring out the window that had given him such a brilliant view of the morning sunlight shimmering on Chatham Strait.

This time, he spied a pair of bald eagles weaving in the wind. They soared, rising and falling with just a slight repositioning of their fully extended wings. They played leapfrog and follow-the-leader, and like children who have grown bored with a game, they abruptly split apart with one heading north and the other south.

While watching the eagles, he mindlessly stroked the hair on his face. Like most Alaskan males over the age of fourteen, he sported a beard. It wasn't because it was stylish or macho. It was more for its convenience and practicality. He hated shaving, and the thick bush of blond, brown, and red hair provided an almost impenetrable barrier between his face and Alaska's third most-despised critter: the mosquito. Unfortunately, the beard did nothing to keep away Alaska's two most bothersome pests: immigrating loud-mouthed Texans who came north to make their fortunes in oil and mining and then repaid their Alaskan hosts by bragging that everything was bigger and better in Texas, and tourists who shuffled off their cruise ships wearing fashionable, overpriced, and impractical outdoor clothing and then asked locals stupid questions like, "Way up here in Sitka, how far above sea level are we?"

A squeal of metal rubbing against metal diverted Kael's attention away from the out-of-doors where he'd have preferred to be. He looked dejectedly back into the room. The source of the noise was a desk chair belonging to his boss, Sam, who was attempting to shift his two hundred and sixty pounds to a more comfortable position. The chair was in obvious agony.

To no one in particular, Sam spoke over the chair's tortured wails. "Why is it that my chair is the only one in this office that squeaks?"

C.B. looked up from his task and said, "Let me put it this way, boss. Elvis' chair made those exact same noises later in his career."

At one hundred and thirty-five pounds, C.B. weighed about as much as one of Elvis' sideburns. He went back to fine-tuning his personals ad.

Kael, meanwhile, had his own way of passing time: He loved devising theories to explain life's little riddles, at least in his own mind. That morning, he'd come up with a doozy. As someone who was considered short by American society's standards, he was developing a theory on height. It simply stated that every man was as tall as the next when each one placed his penis on his head. This one had promise. Sam, who was well over six feet tall, might think differently.

Kael stored that one away for further study and picked up a week-old issue of the *Sitka Daily Sentinel* sitting on the windowsill. It had come out on the last mail flight along with five other back issues. The whole paper was only twelve pages long, but it could stimulate enough new theories in Kael's fertile brain to fill volumes.

He flipped through hoping to find the Police Blotter, a listing of local hooligans who had been apprehended for offenses ranging from domestic violence to dog leash violations. He knew most of the repeat offenders. It was hard not to in a small Alaskan coastal town where few were strangers and spreading gossip was almost as popular as fishing.

Where the Police Blotter should have been, Kael found one of those innocuous filler articles, eleven lines whose sole purpose was to take up white space on the page. Usually they were about the woman in Des Moines who finds a seven-foot boa constrictor in her toilet or the seven year old from Poughkeepsie who drives his family station wagon twelve blocks without hitting anything. This one, however, grabbed Kael's eyes like a bloody roadside accident scene.

## CROCODILE MAN KILLS AMERICAN RESEARCHER
### Associated Press—Bangui, Central African Republic

The body of Molly McGinley, an anthropological researcher from Minneapolis, Minnesota, was found in the Sangha River in the Central African Republic on September 13, three days after she disappeared. Although officials of the American embassy in Bangui ruled the death an accidental drowning, Central African authorities in the town of Bayanga arrested a local man who was accused of being a crocodile man, an individual who commits murder by changing into a crocodile. An embassy spokesman called the charges "unsubstantiated." Ms. McGinley, a PhD student from the University of Minnesota, was studying Pygmy music in the Central African rain forest.

Kael's stomach lurched. He could feel his breakfast of coffee and leftover frozen pizza rising up through his esophagus. He swallowed to stem the tide. It worked, but the foul taste left in his mouth told him that it had been a close call.

He'd expected to see some familiar names in the paper, but not Molly's. The most beautiful morning he'd seen in nine years didn't seem so beautiful anymore.

Ten years earlier they had been fellow Peace Corps volunteers in the same little village in the Central African Republic. Kael had already been there a year when Molly showed up in her tie-dyed t-shirt and Birkenstock sandals—full of energy, enthusiasm, and naivety about saving the world, or at least the little corner she occupied. Kael introduced her around the village and taught her who to trust and who to stay away from. He listed himself in the latter category, but they had become close friends anyway. Unfortunately, like most male-female relationships, it had ended badly. Kael didn't want to point fingers because he knew he'd have to point at himself.

He thought about their one and only night together in the same bed. It had been raining. They had both drunk and smoked more than a heavy metal band. When they'd awakened in the morning wearing only monster headaches, neither one could remember much about the encounter though both agreed that it had probably been fantastic. It had been awkward, but after discussing it over strong coffee and aspirin like mature adults, they decided to forget about the entire incident. Kael had had absolutely no recollection of the night's events, so erasing them from his memory had been one of the easiest tasks he'd had to perform while in Africa. He'd secretly hoped there would be a second time and maybe a third and a fourth—and he'd remember those encounters—but they never happened.

They'd remained just friends right up until their final days with Peace Corps, but what had started out as a difference of opinion, somehow degenerated into ten years of silence, at least on Kael's part. He received the occasional letter from her, but he never once responded. He didn't want to be found, and Hidden Cove, as its name suggested, was a pretty good hiding place.

Kael realized that he wouldn't be receiving any more letters. Dead people wrote even less than he did. And according to the article staring up at him, she was definitely dead. Another accidental drowning or another victim of a crocodile man, depending on one's point of view. In Central Africa accidents didn't just happen. There was always a reason, which usually included black magic and sorcery. Suspected sorcerers were almost as plentiful as the country's humidity and mosquitoes. No one died of malaria or AIDS in the Central African Republic. They died because they had wronged someone who then used the spirit world to achieve retribution.

Central African prisons were stuffed with petty thieves, diamond smugglers, revolution plotters, and innocents who had the misfortune of arguing with someone whose number would soon be up. A family member or neighbor would remember the argument, point a finger, and the suspect would be accused of sorcery and thrown into jail. Justice in Africa was both swift and blind in every perverted sense of the ideal. Molly would be aghast if she knew that some guiltless Central African was now doing hard time because she couldn't swim.

Kael was temporarily pulled away from his thoughts of Molly when he heard Sam throwing darts at the dartboard on the wall above his desk. A passport-sized photo of Sam's ex-wife looked out from the bulls-eye of the dartboard. A dart was sticking out of her forehead.

Sam growled, "And you said I couldn't do anything right."

C.B. looked up from his chore and said, "Hey guys, do you think I'm slightly less rugged than Bruce Willis in *Die Hard*, or slightly cuter than Julia Roberts in *Pretty Woman*?"

Hector, who uttered fewer words before noon than a hibernating bear, stopped sipping his coffee and said, "Slightly less rugged than Julia Roberts... definitely."

Everyone smiled, including C.B.

Sam turned his chair around to face his employees rather than his ex-wife. His chair screamed at being forced to move. He said, "I know you guys have heard the rumor that some corporation wants to purchase Hidden Cove. I talked to headquarters in Juneau and an offer has been made. With the state trying to cut its budget, it wants to get out of the hatchery business and they've found a buyer. It's a group called the Northern Aquaculture Project or NAP. They already own one hatchery in Juneau and one in Sitka and neither one has been producing. They have a mountain of bills and since they're a private non-profit organization and can harvest fish to pay their operating costs, they could conceivably use Hidden Cove salmon to help pay off all their current debts."

The room was speechless. Sudden unemployment can do that.

C.B. broke the silence by saying, "I didn't think it was possible, but this sucks and blows at the same time."

Kael, thinking more of Molly than his own impending layoff, couldn't have agreed more. Life sometimes sucked and blew at the same time, and if anyone needed evidence of that fact, it was right there in black and white on page nine of the *Sitka Daily Sentinel*.

Sam said, "We can talk more about this later. For now, we're still employed and we've got work to do. Let's get that spawning area cleaned up."

Kael got up from his chair thinking that a lot more than the spawning area needed to be cleaned up. He tore the article about Molly from the paper, folded it up, and stuck it in the back pocket of his jeans. Later, when he had a few free minutes, he'd call the one person who might be able to give him more details about Molly's death and the old crocodile man theory.

3

Bolo stood over the lifeless body. If not for the wide-open eyes, one might think he was just napping on a bright red blanket under the shade of a tree. The blanket, however, was a large, expanding pool of blood that almost completely encircled the body. Bolo had never seen so much blood. Could all that have come out of just one body? One of the bullets must have hit a major artery. He had probably bled to death even before he hit the ground.

It had been a perfect ambush. His victim had never suspected a thing. Bolo's sources had told him about this spot. They had also told him that the victim's name was Pablo. Bolo didn't always know their names. It wasn't necessary.

It was time for the mutilation. This was the part that Bolo enjoyed the most. He loved the feel of warm blood splashing on his hands and how the haft of his blade stuck to his palm as Pablo's blood cooled and dried. Bolo's skilled, sticky hands moved like an artist—not one who creates, but one who destroys. He'd done this so many times, it didn't take long. He was a professional after all.

Bolo took the victim's valuables and set them off to the side. They were small, but admirable nonetheless. Their worth wasn't as considerable as others he'd taken throughout the years, but the color was magnificent and would demand a decent price from any buyer.

Bolo couldn't stay to admire his handiwork. He had to get moving. Someone may have heard the shots. He gathered up his bounty and headed down the same path that only minutes earlier had led Pablo into his gun sights.

# 4

Unlike orange juice, Kael couldn't concentrate. Thoughts of Molly and unemployment squatted in his brain. And for some strange reason, he kept remembering two quotes. The first was one made famous by Yogi Berra: "If you come to a fork in the road, take it." The second was an old Arab proverb he'd read that went, "If the water in a pool is still, it becomes stagnant and muddy; if it stirs and flows, it becomes clean again; likewise a man on his voyage." He wondered if NAP's takeover of Hidden Cove was his fork in the road. He also wondered if it was too late to clean up the muddy waters that had silenced two friends for ten years.

While everyone else gathered in the break room for their union-decreed, fifteen-minute, mid-day coffee break, Kael returned to Sam's now vacant office to use Hidden Cove's most recent technological marvel: the telephone. It was a modern satellite system that had only been installed the week before. It was more convenient and more private than the old procedure of going through the marine operator on the single-side-band radio, but to Kael, it was just one more sign that his perfect hiding place wasn't perfect anymore.

He sat at Sam's desk and punched in the long-distance number. After a couple of rings, he heard a voice at the other end say, "Nick Cinzano. Central African Projects."

Kael didn't identify himself. He simply said, "Have you heard this one?"

It was a tradition, mutually agreed upon by Kael and Nick that each new conversation started with an exchange of jokes. It always got both parties in the proper mood.

"Go ahead," said Nick. "Try and make me laugh."

"This macho Texan was having problems in bed, but he was too embarrassed to go see his doctor, so his concerned wife went in his place. The doctor told the wife to have her husband give him a urine sample, a stool sample and a semen sample. When she got home from the doctor's visit, her husband asked, 'Well, what did that quack of a doctor say?' The wife responded, 'He wants to see a pair of your underwear.'"

When Nick finished laughing, he said, "That one was almost as funny as the Republican plan for environmental protection that was announced last week."

"Do you have anything funnier?" asked Kael.

"Of course, and I'll even stick with the Texan theme since I know that brings you great joy. There's this Texan who wants to hunt grizzly bear in Alaska, so he goes to his local sporting goods store to pick out a gun. The Texan tells the man behind the counter that he is going to Alaska to hunt grizzly bear and he wants one of those .44 magnum handguns that Dirty Harry uses in the movies. The salesman informs the Texan that they have a wide selection of .44 handguns to choose from and he would recommend that the Texan file down the front sight right down to the barrel. The Texan asks why and the salesman replies, 'So when the bear shoves that thing up your ass it won't hurt as much.'"

Kael roared. Like most Alaskans, he loved jokes about Texans—telling them and hearing them. Texans were always bragging about how big their state was, so Alaskans would say that if Texans didn't shut their big mouths, Alaska would divide itself in two and make Texas the third largest state. Kael once theorized that if geographers started measuring land masses at low tide, Alaska would then be three times the size of Texas. He even wrote to the American Geographer's Society suggesting this new procedure, but he never heard back. A Texan probably ran the bureau.

Kael regained his composure and said, "Thanks. I really needed that."

"You already heard about Molly, didn't you?"

Kael suddenly got a taste of coffee and pizza for the third time that morning. "I just happened to be glancing through an old newspaper this morning and tripped over an article that read like something right out of *The National Enquirer*."

"I would have contacted you, but you're not the easiest guy to get a hold of."

"What happened?" asked Kael.

"Seems that she was going down river to record some Pygmy music and her dugout canoe overturned. Of course the Central African officials blamed it on a crocodile man. It happened in the reserve I started, so I've been trying to help Molly's folks deal with the Central African bureaucracy. It's been a nightmare. We only got the body back to the states a few days ago."

"I didn't even realize that she was back in Africa."

"She'd only been there a couple of months," said Nick.

Kael wanted to know if Molly had ever asked about him, but that would have sounded selfish. "How did she seem?" was a more acceptable question.

"She hadn't changed one bit from Peace Corps. She still dressed like a deadhead, but she was a consummate professional when it came to her research. She had all sorts of grant money, and in the short time she was there, she made some amazing recordings. I've got a box of her cassettes here in my office. They came back with all of her personal items. I've been meaning to listen to them, but just can't find the time. I should send them to her parents in Minneapolis. Maybe they'd find some comfort in them."

Kael said, "I'm feeling bad about never responding to any of her letters." He didn't elaborate. Nick knew all about it. The three of them had been Peace Corps volunteers together, and Nick was one of the few people Kael had kept in touch with over the years. Kael changed the subject, anyway. "How are the wife and kids?"

"The kids are happy and healthy, but I'm looking for a doctor for Darcy. I want him to tell her that using credit cards can cause cancer. The other day she spent over $2,000 on a wicker couch, and it isn't even all that comfortable. She doesn't quite understand that we conservationists are paid only slightly better than paperboys. She thinks I should sell out and start selling insurance for her father's company up in Connecticut."

"You'd be perfect," said Kael, who waited a full second before adding, "...ly miserable." He knew that Nick wouldn't last a week at a job like that.

Nick had always wanted to be a wildlife biologist, so around the time Kael had run off to hide at Hidden Cove, Nick had enrolled in a doctoral program at Yale. After completing his course work and pioneering field research on the western lowland gorillas of the Central African Republic, he was promptly scooped up by one of the oldest and most distinguished acronyms in Washington, D.C.: TRAP, or the Theodore Roosevelt Alliance for Preservation. Started by Teddy Roosevelt and some of his hunting cronies back in 1913, it had grown to become one of the most successful environmental organizations in the world. Among its enemies, and there were many, TRAP was often referred to as "Those Ridiculous Asshole Protectionists." Kael knew that Nick frequently traveled to Central Africa for his job. That was why Kael had called him. He seemed to be the logical one to contact about Molly's death. The illogical one would have been the crocodile man himself.

Nick asked, "How's Alaska treating you these days?"

"Harshly, but that's why we love living here. Every day's a challenge. Today was especially difficult. Just after reading about Molly, I found out the hatchery is being sold and I'm about to be laid off. If they'd left out the 'off' part, my day would have been much better."

There was a long pause until Nick said, "I just got a brilliant idea that exceeds even my abnormally high standards. We're looking for a new director in Central Africa. You speak the local language and you already know how to get things done over there. Plus, it's another place in which you can be treated harshly, and apparently, that brings you as much joy as jokes about Texans. Are you interested?"

"Are you serious?"

"I try not to be, but sometimes I can't help it. Do you remember Mitchell Wright?"

"Sure. He came in with Peace Corps just before I left. As wide as he was tall and the only thing bigger than his barrel chest was his ego."

"That's him. He did, and still does have an attitude. But he's also a very competent scientist. He's been back in the C.A.R. directing the Doli-Ngili Reserve. We're trying to start similar reserves in the neighboring countries since wildlife frequently crosses international borders. Mitchell is moving down to the Congo to scratch a few backs and rally some support."

"I can't believe you're using Mitchell Wright as your front man. He's about as diplomatic as a pit bull."

"Yeah, but he's a tenacious son-of-a-bitch. Do you know what the difference is between a pit bull and a poodle?"

"What?"

"If a pit bull is humping your leg, you let him finish."

"That was good, Nick. You should have saved it for our next phone call. What kind of person do you need to take Mitchell's place in the C.A.R., a pit bull or a poodle?"

"Actually, we need a pussycat, and I think you'd be perfect. You haven't used up all nine of your lives, have you?"

"No, I've still got three or four left." Kael wondered if Molly had also thought that she had some lives left to play with. "I'll need to ponder this for a while. How quickly do you need someone?"

"We'd like to have somebody in-country in one month. I could give you a couple of days to think it over, but not much more than that."

"Is one month realistic? We're talking shots and visas, and don't forget that I no longer live out of a backpack. I've got a thirty-six foot boat, a dog, winter clothes and a set of matching plates."

"Sell it. Give it away. Put them in storage. Donate them to your favorite charity. Problem solved."

Kael thought about those two quotes again. Taking a fork in the road and flowing to clean up muddy waters. "I admit that I'm tempted, but I'll need those couple of days to think it over, OK?"

"Sure. In the meantime, I'll send you some background information on the project along with a standard TRAP contract that needs only your John Hancock. Have you got a FAX there?"

"No, but we have one in our Sitka office." Kael rattled off the FAX number. "If you send the stuff today, it'll come out tomorrow on the mail flight. I'll let you know by Friday, OK?"

"That sounds good. Take the job, Kael. We could do some amazing things together. Make sure you have a good joke for me on Friday. Talk to you then."

Kael was about to ask if he needed to send an updated resume when he heard the click of a disconnected phone from the other end.

# 5

A slight breeze blew off the river and fanned Bolo's campfire. The flames danced and beckoned. Bolo moved closer to the warmth. Holding the machete up to the flickering light, he tested its edge with his thumb.

He resumed the sharpening process by running the blade over the stone. One hundred times on each side would give it a paper thin edge that could slice through bone. After every few strokes, he paused to re-examine his work and to take a puff from his cigarette. The harsh tobacco burned his throat. He sucked the hand-rolled cigarette down to ash. There were never any butts left. Bolo was a man who took as much as he could get. He lit another.

From across the river came the death-like screams of a tree hyrax marking his territory. The cries grew in intensity. Each one was louder and more horrific than the preceding one. Abruptly, they stopped and the dominant sound of the night became the croaking chorus of a thousand male frogs advertising their presence, not only to potential mates, but also to rival suitors.

The forest at night produced layers of noise. Some were more obvious than others. It took a bit of concentration to pick up the medley of sounds hidden underneath the stentorian calls of the hyrax and frog: a mosquito's buzz; a bat's sonar blip; a large bird's beating wings; and a river gurgling and slapping against the side of a canoe. Bolo's ears picked up every nuance. He could just make out the sound of a tortoise pushing through the dry leaf litter right outside his make-shift camp. Even though tortoise was one of Bolo's favorite meals, he ignored his hunger pangs and continued to hone his blade. He went through three more cigarettes before he was content with the machete's edge. He carefully sheathed it and picked up his rifle, which he wiped meticulously clean with an oily rag. After forty-five minutes of caressing his weapon, he was finally satisfied. He wrapped it in large, broad leaves for protection.

He looked up at the almost-full moon shimmering in a cloudless sky. It was a perfect night for a trip on the river.

He kicked some sand into the fire, which not only smothered the flames, but also consumed the smoke. Within seconds, his arms, legs and torso were covered with mosquitoes. He hardly noticed. He gathered up his machete and gun and slung them over his bare back. He finished up the last few puffs of his cigarette. He was ready. He moved down toward the black river.

He pushed the eighteen-foot dugout canoe away from the sandy bank and into the edge of the current. He stood up in the bow holding a pole as long as the canoe. He stabbed the water with the pole, pushing it deeper until it found the bottom. Putting his weight into the pole, he adroitly made his way to the stern. The canoe sliced forward. He carried the pole back to the bow where he again punctured the water and started the process once more. Poling was much more efficient than paddling, especially when trying to go upstream against the swift, muddy current.

He followed the jagged stream bank, staying in the shallower, calmer water and hiding in the shadows of the trees. He didn't need any night fishermen asking questions. By the time he reached his destination many hours later, the muscles in his shoulders and legs would burn. Even though he was traveling by water, he would hike many miles that evening as he paced from bow to stern and back again with his pole. The trip downstream had been well worth the extra effort, though. He had been paid well for his love of killing.

Kael and C.B. sat on *The Sourdough*'s aft deck sipping their beers and staring at their respective rod tips in an attempt to will them to move. They stubbornly refused.

Kael's golden retriever, Cheechako the Wonder Dog, was asleep in the wheelhouse. She didn't appreciate the fine art of fishing like Kael and C.B. This was probably because she'd once had her nose pierced by one of Kael's treble hooks. It was an unpleasant experience for an animal whose nose is its most important sensory organ. Now, when she spied a fishing rod, she sought a safe haven out of casting distance. Kael liked to brag that Chako would be a great protector on the streets of New York so long as no one attacked him with a fishing rod.

The two fishermen had only wet their lines twelve short minutes earlier, but it seemed an eternity. In the bountiful Alaskan waters, strikes usually occurred within seven to nine minutes. Alaskans were very impatient with their fish. One of the many benefits of being an Alaskan was the knowledge that it never took more than ten minutes for a fish to bite.

C.B. took out his pocket-sized tide table that listed the daily high and low tides. Because Southeasterners' lives revolved around the ocean, they never went anywhere without a tide table in at least one of their pockets.

C.B. studied the page for September. "Yep, just as I suspected. It's a small-dot day."

"Should have known," said Kael.

C.B. was referring to a theory devised by the folks who printed up the tide tables. They attempted to predict daily fishing success according to the phases of the moon. The bigger the dot, the better the fishing for that particular day. There was some scientific validity in that the moon's phases did affect the tides, but that was where the astronomy ended and the astrology began. Kael, C.B. and thousands of other Alaskan fishermen had often filled their freezers with salmon, rockfish and halibut on days when the corresponding dot was no bigger than an amoeba.

It was another gorgeous day in Southeast. The high-pressure systems just kept coming. It had been three whole days since the last substantial rainstorm and Southeasterners were starting to worry that if this trend continued much longer, they might lose their evolutionary advantage: a waxy outer layer of skin that repelled rain like a turtle's shell covered with Lemon Pledge. Kael checked the skin on his arm. It didn't feel as slippery and it actually looked tan. He poured a little beer on his forearm to see if it still beaded up and ran off. It did, so he was satisfied that he hadn't yet dropped a rung on the evolutionary ladder.

He glanced over at the depth sounder. It was still flashing at eighteen fathoms, which was right where they wanted to be. There was an eighteen-fathom hole off Point Lull that produced halibut the size of Cadillacs.

Pacific halibut, *Hippoglossus stenolepis*, were flat, flounder-like fish. They hovered above the ocean bottom gobbling up anything in their path. Today, however, they were ignoring Kael's and C.B.'s attractive jigs. Since nothing was happening below the water, Kael felt the time was right for a conversation. He jumped right into the silence. "I got a job offer."

"Who in their right mind would be foolish enough to hire you?"

"You'd be surprised."

"Are they foolish enough to hire me, too?"

"I doubt it. They want me to go back to Africa."

"Why on Earth would you want to go back to Africa?"

Kael finished the last gulp of his beer and replied, "It's hard to explain. It gets in your blood."

"Yeah, it's called malaria."

"Very funny. Pass me another beer."

C.B. opened up the cooler and pulled out two more cans. He handed one to Kael who said, "I think it's time we got serious about our fishing."

Both men shook their cans, leaned over *The Sourdough*'s gunwales, held their now explosive beers at sea level, and popped the tabs. The combined sound of escaping carbonation was almost deafening. Chako must have thought they were gunshots because she moved farther forward on the boat, burrowing herself deep in the forecastle. To her, guns were almost as dangerous as fishing rods.

Kael said, "There's another reason why I need to go back to Africa. It's sort of a secret."

"Let me guess... you're really an African Princess who's been living in exile here in the Big A. Your loyal followers have staged a bloody coup and have reclaimed the government of your impoverished nation. You are now free to return to the throne to rule with your handsome Prince who has been freed from his prison cell."

"Close." Kael took a mouthful of beer and swallowed. "I have a son in Africa."

"Holy shit!"

"I gather you're surprised?"

"It's not that. I mean, yeah, I'm surprised, but I was commenting on your fishing rod."

Kael looked at his rod to find one end straining the limits of its plastic rod holder while the other end arced downward like an elegant diver penciling into the water. The squeal of line escaping from the reel was like a cry for assistance.

Kael jumped out of his deck chair and grabbed the pole with both hands just in time to hear plastic snapping. He muscled the rod against his abdomen. It was like a squirming puppy not wanting to be held. He took a wide, firm stance and attempted to lift the rod tip out of the water. It didn't budge.

C.B. said, "Don't touch that drag. Let this gal run to Canada if she wants."

"But we don't have licenses to fish in Canada."

C.B. had referred to the fish as a "gal" since it was probably a halibut and female halibut were larger than the males—kind of like Eastern European women.

"What do you think?" asked Kael. "A two or three hundred pounder?"

"Maybe four."

Kael listened to his reel sing as the forty-pound test line continued to fly off the spool. He told himself to be patient. She would eventually tire herself out. His turn to pull would happen soon enough.

After what seemed like an hour, but was probably closer to forty-five seconds, the reel stopped screaming. Now it was Kael's turn to pull. He gently tugged and the rod tip began to rise. When it was pointing to the sun, he dropped it back to its original position while he rapidly reeled in the slack, always making sure to keep tension in the line. A halibut could spit out a limp hook like a professional baseball player did sunflower seeds.

Reeling in his adversary was a long, slow process, but Kael could look down at his reel and confirm that he was making progress. His hands were busier than a Braille speed reader's.

"So, is your kid as ugly as you?"

The ongoing battle with a halibut that probably outweighed either man and quite possibly more than both men together, only allowed Kael to grunt out, "Don't know. I haven't seen him since I left Africa ten years ago, but I'm hoping that ugliness skips a generation."

Kael's arms were beginning to feel stretched to twice their original length. The good news was that they were now long enough to dunk a basketball without jumping from a ladder.

"Have you had any contact with him at all?"

"Not really. I send money to Josie, his mother, and all the other assorted members of a typical African extended family who come out of the woodwork when money appears."

"You can actually send money through the African postal system? I'm impressed."

"No, I have a friend who occasionally travels over there. I pay him here in the states and when he goes over there, he hand delivers the equivalent in local currency to Josie's mom. Stealing is one of the fringe benefits of being a Central African postal worker. In fact, I think it's in their contract. Most letters and packages never arrive at their destinations, and if they do, it can take months. I once got a package for my 23rd birthday that was sent for my 22nd birthday." Kael looked down at his spool and noticed that he was perhaps halfway done if the fish didn't get her second wind and run again.

"Why didn't you say anything about your son before? I told you about that night I spent with the stripper."

"That wasn't confessing. That was out and out bragging." Kael continued to reel down. His muscles were sore and his shirt was soaked with perspiration, but he felt like a marathoner whose endorphins had just kicked in and urged him to run two hundred and sixty miles instead of a paltry twenty-six. "I don't know why I haven't said anything about Josie. We all have secrets. Mine is that I never wanted to be a father and when it happened, I got out of there as quickly as I could. Sending money was about as responsible as I was willing to be. And that's nothing to brag about."

Kael thought about Molly for the umpteenth time since reading about her death. Josie, through no fault of his own, was the reason for the ten years of silent treatment that Kael had inflicted upon Molly. Molly had felt that Kael should have done the right thing by taking his son to the states. Kael had promised to support Josie financially, but that wasn't enough for Molly. In her mind, one had to be totally committed and that couldn't be accomplished from a hiding place halfway around the world. She had been right. Kael knew that now.

He didn't tell this to C.B. Instead, he just said, "Maybe by going back, I can make things right."

"So you are going back?"

"I don't know. I'm supposed to call Washington this evening and give them my decision. If I go, I've got to sell my boat and find someone to adopt Chako, like yesterday."

"Why don't you just leave them with me?"

C.B. said it as nonchalantly as if he were talking about a couple of houseplants.

"That's a generous offer," said Kael, "but your future, like mine, is about as certain as a soap bubble's."

"Not exactly. You're not the only one in demand around here. NAP called me yesterday. Actually, they called Sam and offered positions to any of us wishing to stay on at Hidden Cove, so keeping *The Sourdough* and Chako wouldn't be any harder than watching TV. And it would be a darn shame to break up the set. There's plenty of dock space here and Chako requires less maintenance than a weed. You pay the insurance and let me use the boat every now and then, and I'll take good care of your past while you go in search of your future."

"Let me think about it. Right now I need you to search the water below for our worthy opponent." Kael looked at his spool of line. It was wet, glistening and almost to the top. "She can't be more than ten or twenty yards away. Keep an eye out for a flash of white."

"Want me to get the .22?"

"Not yet. Let's see what we've got first."

C.B. was referring to the common practice of shooting any halibut over one hundred pounds. There were stories of halibut being beaten senseless with a club and hauled into a boat, only to reawaken several minutes later and start thrashing with the power of an unbroken, wild mustang. It could make a mess of a boat by spraying blood and slime everywhere and splintering $200 fishing rods into graphite toothpicks.

"There!" cried Kael. "Off to the right. It's a barn door!"

"Barn door, nothin'. That thing's the whole friggin' barn."

Both men were mesmerized by the halibut's mass. It floated like a treeless island next to *The Sourdough*. She was probably eight feet long and well over three hundred pounds. Before Kael or C.B. could react, she dove for the bottom, pulling line out so fast the Penn reel sounded more like a dentist's drill. The whine was so authentic, Kael's teeth started to ache.

"I think we needed the .22, C.B."

C.B. ran to the wheelhouse, found the pistol in a drawer and returned to stand next to Kael in his best policeman's stance: feet spread, in a low crouch with both arms extended, and pointing the .22 at the water where the monster had appeared only seconds before.

The tug-of-war began again. It gave Kael more time to think about Josie, Molly and crocodile men.

When the halibut bubbled to the surface a second time, C.B. side-stepped to the left to get a clear shot. As he did, he tripped over the cooler tumbling Kael's beer to the deck. Kael watched the contents gurgle out forming a frothy puddle. He suddenly knew what to do.

"Don't shoot!" he yelled.

C.B. relaxed and let his arms drop to his sides.

Kael shifted his gaze from the overturned beer can to the halibut and said, "When I was in Africa, it was common practice to pour a little bit of your warm beer in a glass, swirl it around, and then pour it on the ground. This little ceremony not only cleansed your glass, but more importantly, it appeased the spirit world by letting them have the first sip. I've got to think that the spirits would be pretty darn happy to have some fish with their beer."

"But this is near world-record size."

"I'm guessing the bigger the sacrifice, the happier they are. And I want them to take care of a friend of mine. Crocodiles eat fish, don't they?"

C.B. said, "What do I know about crocodiles?" as he set the .22 down on the cooler. "I know *I* eat fish, but I'm guessing not tonight."

"We'll catch her again when I get back." Kael then reached down and slipped the hook out of the exhausted halibut's upper lip. Its gills moved up and down, searching for oxygen to build up its strength for another run. Kael stroked her along the long lateral line and said, "Go on girl. Now, you've got a fish story to tell."

With a mighty slap of her tail, the halibut drenched Kael and dove straight for the bottom, this time unimpeded by several hundred yards of forty-pound monofilament connected to a one-hundred-and-seventy-pound fisherman at the other end.

Kael watched her disappear, and in her place loomed an image of Molly reaching for the surface. She was dressed in a green-and-orange tie-dyed T-shirt with cutoff jeans and red Converse sneakers. Her blond hair, which Kael remembered reaching down to the small of her back, had been cut to shoulder-length. It seemed so real, he even stuck his hand into the water to help, but she, too, faded below the blue-green swells of Chatham Strait.

"Come on, C.B., let's head home for some hamburgers. I'm so hungry, I'm hallucinating."

C.B. sat down in his deck chair not quite understanding what had just taken place. "I can't believe you let her go."

At first, Kael thought he was talking about Molly, but then realized he was talking about the fish. "Then you probably won't believe this either. I'm leaving *The Sourdough* and Chako in your care and your responsibilities start right now, so get into the wheelhouse and turn this tub of yours around. I'm going to sip a beer, catch some rays and look the part of a rich yachtsman whose only concern is to get back to port in time for this evening's polo match."

"Aye aye, captain," replied C.B. as he saluted and immediately hopped forward into the padded leather chair behind the helm. He beamed like a kid with a new toy.

When C.B. started the powerful Perkins diesel engine, an awakened Chako crawled out from the forecastle to curl up on the rug at C.B.'s feet. It was usually where Kael's feet rested, but Chako didn't seem to mind the difference.

Kael saw this through the open doorway and shook his head. "I always wondered what she'd do in a mutiny."

C.B. reached down to pet his crew's head. "And the tide book said it was going to be a small-dot day." He pushed on the throttle control. The boat moved forward.

Kael thought that was a good direction in which to head.

# 7

It was a lovely morning in the park. The steady rain had abated just before sunrise and the land was now left with a sweet, freshly scrubbed smell as if Mother Nature had just emerged from a long, relaxing bath. Every leaf, flower petal and blade of grass shimmered as the sun's rays reflected off the still-clinging water droplets.

Bolo watched Isabelle lead her younger half-sister Sophie down a muddy path away from the rest of their family. They were headed for a small clearing where the path crossed a stream. A couple of teenagers just looking for berries to snack on and they had no idea that they were being watched.

Besides curiosity and wanderlust, the two sisters shared many sisterly qualities: They were roughly the same height, had similar coloring, and both had the same dark, brooding eyes. They also had big ears, big feet and big noses, which ran in the family.

Isabelle and Sophie looked very much alike, but of the two, Isabelle was the one whose physical appearance most often caught the eyes of men like Bolo and left them temporarily speechless. Isabelle's ears, feet and nose were not her only generous features. When first-time admirers eventually regained the ability to speak, their comments on Isabelle's "development" ranged from, "Look at the size of those things!" to, "God, what a set!"

Sophie's were still small and budding. She was, after all, two years younger than Isabelle.

They arrived at the clearing by the stream and were immediately engulfed by hundreds of brightly colored butterflies flitting between their legs, bouncing off the tops of their heads and resting on any body part that remained still. Sophie quickly escaped to the stream and waded in up to her knees. The older and more mature Isabelle paid the butterflies no attention. She casually made her way over to where the fruits and berries awaited. Sophie stayed in the stream while straining for the fruits that grew along the stream bank.

Both sisters were so busy gorging and enjoying the warmth of the sun on their faces that they never even noticed Bolo hiding behind the tree only seventy-five feet away. He had been there all night—waiting.

He saw Isabelle and knew that he had to have her. He raised the rifle and gently rested the barrel in the crotch of the tree. It was so easy. At only seventy-five feet away, he expertly placed his shot exactly where he aimed—just behind Isabelle's oversized right ear. She dropped to the ground and partially eaten berries spilled from her open mouth.

Confused, Sophie dropped her fruit and reached out to caress Isabelle's face.

Bolo hadn't planned on shooting Sophie. But she was there and she didn't run, so he put a bullet into her brain as well. The butterflies continued to flit between the sisters' legs, bounce off the tops of the sisters' heads, and rest along the entire length of the sisters' forever still and silent bodies.

After four planes, five layovers, six airports, ten bags of salted nuts, nineteen cups of coffee, twenty-seven hours (nine of which were actually in the air), and dozens of reminders to make sure his seat backs and trays were in their full, upright and locked positions, Kael arrived at National Airport in Washington, D.C. with a backpack, a guitar and more than a few reservations. He already missed the familiar smells of salt air, spruce trees and wet dog.

No one from TRAP was waiting to greet him as he disembarked out of gate two. Nick had said that because of budget cuts, their chauffeur-driven limo was only being used for visiting foreign dignitaries, and Kael wasn't foreign enough nor dignified enough to warrant the expense. Kael could only agree.

Nick had told Kael that even if he didn't rate the limo, the Metro didn't care if he was a U.S. citizen and undignified. As long as he purchased a fare ticket, he could hop on the blue line right there at the airport and it would deposit him at the Foggy Bottom – GWU Station. From there, it was a short taxi ride to TRAP's headquarters on Wisconsin Avenue.

The Metro ride to Foggy Bottom was like a high-priced call girl: It was clean, efficient, and came right on time.

Kael then caught a "Yellow Cab" out on Twenty-third Street. Actually, it was orange and black in color, but the company name stenciled on the orange door said, "Yellow Cab." Kael figured lying was the norm in Washington, so he didn't question it.

He was deposited in front of a seven-story, steel and glass stalagmite rising out of the concrete. After paying his driver, he slung his backpack over one shoulder, gripped his guitar case, and walked through the front mirrored doors into an immense lobby of white tiled floors, white walls, white pillars, and a high white ceiling.

A group of people milled about in front of the elevators, so Kael headed in that direction. Next to the elevators he found a building directory. He fingered down the names and saw that TRAP had offices on all seven floors. The Africa Program was located on six.

A bell announced that an elevator had arrived. The white doors opened. One trench-coated gentleman exited and those waiting to go up quickly took his place. Kael was the last to squeeze into the small cubicle with just enough room for his backpack and guitar. He reached over and pressed the button for the sixth floor. He set his backpack gently down and pushed it off to the side. There wasn't enough room for his guitar so he held it close to his body like a small child. With his back to the open doors, he looked straight into the face of a tall blonde with more freckles than most kindergarten classes. She was stunning, but that was how he felt about most tall blondes with the possible exception of Larry Bird.

The elevator doors attempted to close, but something blocked their progress. Kael was facing the other direction so he had no idea what was causing the delay. The tall blonde looked deep into his eyes. In his perfect world she'd lick her full lips and say something like, "Can I buy you a beer later?" Instead, she said, "I think your guitar is caught in the door."

Kael was jolted back to reality. "Oh, sorry." He pushed closer to the tall blonde, pulling his troublesome guitar until the doors were finally able to shut. He looked into the tall blonde's eyes, smiled, and said, "I guess my equipment is too big."

This elicited a few partially stifled chortles from the rear of the elevator. The tall blonde smiled back, just enough to let Kael know that she appreciated the humor, and said, "I seriously doubt that."

The peanut gallery giggled. The only thing better than using a clever line to successfully pick up a member of the opposite sex, was witnessing firsthand an unsuccessful attempt.

The elevator vaulted up. Most of the occupants examined the shine of their shoe tops. Some counted the number of holes in the ceiling tiles. Kael looked straight into the tall blonde's averted eyes and whistled the Rod Stewart version of *Do Ya Think I'm Sexy?*

The elevator bypassed two and three, but came to a roller coaster stop at the fourth floor. The doors opened and Kael stepped back with his guitar to let the tall blonde and several others exit. The tall blonde made no eye contact as she passed. Her cotton dress brushed his pant leg and her scent lingered for a brief moment. She smelled like Ivory soap.

He stepped back into the elevator, but continued to peek around the corner as she headed down the long hallway. He liked the look of her long, prodigiously freckled calves. His eyes were drifting northward when she looked back over her equally speckled shoulder, caught his leer, smiled, and waved. Kael never saw the elevator doors slam shut on his forehead.

"Ouch! This city *is* as dangerous as I've heard." He pulled his aching head back into the elevator. The doors shut, abruptly cutting off the tall blonde's howls of laughter.

The last two remaining passengers, besides Kael, exited on the fifth floor, so Kael rode alone up to the sixth floor. When the ego-deflating doors opened, he shouldered his backpack and grabbed his guitar for the final leg of his journey to Nick's office. He jumped out before the doors could attack again.

At the end of the long hall he found a receptionist blocking his path. She was a large black woman who resembled Idi Amin, but with long, intricately braided hair and wearing a colorful African caftan, probably a size 28 XXXL. Her smile was just as wide.

"Can I help you?"

"Sure. Have you got any aspirin?"

"I think I might." She rummaged through her purse, which would have been too large to qualify as a carry-on bag for most airlines. She dived in up to her elbows and came out with a bottle. "Is Tylenol OK?"

"Perfect."

She handed him two capsules and he swallowed them before she could explain where the water cooler was. "Now, is there anything else I can do for you?"

"I'm looking for Nick Cinzano. My name is Kael Husker. I believe he's expecting me."

"So *you're* Mr. Husker, huh? Dr. Cinzano told me to keep an eye out for you, and to warn you that you'd better have a good joke for him today."

"My jokes are always good."

"According to Dr. Cinzano, they're not nearly as good as his."

"Now that's funny," said Kael.

"Come on," she said behind a smile. "I'll take you to his office. You can leave your bags here if you'd like."

Kael liked. He then followed his guide into the bowels of TRAP's Africa Program. They arrived at an office with an open door. There was no sign of Nick, but the entire state of Rhode Island could have been safely hidden on the other side of that twenty-seven acre caftan.

The receptionist knocked on the door jamb, as if no one would have noticed her slipping into the room. "You have a guest, Dr. Cinzano." She then turned sideways to let Kael pass. He almost had to do the limbo under her protruding bosom to get by.

Nick was already coming around his desk when Kael entered the room. The two old friends shook hands for a brief instant and then released their grips to wrap arms around the other. Nick turned to the receptionist and said, "Thanks for getting him here safely, Delia."

"My pleasure, Dr. Cinzano. I'd better get back to my phones. Enjoy your stay in Washington, Mr. Husker." Delia then beat the odds a second time and made it through the doorway.

Kael looked at his friend whose appearance suggested that he liked having one foot in Africa and one foot in Washington. His dark, full beard was well trimmed and his long, wavy hair was combed back with just a hint of styling gel. He wore a dress shirt and a tie, but the top button of the shirt was open and the tie was loosened. If Nick let the beard grow out, lost the gel, and changed into some ripped pants and a faded t-shirt, he could jump right back into Africa and look just as comfortable.

Nick looked at Kael, opened his palms and said, "Well, what have you got?"

Kael said, "There are these two bear researchers. That's B-E-A-R. And they're working in Southeast Alaska. They're walking down this forest trail, come over a rise, and fifteen feet in front of them they see a big, hungry, snarling brown bear. The bear rises up on his two hind haunches and stretches out to his full ten feet to capture the researchers' scent in the breeze. The one researcher reaches down, quickly removes his hiking boots and replaces them with sneakers. The other researcher sees this and says, 'What the hell are you doing? You'll never outrun a brown bear.' 'I know that,' replies the first researcher. 'All I have to do is outrun you.'"

"Not bad," said Nick. "I'll cut you some slack since you're probably dealing with jet lag. Mine's more of a riddle. How are hemorrhoids and cowboy hats alike?" After Kael shrugged his shoulders, Nick said, "Sooner or later, every asshole gets one."

Kael smiled. "So what's your excuse since you don't have jet lag?"

"A lousy audience," said Nick.

Kael was shown a visually uncomfortable chair facing an intimidating oak desk that was obviously overkill considering the cell-like dimensions of the room and the meager belongings spread out on the desktop: a computer monitor and keyboard, a five by seven family portrait, and three shallow piles of neatly stacked papers. It was like looking down on the Sahara Desert and spotting four or five individual camels in a sea of sand.

Nick squeezed between the desk and the overstocked floor-to-ceiling bookshelves to plop down in his more visually comfortable padded leather chair. "So...no problems getting here from the Great North Woods? You must feel like Crocodile Dundee in the big city."

"It has been an adventure," said Kael rubbing his still throbbing forehead. "I even fell in love on the elevator."

"Was she tall and blonde?"

"Yeah, how'd you know?"

"That's all you ever fall in love with."

"Just to spite you, I might have to start dating dumpy brunettes."

"Please don't. I live vicariously through your dalliances. It's the ultimate in safe sex. You know I'd never cheat on Darcy. My God, if I ever tried she'd cut off my dick and make me eat it on a stale hot dog bun."

Kael laughed. "Glad I could be of service. I wouldn't get a woody over this one though. We only shared a couple of minutes in an elevator and I don't think she was impressed." Kael felt his forehead to determine if an egg was forming. "Besides, I fly out of the country in three days, right?"

Nick nodded. "I've got your ticket right here." He patted one of the lonely piles of paper on his desktop. "I also ran your passport over to the C.A.R. embassy and had it stamped with a valid entry visa." He passed the documents over to Kael.

"Thanks. Is the embassy still a three-ring circus?"

"Ringling Brothers Barnum and Bailey could take lessons. I was over there a number of times trying to get Molly's body back to the states and even though I speak French and Sango, it was like working with the Keystone Cops. Total confusion. I can honestly say I've had more fun shopping with Darcy. I finally did an end run and asked an old friend at the French embassy to help grease the wheels. If not for him, Molly would still be sitting in the chest freezer at the Catholic mission in Nola."

"I thought about sending a note to Molly's folks in Minneapolis, but I didn't know what to say. Not even Hallmark has a card expressing sympathy to the parents of a daughter who gets killed by a crocodile man in Central Africa."

"How about, 'Deepest regrets over the loss of your child. She was special; she was unique; she was reptiled.'"

"Clever, but crass," said Kael.

Nick shuffled in his chair. "I think it's about time I told you something. Molly swore me to secrecy, but now that she's gone, I don't think she'd mind. She was also sending money to Josie. Every couple of months I'd receive a check, which I would then hand deliver to Josie's mother, often at the same time, I gave over one sent by you. This started way back when I began my research right after Peace Corps and it didn't end until a few months ago when Molly started working back over there. All told, it probably came to about five or six thousand dollars. I once asked her why and she replied, 'Because it's the right thing to do.' That was Molly in a nutshell."

Kael stared out the window behind Nick, but his eyes focused on nothing. Not on the treetops. Not on the roofs of other buildings. It was one of those coma-like moments when everything shuts down. Eyes glazed over. Ears cranked up the drawbridge. And the brain hanged a "gone fishin'" sign on the medulla. These momentary lapses of consciousness often occurred during church sermons, Miss America's question and answer rounds, and around the eighth slide of a neighbor's trip to Disney World with the wife, four kids and grandma.

After about five seconds in his personal sensory deprivation chamber, Kael said, "I should have known she'd do something like that. Now, I can't even thank her."

Nick said, "No, but she'd sure get a kick out of the fact that after reading her obituary in a small-town Alaskan newspaper, you called me, which caused me to offer you a job back in Central Africa, which will eventually reconnect you with Josie."

Kael smiled. "She finally got what she wanted."

Nick's hands picked through another neat stack of papers on his desktop until he pulled out a single sheet and slid it over to Kael. "I got a FAX from Mitchell Wright. Central Africa's finest arrested one of Molly's former camp workers and accused him of being a crocodile man." He ran his finger down the FAX and stopped at mid-page. "Says here his name is Assan Séléman. Sounds Arabic. They claim he had a run-in with Molly the day before her death. The proverbial 'smoking gun' in Central African jurisprudence, so he's in jail in Nola making little rocks out of big ones."

Kael snatched the FAX from under Nick's finger and skimmed through. "Did our friend Mitchell do anything to help? We know this Assan didn't change into a crocodile and kill Molly. She fell out of her canoe, right?"

"That's what *we* believe, but we're dealing with a culture that takes a slightly different view of things, as does Mitchell. He probably wouldn't push unless his gorilla research or the project were negatively affected by the arrest."

"Come on, Nick. We've got to do something. You know as well as I do that Molly'd be pissed if we just stood back in the shadows and watched an innocent man rot in prison because of an accident. Can't you hear her screaming?"

Nick cupped his hands over his ears. "No, but I didn't know her as well as you. She was tall and blonde, too, if I recall."

"Yes, she was. She was an inch taller than me and with the possible exceptions of Johnny and Edgar Winter, she had the most beautiful long, blond tresses."

"Not when I last saw her. She'd cut it to about shoulder length. Said it was less of a hassle in the humidity of the forest."

Kael's eyes widened. "Shoulder length? Promise me you won't laugh, but I had a vision of Molly a few weeks ago and she was wearing what she always wore: a tie-dyed t-shirt, green and orange I believe, and cutoff jeans, but her hair was shorter. Now how did I know that?"

"Don't ask me. Every woman I dream about is naked and somewhat blurred from the neck up."

Kael ignored Nick's levity. "Do you know what Molly was wearing when she died?"

"No. I know she'd been in the river for a couple of days, which means her clothes were wet and muddy when she was found. They were probably tossed, why?"

"Just curious. I also remember that she was wearing red Converse sneakers."

"Yeah, so what? Molly never was a fashion plate."

"Remember that joke I told earlier?"

Nick nodded.

"This time, the one wearing the sneakers died. Guess she couldn't outrun the crocodile man."

Nick pointed a finger at Kael, narrowed his eyes, and tilted his head ever so slightly. "You be careful. I see that look of determination in your eyes. It's the same look you get when you spy a tall blonde. I know you and Molly were close once, so do whatever you need to do to feel comfortable with her death. But don't forget that the project is your number-one priority, OK?"

Kael flashed a grin and said, "It's certainly in the top five."

Nick pushed his chair away from the desk and stood up. He buttoned the top button of his shirt and tightened the knot in his tie. "Right now, our number one priority is to put on our sneakers and sprint down to my boss's office. We'll tell him your plane was late."

Kael stood up and stretched his back. The chair was as uncomfortable as it looked. "Anything I should know before I meet him? I mean, since he's the Vice-President for the Africa Region, do I need to kiss his ring or curtsy or give him a gift?" Kael searched his pockets. "I still have a packet of salted nuts from the flight."

"Hold on to your nuts. Just smile, be courteous, and don't bring up the subject of crocodile men. He's a believer like most Africans."

Neither Kael nor Nick had worn sneakers that day so they leisurely strolled down the long white hallway. It was generously decorated with framed TRAP promotional posters full of color, nature and catchy, marketing sight-bytes like, "We're running out of wildlife, habitats and time," and, "If an alarm went off every time a species became extinct, it would sound every ten minutes. Wouldn't that drive you crazy? Wouldn't you want to shut it off? T.R.A.P. does."

One poster, in particular, made Kael stop and taste the full flavor of the message. It was a black and white photograph looking down on five elephant carcasses, two of which were obviously immature adults. All five—even the young ones—had been killed for their tusks. The caption in bright, red letters said, "Ivory, it's to die for."

They continued down the hall and walked past an alcove occupied by an elderly secretary sitting behind a computer monitor. Without stopping, Nick asked, "Is he still in, Edna?"

Edna nodded and said, "He's waiting"

Just past Edna's guard post, Nick stopped in front of a closed door and gently rapped.

"Come in," a voice boomed from the other side.

Nick opened the door and let Kael enter first. Joseph Zimbala was dressed in what appeared to be a tailored three-piece gray suit with a light blue shirt and a matching paisley tie and breast pocket handkerchief. Kael couldn't be certain that the pants completed the outfit because Joseph was seated behind a desk that made Nick's look like something found in a first grade classroom.

Not counting grade school, Kael had never had his own desk, but he had begun to wonder if the size of one's desk was territorial or inversely proportional to the size of one's penis. He thought about asking this of Joseph, but instead, he held out his hand and said, "It's a pleasure to meet you, Joseph. I'm Kael Husker."

Joseph smiled and extended his own hand. "I know. We've been expecting you." After releasing Kael's hand, he walked around the desk, a distance of about a quarter of a mile, and shook Nick's hand.

Very African, thought Kael. With the possible exceptions of clocks and gorillas, Africans shook hands with anything that had them. Kael theorized that that was one of the reasons why so little was accomplished in Africa: people were too busy shaking hands.

Kael noticed that Joseph was wearing another less appealing African badge. It was one often cultivated by those in positions of power: a long pinky fingernail. It announced that the swordsman had attained a certain social status and was, therefore, no longer required to perform manual labor. At least it wasn't painted. Kael decided that a long fingernail was probably like a big desk: it compensated for a short penis.

Joseph ushered his guests over to a casual seating area in one corner of his warehouse-sized office. Generous stuffed chairs in earth tones surrounded a low table made from the cross-section of a tropical mahogany. The two walls in that corner were covered with Joseph's numerous awards and citations. Some were impressive. Most were ceremonial fluff. They ranged from a Presidential commendation as an "Environmental Leader" to a "Devoted Friend of the National Zoo." He was also a "Loyal Member" of an organization known as Z.O.W. (Zimbabweans of Washington) and he was the recipient of a frequent flyer certificate from American Airlines for logging over five hundred thousand air-miles in one year.

"I see you are impressed by my accomplishments."

"Oh, yes," said Kael with tongue in cheek. "You're going to need more wall space pretty soon."

Joseph laughed. It was deep and loud and lasted much longer than the joke called for.

"I should have one more to add after this weekend. I am speaking at the Columbus Zoo on primate protection in Africa. In fact, I leave in a few minutes, as you can see." Joseph pointed to his garment bag sitting next to the four-foot-tall African drum in the opposite corner of the room. "That piece of luggage works almost as hard as Nick and me. It returned from Europe with me only yesterday. I had barely enough time to exchange my soiled clothes for laundered ones to make the Columbus trip. I just wanted to meet you before I left, especially since I won't be back here until after you leave."

"Don't worry," said Nick. "I'll make sure he's appropriately briefed in the next three days. Darcy insisted that he stay with us out in Virginia, so that gives us a full seventy-two hours of uninterrupted time to get caught up."

"Don't monopolize all of his time, Nick. He can't possibly absorb everything in three short days."

Nick nodded.

Joseph tugged at his sparse goatee. It was as thick and luxurious as that of any ninth grader, who in the proper bathroom light and two centimeters from the mirror saw himself as a double for Atilla the Hun.

"I want you to know, Kael," said Joseph, "that this job you are taking on isn't for any Tom, Dick or Larry."

"Harry," said Nick.

"Him, too," said Joseph. He focused his attention back on Kael. "If you ever have any questions or concerns, contact either Nick or me. We are here to support you just as you will be in Central Africa to support TRAP's interests."

Kael nodded as he watched Joseph bring his right leg up and cross it over his left knee. Below the perfectly creased seam of Joseph's right pant leg, his foot was visible as it dangled above the tabletop. He was wearing expensive-looking alligator shoes with tassels.

Kael said, "I do have one question, Joseph?"

Nick's head swiveled in Kael's direction.

"Ask away," said Joseph.

"I've been admiring your shoes."

Joseph smiled and pointed the toe of his shoe up toward the ceiling lights to better accentuate the color and texture. "Yes, they are striking, aren't they? Do you want to know where I bought them?"

"No," said Kael. "I was wondering if they are made from real alligator skin or imitation crocodile man."

Nick looked down at the table like he was counting the rings.

Joseph's smile disappeared. "Crocodile men are no joking matter, Mr. Husker. Americans like you, and even Nick here, look at sorcery and black magic as something found in a Stephen King novel or an innocent costume knocking on your door at Halloween. But it's real, it's frightening, and it kills whether you believe or not."

"So do you believe Molly McGinley was killed by a crocodile man?"

"Let me put it this way: I'm a believer in possibilities."

"Then you must believe in the possibility that crocodile men do *not* exist."

"You're very clever. I like that. Let us hope that you will be as sharp in Central Africa."

Kael smiled. "I'll be as sharp as a crocodile man's incisor."

"Very well," said Joseph. "Be an incisor if you wish. Just stay out of the crocodile man's mouth." He looked at his watch, then stood up and smoothed out the wrinkles in his pants. "You'll have to excuse me, gentlemen, but I must leave for the airport. My flight departs in forty-five minutes."

Nick and Kael climbed out of their comfortable chairs and followed Joseph to the door.

Before Kael left, Joseph shook his hand again and said, "Believe in possibilities, Mr. Husker. That's what the Doli-Ngili project is all about—possibilities."

Kael looked into Joseph's dark eyes and said, "Aren't all environmentalists believers in possibilities?"

Joseph's long slender fingers stroked his pseudo-goatee. "Very well put. I like that. I may even use it in my presentation at the Columbus Zoo." He then offered his hand to Nick. "I will see you when I return next week. What is it you Americans say? Hold down the fort?"

Nick looked directly at Kael and said, "We Americans say a lot of things."

Kael smiled back, softening Nick's glare.

Joseph shepherded his guests through the open doorway and into the hallway although his own alligator shoes remained in the room. He leaned around the corner, looked past Kael and Nick, and said, "Edna, would you please inform the limo driver to come up for my luggage?" Joseph's head popped back into its shell only milliseconds before the door shut.

To the closed door Edna said, "Certainly, Mr. Zimbala," and she reached for her phone.

Kael and Nick shuffled past Edna's desk and headed back down the long, white hallway.

"That went well," said Nick with more than a touch of sarcasm.

"He's an idiot."

"That's a possibility." Both men laughed. "But he's also our boss."

"Now *that's* frightening," said Kael.

"Come on, I'll buy you a cup of coffee."

Killing was Bolo's living. He knew it and he felt no remorse for what he did. It was a job, plain and simple. He provided a service. The money was good and all of it was non-taxable income. He didn't punch a clock; the hours were flexible. He wasn't stuck in an office all day; most of the time, he was outdoors. He could wear what he wanted. Shaving was optional. There were no twice-daily rush-hour commutes to contend with. He frequently traveled internationally. Paperwork was minimal. He was his own boss, even if others assumed he was under their control. The harder he worked, the more money he made. Except for the actual killing part, most people would die for those kinds of working conditions. His victims literally did.

Bolo attributed his phenomenal success to two things: he had brains and balls. He also had beauty, but that quality didn't really count for much in his line of work. A bullet did its damage regardless of whether it was fired by a hunk or a punk.

Bolo had committed unspeakable heinous crimes, but the one thing he would never be accused of was modesty. He was much too smart for that. His superior intelligence made him impossible to catch. He was too methodical, too precise, too perfect in the execution of his professional duties. Sometimes it didn't seem fair that one man should be so much better than everyone else. That was just fine by Bolo, since he never played by the rules, anyway.

He had an adolescent-like eagerness to overstep the bounds of acceptable behavior. Few in his business would have even considered shooting Isabelle's younger sister, Sophie. True, she'd added almost nothing to his profit margin, but her worth was considerable, nonetheless. Her brutal death two short weeks ago would give birth to a legend: that of a cold-blooded killer with absolutely no restraint, no mercy, and no respect for any life but his own.

All of these thoughts raced through Bolo's head just moments before he drew back his machete. He let fly with a mighty downward swing. His perfect form sent the heavy blade crashing through the facial bones of his latest victim. It sounded like wood being split with an ax.

Bolo needed both hands to wiggle free the machete for a second swing. Some might be disgusted by what he was doing, but to Bolo, this was just another day at the office.

# 10

Nick and Kael's quest for a cup of coffee took them down to a comfortable lounge area on the fourth floor. There were two sofas for stretching out, as well as six small round tables with three matching chairs around each table. Along one wall was a large double sink sandwiched between two ornate wrought iron buffet shelves. Mugs, cups, tea bags, cloth napkins, sugar, cream and utensils sat on the oak shelves of one cabinet while the other held two stainless steel water towers. One was labeled "coffee" and the other was labeled "hot water." A man and a woman sat at one of the tables.

"Grab a chair," said Nick. "You take anything in your coffee?"

"A little cream."

"Good for you. I'm still addicted to African coffee, but I'm making progress. I'm down to five sugars."

"Why don't you just pull out your teeth with pliers and be done with it?"

"I haven't got time. With Joseph on the road so often, I'm running the entire Africa Program three out of four weeks."

Kael picked a table at the far corner of the room while Nick filled their drink orders. After Nick returned with two mugs of steaming coffee, Kael asked, "Is Joseph as crazy as he appeared?"

Nick brought his finger to his lips and gave a silent "shh" signal. He subtly pointed to the chattering couple who suddenly stopped conversing and leaned their long-lobed ears in Nick and Kael's direction. Nick said in a loud voice, "Yes, Joseph *is* as *amazing* as he appeared."

Kael smiled.

The couple shifted in their seats and went back to their own briefly interrupted conversation.

In a softer voice, Nick said, "Don't worry about Joseph. Leave him to me. He's administratively challenged and he's got some strange beliefs, but he's..." Nick searched for the right word. "...useful."

Kael took a sip of coffee. He peered over his cup to see two individuals enter the room. His bruised forehead immediately started to throb. It was the tall blonde followed by another woman. Both were laughing. Kael hoped they weren't chuckling about the geek whose head had gotten caught in the elevator doors.

Kael hid behind Nick's large head and said, "Don't turn around, but the tall blonde from the elevator just walked in."

Nick instantly turned around and spotted the tall blonde by the coffee maker. He was grinning as he turned back to Kael and said, "Forget it. It'll never work."

"Why not?"

"Trust me." Nick turned back toward the tall blonde who was now pouring cream into her coffee. "Tallin!"

The tall blonde looked up at Nick. She couldn't see Kael who was scrunched down in his seat hiding behind both Nick and his coffee cup.

"Dr. Cinzano! What brings you down to the fourth floor?"

"Just escaping the chaos up on six. Come and join us. I'd like to introduce you to someone."

The tall blonde spoke to her female companion who replied, "You go ahead. I'll catch up with you back at the office."

The tall blonde made her way back to the last table. She was so busy watching her coffee cup to keep it from spilling that she didn't notice Kael until she was standing within three feet of him. She smiled and said, "How's your head?"

"Not bad. It's been slammed shut between doors much harder than today." Kael stood up to shake her hand.

"Tallin, this is my good friend Kael. Kael, this is my fourth floor friend, Tallin."

Tallin set her coffee cup down and shook Kael's outstretched hand. "I didn't think I'd see you again."

"Are you pleasantly surprised?" asked Kael.

She smiled and sat down next to him. "Yes, I am."

Nick said, "Before you two start picking out a china pattern together, I ought to warn you that it won't work."

Kael looked at Tallin. "It's because I'm leaving the country in three days."

"Well, there's that, too," said Nick.

"What's the other problem?" asked Tallin. "Does he prefer cats over dogs, disco over rock and roll, and NASCAR over any other sport?"

Nick smiled. "I don't think so. What's your last name, Tallin?"

She looked momentarily puzzled like it was a trick question. Finally, she said, "Korne...with a K and a silent e."

"And what's your last name, Kael?"

Kael understood Nick's reservations. "Husker...with an H and an obnoxious r."

"So if you got married, you'd be Kael and Tallin Korne-Husker."

Both Kael and Tallin laughed. "And if we had a kid, we could name him Nebraska," added Tallin.

"It could be worse," said Kael. "I have a friend named Dave Hardy who once dated a woman named Laurel Ann. The relationship was doomed from the start."

Everyone laughed, including the couple at the other table.

Kael continued his story. "He ended up marrying someone else, they had a son, and they named him Partridge or Party for short."

Tallin exploded with laughter. "Party Hardy? I love it!"

"You'd love him. He's a great kid who'd be just as great even if his name was something really ridiculous, like say...Orville." Kael looked at Nick, whose middle name happened to be Orville.

"I disagree," said Tallin. "I don't disagree that Party is a great kid. But I do think there's a lot of baggage that goes with a name. Take it from someone named after a city in Eastern Europe where my parents met. You get certain visual images with names. For example, you'd never see a woman named Bertha accepting the crown for Miss America. And you'd never see a kid named Poindexter throwing the winning touchdown pass in the Super Bowl."

"Could you see yourself dating anyone named Kael?" asked a hopeful Kael.

"Only if Poindexter wasn't available."

"That's OK," said Kael. "You're not really my type. Oh, Nick will tell you that I tend to fall for tall blondes, and that's true, but what I'm really after is a beautiful, rich nymphomaniac who owns a liquor store."

"I'm sorry to disappoint you. I only fit two of those criteria."

Kael sat up straight in his chair. "Hmmm...care to tell me which two? I grade on a curve."

"I don't think so."

Nick stood up smiling. "I'd love to stay and find out how this ends, but I need to get back to my office."

Kael started to rise, too, but Nick placed a hand on his shoulder. "No, you stay and finish your coffee and whatever else you've started. We've still got seventy some hours to talk about the project. You're not even employed yet so they can't fire you. I'll see you in a few." Turning to Tallin he said, "Call me if you need someone to verify any of Kael's questionable claims."

"I will, Dr. Cinzano."

"Please, call me Nick." He turned to leave, but before exiting the lounge, he turned back and said, "Oh, by the way...another piece of data for your name theory, Tallin. Kael's nickname is Pig-Pen."

Kael said, "Thank you *Puru ti kondo*."

Nick smiled back before making a hasty exit.

"What was that you called him?"

"*Puru ti kondo*. It means 'chicken shit,' but there's more to the story than that. When Nick first got to Africa, he wandered through the open air market looking for eggs. The word for egg in the local language of Sango is *para ti kondo*, but Nick went around telling people that he was hungry and wanted to buy *puru ti kondo*. That was thirteen years ago and I think the marketplace is still laughing."

"So how did you get the nickname, Pig-Pen?"

"Don't you read *Peanuts* in the Sunday comics?"

"Sure, but I don't see a cloud of dust enveloping you."

"You didn't know me in my twenties. I was a bit on the unkempt side."

"Unlike now," said Tallin with a smirk.

Kael couldn't stop thinking it might be fun to play connect the dots with Tallin's freckles. It would require several pens. "When you're not theorizing, what do you do with TRAP?"

"Do you want to know what I tell people or what I actually do?"

"Give me both barrels."

"OK. I tell people that I'm a journalist slash writer. Actually, I work for the Publications Department. We make all those colorful TRAP calendars, agenda books, posters and brochures. I occasionally get the opportunity to use my journalism degree. I write articles for the membership newsletter, the TRAPline, and I sometimes write press releases."

"Sounds to me like you *are* a journalist slash writer. Hemingway didn't start out writing *The Sun Also Rises*, but he eventually got there."

"That's true. My dad keeps telling me that a professional writer is just an amateur writer who didn't give up."

"He sounds like someone who would know the difference between eggs and chicken shit."

Tallin laughed. "Now that you know all about me, tell me a bit about yourself."

"Well...I don't own a big desk and I always keep my nails clipped short."

"That's...interesting," said Tallin with a confused look on her freckled face.

"It's my own scientific theory. I'm still collecting raw data so I'm not at liberty to discuss it right now."

"Is TRAP hiring you to study desk size and fingernail length in Africa? It wouldn't be the weirdest grant TRAP has ever awarded."

"How did you know I'm going to Africa?"

"Call it journalistic observation and intuition. You are Nick's friend. You knew about his African market misunderstanding. You are here to discuss a project with him, and he only deals with the Africa Region. And then there's the elevator."

"Elevator?"

"When I left you at the fourth floor, you had to get off at five, six or seven. Seven is where all the top brass have offices. I don't think they'd allow a Pig-Pen up there. The fifth floor is Domestic Programs. You said you were leaving the country in three days, so that leaves six—Africa Region."

"Very journalistic. I'm impressed."

"I'll even go one step further and guess that you're involved with Nick's Doli-Ngili Project in Central Africa."

Kael silently sipped his coffee with his best poker face.

Tallin continued. "I heard they were hiring a new director from Alaska. With that beard, you look like you could come from the Last Frontier."

"Now I'm really impressed. I don't think Hemingway could have figured that one out."

"Hemingway doesn't eat lunch with the secretaries. They talk about everything."

"That's good to know."

Tallin took a sip of her coffee and then said, "Going from Alaska to Africa will certainly be a big change. I can't think of two places more dissimilar, except maybe downtown, tourist-filled Washington and some of the decaying neighborhoods just one or two bus stops from the marble monuments."

"You'd be surprised by how much more alike they are than different."

Tallin raised her eyebrows.

"This isn't a recent big desk and long fingernail type of theory," said Kael. "I've thought about this one quite a bit."

"This should be good. Give me a for instance."

"OK, for starters, Alaska and Africa both begin and end with the letter A."

"So do Alabama, Arizona, Antigua, Albania, Australia and Antarctica."

"That's true, but Alaska and Africa have six letters in their names. The others have seven or more. And did you know that I'm leaving a rain forest in Alaska to work in a rain forest in Africa? One is temperate and the other is tropical, but we're highlighting similarities, so work with me here."

"I'm trying. I really am," said Tallin, "but I have to tell you that compared to your hypothesis, my theory on people's names is a potential Nobel Prize winner."

Kael laughed. "There is *one* big difference between Alaska and Africa though."

"Only one?"

"Yes, only one. There are crocodile men in Africa and none in Alaska."

"Crocodile men?" said Tallin. "A while back, the secretaries were discussing crocodile men during lunch. At first, I thought they were recounting stories of their weekend dating disasters. Male bashing is a favorite topic of lunchtime conversation, especially on Mondays. Turned out, they were talking about a TRAP researcher who was killed by one. The secretaries didn't know very much, just that it had occurred in Nick's project area and that he was pulling his hair out trying to get the body back to the states for a proper burial."

"Did the secretaries say anything else?"

"Delia's comment was funny. She said that the difference between a crocodile man and the loser she had dated that weekend was that she would go out on a second date with the crocodile man."

Kael leaned back in his chair. "The woman who died was a good friend of mine. Her name was Molly McGinley. According to Nick, she fell out of her canoe and drowned, but the Central African officials believe she was killed by a crocodile man—a person with evil, mystical powers who can change into a crocodile to murder his chosen victim."

"And Africans believe this crap?"

"Every last one of them. Even Joseph Zimbala, TRAP's own Vice President for the Africa Region, warned me to be careful."

"Does Joseph also believe in the Easter Bunny?"

"If he does, it doesn't hop around leaving brightly colored eggs. It sneaks into houses on Easter eve and gnaws on its unsuspecting victims like carrots."

50

Tallin laughed. "So did the African authorities catch this crocodile man and make shoes, pocketbooks and belts out of his hide?"

"Unfortunately, he'd already changed back into a regular guy before he was apprehended. He's now doing hard time in the local prison, all because Molly accidentally fell out of her canoe." Kael brought his mug to his mouth only to discover that it was almost empty. "Can I buy you some more coffee?"

"I can't leave yet. Call it journalistic intuition, if you will, but I think there's more to this story." She handed him her cup. "I take mine with a bit of cream."

Going to refill the empty cups, Kael noticed that he and Tallin were the only ones left in the room. The other couple had already gone. When he returned to his seat with two fresh cups of coffee, he asked, "Any guesses as to the rest of the story, Scoop?"

Tallin accepted her steaming cup. "You're going to Africa to find out more about your friend Molly, aren't you?"

"You're good. Nick thinks I'm going back to direct his Doli-Ngili Project, which I am, but I also need to help Molly."

"How? She's already dead."

"You'd have to have known Molly. Her body may have been laid to rest, but her soul won't rest until something is done about the innocent guy rotting in prison for her murder."

"What are you going to do?" asked Tallin. "Find a gopher man to tunnel under the prison walls and break him out?"

"That's an idea, but I have a better one: I have a friend in the Central African police department. He was pretty high up ten years ago. By now, he may be even higher."

"Or dead. There are bleached bones that were African dictators a decade ago."

"That's true, but if he's still alive and still a cop, he'll help. He owes me."

"Why is he so deeply in your debt? Did you save *him* from a crocodile man?"

"Nothing so dramatic. I gave his son a job."

"It must have been one heck of a job for this friend to even consider helping you break someone out of jail."

"Not really. It didn't even pay very much, but the son in question was a juvenile delinquent. Over there, they're called *godobés*, and Bart was a GIT from about age seven. That's *Godobé* in Training. By age fifteen, he had reached the upper echelon of the *godobé* hierarchy and was always the number-one suspect in any reports of thievery or vandalism. Dimassé took no solace in my fervent reminder that at least his son was the best in his field."

"If I were him, and you said that to me, I would have hit you upside the head with my billy club."

"Which is why I would never say that to you."

"You're not as dumb as you look."

"Would it surprise you to learn that I've got a theory on the relationship of physical appearance and intelligence?"

"I'd be surprised if you didn't. Did you give Bart a job as official recorder of your theories? That would certainly be full-time work."

"No. I gave him the privilege of working for me. He'd go out with me on my motorcycle to dispense advice to farmers, assist with pond harvests and stockings, and he'd keep official records for my reports. He helped make my fisheries program one of the most successful in the country. I don't know if it was because he worked so hard or because I'd taken one of the village's biggest fish poachers out of circulation." Kael took a sip of his coffee. "Bart wrote me a few years back to say that he had successfully completed an advanced fisheries course and had become an assistant manager at a large hatchery in the capital city of Bangui. He's married and he named his firstborn son Kael."

Tallin said, "I can see why Dimassé might want to help you. I'm ready to go over myself and seduce the warden as a diversionary tactic while you and Dimassé tunnel under the prison walls."

"A seduction would be nice, but I wasn't thinking of the warden."

Tallin just smiled. It wasn't the reaction Kael was hoping for, but it would do. Getting a pretty girl to smile back at him was always a victory.

He looked into her jade green eyes. The color reminded him of a painting he'd done in the first grade. It had been folded up in 1961 and placed in a cardboard box with other childhood mementos like report cards, his one and only baseball trophy, macaroni art and a hand-made, misspelled Moother's Day card. The box had been found in a long forgotten corner of the attic many years later.

The painting, a two feet by three feet sheet of white paper, had been completely covered with vertical, horizontal and diagonal brush strokes of green paint that was the exact shade of Tallin's eyes. In one corner, Kael's teacher, Miss Walters, had printed in black magic marker, "Green Paper by Kael Husker – Grade 1."

The discovery of Green Paper didn't receive the media attention of, say, an authentic Van Gogh or Matisse bought for fifteen dollars at a garage sale, but it wasn't returned to its box in the attic, either. It was placed in an ornately carved wooden frame and now hung above the mantel in his father's home. It clashed with every other object in the room, but Kael's father, who knew less about art than Chako, said it spoke to him.

Kael's response was, "Weren't you listening when it spoke to you back in 1961? Did it ask to be put in a box for nearly two decades?"

Kael's father had responded with a wee bit of Husker humor: "It's the most creative thing you've ever done, and that alone makes it worthy of display."

"Can I show you something?" said Kael.

Tallin reacted by saying, "This isn't one of those, I'll show you mine if you'll show me yours kind of things, is it? Not that I'd say no, mind you."

"You don't have to expose a thing." He reached into his back pocket and pulled out his wallet. From one of the inner folds, he removed a small, weathered photograph and handed it across to Tallin.

She accepted the photo. "Cute kid. Is he Bart's?"

"No, he's mine."

She leaned forward on both elbows and with the thumb and forefinger of each hand, held the cracked image about six inches from her nose. "He's got your eyes. He might also have your mouth, but I can't tell through that big mustache of yours."

"That picture is five years old. Josie's now ten, so he might actually have my mustache already. We Huskers are a hairy bunch, as you've no doubt noticed."

"You don't have hairy backs, do you?"

"Only the female side of the family. My sister looks like she's wearing a mohair sweater under her halter top."

"A lovely image. So tell me about Josie. I could take a bath in those dimples of his."

Kael was, at the onset, a bit tentative. Sharing was something most men learned in kindergarten, but it only applied to trucks and balls. For the first time, he felt completely comfortable delving into the details he had kept locked away like Green Paper in his own dusty attic for so many years. Maybe it was finally time to hang it over the mantel.

He admitted that he'd left Josie behind because he was young, stupid and wasn't mature enough to be a full-time parent. He wasn't even sure he was ready now. He told her that he continued to support Josie, his mom, Sapu, and a baker's dozen of Sapu's family members by sending over money with Nick. In fact, it was Nick who had taken the small, cracked photograph of Josie during one of his frequent business trips to the

Central Africa. He told her that he was more scared to face Josie than a hungry, ten-foot brown bear. Neither one spoke English, but a bear could only break his body. He admitted that many of his closest friends still didn't know about Josie. He wasn't quite sure how to broach the subject. And finally, he told her about his relationship with Molly, their ten-year silence, and Nick's recent news concerning Molly's philanthropic generosity.

When Kael finished, Tallin said, "So I was right."

"About what?"

"About there being more to the story." She smiled as she gave him back his photo of Josie. "Contrary to what you might think, he's got a good dad."

"If all goes according to plan, he'll have a better one."

Tallin started to stand up. "Speaking of plans, do you have any for Saturday?"

"Are you asking me out?"

"Not exactly. I'll be at the Phillips Gallery on Saturday morning, say ten o'clock. It's a public place and if you happened to be there, too, we could talk about art."

"Art who?"

"Art work."

"Oh, him. Believe it or not, I could use some culture, but after visiting the Phillips, could you possibly show me the liquor store you own?"

"I don't own a liquor store."

Kael gave her a crooked half-smile. "That's encouraging news."

# 11

Bolo sat alone in the dimly lit bar sucking on his beer bottle and pondering who to kill next. For a change, there were a number of worthy candidates from which to choose. He had received information that Charles and Diana had been spotted together again having a bite to eat at the intersection of Sunset Boulevard and Rodeo Drive. Hitting both of them while they bickered over a meal would be a fitting end to their volatile relationship. Their battles were legendary.

Another doomed couple was Ron and Nancy. They were finally back after an eighteen-month absence. Although their whereabouts during that year-and-a-half were unknown, Bolo felt they were probably traveling out of the country. He knew they'd eventually return, and just yesterday, his sources had proven him right. They had been seen somewhere off the Ventura Freeway. Since they were so old, there were good prices on their wrinkled heads. Bolo's benefactors preferred the old ones, but they were getting harder to find. Nowadays, the good died young, the bad died young, and just being average was enough to be at the top of the list.

Bolo took another gulp of flat beer, and from his shadowy corner table, he watched a lone couple on the dance floor—two slender men who shuffled and shimmied to the pulsating rhythm of the music. Electric guitars, brassy horns and syncopated percussion mingled with the odors of stale beer, urine and sweat. Bolo's chair and table vibrated every time a bass note resonated from the hissing, dust-covered speakers.

The dancers were talented. Together, they only required a piece of dance floor the size of a handkerchief. Subtle movements of their hands served to highlight the more graphic gyrations of their hips. They never actually touched, but they came teasingly close.

Bolo despised couples. The specific gender combination didn't matter—male and male; male and female; female and female. They were all abominations.

Bolo was a greedy, single man. His incentives to kill were basic: money and protecting his own interests. These also happened to be his stimuli for getting up every morning with the sun, and rarely with another human being. Destroying a well-known couple like Charles and Di or Ron and Nancy would be doubly satisfying.

Bolo tipped his bottle one last time and drained the warm contents into his waiting mouth. He had a wonderful thought: he'd butcher both couples. It almost brought a smile to his stoic face. He set the bottle down and watched it dance alone across the length of the shaking table. It reached the end, and like a cliff diver perched on the precipice, it stopped as if gathering up courage to leap out into the void. The music ended. The table stopped vibrating. And the bottle balanced precariously on the edge. Bolo stood and slipped silently out of the bar into the humid night air.

# 12

Kael watched the airplane race down the runway. The nose gently lifted off the ground. The tail soon followed and as the plane soared skyward, it gradually banked to the right and out of sight. It was incredible that one hundred and fifty tons of steel could float in the air. What was even more mind-boggling was that in just a few short minutes, he'd be climbing into one of those contraptions and obediently strapping himself in to be subjected to stale air, a bad movie, and emergency instructions should the plane decide to agree with Newton's Laws of Gravity and plummet to the Earth like an apple falling out of a tree.

Nick was standing to Kael's left. His wife and kids had come to the airport, too. They were busy watching the airplanes at another window. Nick reached into his pants pocket and pulled out some change. He held it out for Kael. "Here, take this. French francs and Central African francs. There's enough for a couple of beers in the Paris airport and a beer and taxi ride once you get to Bangui. Mitch should be there to meet you, but one thing we've both learned about Africa is that things rarely go according to prearranged plans."

Kael put the change in his pocket and said, "I know all about CARL."

CARL was a term coined by Nick and Kael, and it had become part of the American expatriate vernacular of the Central African Republic. Thirteen years later it was still being used by Peace Corps volunteers, embassy secretaries and frustrated, American businessmen—all trying to function within the illogical and always chaotic Central African bureaucracy.

CARL was an acronym for "Central Africa Rarely Loses," and it was usually uttered with a symbolic shrug of the shoulders and a smile of expected resignation. Central Africa lost the lottery when it came to competent, honest leaders, but it always seemed to win big when a foreigner tried to get something accomplished within its borders. It made no sense to argue with the ticket agent at the Bangui airport about being bumped from a flight, even with a confirmed reservation. She wouldn't be swayed since it wasn't confirmed with CARL. It was ludicrous to complain to the police about being constantly hassled at their numerous roadside checkpoints. CARL had put them up, and only CARL could take them down. It was worthless to yell and scream in the bank because orderly lines were ignored by everyone, including the tellers. CARL didn't know about lines. Only those who could push and shove through a growing mob and get close enough to wave a deposit/withdrawal slip under the nose of the teller would accomplish any banking business on that day. Smart bankers got behind CARL and followed his blocks like a halfback running off tackle. People noticed CARL.

He was plopped down on the bench next to all non-Central Africans, rumpled, disheveled and spewing out his morning breath as the day started with a cup of too-sweet coffee and greasy *beignets*. He was in the outhouse handing out the sandpaper-like toilet paper. He was under the mosquito net, drooling on the pillow and stealing the covers through another sleepless night. CARL was omnipresent and those who learned to tolerate his annoying intrusions with a casual shrug of the shoulders and a smile were the ones who left the C.A.R. with fond memories of a beautiful country full of gentle people bearing more than their fair share of life's burdens.

Kael heard the announcement that his flight to Paris would soon begin boarding. He asked Nick, "Any last minute instructions?"

"No," said Nick. "You've been briefed. Anything we didn't cover, you'll learn in due time, either through Joseph and me or on your own. The most important thing to remember is to be wary of Bayanga's version of the Three Stooges: the police commissioner, the mayor and the *sous-préfet*. If there were a Dishonesty Olympics, they'd sweep the medals in backstabbing, the lying marathon and the two-faced bobsled."

"How about truth hurdling?" asked Kael.

"In world record time. They are the antithesis of integrity. Unfortunately, we are invited guests in their country and they are the local authorities, so we have to try and work with them, or at least, around them. This has become especially difficult since we now suspect that Moe, Larry and Curly are the three biggest crooks in the Doli-Ngili. They're into everything from illegal diamond mining to poaching."

"I'm half-expecting you to tell me that they are also child molesters, necrophiliacs and non-defensive drivers," said Kael.

"No, but they are the ones who decided Molly was killed by a crocodile man, so they not only hold positions of power, they're idiots, and that's a volatile combination."

"And they're probably on intimate terms with CARL," added Kael. Nick shrugged his shoulders and both he and Kael chuckled.

Nick said, "Pop quiz. What's the first thing you do when you get to Bangui?"

"Have a beer," replied Kael.

"OK, but after that?"

"Have another?"

"No," said Nick. "You get over to the American Embassy and introduce yourself to the Ambassador–the Honorable Daniel T. Saxon. He's anal about protocol so don't forget."

"Is he friend or foe?" asked Kael.

"I'm not sure. Don't be fooled by his captivating charm. Like most career diplomats and used car salesmen, he can flash an ear-to-ear grin while deviously plotting your demise."

"Don't worry, Nick. I can be charming and shallow, too."

"I've noticed. What's going on between you and Tallin?"

Kael narrowed his eyes to visually demonstrate that this type of question was completely out of character for Nick.

"Darcy insisted I ask," said Nick. "She won't be completely happy until all of my single friends are married and producing offspring. You are, at least, halfway there with Josie."

Kael was trying to organize his thoughts for an acceptable response when his concentration was broken by someone calling out his name. He looked over his shoulder, but the terminal was filled with a mass of humanity scrambling to make their flights or sprinting to the baggage claim carousels to see if their luggage had miraculously been sent to the same airport as themselves. There weren't many other Kaels out there. There couldn't be. Very few people named their children after misspelled vegetables. It could have been "Dale" or "Gail."

He turned back to Nick and said, "I'm sorry. I thought I heard someone call my name."

He heard it again. This time it was clearer and closer. It was definitely "Kael." He and Nick turned together to see Tallin's head and a waving arm. She was behind an overweight family of six who were wearing matching Disney World T-shirts and identical Disney World sailor's caps with the built-in green sunglass visors.

Out of the side of his mouth, Nick said, "You heartbreaker, you."

"What's she doing here?" asked Kael. "And I hope that's not her family she's with." Kael was relieved when she broke away from the family and ran up to where he and Nick were standing.

She said, "I thought I'd missed you. The traffic was unbelievable."

She was dressed in jeans and an oversized, gray, hooded Georgetown University Athletic Dept. sweatshirt. Her long, blond hair was pulled back into a ponytail and threaded through the adjustable plastic strap of a Baltimore Orioles baseball cap. It was not exactly an alluring ensemble as defined by *Vogue*, but Kael found himself aroused. It was at that very moment that he realized he'd been in the woods far too long. He didn't even need Frederick's of Hollywood to bring his turtle out of its shell. Nike of Beaverton, Oregon, sufficed.

She smiled at Kael. "Surprise." She hugged him and gave him a peck on his cheek.

Kael didn't know what to say. His vocabulary at that instant was as extensive as that of a rock

Tallin greeted Nick with a sheepish wave and a simple, "Hi."

Nick said, "I've got to hand it to you, Ms. Korne. You're the first person I've met who could make Kael speechless."

Kael regained his powers of communication and said, "Now if we could only find someone who could make Nick say something intelligent."

"Lord knows I've been trying for years."

The voice came from behind Kael. He turned around to find Darcy holding the hands of her two children.

"Which have you been trying?" asked Tallin. "To shut up Kael or to make Nick say something intelligent?"

"Take your pick. I've been trying to censor Kael's constant stream of one-liners for years, and the last intelligent thing Nick said was, 'I do.'"

"Thank you, dear," said Nick. "Tallin Korne, I'd like you to meet my *first* wife, Darcy."

Tallin offered her hand in greeting. Darcy released her grip on her son, Forrest, who suddenly realized he was free and bolted for the window to observe more planes. They were infinitely more interesting than a group of boring grown-ups.

His father reached out, snagged him by a trailing shirttail, and reeled him in to be mercilessly attacked by a tickle monster. Nick then placed his son's squirming body lengthwise across a hip and held him the way a student carries a notebook. He positioned Forrest's dangling head in front of Tallin and said, "This is our son, Forrest, who's almost as fast as the jets he adores."

Tallin tousled the horizontal toddler's hair and said, "Pleased to make your acquaintance."

Forrest looked up to see Tallin standing close to his Uncle Kael. With typical five-year-old frankness, he asked, "Is she your girlfriend, Uncle Kael?"

"One of them," Kael said with a smile.

"He wishes," said Tallin with an even bigger smile.

Nick and Darcy's daughter, Savannah, stepped forward and announced, "I thought *I* was your girlfriend, Uncle Kael."

"You're still my favorite seven-year-old named Savannah who lives in Virginia. That will never change, at least not until next year when you'll be my favorite eight-year-old."

This seemed to appease the little girl who slipped back next to her mother.

The Air France ticket agent made an announcement that they were now ready to begin general boarding starting with the rear of the airplane.

"That's you," said Nick. He reached out to hug Kael with one hand. The other hand held his son who was still balancing on one of his hips.

Kael looked at Nick and said, "I'll call you from Bangui."

"Gee, thanks," said Forrest. "I never talked to Africa before."

Kael then hugged Darcy and Savannah. He turned to face Tallin. "Thanks for coming to the airport to spend another three minutes with me. It was a nice surprise."

"I didn't come just to say good-bye." She took off the Baltimore Orioles baseball cap and handed it to Kael. "It's for Josie. Every American kid should have a baseball cap."

For the second time in less than five minutes, Kael was speechless.

Tallin said, "You'll have to teach him how to mold the brim."

"I will." He looked directly into Tallin's eyes. "Thanks. Now, I don't even care that you don't own a liquor store."

She smiled and opened her arms for a good-bye hug.

Kael held the cap out to the side to keep it from getting squashed between their bodies. He held her for a good five seconds. She still smelled of Ivory soap. That made him smile because he had picked up a few bars the night before to take to Africa, just to remind him of her.

He pulled away and said, "You keep writing. Remember, a writer writes."

"I will," said Tallin. "You write, too."

He made his way to the agent guarding the door. She took his ticket and granted him permission to pass.

Tallin shouted, "Hey, Pig-Pen."

He turned his head at both the sound of his nickname and the sound of her voice.

She was standing with Nick, Darcy, and the kids. They were all waving and leaning over the partition that separated the ticketed passengers from those left behind. She yelled over the din, "I'm not rich, either."

He laughed. It was a good way to begin a journey to Africa. He waved one last time, placed the Orioles cap on his head, and mounted the ramp to his awaiting plane.

# 13

Bolo waited and watched from a safe distance. He was only there to observe. He hadn't even brought his gun—just a small, inconspicuous pair of binoculars worn casually around his neck. They gave him the innocent look of a bird watcher hoping to add the Blue-Breasted Kingfisher to his life list, or that of a wide-eyed Hollywood stargazer eagerly awaiting an up-close encounter with one of his favorite movie starlets.

He didn't look like a killer, which was fine since his mission on this hazy morning wasn't to kill, but to simply see if it would be possible to kill. He wasn't even certain that his chosen targets would show. They could be so unpredictable.

From his vantage point, he had an unobstructed view of *Le Bistro*, a popular local watering hole situated at the busy intersection of Sunset Boulevard and Rodeo Drive. *Le Bistro* was frequented by locals, but it was also known as one of Prince Charles and Lady Di's favorite spots to relax with their entourage when they were in the country. They felt safe here, and *Le Bistro* was big enough to accommodate Chuck and Di's large retinue with abundant space, food and drink.

It was the breakfast hour and *Le Bistro* was already hopping with activity. Through his powerful binoculars, Bolo observed twenty to thirty individuals enter from either Sunset or Rodeo Drive to eat, drink and mingle. Charles and Diana were not among them. Some were alone while others stayed in groups. Some were noisy while others were quiet. Some came and went while others lingered. None noticed Bolo.

The sun was high in the sky when Bolo heard what sounded like a parade of trumpets and drums moving slowly up Sunset Boulevard. As the crescendo of noise approached, many of those in *Le Bistro* momentarily looked up from their food and drink to see what the commotion was. Bolo watched, too, but his interest was more than just idle curiosity. This was a job, so he watched intently through binoculars partially hidden by his large cupped hands.

His sources were right again. He spotted Diana first. She was looking a little thin these days. She was flanked by a cortege of minions and family members including her two young sons, William and Harry. They were getting bigger, but were still too young to kill. Maybe in a few years.

Charles lagged far behind, almost as if he were purposely putting as much distance as possible between himself and the Princess. He was surrounded by a small battalion of cautious but inferior lieutenants shielding their leader from any danger.

The twin lenses of Bolo's binoculars were filled with the clear unmistakable image of Charles' regal head. He really did have big ears.

The procession ambled up Sunset and filed into *Le Bistro* like London commuters queuing up for tickets to ride on "the Tube." Some of *Le Bistro*'s dining assemblage gawked open-mouthed at Charles, Diana and the rest of the royal contingent being herded in like cattle. Most went back to their meals with indifference. This was, after all, a country that had purged any and all affiliation with the "Empire" many years earlier.

Bolo observed that upon entering *Le Bistro*, Diana led her sons to the far end to seek solace from the crowd. Charles paid no discernible attention to them. He was too busy playing the role of the pompous, royal snob—strutting around *Le Bistro* with his nostrils held high in the air. The one time his meandering path crossed that of Diana's, she was less than receptive. Not one harsh word was spoken, but Diana's body language shouted, "Leave me and my sons alone you bloody, big-eared bloke!" She spun away, gathered up her two perplexed offspring and ushered them to a quiet unoccupied corner of *Le Bistro* along the Rodeo Drive side.

Bolo thought Diana would be the easier one to take down. She often isolated herself and her sons from the rest of the group. This would provide Bolo with a clear line of sight. No worthless bystanders to accidentally wander into the path of the bullet.

Another plus was that Diana seemed oblivious to her surroundings where a killer like Bolo might be lurking. Her attention, instead, was focused exclusively on the mothering and nurturing of her two young sons. Bolo wondered how she had managed to live this long being so apathetic about self-preservation. Like most leaders, she probably depended on the vigilance of others for her own security.

Charles, on the other hand, seemed wary. He was constantly moving and surveying every square inch of *Le Bistro*. Once, he even approached to within a couple hundred feet of Bolo's position and stared straight ahead, seemingly right at Bolo. Bolo held his breath. His heart was pounding so loudly, he was certain that Charles could hear it. How could he not with those ears? They stuck out like mammoth side-view mirrors. Bolo thought they'd make a great target: a bulls-eye for a bullet to the brain. Charles held his gaze for a good thirty seconds, then casually turned and walked away.

Bolo slowly and quietly exhaled.

Charles stopped so abruptly, it was almost as if he had walked into a transparent wall. He looked back over his left shoulder and again appeared to glare in Bolo's direction.

Bolo didn't budge. He was certain that Charles couldn't see him. He was too far away and too well hidden. Still, any movement, no matter how innocuous, could catch Charles' eye in the same way a falling star was glimpsed for a brief instant as it plummeted through a twinkling midnight sky. Bolo made a conscious effort to keep his lips from moving as he said to himself that Chuck wasn't as dumb as he looked. Killing him would be a refreshing challenge.

Charles pivoted his head back to its natural forward-facing position and he resumed walking away from Bolo, but with just a bit more speed in his steps. He didn't stop until he reached the far end of *Le Bistro* where he was quickly swallowed up by his cohorts. Even Charles' ears were obscured from Bolo's prying binoculars.

Bolo had seen enough. He knew he had to kill Charles first. He seemed more alert to potential danger than Diana, and once the shooting started, Diana would inevitably rush to protect her family, not herself.

But where to make the kill? Should he shoot them over a drink in *Le Bistro*, or before they entered, while they were still lined up on Sunset Boulevard? Bolo favored the confines of Sunset Boulevard. There, Charles would be more distracted and less aware. This was in contrast to *Le Bistro* where his senses seemed more acute.

Bolo scanned down Sunset Boulevard with his binoculars. After several passes, he found an ideal place for concealment. It was a perfect location. It was high above Sunset and it afforded the shooter equally unobstructed views of *Le Bistro* and Rodeo Drive as well. This was necessary should Charles and Diana decide to take a different route. They could be so unpredictable.

Bolo preferred shooting from above like a hawk swooping down on its unsuspecting prey. Victims rarely looked up. They always expected danger to come at ground level. With a bird's-eye view, the target's head would appear so much larger, like a helium-filled balloon that had slipped through a child's fingers to ascend into the heavens. Bolo was looking forward to piercing the balloons of Charles and Diana with as many large-caliber bullets as it would take to send the pair crashing violently to the ground.

The thought of draining the helium out of Chuck and Di almost brought a smile to Bolo's stoic face. Almost was as close as Bolo ever got to smiling. In fact, almost was an appropriate depiction of Bolo's meager existence. He had almost no body fat, he almost never slept for more than three or four hours per night, and he almost understood the siren-like call of insanity. Every day he navigated those seductive waters by performing insane work under insane conditions for an insane amount of money. What Bolo couldn't fathom was how perilously close the sirens had lured him to the rocks.

He looked as sane as anyone else loitering on the corner of Sunset Boulevard and Rodeo Drive. He waited for Charles and Diana to leave *Le Bistro*. It would go so much more quickly if he could suck on a cigarette, but lighting up here wouldn't be prudent. His sources had warned him that it could be a long, boring stake-out. Chuck and Di could linger at *Le Bistro* for anywhere from twenty minutes to several hours. They could be so unpredictable. It had already been over an hour since they had arrived.

When they finally departed, Bolo would slip away unseen. He'd come back, though, as would Chuck and Di. Only next time, Bolo would return with his gun. Maybe he'd shoot the whole damn family. He could be unpredictable, too.

# 14

Kael stepped out of the air-conditioned cabin of the *Air Afrique* jet and plunged headfirst into the dictatorial Bangui heat. It was oppressive, smothering and merciless. Like most corrupt rulers, the Central African heat had no social conscience. It brought everyone, regardless of status or income, to their scraped and bruised knees pleading for a respite, a soft gentle rain or a refreshing glass of water.

Kael tried to take a deep breath, but it was nearly impossible. The humid air was so saturated with moisture droplets that his lungs rebelled, thinking he was drowning and beginning to swallow mouthfuls of water.

When his coughing subsided, he tried breathing slowly through his nose instead and picked up not only oxygen, but also a long-forgotten fragrance he hadn't experienced for ten years: a mixture of open sewers, diesel fuel and wood smoke all held together by the rancid odor of cassava tubers drying in the hot tropical sun. The unique aroma stunned first-time visitors. It hit one's nose like a persistent left jab, lacking the force of a knock-out punch, but making the person attached to the nose take notice. It was somehow comforting to Kael just as the combination of licorice and Jean Nate perfume reminded him of his grandmother. Not exactly pleasing to the olfactory senses, but soothing nonetheless because it conjured up pleasant memories.

Kael stood on the top platform of a descending aluminum stairway. He waved to the throng of jubilant greeters who were perched on the terminal's second-floor, open-air observation deck. Everyone gathered there because it afforded an early glimpse of an expected, disembarking passenger. It was also close to the airport bar.

Kael scanned the crowd for Mitchell Wright's vaguely familiar face, but it was like looking at a giant *Where's Waldo* puzzle. Up there, on that very observation deck, was where Kael had last seen Josie and his son's mother, Sapu, before mounting a plane to return to the states alone.

Kael waded down the steps leading to the one-hundred-and-twenty-degree melting runway tarmac. It was soft and spongy. The walk to the shoebox-sized terminal of Bangui-Mpoko Airport was a short one, but the oppressive heat made it seem longer. Each step on the melting, pillow-like ground produced an extra ten heartbeats and one pint of perspiration. Gravity was somehow stronger here. It was more possessive and stingy. Everyone moved in slow motion. Kael suspected that if he tried to speak, his voice would come out sounding like an ancient forty-five rpm record played at thirty-three rpm speed. Tallin would love this theory.

Kael and his fellow nose-twitching passengers were escorted to the terminal by a dozen large, camouflage-clad, spit-shined, gun-toting soldiers whose job was primarily to keep all newcomers from wandering into a restricted area. Their secondary responsibility was to intimidate anyone contemplating participation in a *coup d'état*.

Coups were fairly common throughout Africa. In some countries, they occurred with more regularity than leap years. Since achieving independence from France in 1960, the C.A.R. had experienced its share of coup attempts, three of which were successful: Colonel Bokassa's overthrow of Dacko in 1966; Dacko's return engagement with French assistance in 1979, which ousted Emperor Bokassa; and General Kolingba's removal of two-time loser, Dacko, in 1981. One needed a scorecard and a big eraser to follow African politics.

Two of the twelve military escorts were white and both wore red berets perched with jaunty indifference on crewcut heads. They were obviously French Paratroopers who were part of a large military presence. Gallic interests had to be protected, so they had become as commonplace as the heat since the 1979 coup. They barked out orders in guttural French to their ten Central African recruits who were black and wore green berets pulled low over large, frightened eyes. They appeared too scared to even utter the words, *coup d'état*.

Kael smiled at one man intending to soothe his fears, but smiling while in military garb was probably punishable by flogging or having to listen to French music. Kael got no response.

He entered the airport terminal hoping to be greeted by the high-pitched whine of an overworked air conditioner. No such luck. CARL hadn't even installed a fan. It was too bad Bangui couldn't crate up its heat and export it to northern climes. British Thermal Units would certainly fetch a higher price than peanuts or cotton in the international marketplace, and Bangui heat was top-of-the-line, state-of-the-art humidity that few greenhouses could mimic.

Upon entering the terminal, the line of passengers split into two separate entities: those with Central African passports and those without. The foreigners, including

Kael, formed a straight, orderly line for immigration formalities. The Central African contingent rushed forward, pushing and shoving for the exit to see who could get to their baggage first. Kael and the rest of his regimented line watched with awe.

An olive-skinned gentleman standing in front of Kael turned to him and said, "Did someone yell 'fire?'"

Kael smiled and wiped the perspiration from his brow. "No. Maybe they heard the rumor that the baggage claim area is air conditioned."

With only one person to check visas and stamp passports, Kael's line moved so slowly he was afraid his visa would expire before it was his turn. He was glad he had changed into cooler clothes in Paris, swapping his jeans and long-sleeved shirt for lighter, looser tan cotton chinos and a white, three-button, polo shirt. He still wore Josie's baseball cap.

He briefly wondered what project directors were expected to wear these days, but came to the conclusion that he didn't care. This was his nicest, unwrinkled ensemble and it would have to do. He didn't think he could be arrested or thrown out of the country for making an improper fashion statement, but one never knew. People were languishing in African prisons for even more bizarre offenses. Molly's accused killer, Assan Séléman, was a perfect example.

Thoughts of Assan triggered a vision of Molly. It was one Kael had experienced while napping on the plane. The visual image was a close-up of Molly's face. Her eyes were wide open revealing pale blue irises, but Kael couldn't tell if she was alive or not. The lower half of her face—from just below the nose down—was hidden by water.

Kael wished he were submerged up to his nose in water. Maybe he'd hit the ambassador's pool later. It was often available for use by the American community. When Kael was a Peace Corps volunteer, those privileges had been revoked after he and some of his Peace Corps compatriots had sneaked in over a fence one night for some innocent skinny-dipping. Molly, Nick, and three others had been caught along with Kael and all were banned from the pool for the remainder of their Peace Corps contracts. Kael hoped the statute of limitations had expired.

It suddenly hit Kael that Molly *could* swim. He had seen her that night at the ambassador's. He had seen a lot that night. So how did she drown?

He was trying to process this revelation, as well as the significance of his vision, when his concentration was interrupted by someone saying, "*Bonjour, monsieur. Votre passeport, s'il vous plaît.*" It was the immigration official. Kael had reached the head of the line with weeks to spare on his visa.

He handed over his passport and greeted the official in the national language of Sango. *"Bara ma. Mo éké sengué?"*

The official, a small dark man wearing Ben Franklin-style glasses, gave a surprised look and said, in Sango, "You speak our language well. You are not a tourist." He held Kael's passport upside-down and thumbed through it looking for a valid Central African visa.

"No," said Kael, who was pleasantly stunned with the realization that he had picked up every word of Sango the man had spoken. Not bad for being in hibernation for ten years. He was feeling a bit cocksure so he continued, "I'm here to help protect your elephants and gorillas out near Bayanga."

"Why?" said the official who still hadn't found the proper visa. "Elephants trample our fields and gorillas rape our women."

"We all have our faults... and besides," said Kael with an accompanying wink and a smile, "they both eat crocodile men."

"Ah... this is good. We have too many crocodile men."

Kael waited for a reciprocal smile to appear on the official's face—one that acknowledged his appreciation for a good joke—but it never came. He was too busy concentrating on the upside-down passport.

"I can't seem to find your entry visa."

Kael reached out, turned the passport right side up and methodically paged through from front to back until he found it. "Maybe you need a new pair of glasses."

"Yes, ones with prescription lenses. These are just glass." The official stamped the visa and closed the passport.

Kael retrieved his stamped passport, said goodbye, *"Mo douti njoni,"* and walked towards the baggage claim area.

His bags hadn't arrived yet. No one's had. Baggage had to be manually unloaded from the plane by two shirtless adolescents whose mouths worked harder than their well-defined muscles. One would eventually climb up into the cargo hold and hand down a suitcase to his partner who would then carry it balanced on his head to the claim area. Here, it would be dropped onto a low, long, wooden platform to be reclaimed by its anxious owner.

Kael was sweating buckets. The wait wouldn't be so bad if some enterprising Central African had set up a little beer kiosk off to the side. He could make a killing.

The bags finally started to arrive one by one. A mob gathered around the platform, so Kael stood back, leaned against a dingy wall, and watched the proceedings.

He observed, with a slight pang of jealousy, the lucky passengers whose bags came off first. They dragged their ungainly loads across the room to where uniformed customs agents awaited to inspect each piece and to collect the customs questionnaires that had been handed out on the plane just prior to landing. No luggage belonging to Central African passengers was opened or searched. A chalk checkmark scrawled on each bag by an inspector allowed the owner to proceed directly to the main terminal and parking lot hassle-free.

Kael noticed that customs agents only targeted the white French passengers. CARL was obviously on duty. Zippers were opened and hands were thrust into bags to feel for any contraband hidden in socks, underwear and shaving kits. Sometimes, whole suitcases were dumped out on a nearby table for closer inspection. Getting everything properly re-packed amidst the pushing, noise, heat and confusion was stressful for even the hardiest traveler.

Kael had an idea. It had worked before and this appeared to be an ideal situation for further field verification. When his backpack and guitar case came off next-to-last, he felt even more confident with his plan. By now, everyone had gone through customs procedures except for him and one young African woman whose bags came off right after his.

The inspectors were visibly weary from arguing with each disgruntled French passenger to spread out the contents of their matching designer luggage onto a dirty card table. Not one French passenger had cheerily surrendered to the inevitable search. The French, not unlike Texans, could be so haughty, especially when a stranger from one of their former colonies demanded to gaze upon their collection of underwear.

Kael shuffled over to the inspection table. He held the guitar case by its handle, but he was too tired to shoulder the heavy backpack. He dragged it lazily behind like a dog fighting the leash. He handed his completed customs questionnaire to the official who looked to be the most exhausted of the bunch and said, in English, "Good afternoon, sir. How are you doing on this broiler of a day?"

The blue-uniformed customs official glanced at Kael's questionnaire, saw that he had nothing to declare, and then switched his gaze to the backpack and guitar resting at Kael's side. He looked up at his last passenger of the day and said, *"Bonjour, monsieur. Si vous me donnez votre guitare, vous pourrez passer toute de suite."*

Even though Kael knew exactly what the official had said—he wanted the guitar in exchange for a non-inspection—Kael flashed his best look of confusion. It was the same one Chako used when given the command to roll over. Kael said, "I'm sorry, but I don't speak a lick of your lingo. I just assumed you guys spoke English, too."

He had nothing to hide. He wasn't trying to smuggle in drugs or large amounts of cash. He didn't even care if this guy ran his sweaty hands all over his bundle of boxers. His sole purpose, admittedly juvenile, was to test a simple theory: This inspector would be too fatigued and frustrated to patiently deal with a passenger who didn't speak the French language.

This theory was not a new one. Many years earlier, Peace Corps had recommended this ploy to its volunteers for use under certain conditions. For instance, when confronted by crooked Central African cops who sometimes performed random traffic stops for money when their government paychecks didn't arrive, pretending to be a dumb tourist was often the best defense. Extortion wouldn't work if the victim didn't understand he was being extorted. It was like trying to discuss the stock market with a cat.

The official pointed to the guitar and said in a louder, slower voice, "*Votre guitare, votre guitare. Je la desire.*"

"Oh...now I understand," said Kael, in English. From his back pocket he pulled out his flight envelope. He opened it, tore off the two baggage claim tickets and handed them with a smile to the official. "They're my bags, all right. You can check."

"*Mon Dieu,*" said the defeated official who then pulled out a small stick of chalk from his trousers pocket. He slashed checkmarks on both pieces like a chalk-wielding Zorro and said, "*Allez! Allez! Quel idiot!*" He then pointed Kael to the double-wide exit doors.

Kael gathered up the coveted guitar and slung the backpack over one shoulder with renewed enthusiasm. He pushed triumphantly through the doors only to be accosted on the other side by a minimum of nine baggage porters all fighting and squabbling among each other for the opportunity to carry his bags. They surrounded him like hyenas ripping and tearing at a carcass. His hands immediately dropped to protect his most vulnerable area: his wallet. The yelling and jostling provided an excellent distraction for patting down an unsuspecting victim.

The baggage porters were all seasoned young *godobés* with nothing better to do than harass shell-shocked visitors who were still reeling from the long, tiring flight and unconventional immigration and customs procedures. These *godobé* welcoming committees displayed such a perverse bravado that first impressions of Bangui were often referred to as, "first depressions."

Kael knew they would besiege him as long as he remained out in the open, so he tranquilized them with a smile, a few choice curses in Sango, and then crashed through their circle using his guitar as a jousting pole. Once in the clear, he checked to make sure he still had his wallet. It was undisturbed in his pocket, so he headed in the opposite direction of the parking lot. His objective was the airport bar located on the second floor.

Halfway up the wide staircase, he stopped and looked down to see if Mitchell Wright was in the crowd. No Mitchell, but CARL could be seen everywhere, relishing in the disorder.

Kael hadn't expected Mitchell to be at the airport to shake his hand, help him with his bags, and drive him into town in an air-conditioned vehicle. This was Bangui, after all, and Bangui was the birthplace and long-time residence of CARL, who still governed the land no matter which flavor-of-the-month dictator was in charge.

The airport bar hadn't changed. Kael wondered if the dirty tile floor had been scrubbed even once since his departure ten years earlier. Some of those scuffmarks were probably his.

He walked past the long bar, which was sorely in need of a new coat of stain, and wove through a maze of randomly spaced tables, one of which was occupied by the olive-skinned gentleman from the immigration line. Kael nodded and smiled as he stepped around the man's garment bag partially blocking the aisle. He stopped at the last table that looked out on the now-deserted observation deck. He dropped his backpack and guitar to the floor, pulled out a chair, and plopped down with an exaggerated sigh. He was only minutes from a cold beer.

He was busy sorting through a handful of change, trying to pick out the Central African francs that Nick had given him, when he felt someone approaching—probably a waiter—so he looked up ready to place his order.

It was the olive-skinned gentleman who walked up with his garment bag and asked in accented, but grammatically correct, English, "May I sit with you?"

"Sure," said Kael. "Can I buy you a beer? I think I have enough."

"That would be very nice." The short, stout man dropped his garment bag on one chair and sat down in another. He said, "We never did find that air conditioning, did we?"

Kael smiled. "No, and I'm beginning to wonder if we'll ever find a waiter."

The man raised his right arm in the direction of the bar. He snapped his hairy-knuckled fingers several times and released a loud "psst" from his mouth. It sounded like air escaping from a punctured inner tube. "You just have to know how to ask."

Within seconds, a timid young man was at their side prepared to take their order. Kael looked at the olive-skinned man and said, *"Deux Mocafs?"*

Nods were exchanged all around. Just as the waiter turned to leave, Kael stopped him in his tracks by asking, in Sango, if the beer was cold: *"A dé mingui?"*

The waiter nodded and smiled. He then continued on his task.

Kael looked at the olive-skinned man. "Think we'll ever see him again?"

"I think your use of Sango almost guarantees it." He held out his hand. "I am Nasseef."

Kael dropped his change on the table and shook the man's hand. "I'm Kael."

"Your Sango is very good, Kael. Are you an American Peace Corps?" He pronounced the word, "corpse."

"Close," said Kael with a smile. "I used to be a Peace Corpse. Now, my body and soul belong to TRAP."

Nasseef's dark eyes opened wide and his bushy, salt-and-pepper eyebrow, which ran unbroken along the entire length of his lower forehead, raised up slightly, just above the bridge of his large hooked nose. "Ahh...so you must know *Monsieur* Nick."

Evidently, membership in the expatriate community of Bangui wasn't much different from living in a small town like Sitka. There were lots of strange people, but few strangers.

"Better than most. How do you know him?"

Nasseef took out a pack of *Sprint Rouge* cigarettes from his breast pocket. He tapped one out and placed it in the yellowed corner of his mouth while his fingers probed the now-empty pocket for matches. Europeans never asked if they could smoke. They just assumed everyone did. Nasseef talked while he conducted a pocket-to-pocket search. He was very adept at keeping the cigarette dangling precariously from his lips while he carried on a conversation. Kael guessed he had been smoking since he was eight.

"When *Monsieur* Nick was working here, I used to fix his truck. I have a garage. Best garage in all of Bangui. Best prices, too." When he pulled out a yellowed handkerchief from his pants pocket, a book of matches fell out on to the floor. He picked them up and lit his cigarette. "*Monsieur* Nick's truck was very old. He was one of my best customers. He still stops in to see me at the garage when he is here on business. Do you have a truck?"

"I will. *Monsieur* Mitch has it now. Do you know him, too?"

"Not very well. He takes his truck to another garage—one of my competitors who charges very little for an oil change, but overcharges on everything else. Perhaps you will bring this truck to me when it is yours?"

"Perhaps," said Kael as their waiter returned with two, large, green Mocaf beer bottles and two chipped glasses. The bottles looked like they had just stepped out of a shower. They were wet, glistening and covered by tiny water droplets bravely clinging to the surface in a vain attempt to stave off evaporation in the one-hundred-degree heat. The beer looked delicious.

Kael greeted the waiter with one of his favorite Sango phrases: *"Mo si awé?"* You've arrived?

Of course he'd arrived. He was there, wasn't he? It was like waking someone from a deep sleep and then asking, "Are you awake?" The only response was, "Of course I'm awake."

The waiter smiled and gave the only appropriate reply: *"Eh, Mbi si awé."* Yes, I've arrived. He then poured the beers into the chipped glasses, accepted the coins, and left.

Kael loved the simplicity. It highlighted one of the major differences between Africans and Alaskans, one that he neglected to mention to Tallin because he still didn't understand how to interpret the data.

He had once tried the greeting, "You've arrived?" on each individual at Hidden Cove, just to see what kind of reaction he'd get. Sam had predictably responded, "Of course I've arrived. What kind of dumbass question is that?" Hector had also stayed true to form and said, "Yeah, you got any coffee?" C.B.'s reply was typically philosophical: "I'm here physically, but spiritually, I'm still miles from arriving." Chako's response was the most "African." She had wagged her tail at the sound of his voice and then curled up on the floor for a nap untroubled by Kael's query.

His theory on this conundrum was based on the hypothesis that logic could no longer function in Central Africa. It had emigrated long before CARL ever showed up and its desire to repatriate was fleeting, especially after it learned that crocodile men swam in the waters.

Nasseef raised his glass and said, *"Chin chin."*

Kael touched his glass to Nasseef's and echoed the toast, *"Chin chin."*

It was what the French always said when toasting. It simply imitated the sound of two glasses clinking together, but it was a toast that didn't travel well. A friend of Kael's had once traveled to Tokyo and in front of a bunch of Japanese businessmen, had raised his glass of saki with the words, "*Chin chin.*" It was an appropriate toast in France or French-speaking Africa, but not in Japan where it meant, "little penis," not something Japanese men wanted to toast.

The Mocaf was almost perfect. It had three out of four qualities appreciated by discriminating beer drinkers: It was cold, it was carbonated, and it came in big bottles. All it lacked was a distinctive flavor.

He poured a second glass and said, "That's my first Mocaf in ten years. They haven't improved the recipe, have they?"

"No," said Nasseef, "but one has to remember that little in Central Africa has improved in the last ten years. It is like *Monsieur* Nick's truck. I would tell him, 'If you don't keep fixing the little things, they will soon become big things. When the big things are also ignored, the truck is doomed. Not even Nasseef can fix it then.'"

Kael continued to swill the beer. In this heat, cold drinks needed to be consumed before they turned into hot soup. "If you fix trucks as well as you philosophize, you've got my business. How long have you been in Bangui?"

Nasseef kept up with Kael's breakneck pace. Most Europeans living and working in Africa were as accomplished in their drinking habits as they were in their smoking habits.

"Over thirty years," he said. "I came here with my two brothers from Lebanon. We were going to make many francs in the transport business." He laughed, but it was the kind that was more visual than vocal. A smile formed, which made his eyes crinkle up at the corners. "My brothers went back home two weeks after seeing how bad the roads were. I stayed and decided there was more money to be made fixing trucks than driving them. Those bad roads turned out to be my best friends. They have given me many customers."

"And how are your brothers?" Kael poured another glass.

"Yusef, the oldest, still lives in Beirut. Rajan, the youngest, now lives outside Paris with his French wife and their four daughters. I was there visiting with him this past week and I think he is finding that living with five women is much more difficult than starting up a transport business in Central Africa."

Kael smiled. He asked, "Are you glad you stayed?"

Nasseef shrugged what Kael suspected were very hairy shoulders. "I'm glad I don't have four daughters. Are you glad you came back?"

Kael finished what beer was left in his glass and said, "I'm glad I didn't come back just for the beer." He poured into his glass what was left in the bottle. He noticed a small African man approaching with purpose. He came in big strides and his eyes were locked on Nasseef.

"I think you have a gentleman caller," said Kael.

"What?"

Kael pointed and Nasseef turned just as the man reached their table. Nasseef recognized the stranger and spoke in rapid French, "Ah, Simplice. So nice of you to come."

Simplice responded, *"Oui, patron."* Yes, boss.

Nasseef turned back to Kael. "Our taxi has arrived. Can I offer you a ride into town?"

"That would be great. I wasn't sure if I had enough change left to pay for a cab."

"I can exchange some of your American dollars, if you wish. My rates are reasonable and my lines are much shorter than the bank's. I often provide the same service for *Monsieur* Nick when he is in town. He calls me his 'one-stop shopping place.'"

Kael smiled. He finished off his beer in three quick gulps.

Simplice had already grabbed Nasseef's garment bag and was wrestling with Kael's burdensome backpack. It outweighed him by fifty pounds.

Kael tried explaining to Simplice that he was capable of carrying his own backpack.

Simplice grunted and grimaced, but he wouldn't give up, especially with *Patron* Nasseef encouraging him from his corner.

Kael was too exhausted to argue, so he helped Simplice to position the pack properly on the skinny young man's back. Kael cinched up the shoulder straps and waist belt as far as they could go and tried to impress upon Simplice the importance of leaning forward, but not too far. If he tried to stand up straight, the backpack would throw him to the floor for a quick pin.

Simplice smiled the whole time he was being rigged up. With the pack clinging to his back like a grizzly bear to a sapling, he now insisted on carrying the guitar in his free hand. Kael didn't even try to dissuade him this time. He handed it over without comment like a frightened robbery victim. He theorized that Simplice probably needed the weight of the guitar to counterbalance the weight of the garment bag in his other hand.

Simplice followed Kael and Nasseef out the bar, down the stairs, and through the airport's empty main terminal. Even the *godobés* had gone home for nourishment and a siesta. There would be another flight later that evening, and they needed to be strong and well rested for a second shift of intimidation, annoyance and petty thievery.

Nasseef led the trio to one of three vehicles still in the parking lot: a white Toyota Land Cruiser pickup truck. It looked recently washed.

Nasseef opened the tailgate. It was damming back several gallons of soapy water. He was too slow to jump out of the way and the escaping water splashed all over his leather, tasseled shoes. He calmly looked at Simplice and said, "Is this why you were late? You were washing the truck?"

Simplice swayed under the weight of the baggage. A barely audible, "*Oui, patron,*" came out of his mouth between grunts and groans of discomfort.

Nasseef nodded his head and said, "Good job." He looked at Kael and winked. "At least my feet are cool."

Kael helped Simplice crawl out of the backpack, which they then tossed onto a dry section of the bed along with the guitar and garment bag. Simplice turned the keys over to Nasseef and then followed the bags into the bed to sit atop one of the wheel wells. Nasseef closed the tailgate.

Simplice's job changed once again, from chauffeur to pack mule to that of a security guard. His new responsibility was to make sure they arrived in town at their final destination with all three bags still in the bed. Thieves didn't just work under the guise of baggage porters. They were everywhere and their methods were ingenious. An open truck innocently stopped at a traffic light was a prime target for pilferers.

Nasseef unlocked the driver's side door, climbed into the cab and reached across the bench seat to open Kael's door. Kael hopped in. Nasseef turned the key counterclockwise. This produced a clicking sound and also illuminated an orange light above the steering column. The glow plugs were warming up. After several seconds, the clicking stopped and the light was extinguished. Nasseef turned the key clockwise and the diesel engine rumbled to life. His right hand went instinctively to the climate-control knobs on the dash and the cab of the Toyota was instantly flooded with a refreshing blast of arctic air.

Nasseef turned to Kael and said, "At last...we have found the air conditioning."

# 15

Kael, Nasseef and Simplice raced out of the parking lot and headed down the bustling airport access road called *Avenue des Martyrs*. There was virtually no vehicular traffic, but both sides of the pothole-laden road were lined with pedestrians.

Women wrapped in bright patterns of African cloth carried napping babies strapped tightly to their backs. The babies' exposed heads bobbed side-to-side as their mothers power-walked while balancing several hundred board-feet of firewood on their own rigid heads.

Unemployed men in monochromatic leisure suits gathered to gossip, laugh, and create massive sidewalk traffic jams. Small rectangular leather purses dangled from many of the men's wrists. These usually contained identification documents, old letters, pens (which also didn't work), and cutout pictures from magazines of places they'd never visit, people they'd never meet and merchandise they'd never own.

Bald, barefooted children in tattered t-shirts and shorts chased skinny, catatonic, mongrel dogs with sticks. Each cur looked closely related to the next, like they all had the same father—a randy, traveling salesdog of sorts.

Every one hundred meters there was a crudely constructed plywood shack that served as a bar. Most of the customers lounging at the small wooden tables were male and they drank whatever was in season: Mocaf, honey beer, palm wine, or a potent, sometimes lethal, corn whiskey known as *mbako*. The latter was often distilled through scavenged automobile exhaust pipes.

The visual extravaganza taking place just outside Kael's passenger side window was interrupted by Nasseef asking where he would like to be dropped off.

"I need to check in at the American Embassy. Might as well get that over with."

They continued down *Avenue des Martyrs* across *Avenue Koudoukoudou* to where it widened in front of the University of Bangui on the left. It looked as rundown and neglected as the airport.

When they arrived at the intersection of *Avenue des Martyrs* and *Avenue Boganda*, Nasseef pointed to the right and said, "My garage is down there just past the acacia tree."

They turned left on *Avenue Boganda* for downtown or *Centreville*. European influences became more evident the closer one got to *Centreville*. Housing designs changed from bare, mud-brick walls and tin roofs to tall, fenced-in estates with large glass windows hidden behind thick, wrought-iron bars.

*Centreville* was the headquarters for government ministries, presidential palaces, embassies and businesses catering to Bangui's wealthier residents, both foreign and Central African. When Kael was a Peace Corpse, French paté, wine and pastry could be purchased on almost every corner.

Bangui, especially *Centreville*, always had a quaint colonial charm. The sidewalk *cafés*, expensive boutiques and traffic circles full of honking Peugots and Citroens gave the city a distinctive, romantic French flavor. But something had changed during Kael's absence.

Bangui, *La Coquette*, the Flirt, had lost its innocence. The city, which was nestled between green rolling hills and a gentle bend of the Oubangui River, had degraded like a sandcastle in the rain. The streets were now empty and dirty. Buildings were boarded up or falling apart. What was once a vibrant, friendly, whitewashed metropolis had become a decaying slum.

Bangui had gotten older, but like many children, it hadn't matured with its years. The comical, freshly scrubbed, anxious-to-please little brother who was forever trying unsuccessfully to be like "the big boys" had turned into a juvenile delinquent with an attitude.

Kael gazed upon the once lush hillsides rising above the city. They were now brown and denuded with a receding hairline where tall tropical trees had been cut down for firewood. Kael suspected that even the Oubangui was meaner, muddier and more turbulent.

He asked Nasseef, "What happened? The place is filthy."

"Cities age just like people. Some do it more gracefully than others."

Kael shook his head and wondered if Sitka could ever deteriorate to a similar condition.

"I remember when Bokassa crowned himself Emperor and we became the Central African Empire," said Nasseef. "He would cruise the streets in his bullet-proof limousine, and if he spotted a building in need of whitewash, he would stop and have one of his burly bodyguards paint a big red cross on the door of the eyesore. This was a message that the owner had three days to paint the building or he could face the alternative: a long prison term in an unpainted cell. Bokassa was a cannibalistic tyrant, but at least we had a clean city."

Kael wondered how a ruler so concerned with keeping his city clean could have stained those same streets with the blood of his countrymen—many of them children. He didn't bother to pose this question to Nasseef, who was a struggling, local business-man and probably measured the success of his city according to the success of his own garage.

"Just between you and me," said Nasseef, "I used to send Simplice out in the cover of darkness to paint red crosses on vehicles hoping people would interpret it as a message from the Emperor to get their offending vehicles fixed."

They turned right off of *Avenue Boganda* on to a narrower, bumpier side street. Kael couldn't tell if it was a dirt road or a paved one in need of maintenance. Even with the air conditioning on full blast and with the windows closed, Kael's sensitive nostrils picked up the unmistakable odor of urine.

Nasseef must have noticed it, too, as he said, "My definition of an underdeveloped country is a place where one can urinate anywhere."

They drove by a group of African tailors who either had serious nasal blockage, or they had become oblivious to the stench around them. They sat, seemingly unaffected, behind their ancient, foot-pump Singer sewing machines and created clothing on com-mand for Africans of all shapes and sizes, often without the luxury of patterns. African tailors were somehow able to eyeball measurements and were so adept that the finished garment almost always fit perfectly. Why couldn't Central Africans make fashionable, long-wearing cities as easily as they made fashionable, long-wearing clothes?

The Toyota pulled up in front of the American Embassy. It was a boring, block-like structure with as much architectural appeal as a Port-A-Potty. It was heavily fortified by walls, gates, bars and guards dressed in dark blue jumpsuits and carrying big black nightsticks. Where was the traditional, All-American welcome mat?

The embassy's front entrance was partitioned off from the street by a long, straight line of cement blocks the size of industrial washing machines. These had been installed to deter suicidal car bombers. Now, the only way to penetrate the embassy with a car bomb was to drop one on the roof by helicopter. Even then, it would probably get tan-gled up like a netted fish in the maze of rooftop antennas, satellite dishes and guy-wires. Nasseef said to Kael, "If you would like to exchange some American dollars, we can do that now. I checked the rate while in Paris. It was 265 CFA to one U.S. dollar. I will give you 250."

"I thought you said it was 265."

"I have to show a small profit, don't I? It is still much better than you will find anywhere in Bangui."

Kael reached into his pocket and pulled out his wallet. He opened it and removed some American Express Travelers Checks. "How about one hundred dollars worth?"

"Two hundred would be better."

"For whom?"asked Kael.

"For both of us."

Nasseef produced a wad of bills and counted off 50,000 CFA. This was more money than most Central Africans made in a year. What remained in the wad could have kept the Central African government running for several years.

Kael signed over two hundred dollars worth of checks, accepted Nasseef's rough equivalent in Central African currency, and placed the large, colorful bills in his wallet. He shook his banker's hand and said, "Thanks for the lift."

"Thank you for the beer... and for your future business."Nasseef smiled.

Kael hopped out of the air-conditioned cab and was rudely reminded of how hot it was outside. Simplice had already brought both of his bags around to the side of the truck. They sat on the ground as Simplice stood guard over them.

Kael pulled from his pocket what change was left. It could have been worth twenty-five cents or twenty-five dollars. He didn't check and he didn't care. It was Nick's change, anyway. He held it out to Simplice. "*Merci*, Simplice."

Simplice accepted the coins with cupped hands. "*Oui, patron.*"He climbed back into the bed to guard the last piece of luggage and the truck roared off.

Kael's backpack hadn't gotten any lighter. He lifted it to one shoulder, picked up the guitar, and shuffled past three Central African guards who were busy having an animated conversation about somebody's cousin who had died. The three embassy employees didn't even acknowledge Kael's presence. Forget car bombs. Someone without a driver's license could just walk right into the embassy carrying a backpack full of dynamite. He wondered if the guards would even notice the resulting explosion.

He stepped through the front doors to enter a small, air-conditioned waiting room. The room's only piece of furniture was a black vinyl couch. It was the kind that stuck to skin on hot days.

A huge U.S. Marine in full dress uniform stood alone in an adjoining room of bulletproof glass. His outpost separated the waiting area from another door leading to the inner bowels of the embassy compound. He couldn't have been more than nineteen or twenty. Kael's backpack was older than that.

The young Marine spoke through an intercom in the glass. "Good afternoon, sir. How can I help you?"

Kael set his bags down on the couch. "Hi. I'd like to introduce myself to Ambassador Saxon, if that's possible. My name is Kael Husker and I'm the new director of the Doli-Ngili project out in Bayanga."

"Can I see a passport or some other kind of official identification, sir?" He pushed out a drawer similar to those used by cashiers at late-night, self-serve gas stations in the states.

Kael placed his passport in the drawer and asked for a quart of oil, some wiper blades, and a pack of gum.

The Marine said, "That's very funny, sir," but he didn't smile like he meant it. He pulled the drawer to his side of the glass, held the passport right-side-up and compared the photograph to its comedic owner, probably thinking the photo was the funnier of the two. He picked up a phone. The call lasted less than ten seconds. The Marine hung up the receiver and said, "Have a seat, sir. Someone will be here to meet with you shortly."

Kael sat next to his bags on the vinyl couch. Idly waiting for something to happen was as much a part of Central African life as was breathing, perspiring or scratching bug bites. He had just discovered a brand new mosquito bite on his elbow when he heard a buzzer. It sounded like a door release mechanism used to let people enter an apartment building. The buzzing door was the one that led into the embassy catacombs. It opened and a smiling young man wearing the uniform of a bureaucrat—a starched white shirt, a red, white and blue striped tie, gray slacks and black wingtips—entered the waiting room. Kael stood up.

The man held out his hand. "Mr. Husker, I'm Stan Pulaski, the embassy's economics officer. I understand you'd like to meet with Ambassador Saxon."

Kael shook the outstretched hand. "I just arrived and thought it would be a good idea to introduce myself now, since I may be leaving for Bayanga in the next day or so. I'm the new director of the Doli-Ngili project."

Stan smiled and nodded his large blond head the entire time Kael talked. "Yes, yes. We received a FAX from Dr. Cinzano informing us of your imminent arrival. How was your trip?"

"Exhausting, but I'm happy to be back."

"That's right. I heard you were a former Peace Corps volunteer. How's your Sango these days?"

"A little rusty, but it was good enough to get me a cold beer out at the airport bar."

"Great, great." Stan stopped nodding his head the same time he stopped dispensing the small talk. "You've picked a bad time to meet with Ambassador Saxon. His residence was broken into last night and he's a bit... shall we say, preoccupied, with the investigation."

Kael wanted to say, "Finally, an American ambassador has impacted the underprivileged." Instead, he held his tongue like a good loyal subject and said, "I hope no one was hurt."

"No, thank God. The ambassador, his wife, and their son, who's visiting during a break from college, never saw or heard anything. They woke up this morning to discover items missing from the ambassador's bedroom. I can't believe someone could be so brazen."

Kael asked, "Did they take any photographs?"

Stan's eyes widened. "Yes, how did you know?"

"That's pretty common. A photo of me standing next to my jeep is hanging on the wall of some thief's hut."

"Why would anyone steal a stranger's album of family snapshots?"

"Because they don't have one of their own," said Kael.

"That doesn't make any sense."

"Welcome to Central Africa, Stan. Say hello to CARL. CARL, Stan."

Stan smiled and said, "So this is the CARL I've been hearing about?"

"The very same," said Kael. "If it helps, you can tell the ambassador that I was ripped off twelve times during my previous three years here."

"I'm not sure that will make him feel any better," said Stan.

Kael said, "Probably not, but you can tell him that he shouldn't let this one incident taint his opinion of Central Africans. Yes, I was ripped off twelve times, but I was also treated with respect and friendship twelve thousand times. Those help make the occasional appearance of CARL bearable."

Stan said, "CARL doesn't let up, does he?"

"Rarely," said Kael using the R designation from the CARL acronym. "In fact, don't be surprised if CARL hits the ambassador's house again. It's a safe bet he has a friend working there—a cook, a housekeeper, a security guard."

"I'm sure that's being investigated."

"Be patient," said Kael. "It took me twelve times to discover who was ripping me off. Turned out it was my cherubic laundry boy. He finally slipped up when he stole some material from my closet, had a shirt made, and then wore it to my house one day."

Stan chuckled.

Kael said, "Only one way to beat CARL."

"Wait him out?" asked Stan.

"Well, that helps, but while you're twiddling your thumbs, find the humor. It's always there." Kael reached out to shake Stan's hand. "Could you at least tell the ambassador that I tried to perform my responsibilities as a good American by stopping by to introduce myself?"

Stan shook Kael's offered hand. "Of course. And be careful out in Bayanga. I heard about that crocodile man incident. Think CARL had anything to do with that, too?"

"No doubt," said Kael, who retrieved his bags from the couch and exited the embassy with a powerful thirst.

He thought about grabbing a beer in the cramped, little bar at the Minerva Hotel. It was close, and this was where Nick had suggested meeting Mitch in case he didn't show at the airport.

A bed and a shower sounded good, but a sidewalk café sounded better. He wondered if the New Palace Bar was still functioning. It had always been full of Peace Corps volunteers, French soldiers, prostitutes and passersby who were lured off the sidewalks by the music, laughter and a large, hand-painted sign proclaiming, "One quick one couldn't hurt." Kael wasn't sure if it was an advertisement for the bar or the prostitutes.

He hiked past the Mocaf brewery and touched the brim of his cap as a gesture of respect. Mocaf wasn't a great beer, but it was one of the few constants in a country of shortages, setbacks and unpredictability. Mocaf was one of a handful of businesses in Bangui to turn a legal profit every year, and its products could be found in even the tiniest of villages. The appearance of a tall, room-temperature Mocaf at the end of a long day kept many a frustrated Peace Corpse, including Kael, from hopping on the next available flight out.

He passed the Minerva Hotel with its distinctive mustard color. That hadn't changed either, which was reassuring. Even the guy sitting in the shade of the portico looked familiar. His kaleidoscope-like prints made from butterfly wings were displayed to catch the eye of every souvenir-seeking tourist entering or leaving the hotel—all two or three of them.

A street urchin ran out from an alleyway. He planted himself twenty feet in front of Kael and stood defiantly with hands on hips. He looked to be about Josie's age of ten. His gym shorts were the color of dirt and had a rip down the front like a wide-open zipper. They did nothing to hide his blue underpants. His shirt was more holes than material. Kael wondered how this kid knew where to stick his head and arms each morning. His shoes were paper-thin flip-flops. The heel of one was completely gone. The other had a broken top-strap.

Even in this get-up, the kid oozed an air of confidence. Good thing Kael outweighed him by one hundred pounds.

As Kael drew closer, he tightened his grip on the guitar case handle. No way this seventy-pound bully would rip it out of his hand like a woman's purse.

The kid struck suddenly, not with his hands, but with his tongue. *"Touriste! Touriste!"*

Kael wondered if the backpack, white skin and Baltimore Orioles cap had given him away. He stopped to face his taunting adversary. They traded steely-eyed stares like two gunfighters in a dusty cow town street. Kael had an advantage: he'd seen more westerns. He gave his best Clint Eastwood glare and said teasingly, *"Zo ti Bangui! Zo ti Bangui!"* Person of Bangui!

The bully looked startled. He was hit. He obviously hadn't expected the stranger to speak Sango.

Now that Kael had the upper hand, he didn't waste any time. He asked the kid to carry his guitar to the New Palace. It was tempting to make him schlep the backpack, but that would have been cruel as well as optimistic.

The kid smiled. He was all dimples and teeth. His puffed-up chest deflated when his hands left his hips to reach for the guitar. He cradled it with the same care as a mother holding her newborn baby.

African kids were great for running errands. They had few toys and a lot of spare time. They had nothing better to do than respond anxiously to the requests of their elders. Kael had often used them as informal messengers or as go-fers to fetch everything from beer to *beignets*.

During the short stroll to the New Palace Bar, Kael learned that his young porter's name was Dieudonné, which meant "Godgiven" in French. Kael would have believed it if the kid had been able to carry the backpack.

The New Palace Bar wasn't as Kael remembered, but at least the large louvered doors were open for business. The raised cement veranda, which looked out on the street and sidewalk, was cracked and pitted from years of neglect. There were four tables. Three were empty. A young woman who wore an apron and played with a soiled, white dishtowel occupied the fourth. She looked bored. Kael assumed she was the waitress.

The sign was gone. It had probably been burned as firewood years ago. Either that, or one of the prostitutes had taken it to her new headquarters, so to speak.

Something else was missing. Kael shut his eyes. It was too quiet. The street and sidewalk were virtually devoid of traffic. Where was the noise? The laughter? The music?

He missed the rumba-like sounds of contemporary African music pulsating out of abused speakers. He remembered it as an infectious mix of electric guitars, horns, shuffling, syncopated rhythms and high harmonized vocals as intertwined as the colors of a woven basket. There was no other dance music as propulsive or irresistible. All listeners had to move. It started with tapping fingers and toes, but soon spread to dipping knees and hips that couldn't stop shimmying, even if they wanted to.

The absence of music from the New Palace Bar was discouraging to Kael, more so than the abandoned buildings or the denuded hillsides he'd seen earlier that day. Music was the soul of Africa. It was as much a part of the natural surroundings as the chirping of crickets or the harmattan winds whistling through the mango trees.

Molly had understood that. She'd returned to study and record the music of the Pygmies before it was lost forever. It was ironic that the preservationist, Molly, was lost before the music. She was now as silent as the New Palace Bar.

Kael contemplated searching out a more invigorating setting, but he was tired and the pack felt like a Buick on his back. He slid it off and parked it next to one of the three empty tables on the veranda. Dieudonné handed the guitar to Kael who set it next to the backpack. He then invited Dieudonné to sit down and have a soda. More teeth and dimples.

They sat and waited for their waitress who hadn't yet moved out of her seat. She displayed more interest in her dishtowel than in two prospective customers.

Kael projected a short, low-volume "psst" in her direction. She finally acknowledged their arrival and shuffled over with as much enthusiasm as someone headed for a dental appointment.

Kael ordered a Mocaf. Dieudonné requested a Coke. Kael asked their waitress why there was no music.

"The speaker broke," she replied.

"When?" asked Kael.

"Two or three years ago." She ambled away.

Kael turned to Dieudonné. "I guess the speaker repairman is slower than our waitress."

Dieudonné didn't get it. He was too busy enjoying the anticipation of a free Coke.

Kael looked at his young friend and wondered if Josie liked Coke, too. Being one-half Husker, he might have already developed an affinity for beer. Kael hoped not. He, at least, had waited until he was thirteen before trying his first Schlitz in the woods behind his parents' house.

Their waitress returned carrying one Mocaf, one Coke, and what looked to be the same chipped glasses from the airport. She poured the refreshments. She took Kael's money. She gave him his change and walked back through the louvered doors without ever saying a word.

Dieudonné, on the other hand, was bursting with energy. He licked his lips. Both hands wrapped around his glass and he sniffed its bubbly contents. He watched for Kael to give him the signal. He was like an anxious drag racer revving his powerful engine while waiting for the green light.

Kael picked up his beer and held it out. Dieudonné slowly lifted his glass. He was careful so as not to spill a drop. Kael gently touched his glass to Dieudonné's and said, "*Chin chin.*"

That was the green light. Dieudonné roared off. He didn't stop until his glass was finished. He smiled. Victory never tasted sweeter.

Kael refilled the winner's glass and suggested he slow down. "Take your time. It's all yours."

Dieudonné responded by tempering his pace, but Kael could tell it wasn't easy. The boy's hands never left his glass. He maintained a firm grip to discourage anyone who entertained thoughts of stealing his prize.

They drank in silence. Dieudonné examined the bubbles in his Coke while Kael people-watched. The pickings were slim, but wasn't that what one did at a sidewalk café?

Two street cops were coming down the sidewalk. They wore light-blue, ill-fitting uniforms. Their blue beanies were rolled up and stashed under their epaulets. Seeing the policemen gave Kael an idea.

When the cops were almost even with Kael's perch on the veranda, he leaned over the weathered railing and said, "*Excusez-moi, s'il vous plaît.*"

The two policemen stopped to look up at Kael.

Kael switched to Sango. "I was wondering if you know an old friend of mine named Dimassé."

"Of course," replied the shorter one. "He's in charge of the Criminal Division."

The taller one added, "His office is on the hill behind the Presidential Palace, but if you want to see him, you'll have to wait until next week. I heard he's visiting his family in Boda."

"*Merci*," said Kael.

The taller one asked, "Do you want to buy us beers? We are very thirsty."

"*Non, merci*," said Kael.

The two thirsty policemen shrugged their beanie-clad shoulders and continued down the sidewalk.

Kael was, at first, disappointed. He wanted to talk with his old influential friend about Molly's imprisoned killer, preferably before leaving for Bayanga. Who knew when he'd get back this way again? Then he remembered that Mitchell wasn't in Bangui yet. Well, he wasn't at the airport and Kael suspected that he wouldn't be waiting at the Minerva Hotel, either. Kael might possibly have a few days on his own to take a quick side-trip up to Boda to see Dimassé and Josie. Who could fault him for wanting to see his son?

The more he thought about it, the more he liked the idea. It could work if Mitchell didn't show up for a few days. He decided he'd check into the Minerva for the night. He'd give Mitchell until tomorrow morning. If he hadn't arrived by then, Kael would hop a bush taxi for Boda and leave a note explaining his absence. He'd only be gone a couple of days. It was certainly more appealing than hanging out in this ghost town. If he caught CARL snoozing, he might even get back before Mitchell arrived in Bangui.

Kael chugged his beer. He noticed that Dieudonné had already finished his Coke. He had probably tossed down the remainder when he heard the cops say they were thirsty.

Kael said, "So, do you want to carry my backpack to the Minerva Hotel?"

"*Oui*," said the boy.

He obviously had no idea what he was agreeing to do. The Coke must have impaired his judgement and good sense.

Kael said, "No, that's OK. You can carry my guitar again since you did such a great job the first time."

Dieudonné smiled.

Kael said, "You can lighten my load a little, though." He unzipped a lower compartment of the backpack. He reached in, felt around blindly and pulled out a t-shirt. It was bright blue and was emblazoned with the logo of the Alaska Department of Fish and Game. Kael had brought a bunch of these to hand out. He gave it to Dieudonné and said, "Take it. It matches your underwear."

More smiles and dimples. Dieudonné accepted the gift and slipped it on over his other T-shirt. It hung down to his knees.

"Radical, dude," said Kael, in English. He couldn't think of an appropriate translation in Sango.

Dieudonné displayed his excitement by rapidly flicking his limp wrist. This produced a loud snap as his equally relaxed index finger slapped against his thumb. It was as good as a "*Merci.*"

Kael zipped up his pack. He hefted it to his back with a grunt. It didn't feel any lighter. He was now convinced that his theory on the C.A.R.'s stronger gravitational pull warranted further investigation.

He and Dieudonné left the New Palace Bar. Kael decided he liked the old New Palace Bar better. Their waitress looked as excited to see them go as she was to see them arrive. Kael was tempted to say to her, "Come on. Smile. One quick one couldn't hurt."

Kael trudged back down the deserted, litter-strewn streets behind a skipping Dieudonné. As the pair neared the Minerva Hotel, Kael had but one thought: how could cotton socks and underwear weigh so damn much?

# 16

Kael removed the beer bottle from his mouth. It tasted good, even if it was warm. So what if noon was still hours away. The temperature and humidity had already climbed into the nineties. And there was nothing else to do.

He was stuck by the side of the road with seventeen other passengers waiting for their bush taxi's flat tire to be repaired. There was no spare, so the driver and his young apprentice were busy breaking down the rim to patch the inevitable hole in the inner tube.

The beer, a Bass Ale, was compliments of Nick, who had secretly stashed twelve bottles amongst the socks and underwear in Kael's backpack. His business card was attached to one. On the back side of the card, he had written, "And you said you could never get tired of good beer – Nick."No wonder the backpack had been so heavy.

The driver removed the tube from the tire. It already had more patches than a hand-me-down coat in a family with fourteen kids. Dieudonné's old t-shirt probably had fewer holes. Kael and his fellow passengers had gotten two hours out of Bangui before their first flat. At that rate, they should reach Boda within the month.

Kael had spent the night at the Minerva. While searching for a clean shirt to go out on the town, he had discovered the beers and the note. He'd ended up staying in his room trying to lighten his load. When Mitchell hadn't shown by six o'clock the next morning, Kael checked out of his room, left a note at the front desk and found a bush taxi leaving for Boda.

The driver was now trying to glue a patch on top of another patch. Kael shook his head and took another swig of beer. Nothing had changed in ten years. Bush taxis were still C.O.W.'s. C.O.W. was an acronym for "Coffins On Wheels."

Each C.O.W. had a cute name stenciled on its rusted doors. The names were meant to ease potential passengers' fears, but to Kael, they sounded more like the qualities men were looking for in women: *Never Late, Forever Faithful* and *No Problem*. Kael's broken-down heap was called *Without a Care. Without a Spare* might have been more appropriate.

The innocent-sounding C.O.W.s hurtled down rutted unpaved roads with bald tires, mushy steering and jerry-rigged engines held together by wire and rubber bands. The drivers were fearless in their attempts to break the land-speed record. An amazing feat considering that the recommended load capacity of passengers and baggage was usually exceeded by ten adults, three screaming kids, two defecating goats and five, one-hundred-pound sacs of foul-smelling cassava. Evil Knevil would have had second thoughts about hopping into one of these sardine cans strapped to a rocket. Ralph Nader would have preferred commuting to work in a Corvair.

Kael had no choice. Until he got his own wheels, he was at the mercy of the Central African mass transit system.

The patched inner tube held air in the trial run, so it was stuffed back into the tire. The rim was reassembled. Passengers took turns working the foot pump until the tire had just enough air. The wheel was then secured back on the axle with only three lug nuts.

Kael asked the driver, "Where are the other three lug nuts?"

The driver responded, "They're holding on one of the front wheels."

*Without a Care* needed a push start, so the driver requested passenger assistance once again. Everyone pushed. *Without a Care* coughed and sputtered for one hundred feet. Just when Kael decided her name should have been *Without a Prayer*, she roared back to life with a backfire and a puff of black smoke. People hooted as they climbed back into their seats. No one seemed perturbed that they were behind schedule.

Two more flats and seven hours later, *Without a Care* rolled down the final slope leading into Boda. Gravity was now its only propellant since the driver had miscalculated his vehicle's fuel consumption by roughly the length of a couple of football fields. The bush taxi was transformed into a clattering glider. Its speed increased as it drew closer to the rickety bridge at the bottom of the hill. Kael found himself leaning forward. Was it to be more aerodynamic or was he subconsciously beginning to assume the crash position?

They flew across the small bridge with only a brief touch-and-go landing. Several of the taller passengers hit their heads on the roof during impact. *Without a Care's* momentum sent it careening up the road on the other side. The pilot called for full flaps. The taxi coasted to a stop in front of the vacant soccer field. The apprentice jumped out like a paratrooper. He threw a chunk of wood underneath one of the tires to keep *Without a Care* from rolling back towards the bridge. Functioning parking brakes were as common in bush taxis as Corinthian leather seats.

Kael climbed out of the van. He noticed that *Without a Care* had another flat.

The apprentice climbed up to the roof. He began untying and lowering bags down to the growing mob of passengers. Kael's backpack and guitar were the first bags down.

He reached into the backpack for one of the six remaining Bass Ales. He stashed it into his shirt before hoisting the pack to his shoulders. It was now seven beers lighter.

He picked up his dusty guitar case. It would have been nice to leave most of his stuff behind in Bangui, but the hotel manager had refused to guarantee its security. Kael couldn't blame him. After all, the American ambassador's residence wasn't even safe.

Kael bid farewell to his fellow passengers and their flight crew. He had to find Josie and Sapu. Then, Dimassé. But first, he needed sustenance. He retrieved the bottle of beer from his shirt and popped the cap with his trusty Swiss army knife. He toasted Nick before gulping down half the bottle. The rest would be nursed until he reached Josie and Sapu's house back in the *Koufourou Quartier*—a distance of perhaps one-half mile.

Boda hadn't changed a bit. It was still quiet and serene, especially when compared to Bangui. This was his favorite time of the day. The sun was low, only an hour or so from setting, which meant the temperature was cooling down and the mosquitoes weren't swarming yet. The long day of toiling in the fields was done. Plumes of smoke rose from hundreds of individual campfires to swirl above the treetops. Families were gathering around those fires for the evening meal. Static-laden radios played in the distance.

He hiked up a dirt road that led into the *quartiers*, or neighborhoods. Each small house along the road was built by its owner, who obviously had no square, level nor plumb line in his toolbox. The walls were made of sun-baked mud bricks and the roofs were of thatched grass. Often, the more financially solvent homeowners used the profits from the sale of their coffee harvest to replace the thatch with sheets of corrugated tin. It was a local status symbol and the envy of everyone except those who had to sleep under it during a rainy-season downpour. It was like living in a snare drum.

The arrival of a hairy, white stranger was big news to the citizenry of Boda. As Kael passed the houses, curious children abandoned their places by the fire to follow him on his trek. They kept to a safe distance and chanted, "*Mounzou!*" White person!

A few adults recognized him. They called out his name and waved. Some came down to shake his hand. Several of the bolder children offered their hands in greeting, but only after witnessing the success of their parents. They seemed surprised when Kael released their hands with all five fingers still intact. Would Josie's welcome be as tentative?

Kael and his growing entourage of children, none of whom looked strong enough to carry his guitar let alone his backpack, entered *Koufourou Quartier*. He liked this neighborhood. It was Boda's version of suburban serenity. The wind always blew stronger out here. It came rushing down the hills like a cool, clean river. Any noise from the center of town was swept away and deposited somewhere down wind.

As he neared Josie's house, his strides shortened, his heart rate increased to aerobic proportions, and the dust on his hands turned into muddy perspiration. He hadn't felt this nervous since the seconds just before *Without a Care* catapulted over the bridge. That had turned out OK, but could he avert disaster twice in thirty minutes?

He spotted Josie's mother, Sapu, first. She was sitting on a small wooden stool in front of her house. She was peering into a blackened pot. Three round stones supported the pot above the smoky cook fire. While Sapu examined its contents, her teenaged sister, Tara, rearranged the wood and coals to achieve the ideal flame and the optimum cooking temperature. Two other sisters, Anisé and Ebène, sat on woven mats next to the fire. They laughed and gossiped while holding suckling infants to their swollen breasts. Some meals were easier to prepare than others.

Josie was nowhere to be seen.

Kael downed the last of his beer. He gave the empty bottle to one of his young followers. It would be transformed into some sort of toy car or the child's mother would claim it to store salt, palm oil or kerosene. Empty bottles were the African equivalent of Legos or Tupperware.

None of the women seemed to notice Kael or his convoy, so he moved closer. He thought of saying, "Hi, honey, I'm home," but settled on, "What's for dinner?"

All four faces turned.

Tara was the first to recognize their uninvited dinner guest. Her eyes widened and she screamed in a high-pitched falsetto, "Ayeeeeeee!"

Kael was certain that every sleeping dog in Boda was now wide awake.

Tara abandoned her fire-tending duties and ran toward Kael. By now, the others understood who he was, too, and started screaming in harmony.

Kael barely had enough time to drop the backpack and guitar to the ground before Tara leapt into his open arms. She weighed only slightly more than his guitar. The screams, which continued to pour from her mouth, were now in the decibel range of a firehouse siren.

He held her tight, hoping to impede her considerable lung capacity. He spoke in Sango, theorizing she would stop exercising her vocal cords to listen. "Your mouth has gotten much bigger in ten years."

Her screams turned to laughter. She pulled her head off his shoulder and said, "And you've gotten hairier."

He smiled. They kissed the traditional three pecks: right cheek, left cheek and left again.

Anisé and Ebène took Tara's place. One of the babies started to scream, but it wasn't because of Kael's surprise appearance. It had misplaced its mother's nipple. Its piercing wails stopped when Ebène stuffed her leaking breast back into the infant's mouth.

Sapu approached. She was the eldest of the sisters and, in Kael's opinion, the prettiest one. She looked a bit thinner, but that only seemed to further emphasize her mile-high cheekbones. A tear spilled from one almond eye just before she said, "*Mo si awé?*"

He couldn't help but smile. "*Eh, mbi si awé.*"

They embraced. She smelled of sweat and smoke. She had always been slim, but she felt bonier. A carrot had more body fat.

He noticed that the zipper running down the back of her blouse was broken. The material, once a colorful pattern of geometric shapes, was frayed and faded. The closest thing to a gentle-cycle wash in Boda was using a smoother stone in the stream.

When Kael had been a Peace Corps volunteer, the elastic in his underwear had completely disintegrated in two months after just eight washes. His new jeans had survived one full year. They could have lingered another month or so on life support, but he wanted to remember them as they were. He pulled the plug on them one dark day by cutting them up and making rags to clean his motorcycle.

He could hear Sapu sobbing on his shoulder. He stroked the back of her head. Her hair, which had always been painstakingly arranged in one of the intricate African styles, was a mass of loose braids and tangles. Africa, like Alaska, could make even the hardiest of souls feel like a two-month-old pair of underwear. He'd have to remember to pass that one on to Tallin.

He stepped back and held Sapu at arm's length. He wiped away her tears with his thumb. She smiled and shooed away the children who had followed him through the village. They scattered like birds.

While Ebène and Anisé wrestled with his bags and their breast attachments, Sapu led their guest to the fire. Tara emerged from the house with a straight-backed chair, which she placed close to the fire, but on the upwind side of the smoke.

Kael sat down. Tara gave him another hug before squatting down to revive the fire. Sapu stirred something in the pot. The wind shifted and Kael's sinuses were invaded by the unmistakable sting of garlic and hot peppers frying in oil. It all seemed so familiar.

Sapu looked up from her pot and said, "Josie will be here soon. I sent him to the market to buy a can of tomato paste and some peanut butter."

Kael could feel his heart pound at the mere mention of his son's name. How would it react when he actually saw him? He doubted Sapu or any of her sisters knew how to perform CPR, and that made him more nervous.

He scanned the area in the direction of the market, but saw no one resembling a Husker. Would he even recognize Josie? Had it really been ten years? That would be seventy years to Chako, which meant Josie could be an old man by now.

Kael realized that he wasn't thinking rationally, but he couldn't help it. He even thought that this uncomfortable reunion would be so much easier if only they lived on Saturn, a planet that took thirty Earth-years to revolve once around the sun. Ten years here was only four months (one-third of a revolution) on Saturn, and that seemed a more acceptable time frame for a father to not see his son.

He suddenly noticed a child sprinting toward him. The young runner leapt over a garbage pit, sidestepped an outhouse and crashed through a hedgerow of overgrown lemon grass. He didn't stop until he stood panting in front of Kael.

He looked like the negative of a photo of Kael at age ten. His skin was the color of an amber lager—a rich, honey caramel. Curly brown hair with blond and red highlights framed his high, smooth forehead. His pug nose was spattered by an explosion of freckles that spilled out on to his dimpled cheeks. If someone were to put a straw cowboy hat on his head and a Ruger .22 rifle in his hands, he'd look just like Kael in a photo taken on Christmas morning in 1965.

Sapu set down her pot momentarily to stand behind the boy. Her callused hands rested on his shoulders. "Josie, your father is somewhere behind that beard."

"I know," said Josie, whose eyes never left Kael's face. "Some people in the market told me he was here. That's why I ran home."

At first, Kael was impressed by how well Josie spoke Sango, but then realized that it was his son's first language. He wanted to pull Josie close, to envelope him with his arms. Could holding him for ten years make up for ten years of neglect? He was afraid Josie would resist, so he held out his hand for the more traditional African handshake.

"Hello, Josie. You're a good runner. You must be the fastest kid in the village."

Josie gave the tomato paste and peanut butter to his mother. Kael wondered if his son could show the same athleticism with a football in his hands instead of items from a shopping list.

Josie wiped his right hand on the back of his shorts before placing it in Kael's waiting palm. He didn't squeeze and he didn't respond to Kael's compliment. He just stared into his father's eyes.

Kael was surprised at how long and slender Josie's fingers were. They weren't short, fat, big-knuckled, Husker digits. These were made for playing sonatas on the piano. Who was he kidding? Josie probably didn't even know what a piano was. He surely didn't know what a sonata was and chances were good that he didn't know what an American football was, either. If Kael had come from Saturn, they'd have just as much in common.

He released Josie's limp hand and removed the Baltimore Orioles baseball cap from his head. He brushed off the dust and set it on Josie's head. "This is a present from a friend of mine. Every boy in America wears one."

Without warning, Josie rocketed himself into Kael. His skinny brown arms encircled Kael's neck.

Initially, Kael thought he was being attacked by a ten-year-old lunatic. Revenge was a powerful emotion, especially after ten years of fermentation. Maybe, it was something much simpler: Was his son a Boston Red Socks fan?

Josie deserved his pound of flesh, so Kael did nothing until he realized that Josie wasn't striking out. He was reaching out. His head, still clad in the baseball cap, burrowed in to the soft fleshy area between Kael's neck and shoulder. He started to sob.

Kael held him tightly with one arm while the other rubbed his son's trembling back. It was the first mutual hug between father and son, and Kael wished it would never end.

He looked up to see Sapu, Tara, Anisé and Ebène all wiping away tears. Even the babies were crying, though probably for different reasons.

Eventually, Josie stopped sobbing, but his head remained glued to Kael's shoulder. Kael had no intention of evicting his son from his newly chosen place of residence. Kael's stomach, on the other hand, wasn't as sentimental. It gave a low rumbling growl demanding to be fed.

Josie heard it. He stepped back with wide wet eyes and a broad smile. He looked to his mother and said, "Mama, his stomach is crying, too."

Everyone laughed.

Kael rubbed his belly. "It smells Sapu's pot. What's for dinner?"

Sapu said, "Cassava with a simple sauce." She then added as a pseudo-apology: "We didn't know you were coming."

Kael asked, "Is there any meat in the sauce? I'm feeling carnivorous."

Tara giggled. "Simple sauces don't have meat. That's why they're simple."

Kael knew that beef was a luxury few Africans could afford on a regular basis. It was only available at the Boda market if a wandering tribe of Mbororo happened to be herding their cattle nearby. Kael was feeling lucky, so he reached for his wallet and pulled out a one-thousand-franc bill, roughly four dollars. "How about we celebrate and make a difficult sauce? It's on me." He held the crisp note under Josie's nose. He switched to English, "I'll buy if you'll fly."

Josie didn't understand the foreign tongue, but he knew that kids ran errands. He said to his mother, "I saw them selling meat in the market."

Sapu nodded. Josie snatched the money and sprinted off like a thief. He was obviously a carnivore like his father.

When Josie had passed the outhouse, Kael said, "He's a beautiful kid. He looks just like me, don't you think?"

Tara, Anisé and Ebène all giggled. Sapu stopped stirring her pot. "He runs almost as fast as you, too."

Kael knew that she wasn't commenting on his athletic prowess in the short sprint events. She was referring to his performance in the ten-thousand-mile run from Boda to Hidden Cove ten years earlier. Sapu always spoke her mind. It turned off most African men, but it was one of the qualities that had endeared her to him. That and her culinary skills, which were as spicy as her tongue.

While Anisé shifted her ravenous baby from her right breast to the left one, she asked, "Why are you back here in *Centrafrique*, Kael?"

Kael tried to concentrate on the question and not on Anisé's exposed, saucer-sized nipples. He shuffled in his chair like a nervous schoolboy before stammering, "Um...I'm going to be working out in Bayanga."

"Bayanga?" said Sapu. "There is nothing in Bayanga, just a forest full of Pygmies."

"And elephants," said Tara.

"And gorillas that rape women," said Anisé.

"And crocodile men," said Ebène.

Kael smiled. "How do you know there are crocodile men in Bayanga, Ebène?"

"It's a well-known fact that the tribes around Bayanga are not as civilized as we Gbaya. They are full of crocodile men out there."

"Who told you that? The same person who told you that gorillas rape women?"

"No," said Ebène. "Our aunt told us that." Her sisters all nodded in agreement. "As a young girl, she had wandered into the forest. She was missing for three whole days. When she finally reappeared in the village, she was weak and her clothing was torn. She said a gorilla had attacked her. Eight months later, she gave birth to a baby boy." The sisters were still nodding.

"Did the baby look like a gorilla?" asked Kael.

"No. When she found out she was pregnant, she slept with many boys to make sure the baby would be human."

Kael smiled. When he had been living in Boda, many pregnant women had asked him to sleep with them so their babies would have light skin. He had tried to explain that it didn't work like that. None had believed him. Some of the women were quite attractive, but Molly had made him promise to refuse all offers. Peace Corps was there to serve, but there were limits.

Sapu interrupted Kael's thoughts with a question he hadn't expected: "Are you going to take Josie to live with you in Bayanga?"

This query wasn't as easy to answer as, "*Mo si awé?*" Even though he had perfectly understood Sapu's Sango, he responded with, "Huh?"

"I said..." Sapu started to ask the question a second time—Africans were extremely patient with Americans and their well-documented learning disabilities with foreign languages—when Kael interrupted.

"I understood your question. I just don't know how to answer."

"You could start with a yes or no."

"It's not that simple. What if I said yes?"

"I'd say, 'Good. Josie could use a father in his life right now.'"

"What if I said no?"

"I'd say, 'Good. Josie's doing just fine with my sisters and me.'"

Kael smiled. It was vintage Sapu. She never let anyone else's decision, especially Kael's, determine whether she was happy or not. Truth was she wouldn't have asked the question unless she could accept both responses. He doubted Josie was as flexible. Few ten year olds were.

He played with his beard while assessing the situation. If he said yes, he'd be getting a second chance to do exactly what Molly had encouraged him to do ten years earlier. He was being offered a do-over.

Do-overs were created for backyard wiffle ball games. For example, if a hit ball became lodged in a tree, it was a do-over. Do-overs were as common in real life, however, as crocodile men in Alaska; as common as logic in Africa. To ignore a do-over opportunity was not only stupid, it was contrary to the laws of wiffle ball.

Kael leaned forward in his chair. He continued to twirl the tuft of hair beneath his lower lip with his right thumb and index finger. "Does Josie want to be with me? He doesn't even know how to play wiffle ball."

Sapu scrunched up her eyebrows. "What is wiffle ball?"

"It's a game of second chances."

Sapu's eyebrows returned to their normal positions. "Josie is very good at games. He loves soccer. Can't you teach him this wiffle ball?"

Kael's fingers stopped tugging at his beard. "If he'll let me."

Tara broke the sisters' silence. "You have to take him with you, Kael. If he stays here, he'll just become a *godobé* like every other boy."

Kael said, "I happen to know that there are lots of job opportunities for *godobés* at the Bangui airport."

"Josie doesn't need a job," said Ebène. "He needs a father."

"A permanent, full-time father," said Anisé.

Kael didn't know what to say, so he just stared into the campfire. He watched the flames reach up like probing, yellow fingers to stroke Sapu's blackened pot. He nervously picked at his beard. Sure, it was a do-over, but permanent, full-time was something most single young men wanted in their jobs and their fun, not in a relationship.

A sweaty and out-of-breath Josie returned. He handed several kilos of beef wrapped in leaves to his mother. To his father, he presented a big green bottle full of Mocaf beer. "I saw Monsieur Dimassé at the market. When I told him you were here, he bought you this beer and said for you to bring the empty bottle and two full ones to his house this evening."

Kael smiled. "*Merci, jeune homme.*" He pulled out his trusty Swiss army knife with its most important tool: the bottle opener. He opened the bottle and then handed the knife over to Josie. "It's yours if you promise to always have it ready when I need a beer opened."

Josie accepted the gift in his cupped hands. His grin produced two, extra-large dimples in his soft, brown cheeks. He showed off his recent acquisition to his mother and aunts, who all oohed and aahed with appropriate enthusiasm. Ebène's baby wanted to suck on it. Josie's grin didn't fade for several hours. Neither did Kael's.

After a filling meal of bland cassava dipped in a difficult, yet flavorful peanut sauce, Kael and Josie left the women and dishes to make their way to Dimassé's house. Kael borrowed a woven sack, into which he stuffed the empty Mocaf bottle along with the five remaining Bass Ales. Josie wore his new cap and carried his knife in one hand and a flashlight in the other.

They found Dimassé lounging in an Adirondack-style chair next to his campfire. With his three chattering wives and an army of children gathered on mats at his feet, he looked the part of a regal, yet approachable monarch.

Kael and Josie followed their flashlight's weak beam of light. Kael noticed that Josie made certain to keep the flashlight pointed downward like a loaded handgun. Shining it directly into someone's eyes was considered extremely impolite. It was a mistake made only by infants with minimal voluntary muscular control and tourists. Dimassé had once told Kael that patience was required when dealing with both. "One day,"he had said, "the infants would learn and the tourists would go away."

Dimassé, ever-patient, had no choice but to wait his turn to greet his visitors, who were mobbed like Hollywood celebrities by his screaming wives and curious children. The kids seemed more interested in Josie's knife than in the bearded, white stranger being mauled by their mothers.

Kael was still trapped in the embrace of one of Dimassé's wives when he reached out to shake Dimassé's outstretched hand. Dimassé pulled him away from the clutches of his wife and into his own massive chest. Kael felt like a new puppy being passed back and forth for everyone to cuddle.

"I knew you would return one day, *mon ami*,"said Dimassé. "But did you return with my empty bottle and two full ones?"

"No... I brought your empty and five full ones."

Dimassé let out a hearty laugh. His hair was grayer and the lines in his leathered face were deeper, but his laugh was still that of a young man—high-pitched with just a hint of innocence.

Kael said, "I brought two for us and three for your still-lovely, young wives."

The women screamed their approval. Kael wasn't sure if it was for his compliments or the free beers. One of the wives collected their three bottles and the empty from Kael's sack.

Before he could offer the assistance of his son's knife, another wife opened all three bottles with her teeth. Kael's own incisors hurt just from watching. Josie obediently opened Kael's and Dimassé's. He then showed every blade to Dimassé. Both giggled over the tiny scissors.

One of Dimassé's sons brought out a chair and glasses. Kael sat down and poured some beer into one of the dusty glasses. He swirled it around before dumping it on the ground. Maybe, Molly was thirsty. Josie closed his knife to run and play with the other children.

Dimassé dropped back into his own chair. "He's a good boy." He held up his glass of beer, which his own son had already filled. "*Chin chin.*"

"*Chin chin,*" echoed Kael. "Sapu's raised him well."

"Yes, she has, but a boy should be with his father."

"I seem to remember you wanting to kick Bart's butt to the moon."

"Along with everyone else in town."

"How is he?"

Dimassé set his glass down on the chair's arm. "He's made me very proud. He now has two sons named Kael and Dimassé."

"They sound like a handful," said Kael.

"They are, indeed, but Bart deserves double the heartache he put me through. He's in France right now for an advanced fisheries course. His wife and children are all with him."

"He's come a long way."

"I owe much of it to you, *mon ami.*"

"I'm glad you said that. I have a favor to ask."

"Anything. Take one of my wives if you wish."

"No, I'd hate to break up the set. It has to do with an old friend who died out in Bayanga. You even knew her..."

Kael proceeded to fill Dimassé in on Molly's accidental drowning, the subsequent incarceration of Assan, and his desire to free the accused crocodile man from prison.

Dimassé was the most educated and well-traveled Central African Kael knew. He had studied in France, Belgium and had even spent time in several large American cities learning about modern police procedures. Even so, Kael suspected that Dimassé, like every other Central African, still believed in crocodile men.

Dimassé listened to Kael while quietly sipping his beer. When Kael finished explaining the situation, Dimassé asked, "How much does this man's freedom mean to you?"

"It means a lot to me. He didn't kill Molly."

"No, you didn't understand my question, *mon ami.* How much are you willing to pay? I know someone in Nola and my letter to him will get you an open ear, but only money will free this crocodile man."

"You mean a bribe?" asked Kael.

"Not exactly. Those accused of crimes here often receive a sentence of jail time or a healthy fine. If you can pay the fine, you walk. Why do you think Bart never went to prison?"

"I just assumed it was because his father was the police chief."

"That argument worked the first nine or ten times. After that, my wallet did the talking. This is why you won't find many rich men inside Central African prisons."

"It's hard to find many rich men outside of Central African prisons, too," said Kael smiling.

Dimassé laughed. "My country's sad economic state will be much brighter after you have paid Assan's fine. A sorcerer's freedom is very expensive."

Kael nervously asked, "How much are we talking?"

"That depends. My letter of support to Nola's police commissioner, a *Monsieur* Gozo, should count for something. I also happen to know that he's looking for a transfer to Bangui. If I mention something about needing a man of his talents at headquarters, he'll be your friend faster than a horny Bangui prostitute."

"But can I afford his services?"

"What do you care? You Americans are all rich." Dimassé smiled at his own joke. "Besides, he's only half the problem. I should probably write a letter to the *préfet*, too, since he's the top government representative in the region. As such, he has the deepest pockets."

"I thought you said this was a fine and not a bribe?"

"It is, but games are always played under the negotiation table. Backs must be scratched and palms must be greased. It is our way."

"Does the *préfet* want to be transferred to Bangui, too?"

"Probably, but I can't help him with that. I can, however, let him know that he would have a grateful friend high up in the Bangui police department should he decide to help you."

Kael smiled. "And can *Monsieur le Préfet* infer from that generous offer that he would have a bothersome enemy high up in the Bangui police department should he refuse to help me?"

Dimassé winked. "How would I know what the man thinks?"

A childlike smirk took over his face before he took a sip of beer. When he lowered his glass, the sardonic grin was gone and was replaced by a blank stare. It was the look practiced and perfected by those in positions of power. IRS tax auditors had it. So did Marine Corps drill instructors. K-Mart security guards thought they had it.

"With both men on our side, you're still probably looking at 1.5 million CFA. For another one hundred thousand under the table, you could probably get this crocodile man released almost immediately."

Kael rubbed his tired eyes. Roughly six thousand dollars. The same amount Nick had estimated to be Molly's contribution to Josie over the last ten years. It wouldn't bring Molly back, but she might rest easier. He might rest easier, too.

His visions of her were occurring almost daily now. That would be acceptable if the frequent apparitions were more erotic in nature. Since about age twelve, Kael had encouraged images of naked women parading through his thoughts. Trouble was, Molly was always fully clothed in a non-revealing tie-dyed t-shirt, cutoff jeans and red Converse sneakers. She was always in water, too. That was kind of sexy, but rather than reaching out for his penis, she seemed to be clawing through the murky depths in an instinctive attempt to grope for something on the surface.

Dimassé leaned forward and placed a hand on Kael's knee. "If you decide to free this man, which I suspect you will, make sure you get the police commissioner and the *préfet* to sign and stamp an official release form. They outrank the authorities in Bayanga who put this crocodile man in prison." With his free hand, he downed the last of his beer. "Be aware, *mon ami*, that the police commissioner in Bayanga will not be happy that you have gone over his head. I know this man. His name is *Monsieur* Yakonomingui and he is not the forgiving type. He is as crooked as a stick and his history of despicable behavior is as long as an elephant's trunk. You must be careful."

"Sounds like there's some history between you two."

"Yes, and all of it turbulent. I have tried to fire him twice."

"Obviously, you were unsuccessful."

"He happens to be of the same tribe as our President, so for the present, he is virtually untouchable. You should understand that my influence will help to release the crocodile man, but it will not endear you to *Monsieur* Yakonomingui."

"That's OK." Kael placed his hand on Dimassé's. "I already have enough friends."

"But not enough beer." Dimassé held his empty glass high in the air. "Antoinette! We need beer, preferably in big bottles."

Antoinette, the wife that had opened the beers with her teeth, picked out one recruit from the army of children and sent him to the house. A minute later, he emerged with four empty Mocaf bottles. Antoinette unknotted a corner of her *pagne*, the rectangular piece of cloth African women wore wrapped around their bodies like a skirt. She pulled out two, tightly folded, one-thousand-franc bills from her hiding place and handed them to the child, who had to set the bottles on the ground to accept the cash.

Kael held out his woven sack. "*Petit*, use this to carry the bottles."

The child pushed the bills into his pocket and stuffed the sack with the returnable bottles. He sprinted for the bar. He was a young man on a mission.

In Central Africa, there were no laws restricting alcohol purchases by minors. Anyone could buy beer as long as they had the money. Fetching beer was one of the major responsibilities of African children. It was a rite of passage.

Dimassé said, "Your beer was good, but the bottle is much too small."

"Women tell me that all the time."

Dimassé roared with delight. His laugh was the kind that made everyone within a two-mile radius stop what they were doing to turn and look. It was so contagious, most onlookers found themselves smiling as well.

"So, my friend with a little bottle, how long will you be staying in Boda?" He giggled at his own joke.

"I have to get back to Bangui tomorrow. Or... I should say 'we.' Josie is going with me. We'll catch a bush taxi in the morning."

Dimassé winked. "Excellent, but tomorrow is impossible. You must inspect my fish pond and I still have to write your letters. Stay a few days. I will give you a ride back in my Peugot 504."

The offer was too good to turn down. A comfortable seat all to himself versus being wedged in-between a goat and a screaming baby for nine hours on board *Without a Care*. It was not a difficult decision. Mitchell could wait an extra day or two. If he couldn't be patient, he was on the wrong continent.

Kael and Dimassé stayed up late reminiscing. They drank enough beers to make three different kids perform beer runs. Josie opened every bottle with his knife.

Eventually, Josie and his flashlight led Kael back to Sapu's house, where he collapsed into a spare bed. He dreamed of Molly again. Same clothes. Same water. Same groping. Only this time, when her head broke the surface, her face changed into that of Tallin. She screamed, but it had a melodic quality to it, similar to opera or yodeling. It stopped abruptly when she was pushed violently underwater by a pair of hands resting on her shoulders.

The fingers were long and slender. They were piano fingers like Josie's. The wrists didn't quite match; they were too thick and scaly. They widened like funnels into hairless forearms of rough cracked leather. Above the elbows, the hide erupted into a mountain range of armor plates. The dark greenish-gray peaks of protection ran unbroken across the broad shoulder blades and up to the top of its head, where they disappeared under a ten-gallon cowboy hat. Beady yellow eyes peered out from under the brim. It didn't have a nose. It was more of a long tapering snout, like that of a crocodile.

He caught another glimpse of Tallin's frightened face. Bubbles of air escaped from her wide-open mouth and nostrils. The little spheres of life continued to rise long after her face disappeared into the dark depths.

Kael's subconscious recalled that crocodiles preferred to drag their victims down to the bottom. There, they would perform a death roll, twisting violently so their tearing teeth could detach large chunks of flesh. Quite often, the crocodile would simply stuff its hapless victim, still alive, under a submerged stump, where it would rot, bloat and tenderize for a future snack.

Kael was glad he couldn't see that happening. The water was too black, so he could only imagine the ghastly scene occurring just beyond his visionary range.

The steady stream of air bubbles slowed until one final bubble ascended from the darkness. It reached the water's surface, but it didn't burst like the others. It floated. It wasn't clear, either. It was white with teardrop holes covering the top half.

It was a wiffle ball, the same kind he had played with as a kid. The holes allowed the pitcher to throw a wicked curveball, better than anything in Tom Seaver's repertoire.

Kael reached for the ball, but the current pushed it away from his grasp. It bobbed downstream, swirling in the eddies and riding the waves of turbulence kicked up by the wind. It didn't tip. The holes remained on top.

It bounced into a pair of thick, curved, sun-bleached sticks protruding from the turbid water. The ball rolled slightly, allowing a small amount of water to enter the holes. It didn't sink. In fact, now that it had some ballast, it righted itself and seemed even more seaworthy. It continued on its journey downstream.

It reached a wide, gentle bend of the river. The water here was peaceful, inviting, soothing. It was a place to relax, if only temporarily, and to prepare for what lay ahead.

Without warning, the glassy water beneath the ball exploded. The crocodile's jaws rocketed up out of the stillness. They engulfed the ball, snapped shut and slid back beneath the surface. The ball was gone, swallowed up by a monster just like Molly, and now Tallin, too. All that remained was a series of expanding circular ripples. When they reached Kael, he awoke with a sense of despair.

He rubbed his beard. It was wet. So was his pillow. Was it from the river? Was it from the crocodile's splash?

It took a few seconds for Kael to remember exactly where he was and that the river and the crocodile man were just images in a dream. They were probably brought on by too many Mocafs with Dimassé or Sapu's spicy peanut sauce.

He blinked his eyes and two large tears escaped. They rolled down his cheekbones, swung like Tarzan from one whisker to the next, and finally plopped on to the already-damp pillow. That was why everything was wet. He'd been crying. Two more tears welled up. He could feel them flooding his sockets. When this reservoir of water crested, the good people of Boda would need to head for higher ground.

He remembered that when he was a kid, his mom had a special term for these kinds of voluminous teardrops. She'd dab them with an absorbent Kleenex and say, "There, there, Special K. Why all these crocodile tears?"

# 17

Two days after formulating his plan, Bolo returned to the intersection of Sunset Boulevard and Rodeo Drive. This time, he didn't look like an innocent bird watcher. A high-powered rifle took the place of his binoculars. He was a reaper, not a peeper. He came with a death list, not a life list.

He took a position high above *Le Bistro*. It gave him a bird's-eye view of everything, yet he was virtually invisible. He felt like a hawk soaring hundreds of feet above the Earth. He searched for his doomed prey below.

He only had to wait twenty minutes for the arrival of Charles and Diana. They came up Sunset just before sunset. How fitting.

They never made it to *Le Bistro*. Bolo's first bullet pierced the top of Charles' large right ear before passing through to his brain. He never knew what hit him. For a split second, he probably thought it was Diana slapping the side of his head.

Bolo worked the bolt action of his rifle with a fluid motion. It was one he had practiced thousands of times. The empty brass shell casing ejected and another round was chambered. A glance through the scope and just the slightest pressure on the trigger sent a second bullet spiraling out of the barrel at over two thousand feet per second and with over four thousand foot-pounds of energy. It slammed into Charles' royal temple. The slug turned living tissue into a jigsaw puzzle of flesh and bone with many missing pieces. The projectile's lead tip mushroomed out as it crashed through the skull plate and tunneled into the brain like a thick worm.

Bolo fired a third round into Charles' lifeless nerve center just to be sure.

Diana was next. She tried to run while shielding her young sons, William and Harry. No one protected her, so Bolo planted two bullets just behind her frightened eyes. Her bowels involuntarily voided as she fell to the ground. Not very princess-like, thought Bolo. That little fact surely wouldn't be mentioned in the newspapers.

He reloaded. When he looked back through his scope, he saw William and Harry attempting to lift their mother's dead body. They couldn't budge her, but they kept trying. They probably would have continued their struggle for hours had Bolo not stopped them. He didn't want them to be orphans, so he did what he thought was appropriate: He emptied his clip into their soft, adolescent heads. They crashed down on top of their mother who, even dead, broke their falls. Blood, bone fragments, brain matter, urine and excrement from all three pooled together. A red rivulet of ooze snaked along Sunset Boulevard.

Bolo gazed upon the carnage like an artist admiring his nearly completed painting. He'd never done four at the same time. It was a thing of beauty; a powerful statement sure to make him lots of money. "Still Life at Sunset" might be a good title. "Still Death at Sunset" would be an even better play on words.

He inadvertently let the barrel of his rifle touch his bare leg. It was hot enough to startle him and leave a mild burn mark just above the knee. So much for daydreaming. He had too much to do to waste precious time patting himself on the back.

He searched the area where the brass casings had been ejected from the rifle and fallen to the ground. He picked up nine of them. He counted twice just to be sure. He thought he'd fired ten times, but it must have been only nine since there were only nine casings. He tried to remember the sequence: Three for Charles and two for Diana. He was pretty confident with those numbers, but had he used five or just four on William and Harry? It must have been four—two for each one. It was hard to keep an accurate count in the heat of battle. Everything had happened in less than sixty seconds. Still, he couldn't shake the nagging feeling that he was missing one. He combed the area again. nothing. He counted the shiny brass casings again. Still nine.

He hated leaving anything behind, not that it really mattered. He had probably only shot nine times anyway. And even if there were a tenth casing hiding somewhere, it might never be found. hell, he couldn't locate it and he knew exactly what he was looking for.

By the time he left the area, he had almost convinced himself that everything would be OK. Almost.

# 18

Kael's return trip to Bangui in Dimassé's lime-green Peugot 504 was truly, without a care. The closest thing they had to a flat was when Dimassé hit a wrong note while attempting to sing backup to a cassette tape of Bob Marley.

Josie, sprawled across the back seat, seemed more enthralled with the electric windows and door-lock mechanisms than with the passing scenery. On, off, up, down, click, click. Dimassé gave him a half-hour of recreation before overriding all the backseat switches from his driver's-side master control panel. He winked at Kael and said, "The Peugot people are very smart."

Josie then started playing with the manual ashtray covers. They were almost as irritating as the electric door locks. Kael turned to Dimassé and said, "What were you saying about the Peugot people?" Both men had to laugh. Dimassé shrugged his shoulders and turned up the volume of the car stereo. Soon, Josie's ashtray was keeping perfect time with "Is This Love?"

Kael often remarked that Central Africans enjoyed crying and funerals almost as much as laughing and holiday festivals, so it was no surprise that Josie's departure from Boda had been a tearful one. His meager wardrobe—three pairs of shorts, two t-shirts and one pair of underwear—were stuffed into the same woven sack used to carry beer bottles. Kael suspected that people going to spend two weeks at a nudist colony packed bigger suitcases.

Sapu had made Josie promise to write often. She made Kael promise to include money with each of Josie's letters.

When the Peugot finally crawled away from Sapu's house, Kael had reached for his shirt pocket to make certain he still had possession of Dimassé's letters to Nola's police commissioner and *préfet*. He couldn't help but wonder whose life would change most profoundly in the next couple of months. Would it be Assan's, Josie's or his own?

Arriving at the Minerva Hotel in less than four hours was, quite possibly, a world record. Normally, Kael would have been ecstatic. Instead, he said, "Shit," as they pulled into an open parking space. The vehicle sitting next to theirs was a Toyota Landcruiser pick-up with the letters T.R.A.P. boldly stenciled across the door. Mitchell Wright had already arrived. No telling when. It could have been three days ago, or it could have been that very morning.

Kael shook Dimassé's hand." Thanks for the ride, the letters and for not pursuing a professional singing career."

Dimassé laughed. "We all have our shortcomings. Mine is my singing voice. Yours is the size of your bottle."He laughed some more while popping the trunk open.

Kael pulled out his backpack, guitar and Josie's woven sack. He kept the backpack, but handed the other pieces to Josie.

When the trunk was slammed shut, Dimassé backed out of the parking lot. Before zooming away, he leaned his head out of the window. "Remember what I said about our friend, *Monsieur* Yakonomingui. He doesn't have much of a sense of humor."

"I've got enough for both of us,"yelled Kael at the departing car. He put a hand on top of Josie's cap-covered head. "Come on, kiddo. I'll introduce you to Mitch and our hotel room. I have a feeling neither one will be very accommodating."

They entered the Minerva Hotel's dimly lit lobby. To the left, a water-stained coffee table and six low-slung wooden chairs created an informal lounge area that gazed upon the reception desk straight ahead or the bar to the right.

Kael poked his head in the bar and as he suspected, found Mitchell Wright. There was no mistaking that thick upper body. He had been shorter than Kael by an inch or two, but had outweighed him by fifty pounds—all of it in the chest and biceps. That hadn't changed. In fact, Mitch looked even bulkier. His T-shirt was stretched so tight across the pecs, it looked more like a leotard or body paint. He was sitting alone and drinking from a large tumbler of ice and, guessing from the color of the liquid, whiskey.

Kael stepped into the small room. "Hey, Mitch, can I freshen that up for you?"

Mitch looked up from his glass. "Husker? You owe me more than a drink. Where the fuck have you been? I've been here since yesterday."

"Here at the bar or here in Bangui?" Kael asked the bartender for a Mocaf, a Coke and whatever his foul-mouthed friend was drinking.

"You're four fucking days late."

Kael remained calm even though Mitch's speech was obviously slurred. "Good to see you, too, Mitch. What's it been? Ten years? You haven't changed a bit."He wondered if Mitch picked up his rapier-like wit as easily as he picked up his whiskey. Probably not.

Mitch looked at Josie, who was peeking around Kael. "What's with the Pygmy? Is that why you're late?"

Kael guided Josie forward. "This is my son, Josie, and I'm not late. I arrived in Bangui on time four days ago. You didn't get here until yesterday, which means you were three days late."

"Whatever..." He finished off what was left in his glass. His large head seemed to wobble like it was on a spring. "I'm too drunk to argue."

Kael pondered how many whiskeys it took to inebriate a two-hundred-and-forty-pound cinder block.

His drink order arrived, so he and Josie set their bags down next to Mitch's table. Mitch didn't wait for them to sit down. He snatched his new glass from the waiter's tray and threw the honey-colored liquid down his redwood-sized neck. The waiter set the Mocaf, the Coke and two chipped glasses on the table. While the waiter poured, Kael wondered if he was being followed by these glasses. They looked exactly like the ones from the airport and the New Palace Bar. They always traveled in pairs, too. Another theory to run by Tallin.

He picked up his glass and clinked it with Josie's. "Here's to your first drink in Bangui. I had to wait until I was in my twenties." He then said, "*Chin chin*."

Mitch said, "What are you, a fucking frog?"

Kael was glad Josie didn't understand English or the concept of the ugly American. "So what's the plan, Mitch?"

"I'm going to take a siesta. We eventually need to sign the project bank account over to your name. We could have done it this morning, but since you weren't here, we'll have to wait until tomorrow when the banks open up again." He rubbed his head as if trying to strangle a headache. "The fucking bankers here work even fewer hours than those in the states."

"That's because they have less money," said Kael. "Speaking of which, I need some. I've got a TRAP paycheck cut from a French bank, so it's in francs rather than dollars. Will the bank here cash it for me?"

Mitch flashed a smirk. It was the kind despised by parents and teachers. "Sure...as soon as it clears. That could take anywhere from two weeks to two months, depending on how closely related you are to the bank president."

Kael was amazed that Mitch could construct a complete sentence without using the word, "fuck." "What if I'm a perfect stranger with an engaging personality?"

"You're fucked."

Kael tried to formulate a Plan B. In the daily struggle with CARL, alternatives and flexibility were as invaluable as a sense of humor and an ample supply of alcohol. It suddenly came to him. It was brilliant. CARL would be pissed. "Can I borrow the truck for a couple of hours? Josie and I need to run some errands."

Mitch reached into his pocket. He withdrew a ring of keys and dropped it on the table. "Take it. It's yours now, anyway. I'm going up to my room." He got up and left the bar without another word. Not even another "fuck."

Kael had the feeling that he'd just witnessed the ceremonial transfer of power. He wondered if Josie was as moved by the experience. He put an arm around his son. "So, what do you think of your Uncle Mitch? He's quite the raconteur and bon vivant, huh? Some big shoes for your old man to fill. Finish your Coke and we'll check into our room where I'll introduce you to running water, electricity and a little thing called a toilet. I guarantee you they're all more fun than Uncle Mitch."

Two hours later, Kael and Josie hopped into the cab of TRAP's Toyota pick-up. Their hotel room had been the equivalent of Disney World to Josie. He had taken three, long, hot showers. He had worked the light switches until one broke. He had flushed the toilet so many times that Kael had been inspired to write a letter to Tallin theorizing on the economic viability of a theme park entitled either "Plumber's World" or "Six Flags Over Porcelain."

They headed down *Avenue Boganda*. Kael drove while Josie performed his duties as an overeager co-pilot and played with the air-conditioning controls and the wind-shield wipers. Kael put his son's excess energy to proper use by teaching him how to shift the truck's five-speed manual transmission.

Kael would depress the clutch and bark out the appropriate gear. "*Premier. Deux-ième. Troisième.*" Josie, the picture of concentration, would maneuver the large stick shift with both hands. The pink tongue sticking out of the side of his mouth seemed to follow the same modified-H pattern.

Just after the intersection with *Avenue des Martyrs*, Kael had Josie downshift. They passed an acacia tree and turned right on to a long dirt driveway lined with junk: an automobile transmission, suspension springs, a car door and old tires. If there had been a non-functioning snow machine or outboard engine amidst the rusting hardware, Kael would have been reminded of a typically landscaped Alaskan lawn.

Kael and Josie arrived at a gated entrance to Nasseef's garage. A young man in greasy coveralls opened the gate. Kael drove through. The yard was full of automobile carcasses in various states of disrepair. Mechanics swarmed over the vehicles like surgeons removing salvageable parts from some and transplanting their harvests into other less-terminal patients. Kael drove by slowly, hoping the dust he kicked up wouldn't disturb the sterile field.

He stopped in front of a porch where Nasseef sat alone sipping from a doll-sized coffee cup. Kael rolled down his window and poked out his head. "Is it tea time, gov'ner?"

Nasseef smiled. "No, I'm drinking Lebanese coffee. It's very strong like your espresso. Come and join me."

Kael and Josie hopped out of the truck. They entered the porch where Kael shook hands with their host and said, "Nasseef, I'd like you to meet my son, Josie."

Nasseef's bushy eyebrow arched up. "My, my, *Monsieur* Kael. You've been busy." He shook Josie's hand and said in Sango, "I like your hat. You look very American."

Josie smiled and said, "*Merci.*"

Nasseef looked back at Kael. "You still haven't finished the introductions."

Kael was confused. "OK. Josie, this is Nasseef."

"No," said Nasseef. "I mean your truck. Is she mine now?"

"I thought we might work out an arrangement."

"Excellent. Come gentlemen. Sit. Sit." Nasseef ushered them to two empty chairs. He then called into the house. "Simplice, we have guests."

Simplice was on the porch by the time Nasseef said the word, "guests." He nodded at Kael and said, "*Bonjour, patron.*"

"*Bonjour*, Simplice. Don't worry. You don't have to carry my backpack again."

Simplice smiled. "*Merci, patron.*"

Nasseef said, "We need more coffee for *Monsieur* Kael and me. And bring a Coke for *Monsieur* Josie."

"*Oui, patron.*"

After Simplice left, they all sat around the small table. Kael said, "You have quite an operation here. There must be twenty mechanics out in the yard."

"Some are paid employees. Others just like to participate and learn—an informal apprenticeship of sorts."

"Only the knowledgeable ones will work on my truck, right?"

"Of course, and only under my direct supervision. I will even try to be sober."

Simplice returned. On his tray he carried a small coffeepot, another miniature cup and saucer, a bottle of Coke and one of the two chipped glasses following Kael through Central Africa. The other one was probably waiting for him back at the hotel.

Simplice poured the refreshments. Kael's coffee looked like it had just been drained from someone's neglected oil pan.

Simplice wished them, "*Bon apéritif*," and scampered back into the house.

Nasseef held his coffee cup's dime-sized handle between his thumb and forefinger. It seemed out of place in his hairy, big-knuckled hand. "I will tell you what I told *Monsieur* Nick. This coffee is for sipping, for savoring. It is not for guzzling like your Maxwell Home."

Kael nodded. He lifted the tiny cup to his mouth. It reminded him of sex on the beach: somewhat gritty, but enjoyable nonetheless. "That's definitely not Maxwell Home, though I'm sure it's good to the last chunk."

Nasseef set his cup back down on the saucer. "So, what brings you to my garage? Is your truck in need of maintenance? If so, I will bump it to the front of the line."

"No, the truck is fine for now. I've come to see if your bank is still open for business."

"Of course. Do you wish to cash more Traveler's Checks?"

"Not exactly. I've got a TRAP paycheck made out to me in French francs. The bank here will want to hold the check for several weeks until it clears. My problem is that I need local currency now. I was wondering if I could sign the check over to you for the CFA equivalent. It's a lot of money."

"How much?"

Kael removed the check from his shirt pocket. "It's for 662,500 French francs. That's about ten thousand dollars or 2.65 million CFA. The reason why I came to you is that you had at least that much in the bankroll you flashed outside the American embassy the other day."

"And you want this all in CFA?"

"Yes. The banks open up early tomorrow morning. I could meet you there or..."

Nasseef stood up. "Wait here." He walked into the house. A few minutes later he returned carrying a steel-gray strongbox. He set it gently on the table being especially careful to not spill any of the drinks. He inserted a key into the lock and opened the lid. "How much was it? 2.65 million?" He removed a wad of cash several times thicker than the stash he had pulled out of his pocket at the embassy.

Kael was flabbergasted. "You keep that much cash at home? Isn't that risky?"

"No more than leaving it in one of the local banks. I've lived here long enough to have absolutely no confidence in any national institution, especially one that handles large amounts of hard currency on a daily basis. I once banished an apprentice from my garage for stealing and a week later I saw him in my bank working as a teller. I withdrew my money that very day."

Kael held up his check. "If you don't have a bank account, how will *you* cash this?"

Nasseef smiled. "*You* don't have an account and *you're* cashing it. There is a rather substantial underground network of Lebanese businessmen here. We help each other with such matters. I also have a brother in France. Believe me. I will have no trouble cashing your check. I may even realize a small profit. All sorts of games can be played with foreign currency."

Kael shook his head. "You're not going to make any profit from me, are you?"

"Of course I will. I'll pay you the full 2.65 million, but I now know that you will be bringing your truck to me. You have just become a valued customer of *Garage* Nasseef."

Kael signed over the check while Nasseef counted out 2.65 million CFA in ten-thousand-franc notes. Josie stared at the proceedings with the same intensity he had displayed earlier while watching the water swirl around and then disappear from the toilet bowl.

Nasseef had Simplice bring out two containers resembling ordinary one-liter plastic bottles of motor oil. Nasseef popped the false bottoms and stuffed the cash inside. He resealed the bottles before handing them to Kael. "Stick these in a case of oil and no one will know. I can sell you a case if you'd like."

"Sure," said Kael. "We might as well start running a tab."

Nasseef grinned. "See. I am already showing a profit." Kael and Josie finished their drinks. They thanked Nasseef for his hospitality and for the case of motor oil Simplice had deposited on the floor of the truck's cab.

Kael informed Josie that he had a new job to perform during the drive back to the hotel. He was being relieved of his shifting duties in order to keep a strict watch on the motor oil sitting at his feet, in particular two bottles worth considerably more than a full barrel of Saudi Arabian crude.

Josie's eyes widened at the serious nature of his responsibilities. "Do I have to watch them all the way to Bayanga?"

"We'll take turns."

Nasseef had never asked what the money was for. Josie wasn't as restrained. By the time they reached the acacia tree, his curiosity peaked. "Papa, what will you do with those two bottles?"

"I'm going to grease the wheels of justice."

Josie scrunched up his pug nose. He looked as perplexed as Chako the first time Kael had given the command, "Attack!" Words of violence just weren't in her vocabulary. She was a retriever, so she reacted by running around haphazardly sniffing the ground in ever-widening circles. This was, at first, all very confusing to Kael. Finally, he decided that she wasn't dumb. She was probably searching for a small pushpin, "a tack."

Kael patted his son on the knee and gave a new interpretation of his answer. "We're going to help a friend."

Josie smiled. That, he understood.

# 19

When Kael heard Nick answer the other phone thousands of miles away, he said, "Hey, *Puru ti kondo*, I've got a riddle for you."

Nick said, "I really need to start screening calls. Go ahead, Pig-Pen."

"What does Mitchell Wright use for contraception?"

"I don't know. What?"

"His personality."

Nick laughed. "Not bad. Probably not far from the truth, either. I've got one for you. A Texan is trying to impress an Alaskan about the size of his ranch. He says, 'I get up in the morning, hop into my truck, and I drive and I drive and I drive and I drive. Then, I stop for lunch. After lunch, I drive some more. I drive and I drive and I drive and I drive. By the time I stop for supper, I'm still not off of my property.' The Alaskan nods his head and says, 'Hmm, I had a truck like that once.'"

Kael laughed, but apparently not as much as Nick had expected.

"What's the matter?" said Nick. "Don't tell me you have the Bangui Blues already. You've only been there a few days. I'm assuming, of course, that you made it to Bangui. You're not calling from some tall, blond stewardess' apartment in Paris, are you?"

"No, I'm at the posh Minerva Hotel in the heart of downtown Bangui. Your joke was funny—one of your best, in fact, but a cute little brunette is asleep in my bed, so I'm trying to be quiet."

"*Ooh la la.*"

"I'm talking about Josie."

"That's great—not as great as a tall, blond, horny Parisian stewardess, but what is?"

"The love of a good woman like Darcy?"

"I suppose," said Nick. "By the way, Darcy, Savannah, and Forrest all say hi. They've been asking about you every day, as has Tallin. Remember her?"

"Vaguely. Is she tall and blond?"

"I'll tell her you asked about her."

"I wrote her a long letter this afternoon. Josie loves the Orioles cap almost as much as the toilet."

"What?"

"Tallin will explain. It's all in her letter."

"I can't wait," said Nick. "So tell me what else you've accomplished since arriving in Bangui besides writing love letters and luring young boys into your bed with baseball caps and toilets."

"I had a quick drink with Mitch. Rectal exams are more enjoyable."

"Play nice. You only have to deal with him for a little while and then he's off to his new post down in the Congo and you'll probably never have to see him again."

"I'm hoping he's more personable when he's sober. We have some banking to do in the morning."

"So when are you heading out to Bayanga?"

"Tomorrow. After the bank, we'll pick up a few supplies and if all goes according to plan, we should be out of here before noon."

"In other words, you'll be leaving in a few days."

"I'm hoping CARL sleeps in tomorrow."

"Yeah, right," said Nick.

"Any suggestions on how to endure ten hours in a cramped truck with Mitch?"

"Drink heavily."

"It's worth a try. By the way, thanks for the Bass Ales."

"You're quite welcome. Next time, would you prefer a... lighter beer?"

"Very funny."

"That's exactly how I hope to describe your next joke," said Nick. "I've got to run. Joseph is out of town again, so I'm swamped. Thanks for the riddle and the update. Give a big hug to Josie. I'm glad you two are together. I'm sure Molly is, too. Call again when you get back to Bangui."

"Sure. Remind me to tell you the one about the Alaskan who broke the crocodile man out of jail."

Nick said, "What?"

Kael could tell from Nick's tone that he wanted a response. Kael wasn't ready to talk about it yet, so without a word, he hung up the phone.

# 20

Kael awoke to the sound of a flushing toilet—not once, but eight times. His eyes remained closed. He felt the other side of the bed with his right hand. It was warm, but empty. Six Flags Over Porcelain had opened for business.

He reluctantly pulled himself up to sit at the edge of the bed. He rubbed his eyes with one hand while the other reached for his wristwatch on the nightstand. Five fifty-five. Morning light filtered through the thin hotel curtains. He pondered an age-old question: Whose idea was it, anyway, for the sun to rise so early?

He stood up and walked across the floor to the partially closed bathroom door. He poked his head through the opening. "Josie, are you OK?"

Josie didn't answer. He was too busy staring into the toilet bowl. Kael looked in, too. A new, family-size bar of Ivory soap floated in the swirling water. Kael reached in and fished it out. He tossed the perfectly good bar in the sink and said, "There are better ways to clean the toilet."

Josie said, "Your toothbrush made it through."

"Ahh... well, if we still have towels, why don't you hop in the shower."

Josie smiled. His dimples couldn't have been any bigger.

Forty-five minutes later, they were sitting at a table in a busy French *pâtisserie*. Kael was working on his second cup of coffee. Josie was downing his third pastry. He had already inhaled one *pain au chocolat* and one *pain au fromage*.

They waited for Mitch, whom Kael had awakened with a six fifteen phone call. Kael could tell that Mitch's mood hadn't brightened. After twelve rings, he had barked into the receiver, "What the fuck?"

Kael had tried to temper Mitch's rage by inviting him for coffee and *croissants* before going to the bank. Mitch had surprisingly accepted. At least, they sounded like grunts of approval. Kael was beginning to wonder. The seat they had saved for him was still unoccupied.

Kael sat patiently. He watched a parade of people enter the pastry shop to buy *baguettes*, the long, sword-like loaves of French bread. French people definitely looked different from Americans. He started to develop a theory. It began with their style of dress. They rarely wore jeans, or if they did, they were pressed. And they always wore expensive-looking dress shoes with dark, yet almost see-through, socks. Lit cigarettes were in the hand or mouth of eight out of ten *baguette*-buying patrons.

He was just beginning to form a promising hypothesis on hairstyles when Mitch walked through the door. He wore a clean denim shirt and relatively wrinkle-free khaki trousers. His hair was even combed. "Getting married?" asked Kael.

"No, I'm flying down to Brazzaville today."

"You're what?"

Mitch took a seat. "I'm flying down to the Congo today."

"I thought we were driving out to Bayanga today."

"You can if you want. You've got the truck."

Kael tried to remain calm. "When will you be back?"

"I won't. I'm done here." Mitch grabbed a waiter and ordered a cup of coffee.

"I assumed there would be a brief period of transition. Who's going to introduce me to everyone out in Bayanga?"

"There are two TRAP researchers out there as well as a Peace Corps volunteer. They can answer any questions you have. I'm sure Nick has already warned you about the *sous-préfet*, the mayor and the police commissioner. If you think I'm an asshole, wait until you meet them."

Kael rubbed his throbbing forehead. He realized that he should have saved two extra chairs at their table—one for Mitch and another for CARL. On the plus side, Mitch's seat in the cab of the pick-up would be empty all the way to Bayanga. Problem solved. He looked at Mitch. "Can you at least tell me how to *get* to Bayanga?"

"Head southwest. There's a map in the glove box of the truck. One free piece of advice: Take an axe or a bow saw. A chainsaw would be better. The roads go right through the forest. They aren't maintained and they don't see much traffic, so if a downed tree is blocking the way, you'll have to cut it up yourself."

"Does the road go through Nola?"

"Yes." Mitch's coffee arrived. He glared at the waiter and said, "It's about fucking time."

The waiter didn't understand English, so he just smiled back.

Kael decided that Mitch was lucky to be working in a country where few understood his rude comments. One day, CARL would learn English slang and Mitch would become acquainted with the taste of an African fist.

Kael finished his coffee. He briefly considered asking Mitch his opinion on crocodile men, but thought better of it. If a crocodile man were attacking Mitch, Kael had no doubt as to which combatant he would root on to victory. Goooooo reptiles!

While Mitch drank his coffee in silence, Kael and Josie made a list of supplies they would need to pick up: a chainsaw, a backup axe or a bow saw, several cases of tomato paste, a fifty-kilogram sack of rice, assorted shapes of pasta, toilet paper, candy bars, and a new toothbrush for Kael. He reluctantly vetoed Josie's request for a three-month stock of French pastries.

When Kael started naming off household basics like pots, pans, plates, and linens, Mitch mumbled from behind his coffee cup. "You don't need those."

"That's true," said Kael. "They'd just clutter up the place."

Mitch set his coffee cup down. "The TRAP house in Bayanga comes with everything from kerosene lamps to mosquito nets. Project money paid for it all, so it stays with the house and is passed on from one director to the next."

Kael wondered if Mitch would have volunteered that information had he not over-heard their discussion. He doubted it and he let Mitch know this by putting more than a trace of sarcasm in his voice when he asked, "Is there anything else we should know?"

Mitch pushed his chair back. He stood up. "Don't forget to pick up the TRAP mail at the main post office. The key to the box is on the ring with the truck keys. It's Box 499. Come on. Let's get this banking business done so we can both get the fuck out of here."

The bank turned out to be less of an inconvenience than Kael had anticipated. A skin rash instead of a cancer. Sure, there were unruly mobs of customers attempting to storm the tellers' windows. And, of course, no one seemed to know who handled the transfer of an account from one name to another. But one gentleman, who seemed genuinely concerned, had made it all worthwhile with the best line of the morning. After much introspection, he had turned to Mitch and said quite seriously, "It would be so much easier, *monsieur*, if you just didn't leave."

Kael found it all very surreal. He half-expected someone to suggest that it would be far less time consuming if he simply changed his name to Mitchell Wright.

The seventeenth bank employee they met was the Vice-President for New Accounts. Through casual, introductory conversation, it was discovered that he was originally from Boda. It was enough of a connection to keep them from being shuffled off to the office of employee number eighteen.

The Vice-President said, "I don't have the authority to change the name on an account. I don't think anyone does, but I have another idea. We can open a new account in *Monsieur* Husker's name. Then, we transfer the funds from *Monsieur* Wright's account over to *Monsieur* Husker's account. Finally, we close out *Monsieur* Wright's account."

Mitch looked like he wanted to punch something. Kael was afraid that Mitch's target of choice would be *Monsieur le Vice-President*, so he stepped forward and said, "Excellent idea. Now why didn't we think of that?"

The Vice-President smiled, not knowing how close he had come to a massive cerebral hemorrhage. He searched his file cabinet for the appropriate forms that needed to be filled out.

Kael, Mitch and Josie sat down. Kael whispered to Mitch, "It's just like the old saying: Close only counts in horseshoes, grenades, slow dancing and international banking."

Mitch didn't laugh.

Kael and Josie parted ways with Mitch on the outside steps of the bank. Kael bid him good luck in the Congo, though he secretly wished better fortune upon the Congolese. Hadn't those people suffered enough?

Mitch said nothing. He was a man of few words, especially if they weren't made up of four letters. He strutted past a collection of street beggars with an assortment of afflictions ranging from watermelon-sized goiters to one guy who had no lips. They normally leapt upon most foreigners for some spare change, but not one approached Mitch. They were probably just abiding by one of the unwritten laws of panhandling: Never demand anything from those less fortunate. Better to have no lips than no personality.

Kael and Josie ran their errands. They managed to find everything on their list except a chainsaw. Then, he remembered Nasseef. They could stop there after picking up the mail.

There was only one letter in the mailbox, and Kael couldn't even deliver it. It was addressed to Molly from her parents, Mr. and Mrs. Mike McGinley of 5029 First Avenue South, Minneapolis Minnesota 55419, U.S.A. The postmark was from way back in August when Molly was still alive. The handwriting on the envelope had a feminine quality: perfect, round letters like those taught in grade school penmanship classes. It was probably from her mother.

Kael wasn't quite sure what to do with the letter. Normally, he'd scribble "Return to Sender" across the envelope, stuff it in a mailbox, and that would be that. Odds were slim that it would ever make it back to its place of origin. It was a miracle that it had even made it here in the first place. He decided to hang on to it until he could come up with a better plan to get it back to Molly's folks. He folded it up and stuck it in his wallet.

Next stop was Nasseef's. While Kael and Josie sipped cool refreshments on his porch, Nasseef made a couple of phone calls. Within ten minutes, Kael had three different models of chainsaws from which to choose. Nasseef added the cost of the saw to Kael's running tab. It was like shopping from a mail-order catalog.

Father, son, and chainsaw pulled out of Bangui at just after one o'clock. Kael thought it might even be a modern-day record. Bangui shopping expeditions were like banking transactions. They were legendary for taking three to five days longer than anticipated. Often, the frustrated shopper would leave Bangui several days late and still without the supplies they sought. Those people obviously didn't know Nasseef.

According to the neatly folded map in the glove box, the voyage to Bayanga would be roughly five hundred kilometers. The main logging road heading west was either newer than the map or so primitive that the map makers had neglected to include it in the C.A.R.'s official highway system. Mitch had added it to the map in pen. It left the main road south of M'Baiki and picked up another primary, yet still unpaved, route north of Nola. In between, it cut through virgin forest. It would be a feast for the senses, but a nightmare for the truck's suspension.

Kael told Josie that they would probably see lots of monkeys and birds along the way. If they were lucky, they might even glimpse an elephant or a gorilla. Josie seemed excited, but nervous. He informed Kael that one of his mother's aunts had slept with a gorilla. Kael's response was more for his own amusement than for Josie's enlightenment: "Most women probably have at one time or another. Some even marry them."

The ride to Nola was magical. The logging road appeared in their butterfly-splattered windshield right where the map showed it would. It was a combination of slick laterite mud and deep sand with long stretches of kidney-punching washboard, but it was like passing through a primeval tunnel of leaves and light.

Kael and Josie stopped often to gaze up into the dense forest canopy. They found more traffic in the branches than on the road below. Agile-crested mangabeys, black-and-white colobus monkeys, and hornbills were just a few of the overhead commuters. The elephants and gorillas never made an appearance. Neither did the chainsaw. It stayed packed away with the rice, tomato paste, and motor oil.

Kael suspected that if he had never purchased the chainsaw and had attempted to venture through the forest with just a bow saw, he would have encountered dozens of downed trees. That was the way CARL operated. He caused flats when there was no spare. He booby-trapped headlights to malfunction when it was dark. He broke windshield wipers during torrential downpours. He made people believe in crocodile men.

It was already well past dusk when their pick-up rolled into the town of Nola. It wasn't much to look at, especially in the dark. The local architectural style resembled that of every other Central African bush town. It was more temporary than contemporary. Nothing seemed to be built for permanence. Crudely constructed houses of mud brick and palm-frond thatch looked like pup tents dotting the hills under the dim light of the moon.

A washed-out road led Kael and Josie up to a central market place. In the morning, it would be the epicenter of activity. At this late hour, however, it was as lifeless as the tens of thousands of insects squashed against the pick-up's windshield.

A few hundred meters past the empty market stalls was a noisy, well-lit bar. They drove over. It appeared to be the only establishment in town with electricity. A smoking portable generator sat off to one side. With each cough and sputter, the lights dimmed and the scratchy records slowed. A young man danced out of the building to hit the generator with a large hammer. Kael called to him between strikes.

The man ignored Kael's interruption. He continued to tap the asthmatic engine with both ends of the hammer. When the patient didn't respond, he tried using his foot. Three swift kicks against the frame seemed to do the trick. The engine purred.

The successful mechanic approached Kael's truck and asked, "*Oui, monsieur?*"

Kael leaned out the window to shake his hand. "*Bonsoir, Monsieur* Goodwrench. Can you tell me where I might find the Catholic mission?"

"Of course, Father. It's not far."

That was the first time Kael had been mistaken for a priest. And from past experience, "not far" could be anywhere from a few feet to several towns away.

The mechanic scratched his head with the claw end of the hammer. "Go past the market to where the road ends. Turn right. If you come to the river, you've turned left and you'll need to turn around. Go straight until you see the church."

It seemed simple enough. A river was wrong; a church was right. "After I turn right, how far up the road is the church?"

"Not far."

Kael smiled. He deserved that one. He made the sign of the cross with his hand and said, "Bless you, my son."

The mission turned out to be several kilometers past Kael's definition of "not far." After about four kilometers, he started to think that the mechanic was more talented with a hammer than with directions. He decided, however, to push on. When the pickup crested a hill, Josie spotted the church's steeple. It stuck out of the trees like a Saturn rocket aimed at Heaven.

A winding dirt driveway cut through a small grove of tropical fruit trees including mangoes, papayas, guavas and oranges. Kael's mouth watered at the thought of a big juicy mango. Unfortunately, mango season wouldn't be until March or April. Thank goodness beer didn't have a season.

The church was dark. Only one of the half-dozen stone cottages surrounding the church looked awake. Bright light escaped from one small window.

Kael pulled up in front of the cottage and turned off the engine. He suddenly felt tired. The muscles in his shoulders and forearms ached from wrestling with the steering wheel for over eight hours. His eyes burned. His butt was asleep. It dawned on him why he was so exhausted. With no roads at Hidden Cove and only two paved highways running the fifteen miles from one end of Sitka to the other, he probably hadn't driven a car for more than a twenty-minute stint in the last nine years. He looked over at Josie and said, "*E si awé.*"

Josie nodded. "Do you think they have a toilet?"

"Let's go see." Kael and Josie opened their doors and hopped out of the truck's cab.

The night air smelled faintly of pineapple. Kael stepped around the truck and found the source. The walkway leading to the cottage's front door was lined with prickly pineapple plants in various stages of development. Some were as big as footballs. Kael hoped he would be allowed to pick one or two.

The Catholic missions sprinkled throughout Central Africa had an excellent reputation among weary pineapple-craving travelers. They consistently rated higher than their religious competition: the more conservative American Baptists in the east and the American Evangelical Brethren in the west. All three provided a decent bed, edible meals, and friendly conversation. What the Catholics had in their favor was that they were run by the French or the Italians, people who liked their wine, whiskey, and beer almost as much as their God. The American missions were dry, so in Kael's alcohol-saturated mind, the choice was a no-brainer.

Kael knocked on the cottage's heavy wooden door. He ran his fingers through his hair and brushed away some of the dust from Josie's clothes. He was adjusting Josie's baseball cap when the door opened.

The man standing before them filled the doorframe almost as well as the door had. He looked like a homeless Santa Claus. He had a full head of white hair that had obviously been cropped short by someone with no barbering experience. It looked like he had possibly done it himself without the aid of a mirror. His beard was full and white and hid almost everything on his face except the large bulbous nose, upon which sat rectangular wire-rimmed glasses. He wore gray work pants. His belt dangled unbuckled. Gray chest hair sprouted above the low-cut neckline of his dirty-white muscle t-shirt. One meaty hand held up an open book, which he continued to read.

Kael was momentarily tongue-tied. Had he caught Santa going over his list to see who was naughty and who was nice? Kael caught a glimpse of the book's front cover. It was a French translation of a popular Dick Francis novel. He waited for Santa's eyes to look up from his paperback, but when no acknowledgment appeared imminent, Kael cleared his throat and said, "*Excusez-nous, monsieur.*"

Santa held up a finger. It was probably the same one he placed at the side of his nose to rise magically up a chimney.

"*S'il vous plaît.* Just one more second. I'm about to discover who the murderer is."

"The only suspect you can rule out in a Dick Francis mystery is the horse."

Santa nodded, but kept on reading. Kael and Josie stood waiting until Santa hit his own forehead with one of his fists.

"*Incroyable!*" He shut the book the way a priest closed a Bible: slowly, with reverence and respect.

Kael figured it was safe to talk. "Was it who you thought it was?"

Santa smiled. "It never is. Come in, gentlemen." He showed his visitors into a sparsely furnished room and shut the door behind them. The room was brightly lit by an Aladdin kerosene lamp. "Please excuse my unsociable behavior." He held up the paperback. "I get so wrapped up in these things. Let's start over. I'm *Père* Norbert." He held out his hand.

Kael shook hands and introduced himself and his son. "There's no need to apologize, Father. I'm also a big fan of Dick Francis."

*Père* Norbert thrust the novel into Kael's hands. "Then take it. Books were meant to be read and shared. This one's too good to collect dust on some shelf."

Kael accepted the gift. "Thank you. I've never read one in French before. Looking up every other word in my French-English dictionary is one way to make a good book last."

*Père* Norbert chuckled. "I've tried reading Dick Francis in the original English, but I become lost in the slang. Can you explain the verb, 'to get?'"

Kael scratched his beard. "It's like a television, Father. I know how to use it, but I can't explain how it works. The French language can be just as confusing for Americans. For example, why does every noun have to be masculine or feminine? What makes a table feminine and a book masculine? Even my table is feminine. And answer me this: Why is a bra, an obviously feminine article of clothing, a masculine noun—*le soutien-gorge?*"

*Père* Norbert laughed just like Santa. His whole body shook. "I know absolutely nothing about bras. I don't know how to use one and I can't explain how one works."

"Glad to hear it," said Kael.

*Père* Norbert pulled two chairs out from under a scarred wooden table. "Have a seat. You both look exhausted." He turned down the lamp so the light wasn't as intense. "That's better. I keep it high for reading. Can I offer you a whiskey, perhaps? A Coke for your son?"

"Bless you, Father." Kael decided then and there that if he ever found religion, it would be Catholicism. He and Josie collapsed into their chairs.

While *Père* Norbert prepared the beverages, Kael surveyed the room. He'd seen better decorated jail cells. Four straight-backed chairs, two tables, and a small kerosene-run refrigerator were spread out across an undulating cement floor. The four stone walls were bare except for a small metallic crucifix hanging above the doorway to an adjoining room.

*Père* Norbert approached with both hands full of clinking glasses and bottles. He set the refreshments on the table and pulled out an empty chair. Before sitting, he grabbed one of the whiskey-filled glasses. He held it aloft and said, "*Chin chin.*"

Kael picked up his glass. "Amen."

Josie took a sip of his Coke and said, "Do you have a toilet, *Mon Père?*"

*Père* Norbert smiled. "I have an outhouse. Would you like to use it?"

"*Non, merci.*" Josie went back to his Coke.

Kael felt a need to explain. "He's fascinated with the workings of a toilet."

*Père* Norbert sat down. "Wait until he discovers bidets."

"You know," said Kael. "I'd like someone to explain those things to me. And I'll just bet it's a masculine noun."

The whiskey was warm and smooth. Kael didn't know why, but it always tasted better around a campfire or kerosene lamp. Light bulbs and whiskey just didn't mix. He theorized that Thomas Alva Edison was not a whiskey drinker.

*Père* Norbert was. He drained his glass in three quick swallows.

"So, tell me. What brings you to my humble mission? And don't say your truck or my whiskey." He refilled his glass.

"We're on our way to Bayanga. I'm the new director of the Doli-Ngili Reserve."

"Ah... a lovely place at the end of a very bumpy road."

"Sounds like you could be describing Heaven, Father."

*Père* Norbert seemed to mull that one over. He cocked his head to one side and swirled the whiskey in his glass. "I hope there are fewer mosquitoes in Heaven."

"Me, too," said Kael. "I don't know why Noah didn't just smack those remaining two when he had the chance."

"All of God's creatures are precious... but I've often wondered the same thing."

*Père* Norbert asked Kael and Josie to spend the night in the mission's guest cottage. Kael confessed that he had stopped for that very reason, not to mention the whiskey.

*Père* Norbert laughed. "I know. In my twenty-three years of missionary work in Africa, I have never once seen a traveler on my doorstep after nine o'clock searching solely for spiritual guidance. And before you ask, yes, you may take as many pineapples as you wish."

Kael shook his head in disbelief. "You're amazing, Father. I was going to ask you some questions, but we could save a lot of time if you just go ahead and give me the answers beforehand."

"OK. The answer to your first question is, 'Yes, I can refill your glass.'" *Père* Norbert picked up the whiskey bottle and poured.

"Good guess. You can keep pouring, but what I really wanted to know was if you remember a woman named Molly McGinley."

*Père* Norbert set the bottle down. "I hadn't anticipated that one. Was she a friend of yours?" After an affirmative nod, he said, "I remember Molly as having a kind and gentle soul."

"So you knew her before she died?"

"*Oui.* I run a small clinic for the Pygmies. They're pretty much neglected by the country's health care system, so the mission provides them with basic medicines and vaccinations. Molly had some Pygmy workers who were ill. She brought them to me. This was about a month before she died. I only met her that one time, but I liked her. She could hold her whiskey and she seemed... genuine, and those are rare qualities."

*Père* Norbert downed his whiskey in one smooth motion. When he pulled the empty glass away from his mouth, tiny honey-colored droplets were left behind to dangle on his mustache like shiny Christmas balls.

He asked Kael, "Do you believe the old crocodile man theory?"

"Of course not," said Kael. "Do you?"

"No, but we all have illogical beliefs. Mine happens to be the virgin birth. Who's to say which is the more preposterous? Here in Central Africa, the believers in crocodile men far outnumber those who believe that Jesus' mother was a virgin."

"I don't think your bishop would be too pleased to hear that."

"Probably not, but the New Testament says, 'Let us run with patience the race that is set before us.'"

Kael scratched his beard. Wise words, but he had his own race to run. It was a short sprint with two oil bottles full of money in one hand and a couple of letters in the other. He could almost see the finish line where Molly would be cheering him on to victory. "I was told that Molly's body was kept in a freezer here at the mission."

"That's right." *Père* Norbert filled his glass a third time. "One of the researchers, a *Mademoiselle* Schwartz, transported it up. I have one of the few chest freezers in the region big enough to accommodate a human body. I sometimes like my whiskey over ice."

"When you saw the body, did you notice any signs of an attack by a crocodile man?"

"Such as?"

"I don't know. Bite marks? Claw marks? Crocodile hide underneath her fingernails?"

"No, none of that. Her head was bruised, but that could have happened when she fell out of her dugout canoe."

Kael raised one eyebrow. "That would explain why she didn't swim to shore. She either hit her head on the canoe, or... the crocodile man struck her with a blunt instrument before he drowned her."

"Like I said, we all have our illogical beliefs."

"I'm just trying to understand why an innocent man is, at this very minute and in this very town, locked away for being a crocodile man, especially when his victim's body showed no evidence in support of that theory. It's like finding someone floating face down in the middle of the ocean and saying, 'He was obviously hit by a bus.'"

A snort from Kael's right side caused him to turn away from *Père* Norbert. His first thought was that Josie had understood the humor, laughed with a mouthful of Coke, and had painfully sent it surging up through his nasal passages. Coke would now be dripping from his nostrils like a leaky faucet.

Truth was, Josie hadn't heard a word. He was asleep. His head lay across his folded forearms like a passed-out drunk at a bar. A thin string of drool ran from one corner of his open mouth to the tabletop. His glass of Coke had been pushed forward. It was half-full.

Kael looked back at their host. "My son was wondering if he could go to bed now."

"Of course." *Père* Norbert got up. "I should have let you both go straight to bed as soon as you arrived, but I was selfish. I apologize. I see so few visitors out here, I've forgotten how to act with company."

"You didn't have to twist my arm to share your whiskey, Father. And Josie seems quite content. Take it from a biologist. Animals only bed down where they feel safe." *Père* Norbert grabbed a storm lantern and matches sitting on top of the refrigerator. He lit the lamp's wick while Kael finished his whiskey and woke up Josie.

Kael helped Josie to walk in a straight line. *Père* Norbert's lantern illuminated the dirt path leading to another stone cottage hidden behind the church. Inside were two made-up single beds. Josie flopped down on the closest one. Mosquito nets were suspended from the ceiling. They hung like fluffy white clouds above each bed. *Père* Norbert set the lamp down on a wobbly nightstand. A crucifix was nailed to the wall behind the table. Light reflected off of Jesus' polished crown of thorns like a twinkling star.

*Père* Norbert pushed open the shutters at either end of the room. "This should give you some movement of air. The outhouse is out back. Coffee and *beignets* will be served at five thirty. Whiskey at five forty-five." He winked.

"Thank you, Father. I like my coffee with cream, my *beignets* greasy, and my whiskey a bit later in the day."

*Père* Norbert pointed to the empty bed. "Your friend, Molly, slept in that very bed when she visited. I just thought you'd like to know."

Kael smiled. He had finally prevailed. He would be sleeping with Molly a second time. He asked, "Father, do you remember what Molly was wearing when she was brought here after she died?"

*Père* Norbert rubbed his whiskered chin. "We threw everything out. She'd been in the river for several days." He removed his glasses and rubbed the bridge of his nose.

"Now, this could have been from the first time she visited with her sick Pygmies. I'm not certain. Like most old men, I sometimes get confused. She may have even worn the same clothes both times. What I remember are blue jeans cut above the knees for shorts. You Americans love your blue jeans. The cut ends were frayed. She wore a t-shirt that looked as if paint had been spilled on it in a pattern."

"It's called tie-dyed, Father. Do you remember the colors?"

"Orange and green. And she had red shoes. I definitely remember those."

"They're called sneakers... Converse sneakers."

"Her outfit was quite unique."

"You obviously aren't familiar with the Grateful Dead."

"The who?"

"No, that's another band."

"Now, I'm really confused. I should get to bed." *Père* Norbert approached the door. Before stepping through, he turned back toward Kael and said, "If I can misquote Thomas Mann, 'The death of a friend is more the affair of the survivors than of the deceased.'"

"You got that right, Father."

*Père* Norbert said, "God be with you," before closing the door behind him.

Kael removed Josie's shoes, shorts, and t-shirt before pulling the covers over him and tucking in the mosquito net around the foam mattress. He then sat on the edge of his own bed. He ran his hand over the thin cotton blanket. He could almost feel Molly's naked body underneath. Her clothes may have been tossed, but they had somehow landed in his head.

He fell back on the bed. Movement at one corner of the dingy ceiling caught his attention. A common house gecko was busy picking off insects attracted to the lantern's light. With its suction-cup feet, it was able to hang upside-down, leap several inches for a moth, and land back on the ceiling, seemingly defying gravity.

It didn't make any sense to Kael. The gecko should have crashed to the ground. Molly should have still been alive. He should have never left Alaska. He didn't know if *Père* Norbert had accurately recalled what Molly had worn, but his description was exactly what Kael was seeing in his visions: a green and orange tie-dyed t-shirt, cutoffs and red Converse sneakers. Not even Kael could come up with a theory on that one, and he tried hard for the entire ninety seconds before he fell into a deep sleep.

# 21

Bolo was angry. He hated loose ends. They were the footprints of amateurs. Professionals like himself never left anything behind except a dead body, or two, or three, or four...

In the days following the killings of Charles, Diana, William and Harry, he couldn't stop thinking about that missing tenth bullet casing. It bothered him because he'd never felt this way before. It was like an incessant toothache. It never got better. It never got worse. But it was always there.

He replayed the killing scene over and over in his mind. He saw his hand working the bolt action of the rifle. Three times for Charles. Twice for Diana. Those were clear. After that, everything was fuzzy until the image of two dead sons sprawled across the lifeless body of their mother came into focus.

Why hadn't he counted his bullets beforehand? He usually did, but he usually killed only one or two. He'd never killed four before, and he'd never had to remember if he took nine shots or ten. Typically, it was more like two or three. Four, tops.

He closed his eyes. He tried to calm his simmering anger by mentally ticking off the list of arguments he'd been formulating since the killings: 1) There probably never was a tenth brass casing; 2) Even if there was, it might never be found; 3) If it was miraculously found, it didn't matter because it couldn't lead back to him; 4) A brass casing would only identify the caliber of the rifle, and that could already be determined from the bullets in the bodies; 5) Unless the authorities found the rifle, which could possibly be matched up to the bullets and casing, he was safe. And he was one hundred percent certain they'd never find that. Keeping track of one rifle was easier than nine or ten tiny brass casings.

He opened his eyes. He felt better. He'd just have to be more careful next time. Learn from his mistakes and move on, not that he'd made an actual mistake. His obsession with details had either faltered for a brief instant, or it had become even more acute. He couldn't decide which. He knew it wouldn't be a problem with Ron and Nancy. For them, his concentration would be as sharp as his machete.

# 22

Kael heard his headache before he felt it. A whiskey hangover always woke him like a tympanic alarm clock. That was why he tended to stick to beer. It wasn't nearly as noisy.

He applied gentle pressure to his temples hoping to trigger some sort of internal snooze function that would stop the pounding and allow him to sleep for another five precious minutes. It didn't work. It never did.

The French weren't too far off when they described a hangover as a *mal aux cheveux*, a hair ache. Running a comb through Kael's hair would be torture. He wondered if bald Frenchmen could accurately claim to suffer from a *mal aux cheveux* after a night of overindulgence. Being follicle-impaired, were they immune to hangovers? This was worth looking into. Kael's mood brightened. The day was less than five minutes old and he already had the beginnings of a promising theory.

He opened his crusty eyes and focused on the mosquito net dangling directly above. He sneaked a glance to one side without moving his pounding head. No netting. He had forgotten to drop it around his mattress before nodding off. He was probably covered in itchy red mosquito bites. He gently lifted the bass drum between his ears to inspect his ravaged body. He had also forgotten to remove his clothes. He was even wearing his boots, still laced and tied.

He sat up and reached under Josie's mosquito net to nudge the lump underneath the covers. "Time to get up, roomie. We're burning daylight."

The lump shifted its position, but made no attempt to crawl out of its burrow.

Kael shook him again. "Would you believe it's Christmas, and there's a ton of presents under the tree? It looks like one's a bicycle."

The lump dug in deeper.

Kael tickled what he guessed was a foot. "Let's go, kiddo. If you stay in there much longer, you'll get bedsores. I'm already up and dressed."

Josie's head emerged from its cocoon of sheets and blankets. He mumbled something unintelligible and then tried to slide out of bed without first lifting the mosquito net. It caught him like a bug in a spider's web. Kael decided that Coke drinkers, like whiskey drinkers, preferred to ease into the day around the crack of noon.

A pail of water, a bar of soap, and two hand towels were found loitering next to the outhouse. Kael and Josie got cleaned up by washing the parts that weren't covered by clothes.

Kael finished "showering" first. He then went out to the truck. He didn't notice any activity in *Père* Norbert's cottage as he rummaged through his backpack looking for clean shirts. If he and Josie were going to meet with the police commissioner and the *préfet* this morning, they had better be presentable. He found a red Alaska Department of Fish and Game t-shirt for Josie, and a tan, slightly wrinkled collared shirt for himself. Tucked in, they would do.

The truck looked exactly as it had the night before. He peeked behind the front seat. The two motor oil bottles full of money were undisturbed under a bunch of soiled rags, discarded candy wrappers, the bow saw, a foot pump, and three other "real" oil bottles. He had even dripped a bit of thirty-weight over the bottles thinking no one, not even a thief, would pick up a slippery, dirty bottle behind the seat when there was a partial case of clean bottles sitting in the truck's open bed. Besides, thievery was like cold Mocaf: it diminished the farther one got from Bangui.

Josie, who approved of his father's choice in upper body wear, joined Kael at the truck. He told Kael that his favorite color was red.

*Père* Norbert wasn't in his cottage. They tried the church next, but that, too, was empty. Josie pointed out a front door ajar at one of the other outbuildings. As Kael approached, he knew they had found the right place. The aroma of freshly brewed coffee skipped through the open doorway like an enthusiastic child greeting expected visitors.

The door squeaked when Kael pushed on it. "*Père* Norbert?"

"*Oui?*"

Kael stepped into the room. The first thing he noticed was a big copper-colored chest freezer against the far wall. Filled with water, it could have doubled as a lap pool. No doubt this was where Molly's lifeless body had been kept. He pictured her lying inside, her head resting on a rump roast, her long arms and legs curled around frozen bags of Green Giant mixed vegetables.

"Kael! Josie! *Bonjour*! I was just about to come and wake you two. You already missed the first pot of coffee, but I'm almost ready with the second." *Père* Norbert was pouring hot water through a drip coffee filter. He held his nose above the rising steam. "Why doesn't coffee taste as good as it smells?"

"I don't know," said Kael, "but the same is true for soap, perfume, and any hot meals served on airplanes."

He and Josie sat down at a long table in the center of the room. It was set up with two tin mugs and two bowls of fresh sliced fruit: bananas, pineapples, and papaya. Between the bowls was a tray containing one open can of powdered milk, another of Nescao chocolate mix, and a third full of sugar cubes.

Kael figured they were in the mission's kitchen facility. Along with the freezer, there was a refrigerator identical to the one in *Père* Norbert's cottage, a stove—the kind with refillable gas bottles—and open shelves full of dry goods and tall stacks of plates, glasses, pots and pans. The ever-present crucifix looked down on the dishwashing area: a free-standing, laundry-room style sink with no pipes to bring water in. A thirty-gallon plastic barrel stood nearby. It held water probably collected from a nearby well and hauled to the kitchen one bucket at a time.

Kael had to hand it to missionaries. Theirs was not a life of conveniences, yet they were as dedicated as any good hunting dog, Chako excluded. What truly amazed Kael, beyond their vows of celibacy or their unwavering allegiance to promote the teachings of a poor, non-union carpenter to believers of crocodile men, was that missionaries didn't just sign a one-year or two-year contract like TRAP employees or Peace Corps volunteers. They did it for ten, fifteen, twenty years or longer. Hadn't *Père* Norbert mentioned that he'd been doing it for twenty-three years? The closest Kael could come to any comparable accomplishment was that he'd been using the missionary position for almost nineteen years.

*Père* Norbert approached. He grasped two dented aluminum coffeepots in one of his massive hands. The other hand held a tin cup from which he sipped. "I have coffee for you, Kael, and hot water for Josie, so he can make hot chocolate."

Josie beamed. "*Merci, mon père.*"

"Swiss chocolate was my favorite drink when I was your age, *petit*. Now, as an old man, my international loyalties have shifted a thousand miles west to Irish coffee." He held up his cup and winked at Kael. "Care to travel to the Emerald Isle with me this fine morning?"

"I think I'll stick to coffee with a little powdered milk, thanks. I've got to drive to Bayanga." Kael didn't mention that his head was still throwing a temper tantrum over last night's wee voyage.

"Very well," said *Père* Norbert. "There's always room on the plane should you change your mind."

Kael helped Josie to mix up his hot chocolate. When it came to adding the sugar, Josie's African sweet tooth took over. He dropped six cubes into his cup, one at a time. They plunged into the brown water like kamikaze pilots fulfilling an objective despite certain annihilation.

Kael asked Josie, "Why did you use six?"

"I was being polite," he said.

"Well, don't be polite with the fruit," said *Père* Norbert. "Eat it up. I've already had mine, so what's there is all yours."

Before attacking the fruit, Kael asked, "What can you tell me about Nola's police commissioner and *préfet*, Father?"

"They're not Catholics." *Père* Norbert sipped his coffee. "They're pretty much your typical African *fonctionnaires*: good liars, excellent schemers, motivated by greed and whatever will get them reassigned to Bangui. It's my opinion that most of Nola's citizens would prefer them there also."

"That's just what I wanted to hear."

*Père* Norbert asked, "Why do the police commissioner and the *préfet* interest you?"

"I'm hoping to meet with them this morning. I want them to free the crocodile man."

"Molly's crocodile man?"

"Of course. I can't save everyone. That's your job."

*Père* Norbert smiled. "That's what I thought when I first came to Africa. Now, each day I try to accomplish just two things and one of them is buying bread."

"Very well. My two objectives today will be to liberate an innocent man and to drive to Bayanga. Josie's will be to consume his weight in sugar, which he has already done, and to drive to Bayanga. We may even buy some bread on the way."

"Have you got some money?"

"Sure," said Kael. "Bread doesn't cost that much."

"No, I mean to free Molly's crocodile man. As I said, the police commissioner and *préfet* are typical government workers. They haven't received paychecks for three or four months and they're probably getting desperate. If you have money, you could probably buy a crocodile man at a bargain price."

"Excellent. Maybe I'll buy two." Kael took a mouthful of coffee. Powdered milk was a poor substitute for real cream. "I've also got letters from Bangui's police commissioner. He offers professional favors if the Nola authorities will agree to my request."

*Père* Norbert raised one white eyebrow. "You have friends in high places."

"Not quite as high as your friends." Kael pointed to the crucifix on the wall. "I just want to pay the legal fine. The letters are my guarantee that I'll be seen immediately. You don't want Josie and me hanging out here at the mission for days, maybe weeks, waiting for the rusted wheels of Central African justice to turn on their own, do you?"

"Heavens, no. I haven't got enough sugar or whiskey."

"And the police commissioner and *préfet* don't have enough money, so everybody wins."

Kael got directions to Nola's administrative offices. Not once did *Père* Norbert say they were "not far." He even offered to keep Josie at the mission while Kael attended to his business. Kael accepted for practical reasons: No human being could sit still in an office setting after consuming two large hot chocolates laced with twelve sugar cubes.

Kael collected his letters and placed them in his shirt pocket. He then transferred the money from the oil bottles to a small fanny pack, which he wore hidden underneath his untucked shirt. He could always tuck it in once he reached his destination unmolested.

All of Nola's government offices, including those of the police commissioner and the *préfet*, were inconveniently located on the other side of the river. Central African bureaucrats were not known for their accessibility, but the use of a moat verged on the ridiculous. There were no bridges. The only way to cross with a vehicle was by an ancient, two-car-capacity ferry that was powered by the river's swift current. Situated just right in the muddy flow, the ferry would slide crab-like along a thick cable suspended between two trees on opposite banks.

Kael briefly thought about leaving his truck behind and just hitching a ride with one of the enterprising canoeists who loitered at the river's edge and charged one hundred francs per crossing. It would have been quicker, but Kael decided that a stranger's truck full of supplies and knowingly abandoned for a couple of hours would be too tempting for someone who eked out a living at one hundred francs a pop. Besides, the ferry was on Kael's side. This was surely a sign since CARL usually insisted that a ferry be waiting on the opposite bank of the foreign traveler.

Kael didn't need further confirmation of his suspicions, but was given one, anyway: Halfway across the river, the ferry operator interrupted his running monologue about the workings of his craft by saying, "You were smart to bring your truck. Some of those paddlers are from Cameroon and the Congo. They come upriver to steal from us."

This was a common excuse among Central Africans. Many of their problems were blamed on foreigners. The thieves and diseased prostitutes in Bangui were all from

Zaire. Poachers and highway bandits came in from Sudan, Chad and the Congo. And most everything else was France's fault. The times when one Central African pointed a finger at another Central African were rare. Typically, the accuser and the accused were from different tribes. The Pygmies and the Muslims were the handiest targets because they were different. Everyone agreed that there were crocodile men, but they were always from a neighboring tribe. Never from their own. Molly's crocodile man, Assan Séléman, sounded Muslim. Kael wouldn't be surprised if he turned out to be a Muslim Pygmy with a French grandfather who had slipped into the country illegally through Zaire with his diseased Sudanese wife.

The ferry waddled across the river. The current was deceiving. It didn't look fast, but when Kael dropped a stick onto the muddy surface, it bobbed away in a matter of seconds. Was that what had happened to Molly? Was the turbulence too much for her when she fell out of her canoe? Kael and his pickup were deposited on the opposite bank.

He slipped the operator a one-thousand-franc note and promised, "There's another one if your ferry is waiting on this side when I return in an hour or two."

The man smiled while holding the bill like water in his cupped hands. "For two thousand francs, *monsieur*, I will not budge from this spot until you tell me to."

Kael hoped his money would be as persuasive with the police commissioner and the *préfet*. He had about two and a half million francs available for the crocodile man negotiations. He shouldn't need that much. Dimassé had thought one and a half million would be more than enough.

The decision to see the police commissioner, *Monsieur* Gozo, first was an easy one. In the strict Central African hierarchy, he was an underling to both the *préfet* and Dimassé. Therefore, a personal letter from his boss in Bangui, Dimassé, would make quite an impression and it would put him securely on Kael's side before they met with the *préfet*. *Monsieur* Gozo's reassignment to Bangui, according to the letter, would depend on his helping Kael with the quick release of the crocodile man. That, and some spending money for a man who hadn't been paid in four months, would be potent motivators.

Kael's leverage on the *préfet* wasn't as strong. Dimassé had no direct power over the *préfet*, but a pledge of favorable treatment from one of the country's top policemen was like a "get-out-of-jail-free" card.

Kael arrived at the *Commissariat de Police* just in time. It would not be around for long. The one-story wooden structure was bent over, leaning against a mango tree for support while it gasped for breath and searched for a soft patch of grass on which to break its fall. The rusted aluminum roof looked like a swaybacked mule. Every piece of wood, which included the paint-peeled outer walls and the rotting doors and shutters, was covered with the raised meandering freeways of ravenous termites. They munched with fervor like a horde of American teenagers pillaging an all-you-can-eat pizza buffet. Kael could almost hear the building being digested.

He didn't knock on the open door for fear that it might break away from its hinges. Instead, he announced his presence the way an African would: he clapped his hands and said, "*Ko ko ko.*" He then remembered to tuck in his shirt.

A small, blue-uniformed police officer who resembled Barney Fife with an afro, appeared in the doorway. He stood with both hands on two bony hips. His black imitation-leather holster was empty, which didn't surprise Kael. Due to the high number of *coup* attempts, the President only doled out guns to his most-trusted personal security forces. Bullets were even scarcer. Kael had once encountered a Bangui street cop with a water pistol in his holster, and it didn't even have water in it.

"*Bonjour.*" Kael reached out and shook the policeman's hand. "I'd like to see *Monsieur* Gozo if it's not too much trouble."

The officer returned his hand to his hip, close to his holster in case there was trouble.

"He's occupied right now. You can wait or come back in a couple of hours."

Kael wasn't about to be given the brush-off. He could easily go over this guy's head, which hovered at just over five feet. "Could you inform *Monsieur* Gozo that I've brought him an important letter from *Monsieur* Dimassé? It has to do with a possible reassignment to Bangui."

The man eyes bugged out at the mere mention of Dimassé. He held out a quivering hand. "I'll see that *Monsieur* Gozo gets the letter."

Kael smiled. "*Merci,* but I promised Dimassé that I'd deliver it personally. We're friends."

"I see." The officer stepped back. "Come in. I'll tell the commissioner you're here."

Kael entered the room. Sunlight leaked through the holes in the roof, but there was not much to see. The room was devoid of furniture. He suspected that any chairs and tables had been eaten by the termites as *hors d'oeuvres* before feasting on the main course.

The floorboards creaked as Barney Fife snuck back to an adjoining office. He timidly inched his head into the office's open doorway and said, "*Excusez-moi, patron.*"

Kael couldn't hear much of what was said after that. There was a lot of "*Oui, patron,*" "*Non, patron,*" "Dimassé," and "Bangui." Barney turned to face Kael. He held his hand up as if to wave hello, but then brought his fingers down forming a loose fist. This was the Central African gesture to "come." Kael wondered if this signal would work on Chako. Nothing else seemed to, although he was able to reel her in the time his treble hook pierced her nose.

The police commissioner's office was a walk-in closet with a window. Kael shook the commissioner's hand and introduced himself. The commissioner was a smallish man with a shaved head. He was dressed in a blue uniform with a frayed collar and sleeves.

"*Bonjour*. Please sit." The commissioner pointed a finger at a small bench in front of his desk. "My lieutenant says you've brought me an important letter from Bangui."

Kael removed the letter from his shirt pocket and handed it to the commissioner.

"I apologize for the cramped quarters, *Monsieur* Husker, but this is the only room that doesn't leak when it rains."

"Why don't you get the rest of the roof repaired?" asked Kael.

The commissioner sliced open the envelope with a knife. "Why fix the roof when the termites are turning everything beneath it into sawdust? What we need is a new building and we don't have the money for that."

"Hmm," said Kael. He watched the commissioner read the letter, which basically said, "Having a wonderful time in Bangui. Wish you were here." Kael wondered if *Monsieur* Gozo was already visualizing his large, new office in Bangui—one without a leaky roof.

The commissioner looked up from his one-way ticket out of Nola. "So, you are friends with *Monsieur le Commissaire* Dimassé?"

"Like this," said Kael holding up two crossed fingers.

"And you would like to free a crocodile man...this Assan Séléman?"

"*Monsieur* Dimassé and I would like to free him. We have money to pay his fine." Kael hoped that if the man perceived it to be Dimassé's money, or at least some of it, he wouldn't be nearly as greedy. "*Monsieur* Dimassé has also written a letter to the *préfet* asking for his collaboration in this matter. If you were to introduce me, I could deliver the letter and the three of us could work together to come up with a reasonable plan for Monsieur Séléman's release." Kael used the word "plan" rather than "amount." It was like substituting the word "fine" for "bribe." After all, Dimassé had said that games were always played under the negotiation table. It was their way.

The commissioner stood up as if he had been ejected from his chair. He still managed to hang on to his letter, though. "If we go now, we can probably catch the *préfet* before his morning gets too busy."

Kael hadn't seen this much enthusiasm since Josie had discovered the toilet. It could all end up like his toothbrush, however, if the *préfet* didn't want to play. As he got up, he asked, "You know the *préfet*. Do you think he'll be on our side?"

The commissioner smiled. "If you have money to pay the fine, *monsieur,* then you will have a crocodile man and I will be on my way to Bangui."

The two conspirators exited the office. Barney was left in charge, but Kael thought the termites already had complete control of the building.

The commissioner said that the *préfet*'s office was "not far," so Kael offered to drive. He hadn't even shifted into third gear yet when he was directed to pull in front of a large house.

The commissioner announced, *"E si awé."*

Kael looked past the commissioner to his side-view mirror. He could clearly see the reflection of the commissioner's office. He could even make out Barney standing in the open doorway. What made it that much funnier was the warning inscribed at the bottom of the mirror: Caution—Objects May Be Closer Than They Appear.

Kael got out of the truck. He waved to Barney, who returned a half-hearted salute.

The commissioner, who was already halfway up the stairs to the *préfet*'s office, shouted back to Kael, "I told you it wasn't far. Come on. We can't let that crocodile man spend one extra minute in prison."

Kael smiled because he knew what the commissioner was really saying: "Come on. I can't spend another minute in this town." Kael touched the letter poking out of his shirt pocket. With his other hand, he patted his fanny pack. He took a deep breath and climbed the stairs.

The *préfet, Monsieur* Nzapa, was of average height, but suffered from a diminutive fashion sense. For starters, his leisure suit, the accepted uniform of Central African *fonctionnaires*, looked like a leftover from the disco era. It was a two-toned brown number that would have looked better on a couch or as draperies. The top had short sleeves, wide lapels and buttons the size of hubcaps. The matching pants widened into what Kael remembered as, "elephant bell-bottoms." The *préfet*'s shoes were completely hidden beneath the flare of his pants. Kael guessed they were platforms to complement the outfit.

The commissioner performed the introductions. He presented Kael as, "a close friend and messenger of *Monsieur le Commissaire* Dimassé."

The *préfet* nodded as if he were familiar with the name. He shook Kael's hand. *"Bienvenu, Monsieur* Husker. How can I help you and *Monsieur* Dimassé?"

Kael removed the letter from his pocket. "First, you can read this."

The *préfet* accepted the letter. He showed Kael and the commissioner to two empty chairs facing his desk and a large framed portrait of the President, which hung on the wall. The *préfet* sat underneath the almost laughable likeness of the current dictator-of-the-month. His Excellency's expression was too dramatic, like a bad actor playing the part of a tyrannical ruler. He wore so many medals, he looked like a tacky Christmas tree. And his infamous receding hairline and pockmarked complexion had been, respectively, pushed forward and smoothed out by an artist too afraid to paint what he really saw. By official decree, this caricature was to be openly displayed in all government offices and places of business. Failure to do so was an act of treason, for which there was no alternative fine. Better to be a crocodile man than an art critic.

While the *préfet* read Dimassé's letter, Kael turned his attention to the *préfet's* impressive desk. In square footage, it was bigger than the police commissioner's entire cubby, and Kael had no doubt that the commissioner had already made this same observation. Today, however, it probably didn't bother him as much, so Kael held off from telling him his big desk/little penis theory. Maybe later, if the *préfet* screwed up this crocodile man deal.

The *préfet* stopped reading. He set the letter down on his desk and asked the commissioner, "What is the fine for a crocodile man?"

"That depends, *patron.*"

"On what?"

"On what we want it to be, *patron.*"

The *préfet* rubbed his chin. "This is very unusual, especially for such a serious offense."

"*Oui, patron*, but I also received a letter from *Monsieur le Commissaire* Dimassé. He informs me that even though the standard fine for a crocodile man is around three million francs, this is negotiable. The reason is that most crocodile men can't afford such stiff fines, so they all go to prison and our... administrative coffers... remain empty. The new directive, according to *Monsieur le Commissaire* Dimassé, leaves the amount of the fine up to our discretion. *Bien sûr*, our decisions should always take into consideration the welfare of... the general public."

Kael was impressed. Commissioner Gozo had set the stage for a relaxed session of bribery without once uttering the word.

The *préfet* picked up his letter. He skimmed it over once more before asking, "Why are you so interested in this particular crocodile man, *Monsieur* Husker?"

"We believe he is an innocent man." Kael hoped the *préfet* would interpret "we" as including Dimassé. In actuality, Kael meant it for himself and Chako. "The woman he is accused of killing was a close friend of mine. She simply fell out of her canoe and drowned. It was an unfortunate accident that has been made more tragic by the imprisonment of *Monsieur* Séléman. My friend, Molly, loved your country. She came here to help, not to destroy a man's life." Kael noticed a chipped glass on the *préfet*'s desk. It was the same one that had been following Kael from bar to bar. It had somehow made the journey to Nola, and it gave him an idea. "*Monsieur le Préfet*, when you go to the bar and your server brings you a big bottle of Mocaf and a dusty glass, what's the first thing you do?"

The *préfet* seemed to mull over Kael's query by puckering his lips. "I pour a small amount of beer into the glass, swirl it around, and dump it on the ground."

"Do you do this just to clean the glass?"

"No, it's also done to satisfy the thirsty spirits of our ancestors."

"*Exactement*," said Kael. "Molly's spirit also needs to be indulged. Unfortunately, a glass of beer won't do it. Freeing *Monsieur* Séléman will."

The *préfet* looked at the police commissioner. "I'm afraid if we release this man, your counterpart in Bayanga, *Monsieur* Yakonomingui, will need several beers to calm his spirit."

"I'm buying," said Kael with a grin.

"And just how much are you prepared to pay?" asked the *préfet*.

"I'd be willing to give him a case or two, and I'm not just talking Mocaf. I'm thinking Guinness or Cameroonian '33' if he prefers."

"*Non, non, non*," said the *préfet*. "I meant for *Monsieur* Séléman's fine."

Kael knew that, but he theorized that if he didn't throw out an occasional wisecrack, he'd start to dwell on how serious the situation really was. He was bargaining for a man's life and a woman's spirit, and he didn't have three million francs.

"Well, we (he and Chako) want to be fair. Even *Monsieur* Dimassé thinks the current fine of three million is way too extravagant. How does one million sound?"

"Small," said the *préfet*.

"It's a lot bigger than your last paycheck that you didn't receive," said Kael.

The commissioner nodded his head. "That's true, *patron*."

Kael had an inspiration. He unbuckled his fanny pack and plopped it down on the desktop. It sounded heavy. He slowly unzipped it and the colorful stacks of money burst out almost as far as the surprised eyes of the *préfet* and the commissioner.

"I have the cash. No checks. No installment plan. No *bon pours*. No "half now and half later" crap. I'll even throw in another five hundred thousand if *Monsieur* Séléman is released immediately and if both of you sign and stamp an official release form. I don't need a receipt."

The *préfet* and the commissioner continued to stare at the money. Eventually, they looked at one another and like puppets on the same string, they nodded their rich little heads.

"*D'accord,*" said the *préfet*. "*Monsieur* Gozo, you will take my car to the prison and return with *Monsieur* Séléman. Don't forget to stop at your office and pick up a rubber stamp. I will have my secretary type up a document. In the meantime, *Monsieur* Husker, can I interest you in a cold beer and a dusty glass?"

"I'd like that almost as much as Molly would."

# 23

Kael had just finished his beer when Commissioner Gozo returned. He stuck his head into the *préfet's* office and proudly announced, "I have the prisoner and the stamp, *patron.*"

"Very well," said the *préfet.* "Bring them in."

The man who stepped through the doorway with the commissioner was a contradiction. Physically, he looked frail. His brown rice-paper skin was stretched tightly across high, sharp cheekbones. His hair had the reddish tint of malnutrition. But his clear, soft-brown eyes, which calmly scanned the room, suggested a still-vibrant inner strength of spirit. In a subdued voice, he said, "*Salaam aleikum.*" Peace be with you.

The *préfet* just nodded, but Kael responded with one of the handful of Arabic phrases he'd picked up, "*Wa aleikum as-salaam,* Assan." And on you be peace, Assan.

The prisoner smiled.

Kael theorized that Assan was probably like most Muslims he'd met in Central Africa. They were quiet, unassuming, and accepted their own misfortunes as part of Allah's greater plan. The followers of Islam believed that every event, every turn of fate, was determined by God, Allah. If Kael were to say, "See you tomorrow, Assan," he would undoubtedly respond, "*Inshallah.*" If Allah wills it.

Kael wasn't sure if Assan knew yet what was happening. He stood alone off to one side while the *préfet,* the police commissioner, and Kael gathered around the desk to sign the freshly typed release form and two smudged carbon copies. Kael noticed there was no mention of the exact amount of the fine—just that a fine had been paid in full and that *Monsieur* Assan Séléman was a free man. This probably meant that very little, if any, of the one and a half million francs would appear in Nola's administrative ledger.

There was still one more thing to do before the document could be considered legal and binding: it had to be rubber-stamped. The more times the better, so the *préfet* and the police commissioner pounded each copy several times with their official endorsements.

Kael thought it funny that so much faith was put in rubber-stamp approval, especially since there were guys on Bangui street corners who, for a reasonable cost, would hand carve any rubber stamp request out of pieces of old tires. When the rubber stampers had finished, he snatched the original release form from the desk, folded it, and stuck it in his empty shirt pocket before opening up his fanny pack. Since the money was in convenient bundles of five-hundred thousand francs each, it was easy to extract three without letting the *préfet* or the commissioner see how much they could have had. He stacked the money in the center of the *préfet's* desk. It looked nice against the red mahogany, like a picture in the right frame.

Kael stood up. "It's all there: one and a half million francs. *Monsieur* Dimassé and I appreciate your cooperation." He shook their hands before heading over to where Assan stood leaning against the far wall. He held out the folded release form and said, "You're a free man."

Assan looked at the piece of paper. He didn't cry. He didn't scream out with joy. He didn't leap into Kael's arms. He didn't even smile. He simply said, "*Allah akbar.*" God is great. He then grasped Kael's hand.

With the release form crumpled between their two palms, Assan gave Kael a traditional handshake of respect by holding his own thin right wrist with his left hand. It was the best handshake Kael could remember, and that included the one Chako had performed on command in front of all of his friends. "Come on. I'll give you a lift into town." He made sure that the release form remained in Assan's grip.

When they got outside, Assan asked, "But where will I go?"

"That paper you're holding says you're free to go wherever you like," said Kael.

"Then, I will go with you."

Kael opened the passenger-side door for Assan. "Not a good idea. I'm headed for Bayanga and that's where you ran into trouble in the first place. If I were you, I'd pick somewhere far away from *Monsieur le Commissaire* Yakonomingui—maybe Hawaii or the Seychelles." He shut the door and ran around to the other side of the truck. He climbed in behind the steering wheel. "At the very least, I'd pick a place that didn't have crocodile men."

Before starting the truck, Kael opened up his fanny pack and removed one hundred thousand francs. According to Nick, Molly had contributed five or six thousand dollars to Josie over the years. Using the higher figure, that converted to almost 1.6 million francs. Since he'd just paid 1.5 million for Assan's release, that left one hundred thousand to even the score. He handed it over to Assan. "This won't get you to Hawaii, but it will help you to get somewhere."

"*Allah akbar.*" Assan smoothed out his wrinkled letter before accepting the money, which was eventually slipped into a fold for protection.

Kael might have done it the other way: wrapping the more valuable letter, which cost 1.5 million francs, in the money, which was worth a measly one hundred thousand. He didn't say anything. Assan was now free to make his own decisions.

They traveled in silence during the short trip to the ferry. Kael thought about Molly and the time they'd gotten caught in a flash rainstorm while cruising on his motorcycle. There had been no thunder, no lightning, and no shelter, so they'd simply stopped the bike and raised their faces in resignation to the leaky sky. The drops were so big and loud, it had been like standing under a cool waterfall. The storm had passed as quickly as it had arrived and with its departure, he was finally able to hear Molly whooping and hollering from the seat behind him. He had turned to face her. Her hair was plastered to her head. Raindrops clung like tiny icicles to her nose, eyelashes and earlobes. She smiled and said, "Wasn't it great? I feel so clean."

He wondered if she felt clean today.

As promised, the ferry was waiting on Kael's side, so he handed over another one thousand francs to the grateful operator. It was a small price to pay for the satisfaction of beating CARL on both sides of the river. As far as Kael knew, such a feat had never been accomplished before by any foreigner. It was turning out to be a big-dot day.

The truck bounced to a dusty stop in front of the busy market place. It was jam-packed with buyers and sellers. Most were women and children. Some walked right up to Kael's open window and offered to sell him bananas, fish, mushrooms, and caterpillars.

Kael said, "*Non, merci,*" and rolled up his window. He turned to Assan, who hadn't said a word since accepting the money outside of the *préfet*'s office. "This might be a good place for you to get out. The bush taxis usually leave from the market."

Assan nervously played with the letter and money. He rolled it up. He flattened it out. He tried to pull it like taffy. "You said I could go anywhere?"

"That's right," said Kael.

"Then I want to go to Bayanga." Assan held up the money and smiled. "I can pay you."

Kael laughed. "You don't need to pay me, Assan."

"But I need to repay you... for your help. It is Allah's wish and I can not disobey him. I am a good chauffeur-mechanic, a competent cook, and a very hard worker. Just ask the prison guards. I was their best laborer."

"That's quite the recommendation," said Kael. "What about *Monsieur* Yakonomin-gui and the other stooges who put you in prison?"

"Allah and this letter will protect me."

"Where was Allah the first time?" asked Kael.

"He was searching for you."

"*Allah akbar*," said Kael as he shifted into first gear. "Next stop—the Catholic mission."

*Père* Norbert and Josie were found lounging in the mission's kitchen. The coffeepot was still on and the whiskey bottle, which sat in the middle of the table, looked lighter by about two or three fingers. Kael hoped the good Father had left Josie behind in Switzerland while he continued his pub tour of Ireland.

Josie popped out of his seat when Kael and Assan entered the room. "Papa, *Père* Norbert gave me four big pineapples to take to Bayanga."

"That's great," said Kael. "Did you say thank you?"

"No, he was saying thank you to me for hauling water up from the well."

"He's a good worker," said *Père* Norbert. "It looks like you are, too. Who's your friend?"

Kael stood aside. "This is Assan Séléman, the gentleman we spoke of earlier. Assan, this is *Père* Norbert and my son, Josie." Assan stepped forward to shake their hands. Both got handshakes of respect.

Josie asked, "Are you really a crocodile man?"

Assan smiled. "No, *petit*, I'm just a man."

"A very lucky man," added *Père* Norbert, who winked at Kael. "Are you a thirsty man, Assan? I have coffee, hot chocolate, and thanks to my little helper, cool water fresh from the well." He placed his large hand on Assan's bony shoulder. "I know that Islam forbids the consumption of alcohol, but after what you've been through, young man, I wouldn't blame you if you preferred a shot of whiskey with a beer chaser right now."

"*Non, merci*," said Assan. "If it's no trouble, hot chocolate sounds good."

"I'll make it," volunteered Josie. "How many sugars do you want? I like six."

"Me, too," said Assan.

Josie beamed. "That's the polite number, too."

*Père* Norbert poured Kael some coffee. With his other hand, he held up the whiskey bottle. "I know it's not against your religious beliefs. Besides, now you have something worth celebrating. To Molly... may she rest in peace."

Kael sat down. "There's nothing quite like an Irish wake performed by a French priest. Go ahead. Top it off, but before you fill my cup, could you pour a small amount of whiskey on the floor?"

*Père* Norbert said, "You do realize you're asking me to perform a mortal sin, don't you?" But he did it anyway.

"Chin chin," said Kael.

*Père* Norbert turned his attention to Assan, who was just sitting down to the table with his hot chocolate. "So, Assan, what are your plans now?"

Assan stopped slurping his drink and said, "I'm going back to Bayanga."

*Père* Norbert raised his eyebrows. "Back to Bayanga? Do you think that's wise? You have powerful enemies there."

"Allah will protect me," said Assan between sips.

"True," said *Père* Norbert, "but let me tell you a little story about a man whose faith in God was as strong as yours. One day, there was a terrible rainstorm. The man went outside, and the floodwaters were up to his knees. A rowboat came by. The people inside the boat said, 'Hop in. We will take you to safety.' The man replied, 'No, thank you. God will provide.' A few hours passed, and the floodwaters rose to the man's waist. Another rowboat approached. The occupants of the second boat said, 'Hop in. We will take you to higher ground.' The man replied, 'No, thank you. God will provide.' Several hours later, the floodwaters reached the man's chin. A helicopter flew overhead. A rescuer leaned out and yelled, 'We'll lower a line. Grab on and we'll haul you to safety.' The man yelled back, 'No, thank you. God will provide.' The floodwaters continued to rise until they covered the man's mouth and nose. The man couldn't swim, so he perished. When he reached Heaven, he said to God, 'I'm a bit confused. I always thought God would provide.' God's reply was, 'Who do you think sent the two rowboats and the helicopter?'"

"That's a good story," said Assan, "and I see what you mean. Allah has sent me *Monsieur* Kael. He is my rowboat, and this is why I must go with him. Allah won't have to send me another rowboat or a helicopter. Besides, Allah already knows I'm afraid of flying."

*Père* Norbert turned straight-faced to Kael and said, "This is why I love Africa."

The whiskey tasted surprisingly good at that hour of the morning, but Kael stopped after one Irish coffee. The road to Bayanga would be challenging enough without moving potholes. The only thing that would be loaded were the pineapples in the back of the truck.

Everyone thanked *Père* Norbert for his hospitality and all promised to visit again. Kael searched for and found an Alaska Department of Fish and Game t-shirt big enough for their host. It was neon pink, but the only XXXL he'd brought.

*Père* Norbert didn't seem to mind the loud color. He immediately put it on and said, "I love it. It's just the right size, it smells fresh, it has no holes except for where the arms and head go, and it matches the red in my nose. I'll wear it when I perform mass on Sunday."

Kael said, "Under your robes, right Father?"

"Or over," said *Père* Norbert with a wink. "It depends on how many Irish coffees I have that morning."

Kael, Josie and Assan hopped into the cab of the truck. They waved good-bye until *Père* Norbert's pink-clad mass disappeared from view.

The road to Bayanga was an adventure. Only four-wheel-drive vehicles could conquer the deep, canyon-like ruts, the mud puddles big enough for championship water-skiing, and the stretches of sand seemingly as long as the California coastline. Once, while attempting to negotiate a harrowing incline where the road had washed away, Kael had thought the Toyota would tip over like a clumsy turtle.

The truck managed to stay on all four wheels, but after leveling out, Kael noticed that the Toyota's temperature gauge was in the red zone. He parked under some shade and killed the feverish engine. "Houston, we have a problem." He pointed to the offending gauge.

Assan saw the needle. He said, "If you open the hood, I'll check the radiator."

While Kael pulled the hood release knob, he inwardly rejoiced that Assan hadn't suggested, as most Africans would, that the problem was the spark plug. "*C'est la bougie,*" was the preliminary diagnosis of every amateur African mechanic. Kael happily joined Assan at the front of the truck.

The hood wasn't open for five seconds before Assan said, "The problem is butterflies."

"Butterflies?" said Kael, who was thinking "*C'est la bougie,*" wasn't so bad after all.

"Butterflies have clogged your radiator. The air can't pass through the fins, so the engine overheats and the water boils out."

Kael examined the front of the radiator. It was covered with butterfly wings and other cooked body parts. He remembered all the butterflies that had been squashed on his windshield when he and Josie had arrived in Nola. "Can't we just brush them off?"

"Some," said Assan, "but to get at all of them, we'll have to remove the radiator. Do you have tools?"

"Yes, they're in the back of the truck. Josie, can you bring us the green tool box?"

It took just over an hour to liberate the radiator from all of the screws, bolts and hoses. Kael figured they'd wasted at least fifteen minutes just swatting at the sweat bees. They homesteaded on exposed human skin, a delicacy in the forest. They didn't bite or sting. They were just a nuisance wanting to lap up the salt found in human sweat. Obliterating one only seemed to signal two others to take their fallen comrade's place. They were especially fond of the moisture produced near the eyes, nose, mouth and ears.

Of the three main courses, Assan was, by far, the most skilled at ignoring the thirsty pests. Kael theorized that Assan handled them the same way he had endured prison: with a resolve that Allah was testing his worthiness. Assan never complained.

The radiator, Kael found out, was completely plugged with butterfly parts as well as hundreds of thousands of seeds hitching a ride in search of a place to germinate. Assan seemed to know what he was doing. He informed Kael that the best way to remove everything foreign was to dip the radiator in a fast flowing stream, or hit it with a high-pressure water hose. They had neither, so Assan suggested using the foot pump. The short bursts of air would clean all the choked fins. Josie was more than happy to provide the leg power.

The clean radiator was re-installed. Kael was happy to note that when the job was completed, they had no extra parts. "Always a good sign," he said to Josie. Unfortunately, they had no water to refill the radiator. One small jug of drinking water wasn't nearly enough, and there were no villages nearby. The last stream they'd crossed was twenty kilometers back. Assan said the next one was ten kilometers ahead. Kael suggested a mud puddle, but then remembered that the last one was farther back than the stream. He was about to resort to urinating in the radiator when he realized how foolish that idea was. Most males had a hard enough time hitting a big toilet bowl let alone a three-inch round opening for a radiator.

Assan asked, "Do you have a machete or a saw?"

"Behind the seat," answered Kael.

Assan found the bow saw. He walked off into the forest's thick vegetation. Kael briefly wondered if he was coming back. Several minutes later, Assan emerged carrying what looked like two giant sausage links, one across each shoulder. He asked Kael to start the engine. Then, he gave one of the sausages to Josie to hold horizontally. It was a three-foot long vine as thick as a man's calf muscle. Water dripped from its cut ends.

Assan positioned the other sausage link above the radiator opening. He tilted it up allowing the water to pour from one end. Kael was amazed at how much water gushed out. When it slowed to a trickle, Assan threw the vine aside and followed the same procedure with Josie's vine. When the radiator filled to the top, Assan lifted the vine to his mouth and drank. He offered it to Kael and Josie, who both accepted. It tasted clean and cool.

Assan tossed the vine into the roadside brush. "Some forest trees are very smart. They store water in their branches in case of a drought."

"Or in case of an overheated engine," added Kael.

"*Allah akbar*," said Assan.

Josie wanted to sit in the open bed of the truck for the remainder of the journey. He said it would give him a better chance to spot an elephant or a gorilla. Kael didn't have the heart to tell him that his chances would probably be better facing forward while looking through the windshield of the cab.

Large animals like elephants and gorillas were sometimes glimpsed on the road, but they didn't hang around for long. As soon as they saw the truck or heard the engine or smelled the diesel fumes, they would flee into the cover of the trees. Even five-ton elephants became invisible within seconds once they crashed through the dense roadside foliage.

Josie's request, however, provided Kael with an opportunity to talk with Assan alone, so he said, "Great idea. If you spot anything, tap on the roof. We want to see an elephant, too." He piled up his backpack and some of the supply boxes to form a comfortable perch in the truck's bed. He even looped a pair of Minolta pocket binoculars around Josie's neck.

Before leaving, they sliced up one of *Père* Norbert's pineapples. It was sweet, messy and refreshing—not unlike *Père* Norbert himself.

They weren't moving for more than a minute when Kael asked Assan, "So, why did Commissioner Yakonomingui arrest you for Molly's death?"

Assan continued to look out the windshield. Kael didn't think he was just being vigilant in the search for elephants. He seemed uncomfortable, but he answered the question anyway.

"He said it was because I'd had an argument with her the day before she died."

"Did you argue?" Kael asked.

"Yes."

"About what?"

"I didn't want her to go downstream by herself."

"Why not?"

"Because the river is dangerous," said Assan, "especially for those unfamiliar with it. There are many hazards, like currents, eddies, sandbars, and hippos."

"Let's not forget crocodile men," said Kael, but Assan didn't seem to hear.

"*Mademoiselle* Molly had put an outboard engine on her canoe. It was very fast, but also very tippy. I told her I would accompany her, but she insisted on going alone. I couldn't change her mind."

Kael knew all about Molly's stubborn streak. "Americans need space sometimes. We need to be by ourselves. It wasn't your fault, Assan."

Assan looked directly at Kael for the first time during their conversation. "Sometimes, I think if I had been more forceful, even if she was my boss, maybe she'd have taken me and she'd still be alive."

"Or you would have drowned with her."

"*Inshallah*," said Assan.

"Did Molly often travel by herself?"

"Not usually. She needed her Pygmy guides to help find the Pygmy camps deep in the forest, as well as to translate her requests to record their music. The night before she went downstream, she returned from a week-long recording trip with five Pygmy guides. I stayed behind to watch over her camp."

"Maybe Molly went downstream by herself to take a break. After all, you said she'd just returned from a recording trip, right? Did she take her recording stuff with her downstream?"

"No, she left it in camp."

"Well, there you go," said Kael. "She probably just needed some space."

Assan just nodded his head. "Why did you pay my fine, *monsieur*?"

Kael smiled. "It was the right thing to do. I was Molly's friend. I think you were, too." He felt compelled to make a full confession. He didn't think Assan would label him as a crazy person. "Ever since I heard about Molly's death, I've been seeing her in my dreams. She's in trouble and she seems to be reaching out for my help. I think you were a loose end for Molly, and Molly hated loose ends. Getting you out of prison will, I hope, let Molly and me rest in peace."

"*Insahallah*," said Assan.

A loud banging on the roof startled Kael. He braked and leaned out the window. "What's up? You want to come up front?"

A little voice from the back said, "Elephant."

Kael looked forward. Nothing. He glanced in his side-view mirror. There was something on the road about fifty yards back. It was big. He turned off the engine before quietly opening his door and stepping out.

The elephant was standing in the middle of the road. He had huge, inwardly curving, creamy yellow tusks. His long trunk was raised like a periscope to sniff the air for danger.

Kael whispered to Josie, "He's trying to figure out who's using his road."

Josie watched through the binoculars. "He popped out of the trees right behind us."

Kael borrowed the binoculars from Josie. As he focused, he asked, "Do you know how to catch an elephant?"

"No," said Josie. "This is the first elephant I've ever seen."

"It's simple," said Kael. "You just look through the wrong end of the binoculars, pick him up with tweezers, and put him in a jar."

Josie giggled. The elephant continued to sniff the air as he lumbered across the road.

Looking through the binoculars, Kael said, "This guy's been in a few brawls. He's got a ragged scar low on his left flank. Can you see it? It looks like a backward question mark. He's also got two big notches in his left ear."

"He probably got them fighting over a female," said Assan, who was now standing on the other side of the truck. "Males battle over the right to mate with the best females."

"Are we talking elephants or humans?" asked Kael.

"Elephants," said Assan, "but I, too, have scars."

"Join the club," said Kael.

Josie paid no attention to the sob stories of his lovelorn traveling companions. He was too busy holding his arm up against his face to imitate the elephant's constantly moving trunk.

Kael handed the binoculars back to Josie, who looked through the wrong end and pretended to pick up the elephant with his fingers. He couldn't help but giggle.

Kael said, "Do you know what the elephant said to the naked man?"

"What?" asked Josie.

"How do you breathe through that little thing?"

Josie laughed. Assan smiled. Kael was pleased. It had been a good first dirty joke between father and son. Not too graphic, but slightly risqué. Penis jokes hardly ever missed.

The elephant was the only one that wasn't impressed with Kael's stand-up routine. Just after the punch line, he defecated on the road, lowered his head, and pushed through an opening in the trees.

Kael yelled after him. "No wonder you're an endangered species. You have no sense of humor." He looked at Josie. "Let's hope the audiences in Bayanga are more appreciative of a good elephant joke."

An hour later, Bayanga appeared like the elephant. It was suddenly there. It wasn't sighted from far off like an approaching boat on the ocean's flat horizon. There was no such anticipation in the forest. Things were too well hidden in the trees. Whole villages crouched down under camouflage. Without warning, they would emerge from the thick roadside vegetation like a curious, bumbling animal. A surprised elephant, however, had options: it could attack, or more likely, it could defecate and drop back behind the curtain of plant life. Villages were more vulnerable. They didn't have the luxury of locomotion. Their only option was to remain frozen like a frightened fawn. If discovered, they were doomed.

Such was the saga of Bayanga. According to the background information Nick had given to Kael to read, Bayanga was a boomtown gone bust. Bayanga originated as a small fishing village of about ten crude huts along the pristine, tree-covered beaches of the Sangha River. It was home to a few Sangha-Sangha fishermen, roving bands of Pygmies, and the largest concentration of forest wildlife on the continent.

This slow-moving bend in the river changed almost overnight when a Yugoslavian group exclaimed, "There's wood in them thar hills." Reminiscent of the Yukon gold rush days, people from all corners of the country came to make their fortunes harvesting timber. Bayanga soon became a company town of four thousand inhabitants, most of whom came from the treeless savanna towns and saw the dark forest as an evil place taking up space better suited to cassava fields and coffee plantations. They pledged their allegiance to a sawmill that provided them with rent-free, tin-roofed houses, a fully staffed, complimentary health clinic, a sparkling new primary school, and big paychecks whose sole purpose seemed to be the support of the region's other thriving industry: alcohol consumption. To Kael, it sounded suspiciously like the developers in Alaska. Oil, timber, fish and precious metals were hauled out, while booze and Texans were piped in.

Just when Bayanga's mill workers were becoming comfortable with their new and improved, albeit alcohol-impaired lives, timber prices dropped dramatically. The Yugoslavs could no longer pay their transport costs, the national taxes, or the high salaries. They convinced the government to temporarily postpone the collection of taxes until the market improved. Loyal workers, who feared a shutdown, did their part by volunteering to man the saws without pay. The trees fell and were shipped down river to market in the Congo, but the money never made it back to Bayanga. So while the broke and tired rank-and-file slept under a noisy, roof-pounding thunderstorm, the Yugoslavs quietly slipped out of town.

Workers, many of whom were owed up to three years of back wages, waited for the next group to come in and return Bayanga to prosperity. The memories were too good to give up. Besides, the unemployed had no money to return home. Many turned to poaching as an interim occupation until the next logging company fired up the population and the band saws once again. Rumors of a town full of poachers guaranteed that Bayanga would soon be discovered by some international conservation organization. Thanks to Nick, TRAP happened to get there first. They planted their flag and claimed it in the name of conservation, a word not generally appreciated by unemployed loggers.

Kael drove slowly down the main north-south road that skirted town. It was no more than two parallel troughs running through deep, fine-grained sand. It was the kind that swallowed up bicycles and slow-moving cars with bald tires. Kael shifted the truck into four-wheel high just to be safe.

Assan pointed out some of the local landmarks. "That road takes you to the bar and the market. That road leads to the offices of the *sous-préfet* and Commissioner Yakonomingui."

Kael made a face. "Let's steer clear of them—for now, at least."

"You show the wisdom of Allah," said Assan. "You will want to turn right up here. It will take us to the sawmill property."

"Why do we need to see the sawmill? I'd rather see the bar."

"This is where your house is. TRAP is renting one of the expatriate residences while the mill is shut down. It's very nice. Right on the river."

"Is it close to the bar?" asked Kael.

"Not far," said Assan.

Kael groaned.

The TRAP house sat on the edge of the riverbank like a lazy fisherman waiting for a nibble, but secretly hoping nothing would. It rested undisturbed beneath the shade of a large tuft of bamboo that was twice the size of the house. When Kael killed the Toyota's engine, the only sound was the creaking of the individual bamboo stalks leaning to indicate in which direction the river breeze was blowing: south-southeast at about five knots.

"Not bad," said Kael. Accompanied by Assan and Josie, he walked up to the front door of his new digs. It was padlocked, so he started trying keys from the key ring that Mitchell Wright had given him. He found the right one on the third attempt. He pushed the door open and said to Josie, "*E si awé.*"

While Kael's eyes adjusted to the darkened room, Josie rushed past him like a bat entering a familiar cave in search of food. Kael figured his son's sonar was seeking out another item necessary for survival: a flush toilet of his very own.

Assan followed Kael into the room. He said, "We can open the shutters for light and a cool breeze coming off the river."

"*D'accord*," said Kael, whose eyes were just starting to distinguish the shapes in front of him as furniture. "Now, all we have to do is find the shutters."

The room was suddenly flooded with sunlight. Assan stood next to an open, unscreened window. "*Voila.*" He unlatched a second louvered shutter almost as big as the door. It swung out allowing more light to shine in. He then went to the back of the house, the side facing the river, and threw open the two shutters along that wall. A gentle crosscurrent of air wafted through the room.

Josie entered from an adjoining room. "There's a toilet in here, but it doesn't flush."

"Bummer," said Kael.

Assan said, "When the Yugoslavs lived in these houses, they had running water, electric lights, and air conditioning. It was like Bangui. Now, the pipes are rusted and the generator that works the water pump and the electricity is no longer maintained. I could fix it, but it requires many liters of diesel fuel, along with the permission of the *sous-préfet.*"

"Why do we need his OK?" asked Kael.

"Because TRAP is only renting this house from the government. And since the *sous-préfet* is the highest-ranking local government representative, he is your landlord. He doesn't have electricity or running water at his house. No one in Bayanga does, so he won't allow you to have any. It would mock his authority."

"Wait until he hears I went over his head to free you from prison."

"*Allah akbar,*" said Assan.

Josie interrupted to ask, "Can we fix the toilet?"

"It still works," said Assan. "You just have to pour in a bucket of water to flush."

Josie ran off, no doubt, in search of a bucket of water. Assan followed to help.

Kael took a good first look around his new house. It was clean and orderly. Everything was in its place. Mitchell Wright hadn't left it like a typical renter who was headed out of the country and couldn't care less about his security deposit. The main living area contained a futon-like couch and two easy chairs in the same simple style. All three pieces were probably crafted by the same local woodworker who was more than likely an unemployed mill laborer. The thick foam seat pads and back pillows were covered in assorted colorful African fabric. Nothing matched. Stripes mixed with paisley. Rich dark purples sat between olive greens and neon blues. One pillow was covered with a tacky fuchsia and mauve cloth promoting a local condom called "Prudence." The slogan read, "Love with Prudence."

Kael liked the Bohemian style. It was inviting and said, "Flop down. Try me out. Get comfortable." So Kael did. From where he sat, he could see bookshelves devoid of paperbacks, but home to two storm lanterns. The dining room, which was just the back part of the living area, held a sturdy wooden table and four chairs. The tablecloth was another African print glorifying the President's portrait and one of his equally unattractive first wife.

Kael realized that every day, he and Josie could dine with the country's current dictatorial rulers. He was about to get up to check out the other rooms when he heard three claps in unison with the words, "*Ko ko ko.*" The sounds came from the open front doorway. No one poked a head in, so Kael left the comfort of his couch to greet his first official visitor.

A bandy-legged stick of a man with gray hair stood off to the side. He wore a tattered outfit of shorts and shirt that were six months past the stage of being used for rags. He was barefoot, and a machete was tucked under one arm.

"*Bonjour,*" said Kael.

"*Bonjour,*" replied the man.

They shook hands.

"Who are you?" asked the man.

"Isn't that supposed to be my question?" asked Kael with a smile. "I mean, you did knock on *my* door."

"This door belongs to the sawmill," said the man grasping his machete, "and I am the day guardian. My name is Jacques, and it is my job to make sure no one vandalizes the property."

"At ease, Jacques. My name is Kael. I work for TRAP and it's my job to make sure no one vandalizes the forest."

"Where is *Monsieur* Mitchell?"

"In the Congo. I'm his replacement."

"Good. I didn't like him."

"Me, neither," said Kael with a wink.

"He was very rude," said Jacques. "He never once invited me in."

"Well," said Kael, "let's not continue that tradition. Please, come in. Have a seat. I welcome all strangers with machetes into my home." He showed his guest to a chair.

Jacques sat just on the front edge of his seat. "Do you have any beer?"

"I wish," said Kael, who wasn't surprised by Jacques' blatant request. Central Africans were not shy when it came to asking for material things. They knew that most Americans were easy marks. Peace Corps volunteers had an especially hard time saying, "No" to a barefoot, undernourished old man wearing rags.

Assan and Josie entered the room. Josie announced, "The toilet flushes with a bucket of water."

"Great," said Kael. "Say *Bonjour* to Jacques. Jacques, this is my son Josie and our friend..."

"Assan!" said Jacques completing Kael's sentence as he shot up out of his chair. "What are you doing here?"

"*Allah akbar.*"

"But I thought you were in prison in Nola."

"I was released this morning. Now, I work for *Monsieur* Kael."

"*Bonjour,*" said Josie standing with an outstretched hand before Jacques. "We both like six sugars in our hot chocolate. How many do you like?"

Jacques shook his hand. "Four if I'm making it. Eight if someone else is." He pointed at Josie's chest. "That's a nice t-shirt. Can I have it?"

Josie gave a worried look at his father that said, "Do I have to?"

Kael said, "That was a present from me. Give us some time to unpack, Jacques, and I'll see if I can't find one for you, too. OK?"

"*D'accord,*" said Jacques. "I have to be going. I'll stop by tomorrow for my t-shirt. Maybe then you'll have some beer, too."

Jacques departed, but as he walked to the doorway, his sunken eyes remained fixed not on Josie's coveted t-shirt, but squarely on Assan. When Jacques was out of earshot, Kael said, "It's not too late for Hawaii, Assan."

"*Inshallah.*"

"OK," said Kael, "but Jacques didn't seem too excited to see you out of prison,"

"That's because he works for the *sous-préfet*, and it is now his unfortunate duty to pass along some disturbing news to his boss."

"That you are a free man and flaunting it back in Bayanga?" said Kael.

"That's part of it. The other bad news is that you have arrived."

"Me? What did I ever do to the *sous-préfet* except go over his head to help an innocent man?"

"You work for TRAP," said Assan.

"So?"

"So, the *sous-préfet*, the mayor, and the police commissioner see TRAP as their enemy. A new director means a continued effort of anti-poaching and anti-logging. If TRAP leaves, the *sous-préfet*, the mayor, and the police commissioner will rule this forest again. Their poaching will go unchallenged. They also feel that as long as TRAP is still here, no new logging companies will return to Bayanga. There is no profit when you cut according to the regulations. That's why Jacques is here: to spy on TRAP. You will be seeing a lot of him."

"Along with his friend, CARL, no doubt," said Kael.

"Who is CARL?" asked Assan.

Kael smiled as he raked a hand across his scalp. "It loses something in the translation. Let's just say that unlike the *sous-préfet*, CARL wants us here in Bayanga, but it's only to toy with us."

The only perceived reaction from Assan was a simple nod of his head. He and Josie then left the room without a word. Assan still didn't know who CARL was, but Kael theorized that it didn't really matter. In Assan's mind, he would meet CARL only if Allah deemed it necessary. *Inshallah.*

Assan re-entered the room. He was loaded down with a box of supplies under one arm, a guitar under the other, and Kael's backpack slung over one listing shoulder.

"I thought I'd unload the truck, *monsieur.*"

"You didn't have to do it all in one trip," kidded Kael.

"I didn't. There's still some left. Where should I put this?"

"Just set it on the floor for now. We'll figure out where everything goes later. Where's Josie?"

Assan gently slid the backpack and guitar to the floor. "He's in the bed of the truck helping to unload the supplies."

"Great. With the three of us, it shouldn't take long. And then, we can all go for a swim."

Assan set the box down next to the guitar. "Are you sure you want to swim with a crocodile man, *monsieur?*"

Kael smiled. "One who fixes and unloads trucks can't be all bad. Are you sure you want to stay in Bayanga?"

"*Inshallah,*" said Assan.

As the two new friends walked outside, Kael said, "Allah wants you to carry the heavy things."

# 24

Bolo hated waiting. It was almost as infuriating as sloppy workmanship, although he had finally convinced himself that he'd only used nine cartridges instead of ten. He vowed that next time there would be no mistakes, no second guesses, no doubts. No way. His rifle was oiled, his blades were sharpened, and his cartridges were counted, more than once. All he needed now were Ron and Nancy, but they were nowhere to be found. His sources had been checking all their usual haunts from the Ventura Freeway south to the San Diego Freeway. Nothing. He was working with idiots.

Another thing Bolo despised was having to depend on others for information, but he realized they were necessary. Alone, he couldn't possibly keep track of all the names on his list. Especially now. Incompetent or not, those extra pairs of observing eyes made his job easier... usually.

Right now, however, they were testing the limits of his patience. They couldn't even keep up with a couple of wrinkled old geezers like Ron and Nancy.

Bolo wanted to wring their little necks. He was aching to make a kill. He had told them it didn't even have to be Ron and Nancy. Any name and location would do. When he was feeling this anxious, there was no such thing as too small or too insignificant. He just wanted to squeeze the trigger and see his unsuspecting victim get knocked to the ground by the destructive force of a piece of lead weighing no more than a few ounces. Such power! It was an incomparable high and Bolo was addicted.

His cravings wouldn't allow him to sit still awaiting word from his sources, so he collected his killing tools and headed out in no particular direction. As he walked, he thought to himself, to hell with Ron and Nancy. They couldn't avoid the public eye forever. They'd eventually come out into the open. And when they did, he'd be there. Until then, he'd have to stay sharp.

It only took an hour to find a temporary substitute for Ron and Nancy. She was alone. She was young. She'd never see her family again.

Bolo raised his rifle. The polished stock felt comforting against his right cheek. To accommodate for such a long-distance shot, he positioned the cross hairs of his scope a little high on the target's skull. This would be good practice for Ron and Nancy, since he didn't know how close he could get to them.

A deep breath, a partial exhale, just the slightest pressure on the trigger, and she dropped seemingly instantaneously with the rifle's deafening retort. She lay in a heap. There were no moans, no final gasps of air, no signs of life. The only movement from the body was a stream of blood exiting from her massive head wound. It was as red as the blood temporarily pulsing through the bodies of Ron and Nancy.

Bolo ejected the brass cartridge from the rifle's chamber. It fell at his feet. He picked it up and thought: one bullet, one body. No miscount there.

He wouldn't brag to his sources about this one, though. They hated it when he free-lanced by not sticking to the names on the list. They had no idea how many he'd killed without their approval.

He pocketed the cartridge. He thought briefly about practicing his carving skills as well, on the victim, but decided she wasn't worth his time. He walked briskly away. He felt much better.

# 25

He dreamed of Molly again: a subconscious rerun featuring the same clothes, same water, same groping, and the same melodic screaming that ended when the same armor-plated crocodile man pushed her under. It was even more frightening this time, however, because Kael had been certain that with Assan now free, the nightmares would end. What was going on? Kael didn't even have a theory.

He couldn't get back to sleep, so he lit a lantern and tried reading *Père* Norbert's borrowed paperback. It was a typically fast-paced Dick Francis mystery full of murder, horses and lush English countryside, but it still couldn't distract him from thinking about Molly. To Kael, every female character in the story looked like Molly. He even pictured the horses wearing tie-dyed t-shirts and red Converse sneakers instead of riding blankets and horseshoes. After a couple of chapters, he realized that he couldn't recall what he'd just read—only that it had something to do with a murder and horses – so he put the book down.

He passed the next hour beneath his mosquito net listening to the exotic noises of the African night. Frogs and crickets bantered back and forth. The din of a jungle cocktail party was occasionally interrupted by the muffled snorts and grunts of a species more highly evolved than amphibians or insects. At first, he thought the noises were originating from the clogged nasal passages of Assan or Josie, who were asleep in the other two bedrooms, but there was no rhythm to them. He sat up in bed and decided they were coming from the direction of the river and were probably hippos. He fell asleep thinking about Molly again.

He was awakened at dawn by one of the most annoying calls in all of Africa.

"*Ko ko ko.*"

Someone was at his front door. He stepped into a pair of jeans and stumbled out towards the sound. He unlatched the door, which swung open to reveal the source: it was Jacques, the day guardian/spy. He stood at attention with the machete safely at his side.

"It's a little early to be gathering information, isn't it?"

"*Pardon, monsieur?*"

"Oh, nothing. *Bonjour* Jacques. What can I do for you?"

Jacques extended a hand containing a thin strip of paper, which Kael accepted. At first, he thought it might be Jacques' t-shirt size or a list of his favorite beers to keep in stock for future visits. Unfortunately, it wasn't that funny. It was a summons. Kael's presence was requested at the office of the *sous-préfet*, *Monsieur* Wabunda, promptly at eight o'clock that morning.

Kael looked directly at Jacques. "How did the *sous-préfet* know that I had arrived?"

Jacques didn't bat an eye. "I don't know, *monsieur*."

It was no big deal. Kael would have to meet the *sous-préfet* eventually, with or without Jacques' help.

"Do you have my t-shirt yet, *monsieur*?"

"Not yet." A spy working for the other side didn't deserve a Fish and Game t-shirt.

"I'll have it for you next time, providing you don't "*Ko ko ko*" at my door at five thirty ever again."

"*D'accord, monsieur*. What about my beer?"

"Your beer can knock on my door any time," said Kael straight-faced. It was in direct contrast to the fissures of confusion beginning to form across Jacques' burnished brow. Before he could vocalize his bewilderment or ask for something else, Kael held up the summons and said, "*Merci*. Tell *Monsieur le Sous-Préfet* that I bring greetings from *Monsieur le Préfet*. He and I got acquainted yesterday and he was very supportive of my ideas." Kael neglected to tell Jacques that the reason for the *préfet*'s enthusiasm was one point five million CFA split two ways. For that kind of money, even someone like Mitch could have influential friends.

Jacques backed away from the door with his head slightly bowed. It seemed as if Kael's supposed connection to the region's highest ranking official had made an impression, and there was no doubt that the *sous-préfet* would be made aware of this relationship before eight o'clock. Kael felt a little better about the summons since he wouldn't be going in alone. He now had the *préfet* on his side. At least, that was how the *sous-préfet* would interpret this conversation. Intimidation was like fire. It could burn out of control, but when used properly, it was a wonderful tool.

Two hours later, Kael promised Assan and Josie that he wouldn't be long at the *sous-préfet*'s. Josie vowed to catch a fish before his father returned.

Kael asked, "Are you confident of success because it's a big-dot day?" He hadn't yet explained to his son the meaning of the term, but Josie didn't let that stop him from answering.

He shrugged his bare shoulders and said, "No, I'm a good fisherman, and Assan says the river is full of fish."

Kael rubbed the top of his son's head. "You be careful. Some of those tiger fish and Nile perch are bigger than you are."

"I'll watch him, *monsieur*," said Assan.

"OK, but if he falls in, promise me you'll do more than watch."

"Of course," said Assan. "I would perish before I would allow your son to come to any harm."

"Actually," said Kael, "I'd prefer that no one dies while I'm gone. *D'accord?*"

"*D'accord, monsieur.*"

Kael turned to leave. He knew that Josie would be fine with Assan, just as Molly would have been had she allowed him to go with her in the canoe that day. It was ironic that the only man who could have saved Molly was, instead, arrested for her murder. The whole thing stunk of CARL.

Kael arrived at the *sous-préfet*'s right at eight. It was a typical government structure: chipped cement over cinder block, painted white with green trim peeling under a rusting tin roof. No one was home, so Kael sat in the shade of a nearby mango tree.

He contemplated how long it would take before his host showed up. Most Central Africans used specific, European-style times, such as eight o'clock, as mere approximations. An eight a.m. meeting could start at eight thirty, nine o'clock, ten forty-five, or not at all if the palm wine was flowing and free.

To pass the time, he chatted with passersby. One bent-over old woman from a neighboring house approached with a straight-backed wooden chair that may have outweighed her. She set it down next to Kael and said that it was much more comfortable than the root he was presently sitting on.

He thanked her and said that he was waiting for the *sous-préfet*. She nodded and went back to sweeping up the goat droppings on the small plot of dirt in front of her house. Her brush strokes left a herringbone pattern in the dust.

A few minutes later, a child of five or six came out of the same house. She was cradling a tin mug in her small hands. She walked up to Kael.

"It's coffee. My grandmother sent it over."

"That's very nice of your grandmother," said Kael accepting the mug. "Tell her I said *merci*." The girl nodded. "And tell her I think her grand-daughter is very pretty."

The little girl giggled and ran back to her house. Her tiny footprints added gentle touches of imperfection to her grandmother's uniformly swept dirt.

Kael sipped his sweet coffee. He was reminded of Molly, who used to cynically call this local brew, "a cup of African politics," because all that sugar still couldn't hide the basic bitter taste left behind by the lower-grade coffee bean.

He poured a little on the ground. "I'll give you more if you promise to stay out of my dreams." He looked up to see a man standing in front of the *sous-préfet*'s office door. He inserted a key into the lock, pushed the door open, and kicked a small wedge underneath to keep it from shutting again. Kael glanced down at his wristwatch. It was eight forty-two and it appeared that the *sous-préfet*'s office was now open for business.

Kael stood up. He took a few more gulps of coffee before setting the mug on the chair. He walked over to the office's open doorway and poked his head in. "*Monsieur le Sous-Préfet?*" The man who had unlocked the door sat behind a little desk. He didn't look up, even though he appeared to be doing nothing.

"He will be here soon."

Great, thought Kael. "Soon" was, no doubt, in the same category of non-specific terms as "not far" and "eight o'clock." Kael kept his cool. "My name is Kael Husker. I was supposed to have an eight o'clock appointment with the *sous-préfet*."

The man looked at his watch. "You're late. It's eight forty-three."

Kael smiled. "I've been waiting since eight."

"You can take a seat in his office."

Kael was escorted into a dark back room. The man opened a window shutter for light. The room wasn't much to look at. All four walls were bare except for the same airbrushed portrait of the dictator hanging above a desk. There were four chairs in the room. One was behind the desk and three others were lined up to face the front of the desk.

The man said, "Sit anywhere, except behind the desk. That's the *sous-préfet*'s chair."

The man departed without comment. There were no magazines to read so Kael sat quietly in the middle chair. After several minutes, a different man entered the room. This man was taller, thinner, and was dressed in a yellow leisure suit. He looked like a ripe banana. He was followed by two shorter gentlemen: one was a muscular guy in a light-blue uniform, and the other, the skinnier one, was wearing blue jeans, a long-sleeved western-style shirt, and a straw cowboy hat. The ensemble wasn't quite complete, however. Flip-flops adorned the skinny cowboy's feet rather than pointy-toed cowboy boots.

Kael stood up. His first thought was that these had to be three members of the musical group, The Village People. Maybe, like many dying bands, they had to resort to touring in out-of-the-way locales like Central Africa to search out new fans. It was the only logical explanation.

The banana said, "Sit down, *Monsieur* Husker." The banana sat behind the desk. The two others took their places in the empty chairs at either side of where Kael was sitting. "I am *Monsieur* Wabunda. Now that you are here in Bayanga, I am your *sous-préfet*. My friends are *Monsieur* Yakonomingui, your police commissioner..." The man in the uniform nodded. "...and *Monsieur* Likéké, your mayor." A tip of the hat.

Kael realized he was in the presence of The Three Stooges. He reached out and shook each one's hand enthusiastically, starting with the *sous-préfet* and ending with the mayor. "I'm so pleased to make your acquaintance. I've heard so much about you, I feel as if I already know you." He turned to the *sous-préfet*, *Monsieur* Wabunda, the top banana. "Thank you for inviting me this morning, and it was nice of you to include your friends. Meeting you all at once like this will save me a considerable amount of work." He looked from the police commissioner to the mayor. "Now I won't have to visit your offices to introduce myself. That will leave me with more time to protect the forest. Already, we are collaborating."

"That's more than your predecessor, *Monsieur* Mitch, ever did," said the police commissioner.

The two other Stooges nodded in agreement. Kael wanted to be as diplomatic as possible in his response, but defending one asshole to three others was ludicrous, at best. He decided to just stick to the facts. "*Monsieur* Mitch is now working in the Congo. You'll probably never see him again. I, on the other hand, will be very visible as the Doli-Ngili Reserve's new director, and I promise to be as cooperative as you."

The *sous-préfet* said, "We are very glad to hear that. Why, then, do you employ a sorcerer who we arrested for the murder of one of your fellow Americans?"

"I'm an equal opportunity employer," said Kael. "Assan has a prison release form signed and stamped by Nola's *préfet* and police commissioner." Kael wasn't sure if the Stooges knew yet who had paid Assan's fine. Why tell them more than he had to? "It is my belief that Assan committed no crime. He is not a crocodile man. He is, however, a very talented mechanic and cook. As far as I can tell, his only fault is that he doesn't drink beer."

"He drinks the blood of his victims, instead," said the mayor.

Kael wanted to laugh, but the mayor's stony stare suggested he genuinely believed what he had said. He was, Kael decided, as serious as one could be while wearing a cowboy outfit with flip-flops. With tongue in cheek, Kael said, "Thank you for the warning, *Monsieur le Maire*."

The mayor nodded earnestly.

Kael watched Police Commissioner Yakonomingui pull out a single cigarette from his breast pocket. The guy had Popeye-like forearms. His cigarette, however, was bent and flattened. He rolled it on the desktop. Kael assumed that he was attempting to re-shape the deformed cylinder before popping it into his mouth. Instead, he rolled it so hard, the tobacco burst from its white paper skin. With one meaty hand, he brushed the mess to the floor where it fell at Kael's feet.

Kael got the distinct feeling that he was being sent some sort of subtle message like, "Don't joke around with me or I'll roll you across this desk and make the stuffing come out of you just as easily." It probably wasn't the time for a wisecrack, but he couldn't help himself. He smiled at the police commissioner and said, "That's one way to prevent cancer." When the commissioner didn't respond, Kael decided to push him even further. "Did I mention that *Commissaire* Dimassé is a very old and dear friend of mine?"

The compact, muscular body of Bayanga's police commissioner seemed to swell to a point where it tested the constraints of his tailored uniform. Just before buttons would pop and seams would tear, the *sous-préfet* defused the situation with a little diversionary ego stroking.

"Did you know, *Monsieur* Husker, that since Commissioner Yakonomingui arrived in Bayanga, the incidence of theft has gone way down?"

The smart aleck in Kael wanted to say, "And poaching has gone way up," but this time, he held his tongue. "That's great. So I can leave my front door unlocked?" He looked right at the police commissioner, who appeared to have regained his composure.

"It's never wise to tempt fate, *monsieur*. You may be one of the unlucky ones."

"On the contrary," said Kael. "With a known crocodile man living under my roof, my house is probably the last place a thief would invade."

The *sous-préfet* leaned across his desk. "May I remind you that it is not your house. It belongs to my government."

"Only until the next logging company arrives, and that could be soon," said the mayor.

The word "soon" eased any worries Kael might have had about being evicted from his house.

"This town needs logging," continued the mayor. "There are a lot of trees and a lot of able men without jobs." He pushed his hat up higher on his forehead. Then he leaned forward to rest his elbows on his knees. "I worked for the Yugoslavs myself, you know. I was a roll-taker."

"What's a roll-taker?" asked Kael. He'd never heard that logging term before.

"I took roll. I called out the names of workers on a list to see if they were present. If they were, I put a check mark next to their name. I got the job because I could read and write and I had a loud voice."

"What did you do the rest of the day—after the roll was done?" asked Kael.

"We had many people working different shifts. My job took all day."

Kael wasn't surprised. From what Nick had told him, the logging company had employed anyone who could breathe. They didn't even have to breathe very well. The story on the mayor was that after logging operations had folded, he had been elected in a landslide victory by promising the return of logging to the region. He had even convinced the voters that they should finance a campaign to lure another logging company to Bayanga. Taxes were raised. Bayangans didn't complain because they believed that their collective future depended on the forest sounds of chainsaws and someone yelling, "Timber!"

Logging had yet to return to Bayanga, but the mayor somehow ended up with a brand new red Suzuki motorcycle. Even more discouraging to Kael was that several years later, the mayor was re-elected in another landslide. The little guy under the cowboy hat had to be one sugary sweet coffee bean.

In the land of CARL, most believed that despicable behavior by an elected official was an accepted perk of the position. An honest politician was not only an oxymoron. He was a moron. He was surrounded by so much corruption that if he didn't take advantage of certain situations, someone else surely would and someone else's family would eat better than his own. Therefore, Mayor Likéké had only done what any mayor in the land of CARL would do.

Staring into the mayor's bloodshot eyes and smelling his whiskey-scented breath, Kael wondered if the electorate had also obligingly picked up the tab for his drinks that morning.

When the *sous-préfet* folded his hands on his desk, Kael's attention was drawn to a bright flash of red. On the *sous-préfet's* left hand was a polished, buffed, and obviously pampered pinky fingernail that was probably longer than the man's penis. It looked perfect for picking a lock, for stabbing peas off a plate, or for stirring a mixed drink. It certainly wasn't conducive to performing any kind of manual labor more strenuous than picking one's nose. The *sous-préfet* opened his mouth and proved that his brain worked just as hard as his muscles.

"Do you work for the C.I.A., *monsieur*?"

Kael smiled. Central Africans commonly believed that their country was some sort of strategic target in America's quest to rule the world. Therefore, any Americans working there had to be spies with instructions to conduct preliminary surveillance prior to the inevitable invasion by ground troops. Kael didn't want to argue, so he just responded, "Not anymore. Now I work for TRAP. Our sole purpose is to help you protect your natural resources."

"That sounds very nice," said the police commissioner, "but isn't your true mission to keep logging from returning to Bayanga?"

"Not at all," said Kael calmly. "We don't want to see another crooked logging company return to Bayanga. The last one paid no attention to the harvest regulations, they stopped paying their taxes and worker's salaries like that of *Monsieur le Maire*, and they skipped town in the middle of the night without saying good-bye. Do you want to be treated that way again?"

After several seconds of silence, the mayor said, "It depends on how much they pay us." The *sous-préfet* and police commissioner both nodded their heads in agreement.

Kael thought about telling them that without a forest, the American invasion would be much easier. A flat, treeless country was perfect for C-130 landing strips. In addition, U.S. Marines and Army Rangers would have no problem rounding up Central African prisoners, since there would be no place for them to hide. He scratched his beard while searching for a more practical example. "You have to look at the forest like a pond full of fish. If you remove all the fish, you will have nothing left to eat."

"But we don't eat the trees," said the *sous-préfet*.

"Sure you do," said Kael. "You eat the fruits, don't you? And some roots, bark, and leaves found only in your forest provide strong medicines against malaria, cancer and..." His voice softened to a whisper "...male impotence."

All three Stooges nodded solemnly, but only after hearing that last and most serious ailment. It was enough of a positive reaction to make Kael forge on.

"Don't forget about meat from the forest. You eat bush pig and duikers, right? They only live here in your forest. What will happen when they are gone? What will your children and grandchildren eat then?"

"Elephants and gorillas," volunteered the mayor.

Kael shook his head. "Those are protected species. You can't eat them."

"Not even if they taste good?" asked the sous-préfet.

"Not even if they walk into your kitchen and sit down on your dinner plate," said Kael.

"But gorillas rape our women," said the mayor emphatically.

"And elephants trample our fields," added the police commissioner.

The *sous-préfet* slammed his flattened right hand down on the desktop. "And I'll just bet they both eat those trees that help with, you know..." He whispered, "male impotence."

Kael laughed. He couldn't help it. These guys were funnier than the original Three Stooges. "Gentlemen, there are apparently a lot of misconceptions about elephants, gorillas, their inappropriate dating habits, and the subtle differences between TRAP and the C.I.A. Actually, I'm glad to hear it because that means I have a job to do."

"And what exactly would that be... other than employing crocodile men?" asked the police commissioner.

"My goal here is to help you and the good people of Bayanga understand that your forest is important, and not just for logging. Sure, the logging company gave you jobs and paid you exorbitant salaries, but that didn't last for long. When your own government, which you three all work for, decided to shut them down for not paying their taxes or your salaries, they cowardly snuck out of town in the middle of the night. If you ask me, impotence is manlier than what they did. They didn't even stick around for roll call the next morning, did they *Monsieur le Maire*?"

The mayor shook his head. "They even took my clipboard."

"Right now," said Kael, "they're probably ripping off some other African town. They didn't come to Bayanga for your benefit, gentlemen. They came here for their own."

"Why should TRAP be any different?" asked the police commissioner. "*Monsieur* Mitch certainly didn't act like our friend when he was here. His anti-poaching patrols arrested many men who were out of work and only wanted a little meat to feed to their suffering children. I would like to remind you that *Monsieur* Mitch also left without saying *au revoir*."

"Did he owe taxes or back wages to anyone in town?" asked Kael. No response. "Did he lie to you?"

"He never talked to us," said the *sous-préfet*.

"So he was guilty of bad manners," said Kael. "And the poachers he arrested were disobeying the laws and regulations as specified by your own government. TRAP is not against hunting. We don't care about the local guy who wants to occasionally feed his family with bush meat. That's small change. The poachers we arrest are the ones with guns who kill protected species, or the ones who set hundreds of wire snares throughout the forest and then surreptitiously send truckloads of meat out to other towns up north for a tidy profit."

Kael surveyed the room. He was talking about people like The Three Stooges. He wondered if they understood that. He'd reached his limit for nonsense so he stood up and reached across the desk to shake the *sous-préfet*'s hand. "Thank you, *Monsieur* Wabunda, for setting up this little meeting. It was nice of you to think of me. I found it very informative." He released the *sous-préfet*'s large hand that seemed to pump in unison with each nod of his pinhead. Kael then turned his attention to Commissioner Yakonomingui. "I hope we now know what to expect from each other."

"In my line of work," said the commissioner, "I've learned to expect the unexpected. You might be wise to do the same."

The commissioner's handshake was vise-like, as expected. Kael snaked his hand out before any fingers were broken. He thought he detected a hint of macho superiority in the bone-crushing gesture, along with the accompanying smile on the commissioner's face, so he said, "I'll pass along your regards to *Monsieur* Dimassé."

Kael watched the police commissioner turn into a ninety-nine degree centigrade pot of water. On the surface, he was calm and still. Below, however, the first bubbles of turbulence were beginning to rise. He was only one degree from boiling over. Kael debated whether to turn the burner up or down. The news that he and Dimassé had paid Assan's fine would certainly accomplish the former. He'd never realized just how much fun cooking could be.

The temperature in the room was lowered when the mayor offered his hand to Kael and said, "Why don't we all go over to my bar for a beer?"

"You own a bar?" asked Kael, shaking the man's hand with a newfound respect.

"The only bar in town with electricity," said the mayor. "It's called 'The Chainsaw Bar.' We serve cold 33's. I have them trucked in from Cameroon every week."

Kael knew that those trucks didn't go over to Cameroon with just empty bottles. That had to be how they transported the meat out. "A cold beer sounds delicious, but I should get back home to my son. Can we do it another time?"

"Of course," said the mayor. "Any time you wish. We open at seven every morning, and the music and dancing don't stop until well after midnight."

The *sous-préfet* scurried around his desk. With a slight bow and an exaggerated wave of his arm in the direction of the doorway, he said, "I'll show you out, *monsieur*."

"*Merci*," said Kael. He followed the *sous-préfet*, leaving behind the mayor and the police commissioner. He was led past the idle receptionist and out the front door. Kael noticed that the chair and coffee mug had already been collected from under the mango tree.

A few steps away from the office building, the *sous-préfet* stopped. He leaned in toward Kael, and in a soft voice, he said, "I wanted to speak with you alone."

"Sure," said Kael thinking maybe the *sous-préfet* was about to ease his conscience by blowing off the lid on The Three Stooges' poaching operation.

"I was wondering if you could get me a job with the C.I.A. I think I'd make a good spy. I have a high school education, and I know how to blend in unseen."

Kael looked at the banana-yellow leisure suit and thought, in a fruit bowl, maybe. "I'll see if I can get you an application."

"*Merci. Merci beaucoup.*"

Kael walked away, certain he now had a new riddle for Nick the next time they talked on the phone: What was the difference between Elvis and a smart *sous-préfet*? Elvis had been sighted.

Kael's meeting later that day with the American contingent stationed in Bayanga went much more smoothly. Not one person present thought gorillas raped women or that a crocodile man had killed Molly, yet everyone believed wholeheartedly in CARL.

Two researchers and a Peace Corps volunteer, all women, arrived at Kael's doorstep unannounced during the afternoon siesta. Kael sent Josie out for beers while everyone got comfortable on the breezy back deck overlooking the river. Kael filled them in on his first meeting with The Three Stooges earlier that morning.

The Peace Corps volunteer, Paige Marie Turner, was a spindly twenty-one year old fresh out of Indianapolis, Indiana. She was convinced that each one of The Three Stooges was suffering from some as yet undetermined tropical affliction that skewed their judgement and logical thinking processes. As evidence, she pulled out a thick reference book from her backpack: *The Encyclopedia Of Infectious Tropical Diseases: The Unabridged Edition*. "The answer is somewhere in here. I'm sure of it."

"Check under A for Assholes," suggested the elephant researcher, Zenith Rocco, a tall sturdy New Yorker.

The gorilla researcher, Ms. Bermuda Schwartz, a long lanky brunette from Los Angeles, said, "I'd put my money on something sexually transmitted like the latter stages of syphilis, or some new strain of the HIV virus, or just plain dumb parents."

Kael found all three women to be intelligent and entertaining. "So tell me," he asked, "how did you all end up here?"

Zenith said, "Nick recruited Bermuda and me out of Yale's Graduate School of Forestry."

Bermuda said, "It was either here or the real world, and I wasn't ready for that yet."

Paige closed her encyclopedia. "I like the diseases."

Josie arrived with the beers. While he was opening and pouring, Assan slid out of the kitchen with a large platter of golden fried plantains. The women cheered.

"What was that for?" asked Kael.

Zenith said, "You've obviously never tasted Assan's plantains. They're the best. He used to make them out at Molly's camp when we'd visit."

"How often was that?" asked Kael.

"More often than we visit Zenith's camp," said Bermuda. "Her cook is lethal. We used to call him 'Dexatrim—The Appetite Suppressant,' but after tasting his lasagna surprise, we upgraded him to 'Dexatrim II–The New and Improved Appetite Assassin.'"

Kael looked in Zenith's direction. "Why don't you hire someone else? There are plenty of talented cooks in this country. I found mine in prison."

"Are you kidding?" said Zenith. "I've already lost fifteen pounds and I've still got another fifteen to go."

When all the glasses were full, Kael picked his up and said, "Chin chin." Then, after seeing the river in the background, he added, "To Molly."

The three women raised their glasses and echoed, "To Molly."

Kael waited until everyone had a few gulps before asking, "What do you three think really happened to her?"

"She fell out of her canoe and drowned," said Bermuda between sips. "You don't need a crocodile man for that kind of accident to happen."

Zenith said, "You put a tippy canoe with a large outboard engine on a fast-moving river and sooner or later, someone's going to get wet."

"But that doesn't explain why she didn't swim to shore," said Kael. "She was a good swimmer."

"Maybe she hit her head on the side of the canoe or on a rock when she fell out," said Zenith.

"Or maybe the current was too strong," said Bermuda.

"Or just maybe," said Paige, "her body was already weakened by the presence of parasites." She put down her beer and held up her book. "My encyclopedia says that the latter stages of amoebic dysentery or shistosomiasis, which are commonplace here, could have rendered her virtually helpless against a raging river."

"Or she may have just eaten a seven-course meal at Zenith's," said Bermuda.

Kael yelled for Assan, who had returned to the kitchen. When he stepped back out on the deck, Kael asked, "Was Molly sick before she left to go down river by herself?"

"*Non, monsieur.* She was quite healthy. She had just returned from a week-long recording trip in the forest and had probably walked over seventy kilometers. She was very fit."

Bermuda said, "Her Pygmy guides used to call her *Njokou,* their word for elephant, because she was so strong and fearless."

"She was also a damn good researcher," said Zenith, "even if she wasn't from Yale."

"She wasn't even Ivy League," said Bermuda.

"Neither am I," said Paige.

"That's why we speak very slowly and use few polysyllabic words when we're around you, dear," said Zenith half-grinning.

Something in Zenith's crooked smile made Kael wonder if her bite was truly in jest or if there was something else there. He remembered that Nick often talked about the competitive nature of researchers, especially the good ones. They fought over grades, limited openings at the best graduate schools, the most prestigious grants, and the race to publish their findings before anyone else.

"I'll have you know," said Paige, "that Ball State University is one of the leading institutions of higher learning in the State of Indiana."

"Yeah, right," said Zenith. "I heard the *sous-préfet* was accepted there."

"That's true," said Kael trying to avert an all-out cat fight, "but it was only as a specimen for the medical school. Underneath that atrocious yellow leisure suit is a walking laboratory of undiscovered tropical diseases. Right, Paige?"

Paige smiled. "At least two or three volumes worth, I'd say."

Kael figured if he could get Zenith talking about her research, she might quit teasing Paige. "Fill me in on your work with the elephants. It must be fascinating."

Zenith immediately transformed into a serious professional scientist. She set down her beer and straightened up in her chair. "Basically, I'm studying their ranging or migration patterns. I've set up treetop observation sites at different clearings throughout the forest where they like to congregate. There, they socialize, drink and bathe in the muddy pools, and feed on the mineral-rich soils. They don't even know I'm watching. I'm attempting to identify individuals through unique tusk, tail and ear features. So far, I've cataloged over three thousand different elephants that either live in or pass through the Doli-Ngili Reserve."

"That's amazing," said Kael. "Since you're our resident elephant expert, I've got a question for you. What do you do to an elephant with three balls?"

Zenith puckered her lips seeming to mull it over. "Well, to be honest, I've never encountered that particular anomaly in my research, but he'd certainly be easier to identify. Those things are as large as cantaloups. What would *you* do to an elephant with three balls?"

"Walk him and pitch to the giraffe," said Kael.

"I saw that one coming," said Paige with a grin, "and I only went to Ball State."

"That explains it right there," said Bermuda.

"I'm sorry, Zenith," said Kael, "but if you can't tell your elephant jokes to an elephant researcher, who can you tell them to?"

"Gorilla researchers," said Bermuda.

"Don't forget Peace Corps volunteers," said Paige.

Zenith flashed her crooked half-smile and said, "That's OK. Nick already warned us that you were a comedian. He also said if we were ever offended, we should retaliate."

Kael said, "Give it your best shot."

"OK. What does a woman do with her asshole every morning?"

"I honestly don't know," answered Kael.

"Packs up his lunch and sends him off to work," said Zenith.

The other women cheered. Kael could count, so he knew when he was outnumbered. He made the wise decision to keep his mouth shut.

"Hey," said Zenith, "if you can't tell your man jokes to a man, who can you tell them to?"

"Gorilla researchers," said Bermuda.

"Don't forget Peace Corps volunteers," said Paige.

Josie brought out more beer to refill empty glasses while Assan cleared away the pillaged platter of plantains. He replaced it with a brightly colored ceramic bowl of steaming hot chickpeas still in their softened shells. Next to beer, they were Kael's favorite African snack.

After Assan had returned to the kitchen with Josie, Bermuda said, "Assan's a good guy. There's absolutely no way he was involved in Molly's death. His arrest and imprisonment were tactical ploys by The Three Stooges to make TRAP look bad, like we're nothing but a bunch of crocodile men and murderers."

"And don't forget C.I.A. spies," said Paige.

Kael said, "When you're not spying, Paige, what else do you do? You're an environmental education volunteer, aren't you?"

"Technically, yes," said Paige, "but my true passion is diseases."

"Your own or just diseases in general?" asked Kael.

Zenith laughed. "She thinks she has every frigging one, so it really doesn't matter. Last week it was rabies. This week it's scabies. What's next... babies?"

"Let's hope that's not contagious," said Bermuda. Then, in a sing-song lilt, she chanted, "Rabies and scabies and babies, oh my!"

Kael asked, "Other than acquiring a first-hand knowledge of rabies, scabies and babies, what else have you accomplished as a Peace Corpse?"

Paige removed a compact thirty-five millimeter camera from her backpack. "I've taken a lot of pictures. Most are of diseases. I've got some great shots of goiters. Some are as big as basketballs. You want to see them?"

"Only if they're hidden behind turtlenecks," said Kael. He theorized that Paige's idea of a fun date would be to see the movie, *Saturday Night Dengue Fever*, followed by a trip to the hospital for a blood analysis, a urinalysis and a stool sample. "Have you done anything remotely related to environmental education?"

Paige shrugged her shoulders. "Not in the traditional sense, although diseases are certainly part of our environment."

"More for some than others," said Kael.

Bermuda said, "That particular aspect of the project wasn't a priority for Mitch. He was more into his research and anti-poaching."

"Well," said Kael, "after meeting with The Three Stooges this morning, it's apparent to me that we need to do some serious educating."

"I can show them my pictures," said Paige.

That gave Kael an idea. "Pictures would be good. Slides would be better. We could invite the whole village."

Zenith said, "Do you really think that many people would want to see Paige's goiters?"

Kael said, "When I was a fish volunteer, I used slides to teach farmers about pond fish culture. The projector hooked up to a truck battery, so I could take the show any-where. You wouldn't believe the crowds I drew. Entire villages turned out. The reason was simple: There was nothing else to do. My slides were the only game in town."

"And you think we could do the same thing with my goiter pictures?" asked Paige.

"Definitely not," said Kael, "but if we showed slides that helped to explain the Doli-Ngili project and exactly why we're here, we might get a few more people on our side. Right now, The Three Stooges are telling everyone that we're C.I.A. operatives sent in to recruit crocodile men as part of our larger mission to eliminate logging in Bayanga. Moe, Larry, and Curly didn't exactly come right out and say it, but I'm sure they're spreading rumors that we are somehow encouraging elephants to destroy their fields, and instigating gorillas to rape their women."

"That's ridiculous," said Bermuda. "Whenever I see a gorilla in the forest, it runs away."

"Have you thought of changing your hairstyle? asked Zenith.

"I already have," said a smiling Bermuda. "Before, they'd scream first, and then run. Now, they just run."

"Men!" said Zenith with feigned attitude.

"Thank you for that insightful social commentary," said Kael. "Now, why don't you channel that frustration into a slide show that has the potential of destroying the evil plans of not one, but three despicable men?"

"When you phrase it that way," said Bermuda, "it sounds like fun."

Zenith asked Paige, "Have you got any pictures of castration?"

"No," said Paige.

"Good," said Zenith. "We might be able to supply you with three."

Kael noticed that same crooked smile evident on Zenith's face. He felt his own tes-ticles retract as if trying to burrow into his abdomen for protection. "Now that we're all sufficiently motivated, we need slides—lots of them. Paige, you're our photographer. I'll give you all the film you need as long as you take pictures that promote TRAP's mission of protecting the forest rather than cutting it down. A *few* pictures of diseases are fine if you can make a connection to conservation." Paige nodded, so he turned his attention to Zenith and Bermuda. "You two *must* have slides of your research."

"A few," said Zenith.

"More than a few," said Bermuda.

"Good," said Kael. "We can use those to dispel some of the rumors flying out of the *sous-préfet's* office."

"What about a script?" asked Paige.

"Thank you for volunteering," said Kael. "In the next few days, I'll come up with some preliminary ideas of things we want to cover. You can then develop a storyline. Let's make it educational, entertaining, and easy to understand. Remember, our audience includes the *sous-préfet.*"

"And a cowboy who wears flip-flops," said Zenith.

Kael washed down some chickpeas with the last of his beer. "The Three Stooges may not be the sharpest tools in the drawer, but they still have one big advantage over us."

"I know," said Paige. "Their immune systems are better suited than our own to combating the diseases over here."

"OK," said Kael, "I guess they have two big advantages. The other is that CARL is on *their* side."

Everyone shrugged their shoulders without uttering a word. Some things, like the sun rising in the east, setting in the west, and always shining on CARL, were indisputable.

# 26

Bolo sucked the death out of his cigarette. The acrid smoke followed a well-worn path across his tongue, down his throat and into his expanding lungs. He held it there until his insides felt like they were on fire. Then he slowly exhaled, almost expecting flames to shoot out from his nostrils.

This was a cigarette of celebration, not that he needed any excuse to smoke. It was one of the few pleasures he had left along with drinking, killing, and getting good reports from his sources. The latter happened so rarely these days, he'd begun to wonder why they should continue to reap some of the benefits of his hard work. They were incompetents. He had been convinced of that fact from the very start of their relationship, but today, they'd actually done something right. Ron and Nancy had finally been spotted.

The message had been short, but sweet: "Ron and Nancy. The Big Apple. Broadway and Forty-Second Street."

His cynical response had left no doubt as to his confidence in their abilities: "Are you certain you've got the right Ron and Nancy?"

"Absolutely."

"And you're sure about the location?"

"Of course."

Bolo had let the conversation die there. He hadn't told them when, or even if he'd be arriving at the disclosed location. Some things were better left unspoken. Keeping secrets, even from his fellow collaborators, was why he'd been able to succeed at this kind of work for so long. They didn't know the half of what he'd done, or what he was planning to do. He wanted to keep it that way.

He took another long drag on his cigarette. He seemed to think better when he was smoking. Black lungs made for a clear head.

If he'd learned anything from the Charles and Diana killings, it was that he had to be thorough. At the time, shooting William and Harry along with their parents had felt like the right thing to do. He'd gotten caught up in the heat of battle. Too caught up, maybe, because with so many bullets flying, he'd lost count. He still didn't know for sure if he'd fired nine or ten. All that mental aggravation over one bullet and the deaths of William and Harry hadn't even increased his profit margin. That was the worst part. They were so young their worth was negligible.

Ron and Nancy were a different story altogether. There was good money on their gray heads. Bolo realized that he couldn't let their substantial price tags cloud his concentration, though. This particular job would be perfect, precise, and professional. He promised.

It would take him at least a couple of days to get up to The Big Apple unnoticed. He didn't just want to drop everything and travel all that way only to discover that Ron and Nancy had already left. That would be overanxious, and overanxious wasn't thorough. First, he needed his sources to establish a pattern for Ron and Nancy. One sighting wasn't enough, but several over the next two or three weeks meant that the elusive couple was probably sticking around for a while.

Second, he needed to check out the sniper possibilities around Broadway and Forty-second. He was already familiar with the general layout. He'd been there many times, and he recalled that there were a number of perches near that intersection that might work. He just had to pick the one that best suited his purposes. He preferred something high and hidden.

He'd already convinced himself that he'd be doing Ron and Nancy a big favor by planting bullets deep in their failing brains. They were no longer leaders. They were followers. They weren't contributing to society anymore. Others had to care for them. They were old. They had to be well past seventy. Ron, in particular, had already smashed the odds. He was, by some estimates, plodding past eighty. Neither one had much longer to live, even if they went naturally. A few years, tops, thought Bolo, so why not make some money from their slightly premature deaths? If he didn't, someone else would. What was left for them, anyway? The complete loss of their teeth? Painful arthritic joints? Obliteration of their legendary capacity to remember? A slow agonizing end? Not if Bolo could help it. He snuffed out his cigarette and decided that Ron and Nancy would go out with a bang, not a whimper.

# 27

The road out to Zenith's research camp wasn't much more than an elephant trail carved through the forest. Branches of wild ginger—a favorite food of gorillas—slapped at both sides of Kael's truck. It was like driving through an automated car wash without the soap and water. The road, which was difficult to discern through the brush-covered windshield, was so bumpy and pitted Kael had to keep both hands constantly on the steering wheel just to persuade the front tires from veering off into the trees. This seemed ridiculous to Kael, especially since top speed was roughly that of a snail with a limp. He glanced over at Josie, who was bouncing on the passenger seat like an overinflated basketball.

"We're moving forward more slowly than evolution."

Josie, who was nearly launched into orbit after one particularly severe jolt, smiled. "This is fun."

"Hmm... more fun that a barrel of toilets."

They soon came to a fork in the road. Kael had been told by Assan that Zenith's camp was to the left and Bermuda's was to the right. Not unlike his political leanings, he steered left.

The road cut deeper into the forest like a jagged knife. Kael pressed on. He was determined to find Zenith's camp. Besides, returning to Bayanga was not an option since there was no place wide enough to turn around.

He was busy eyeing the temperature gauge, willing it to stay within the normal range, when he heard Josie announce, "*E si awé.*" Returning his attention to the windshield, Kael spotted a brown truck parked at the far end of a cul-de-sac. It was no mirage. This was, indeed, the end of the road. He pulled up next to the other vehicle. It wasn't just a truck. It was a showroom-new, top-of-the-line, four-wheel-drive Toyota Land Cruiser Station Wagon—forty thousand dollars worth of luxury automobile that could climb the side of a building.

Josie couldn't have been more impressed if it were a flush toilet on wheels.

"Wow! Why don't we have a truck like that?"

Kael wondered the same thing. "I don't know. Maybe I should have gone to Yale."

"Is that where they sell them?" asked Josie.

Kael smiled. "You could say that."

They hopped out of their own primitive transportation for a closer inspection of the competition. There was nothing quite like a shiny, new, overpriced automobile to get two males breathing heavily. Kael had a theory that men liked ogling cars more than women. Both could be beautiful, stylish and sexy, but all cars, unlike most intelligent women, yielded to a man's total control. No questions, no arguments, no discussions. Such behavior was empowering to men, who also appreciated the concept of an unconditional warranty. If there was even the slightest bit of hesitation on the car's part, it could be returned and repaired free of charge.

Kael was surprised to find the station wagon locked up tight. Who was going to steal it, a delinquent gorilla? It was a bit like the Apollo astronauts locking up the lunar landing module before going out for a moonwalk.

On the other side of the truck Kael discovered a footpath. It started at the edge of the trees and snaked through a forest thick with old-growth mahogany and ebony trees. Some had to be over a hundred feet tall. Along with chainsaws that never needed sharpening and the world-wide elimination of environmentalists, these towers of timber were what loggers dreamed of: big expensive trees standing right next to an already existing road.

Kael whistled to Josie, who abandoned the car to sprint down the path ahead of Kael. Kael warned the blur that shot by him to keep an eye out for snakes.

It was a short hike to Zenith's camp, which was comprised of four round grass-thatched *paillotte* huts without walls. They were lined up like open upright umbrellas in a small man-made clearing of the rain forest.

Out of place amidst the bush motif of living were a series of solar panels fanning across the roof of one of the *paillottes* and a thirty-foot fiberglass flag pole flying a blue-bordered pennant with a big blue Y in a field of white. Kael quickly deduced that it didn't stand for Harvard.

He heard a sickly dog barking. A few paces ahead, Josie had knelt down to inspect something next to the path. He started giggling.

Kael approached. He saw and heard what Josie found so entertaining. It was a small plastic dog about eight inches high. It was also the source of the barking. Kael smiled. He had never actually seen one of these, although he'd often encountered the riotous advertisements for them in the back of magazines: twenty-one bucks for a motion sensor and a tinny recording encased in a plastic pound puppy that was guaranteed to keep intruders away. Batteries not included.

Kael looked up to see Zenith, rifle in hand, coming down the path from her camp. He held up his hands in total surrender.

"Please lady, call off your dog!"

Zenith flashed a look of disgust as she realized who her trespassers were. "Don't make any sudden movements. He's a trained killer."

"Only until his batteries die," said Kael, "and it sounds like that could be any second now."

"Then my fine for trespassing is four D-cell batteries," said Zenith. She waved them forward.

As soon as Kael and Josie were ten feet past the dog, he stopped barking. Either they were out of his motion sensor's range or his batteries had mercifully died. When they got up to where Zenith stood on the path, Kael said, "That's quite the watchdog you've got there."

Zenith nodded. "He did his job, even if he is a bit annoying when he does it. My worrisome mother sent me a litter of six after I'd mentioned to her that elephants were wandering into my camp at night. At first I thought her idea was crazy, but I set them up around the perimeter and since then, not one elephant has barged in uninvited."

"Just directors and their sons," said Kael.

"Yeah," said Zenith holding up her gun. "That's why I have this."

"I noticed," said Kael, "but it looks like a toy. Was it made by the same company that produced your watchdog? Don't tell me. You pull the trigger and it sounds like a bullet firing. That is, if the batteries aren't dead." He watched her pat her rifle in much the same way one would comfort a warm puppy.

"It's no toy. It shoots darts for taking elephant skin samples. The dart falls to the ground with a tiny core of skin. Through mitochondrial DNA analysis, I can tell who's related to whom."

"Well," said Kael, "don't shoot. I'll tell you right off that Josie and I are related."

Zenith looked from Kael to Josie and back to Kael. "No doubt about that. Come on up to camp. I've got coffee and canned sardines. They're the only two items on the menu that Dexatrim II can't ruin."

"The coffee sounds great," said Kael, "but I'll pass on the sardines. I've got a theory that the human body can only consume a certain number of sardines from a tin. I don't know the exact amount, but I reached it sometime during my third year as a Peace Corps volunteer."

Zenith nodded. "As a scientist, I can appreciate your hypothesis, but if you had a cook like mine, you might re-think your theory."

"Wouldn't matter," said Kael. "When your number's up, your number's up."

Zenith had Kael and Josie wait in the living room/office *paillotte* while she went off to prepare the coffee and sardines in the kitchen *paillotte*. The two remaining *paillottes* were set up as bedrooms.

The chair Kael picked to sit in was comfortable and similar in style to the ones in his new house. The only difference was the fabric covering the foam pads. Zenith's patterns and colors were much more in line with tasteful decorating. "No promotional condom cloth here," he said to Josie, who just smiled back from where he sat paging through a Yale University alumni magazine.

One end of the *paillotte* was set up as an office. A large red mahogany table held several foot-high stacks of papers, cups of pens and pencils, boxes of assorted sizes, an open IBM notebook computer, and a Motorola single-side-band radio. It was the exact same model as the one sitting in the office at Hidden Cove.

Zenith arrived with the mid-morning refreshments. "I've got coffees for us and a hot chocolate for Josie. Sorry, no marshmallows. The sardines are for Josie and me. The boiled peanuts are all yours. You haven't reached your limit on those, I hope."

"Not yet," said Kael.

The coffee was good. Zenith had prepared it the way Arabs did when they weren't drinking tea. There was just a hint of black pepper.

"What's the range on your radio?" asked Kael.

Zenith swallowed her sardine before answering. "On good days, I can reach Bangui. The American embassy likes us to occasionally check in."

"Us?" asked Kael.

"Bermuda and me. She has a radio, too, just in case there's an accident or an emergency or some juicy gossip to pass on. We talk to each other every night. It fools us into thinking we're not really that isolated and alone."

"But you have a dog to keep you company."

Zenith frowned. "A dog is *man's* best friend, not woman's."

"How about your cook, Dexatrim II?"

Zenith rolled her eyes. "He's a better cook than conversationalist."

Kael had to laugh. "Did it ever occur to you that if you're not into loneliness and isolation, elephant field research might be the wrong choice for a profession? I mean, it's kind of like a car mechanic who doesn't like having dirty hands."

"You know," said Zenith, "with a Bronx accent, you'd sound just like my mother."

"Sorry," said Kael. "Don't you hate it when your mother's right?"

Zenith pinched the head off a sardine. "You can't imagine." She popped both pieces into her mouth and noisily gobbled them down. "I don't plan on being out here forever. I'll do my research, publish my data, and get my doctorate. Then I'll teach at an Ivy-league school, preferably one located in a large overpopulated city. Dartmouth, Cornell and Princeton are out. Too rural. Brown and Yale are possibilities, but I'd prefer Columbia, Harvard or Penn, in that order."

"I take it Ball State is out, too?"

Zenith arched one eyebrow. "A whole classroom of Paiges? I don't think so. I'd rather be isolated and alone."

"I'll admit that Paige is a bit eccentric," said Kael, "but *anyone* choosing to live and work here *has* to be somewhat abnormal." He looked straight at Zenith. "Some of us use battery-operated guard dogs for protection, while others cope by taking their temperature every two hours. My new best friend is a crocodile man. Josie's is a flush toilet. We're all certifiable."

"Point taken," said Zenith. "At least we're not from Indiana."

Kael smiled. "I suspect that the Hoosier State is just as happy about that fact." He grabbed a handful of boiled peanuts. "Believe it or not, Paige has come up with a clever script idea for the slide show. It's got all the ingredients of a classic Shakespearean storyline: greed, deceit, murder and parasitic infestation."

"That certainly sounds like Bayanga... and Paige."

"Now, all we need are some slides of elephants and gorillas." Kael wiggled his eyebrows up and down at Zenith, who got up without a word and walked over to her desk. She returned with a small cardboard box that she tossed at Kael. He caught it in the one hand not full of peanuts.

"There are twenty good elephant shots in there, and I want every one back when this silly slide show of yours is done."

"*D'accord,*" said Kael. He opened the box and began examining the slides. Josie wanted to see, too, but as hard as he squinted, he couldn't make out the tiny images of elephants caught on film.

After holding several different slides at varying distances against assorted backgrounds, Josie gave up saying, "I think I see them, but it's like looking through the wrong end of the binoculars."

Kael tried explaining about projectors and light, not an easy feat in Sango, but Josie's attention had already refocused on his neglected life-size sardines and hot chocolate.

Zenith said in Sango for Josie's benefit, "Why don't we go see some real elephants?"

Josie's head popped up like a jack-in-the-box. "Really?"

"Sure," said Zenith. "There's a footpath that leads to a large clearing only fifteen minutes from here. Elephants like to hang out there. We could watch them from my observation tower."

Josie's wide eyes turned to his father. "Can we?"

Kael stood up. "Last one there has to marry the *sous-préfet*."

Josie giggled. Zenith made a face before saying, "Since I know the way, I should lead. You two stay right behind me at all times. It's easy to get lost out there."

Kael smiled. "I'm touched by your sudden concern for our safety."

Zenith stood up and shrugged her shoulders. "That's just the way I am—always putting the welfare of others before my own."

"As long as you're still first in line," added Kael.

"Of course. Let me just grab my backpack."

Zenith was right. The footpath out to the clearing was fifteen minutes of confusion. It stretched through the forest like an out-of-control vine. With no compass, Kael didn't know if they were heading north, south, east or west. At times, it seemed like they tried all four.

The thick canopy of trees overhead made simple navigation by the sun or stars an impossibility. Like geese flying south on a foggy, fall day, one just had to know the way. Or, as in Kael's case, one just had to be smart enough to keep the lead goose in sight.

Kael called ahead to Zenith: "When geese fly in a V-formation, do you know why one side of the V is almost always longer than the other side?"

Zenith thought about it for a few seconds before asking, "Does it have anything to do with wind resistance?"

"No, it's because there are more geese on that side. Lead on."

One hundred feet ahead, the forest opened up, but all Kael could make out through the last line of trees were lots of large gray rocks. His view of the clearing was further obstructed by Josie and Zenith on the trail in front of him. He said, "I wonder if the *sous-préfet* would prefer a large wedding or a small intimate gathering of just family and close friends."

Zenith turned and whispered, "The quieter we are, the more we'll see. My tower is just ahead on the right. I'll climb up first. Then Josie. Kael, you bring up the rear." She smiled before asking, "Can I be a bridesmaid?"

Kael made sure to keep his voice low this time. "Go ahead and gloat, missy. I'll have my revenge. Just wait until you see the dress I'll make you wear. It has puffy sleeves."

Zenith smothered her laughter with both hands before resuming her role as the lead dog.

The tower was a platform thirty feet straight up in the branches of a large tree. A homemade wooden ladder with rotting rungs connected the platform to the ground.

"Is this safe?" asked Kael.

"As long as you don't fall," replied Zenith, who started to climb up hand over hand.

Josie's foot quickly replaced Zenith's on the bottom rung. Like most ten year olds, he had no fear of climbing trees. His only concern seemed to be getting to the top in world-record time.

Heights had never affected Kael before, but the sight of his own son scampering up a rickety ladder like Spiderman made him more uncomfortable than a Texan in a humble contest. He waited at the bottom with arms outstretched like a gymnastics spotter. If Josie slipped and plummeted to the ground, Kael would be there to break his fall. With the possible exception of his first rectal exam, it was the longest twenty seconds of Kael's life.

Only after Josie pulled himself safely up on to the platform and inside the guardrail did Kael begin his ascent. When he reached the top, Zenith was softly singing, "Here comes the bride... all dressed in white..."

Kael wagged a finger in her direction. "Keep it up and I won't throw the bouquet your way."

"Promise?"

"No," said Kael struggling to his feet, "but here's an idea. When the sous-préfet walks down the aisle, maybe you could sing, 'Here comes the fellow... all dressed in yellow.'"

"I like it," said Zenith.

Kael looked past Zenith to the other side of the platform where Josie stood leaning over the guardrail. Kael might have been concerned had it not been for the scene playing out just beyond his daredevil son.

In the clearing below, the large gray rocks, which Kael had glimpsed earlier, were now behaving more animal-like than mineral-like. They were walking, running, eating, and drinking. Some were bathing. Others were playing. In short, they were acting like elephants. There were forty or fifty of them, and they didn't seem to know or care that they were being observed.

Kael could only say, "Wow!" He then sidled up to his star-struck son, nudged him with an elbow, and leaned over the guardrail for a better view.

Upon closer inspection, the elephants weren't the only live entertainment in the clearing. A pair of sitatunga antelope, a male and a female, sprinted through a shallow marsh so effortlessly, they appeared to be gliding on ice. They stopped midway to take a drink and leisurely wade in the ankle-deep water.

Five forest buffalo, redder and slightly smaller than their savanna cousins, looked up from their grazing to see why the sitatunga had run. Something must have told them that there was nothing to fear because their twitching snouts soon returned to the ground to finish their breakfast.

A solitary giant forest hog rolled around in a small pool of mud and muck. Its snorts of contentment got louder the filthier it became.

Zenith thrust a pair of pocket-sized binoculars between Kael and Josie. "If you look into the trees at the far end of the clearing, you'll see hundreds of gray parrots. They're easy to spot with their red tails."

Josie grabbed the binoculars first, but not before Kael noticed that they were manufactured by Zeiss. A thousand dollars worth of German optical precision and Kael imagined Josie accidentally dropping them thirty feet to the unforgiving forest floor. He placed the strap around Josie's neck. "Just to be on the safe side."

"Don't worry about it," said Zenith. "I've got two more pairs back at camp along with a couple of spotting scopes. Out here, you've got to factor in disasters with your equipment."

"That could be sound dating advice for most men."

"*All* men is more like it."

Josie interrupted to announce, "The elephants are eating dirt."

"I guess they've reached their limit on sardines, too," said Kael.

"Actually," said Zenith, "they're eating the dirt to get at the salt and other minerals found in the soil. It's full of nutrients. That's why they come to these clearings: to eat, to drink, and to socialize. It makes for a near-perfect spot to do my research."

Kael watched six bush pigs march out of the trees. They paraded across the clearing in single file to the other side, where they disappeared back into the forest. He noticed that Zenith was busy scribbling in a worn spiral notebook.

"Field observations?" he asked.

Zenith continued to write. "Yeah, I normally enter data directly into my computer, but for short show-and-tell trips like this one, I just bring a low-tech pad and pencil. That way, if I see something of interest, I record it and enter it into the computer when I get back to camp."

"So, what did you see?"

"Possibly a new elephant. See that big bull all by himself at the edge of the trees?" She pointed a finger. "He doesn't look familiar. He may be entirely new to the area, or he may be a transient that is already part of my database, but hasn't been around for a while. I'd guess that he's a savanna elephant."

"How can you tell?" asked Kael. "Has he got a Southern accent?"

Zenith furrowed her brow. "Southern accent? Oh, I get it. No, he's not from Georgia, but look at how big he is compared to the other elephants. The forest variety are generally smaller. Next, look at his tusks. Would you say they curve in or out?"

"Out," said Kael.

"Correct. Forest elephants tend to have inward-curving tusks. That trait, along with their smaller stature, is an adaptation that makes it easier for them to maneuver through the tight confines of the forest."

"So, is this guy lost or just on vacation?"

"Neither," said Zenith. "He's part of a trend, and I'm hoping to publish a paper on it. I'm finding a lot more savanna-type elephants in the forest. My theory is that they're being slaughtered so easily in the wide open savannas up north that they're migrating down here to the forest where it's easier to hide and where the poaching pressure isn't nearly as intense." She borrowed the binoculars from Josie. "Aha... just as I suspected. His tusks lack the creamy yellow coloring typical of forest elephants." She made a notation in her field book. "I've been told that ivory carvers actually prefer the tusks from a forest elephant."

"Because it's harder to acquire?" asked Kael.

"No, because it's slightly denser. Apparently, that makes it easier to carve more intricate patterns, which can fetch a higher market price."

Kael said, "Don't let Josie hear that yellow teeth are a good thing."

"I can keep a secret," said Zenith, "if you can convince your friend, Nick, that my request for radio telemetry equipment is essential to my research."

"Is it?" asked Kael.

"Of course," she said handing the binoculars back to Josie. "If I had a state-of-the-art global positioning satellite system, I wouldn't have to sit in a tower all day. I could put transmitters on, say, a hundred random elephants, and track them by computer from my apartment in Manhattan."

"Sounds expensive, and I'm just thinking about the monthly rent on an upper east-side apartment."

"I'd settle for something in the Village," said Zenith.

"The ultimate sacrifice."

"Hey," said Zenith, "when I came on board, Nick promised that there was plenty of grant money available through TRAP for cutting-edge research projects like mine."

"Think back. Was the word 'Manhattan' ever mentioned?"

Zenith scratched her head. "I think so. We were in a bar in New Haven called Toad's Place. Nick ordered a beer. I ordered a Manhattan and I distinctly remember him saying he'd get it."

She winked at Kael, who was not to be outdone when it came to telling funny stories. He said, "That reminds me of the joke about Mickey Mouse requesting a divorce from Minnie. The judge, the honorable Donald Duck, threw the case out of court on the grounds that Minnie was not legally insane. Mickey stood up and said, 'I didn't say she was insane, your honor. I said she was fucking Goofy.'"

Zenith laughed. "So, you think Nick was talking about the drink and not the city, huh?"

"I think," said Kael, "if you want to study elephants in New York, you should get a job at the Bronx Zoo."

Josie announced that some strange new animals had entered the clearing. Kael looked in the direction at which Josie's binoculars and pointing finger were aimed.

"My God," said Zenith snatching the binoculars away from Josie. "That's a herd of bongo... twelve of them. You don't see that very often."

"Especially in New York," said Kael, helping Josie to extricate himself from the binoculars' strap that was now wrapped around his neck like a noose.

Zenith said, "Don't pull. You'll get your turn."

With Josie liberated from an early death by hanging, Kael explained to him that the bongo was the largest forest antelope and could weigh well over five hundred pounds. Its long horns and white-striped hide were coveted as trophies by big-game hunters.

Josie's only question was, "Does it taste good?"

"Very," said Zenith, who offered no further elaboration.

Kael said, "I take it Dexatrim II had nothing to do with the preparation."

Zenith continued to observe the bongo through the binoculars. "You got that right."

The bongo gingerly stepped through the open clearing. The farther they got from the safety of the trees, the more they looked like they were tiptoeing through a mine-field. They occasionally grazed on some grass, but they never lingered in one spot for too long. And for every bongo feeding, there were two keeping their heads up, alert to any potential danger.

"See how they feed as a group?" whispered Kael. "They look out for each other. Everyone gets a turn to eat under the watchful eye of the herd."

Zenith handed the binoculars over to Josie, but spoke to Kael. "Do you think they conform because they have to or because they choose to?"

"I don't think they have much of a choice," said Kael. "It's all instinct. Their survival is dependent on the herd's well-being."

"One for all and all for one," said Zenith.

Kael smiled. "At least until a hungry leopard enters the scene. Then it's every bongo for himself."

"Then self-preservation is acceptable behavior, too?" asked Zenith.

"You'd know all about that," said Kael.

Zenith furrowed her brow. "What do you mean by that?"

"I'm the one marrying the *sous-préfet*, not you."

Zenith smiled. "That's true."

The remainder of the herd's slow dance across the clearing was observed in silence. When they finally merged with the trees on the other side, Zenith spoke.

"We should probably get back to camp. I've got a ton of work waiting for me."

Kael nudged Josie and said, "Ready to go?"

Josie removed the binoculars from his eyes. "But I haven't seen a gorilla, yet."

Zenith said, "I'm sorry, but I've only seen gorillas out here once. They don't like the clearings as much as the other animals."

"Why?" asked Josie.

"Well," said Zenith, "they're very shy and they feel safer in the forest."

That seemed to be enough of an explanation for Josie. He gave the binoculars back to Zenith and said, "*Merci.*"

"You're very welcome." She turned to Kael and asked, "At what age do boys lose their charm?"

Kael winked. "Some of us never do."

"Yeah, right." She started to return things to her backpack.

Kael asked, "Do you think Bermuda could help two charming boys to see a gorilla?"

"Possibly, although she doesn't see them very often, either. She's finding that when elephants move into an area, gorillas leave."

"Why? Do their property values go down?"

"No, but I'll mention that to her. She thinks it's more a problem of space. Both are large mammals that require lots of real estate around them to feel safe. My elephants come from as far away as Cameroon, the Congo, and northern C.A.R. Bermuda thinks they're elbowing her gorillas farther east."

"And you're still friends?"

"One for all and all for one."

"So," said Kael, "Yale blood is not only blue. It's thick."

Zenith buckled up her backpack. "Just like Dexatrim II's gravy."

Kael's stomach lurched. He pictured sardines floating in a thick blue gravy. "Sorry we can't stay for lunch."

"Another time, perhaps." Zenith shouldered her backpack before sitting down beneath the guardrail at the edge of the platform. She placed her left hand and foot on the ladder. "I'll go down first."

"Hold on," said Kael. "If your elephants are chasing away Bermuda's gorillas, doesn't that screw up her research?"

Zenith reached across the ladder with her other hand and foot. She was now in position to climb down. "Not if her dissertation is on the ranging habits of lowland gorillas and how they're affected by the presence of other species, which it is. She just has to come up with data to support her thesis, which she is, so she's pretty happy about it, actually. Can we go down, now?"

"After you," said Kael. He had Josie follow her, but only after making him promise to touch each and every rung on the way down. Otherwise, his world-record descent would be declared invalid.

Left alone atop the tower, Kael took one final look at the big gray rocks below.

It suddenly struck him that as the new director of the Doli-Ngili Reserve, he was in charge of all this, or at least as much as Zenith and CARL would allow.

His roving eyes caught Zenith's new elephant, still standing by himself at the edge of the trees. He hadn't budged from his spot, either, and like Kael, he seemed to be uncertain about what to do next—whether to venture farther into the clearing or retreat back into the forest. Kael's decision was made easier by Zenith impatiently pleading from the ground.

"Come on, Husker. You've got a wedding to plan."

Kael slowly peered over the guardrail to where Zenith stood with hands on hips. "If the *sous-préfet* thinks I'm going to organize this all by myself, he's sorely mistaken." With both hands on the guardrail, he lowered himself to a sitting position at the edge of the platform. His legs dangled next to the ladder. The distinctive whooshing sound of a hornbill flying overhead caused him to look up. He caught a glimpse of tail feathers just before they dipped into the treetops. Something closer came into focus: crudely carved into the underneath side of the wooden guardrail above his head were the initials, "M.M."

M.M.? Mickey Mouse? Minnie Mouse? Or Molly McGinley? Kael traced the "M.M." with his finger. It was Molly, all right. She'd left her mark hidden in this piece of wood in much the same way she'd etched her image into his nightmares. Both had gotten his attention, not to mention six thousand dollars of his own money he'd spent to free Assan from prison.

"What more do you want from me?" He thought he'd spoken softly to himself, but he must have said it with enough volume to carry at least thirty feet because Zenith answered.

"Getting down would be a good start."

Kael recovered quickly. "Play any tune by K.C. and the Sunshine Band and just watch me get down."

"You're testing my patience," said Zenith, "not to mention my limited knowledge of disco-era musical groups."

Kael shook his head in mock disgust. "What *do* they teach you kids at Yale?" He climbed down singing the chorus to *Shake Your Booty*. It had been one of Molly's favorites.

# 28

Bolo concentrated. In more ways than one, he was trying to get into the heads of Ron and Nancy. A worn map was spread out on the ground before him. It was his own personal travel diary of all of his targets over the last five years. Ron and Nancy were there. So were Charles and Diana, along with dozens of others.

Specific locations where each had been observed were noted with a date and time, and highlighted using different colored markers. Ron and Nancy sightings were in red; royal blue seemed appropriate for Charles and Diana.

Bolo picked the royal blue marker out of the box. He broke it in half. He wouldn't need that color any longer.

He circled the most recent red entries in pencil. There didn't seem to be any discernible pattern. Back in October, they had both been seen for the first time in eighteen months on the Ventura Freeway. Less than one month later, they were spotted walking down Broadway near Forty-second Street. Now, one source had Ron, without Nancy, at Central Park, while another source swore Ron was with Nancy on the same day, just two hours later at the Hollywood Bowl. For such an old geezer, he still managed to get all over the map.

Bolo appreciated the occasional challenge of a worthy adversary like Ron. There weren't too many octogenarians that could stay one step ahead of him.

He studied the map. There had to be something there that wasn't random. We were all creatures of habit. Maybe the clue to finding Ron and Nancy wasn't in what they'd done recently, but in what they'd done historically.

Suddenly, he saw it. Three dates highlighted in red were grouped together: January 12, January 8 and January 4. In three out of the last four years, within two weeks of New Year's Day, Ron and Nancy had been seen at Venice Beach. It wasn't much, but it was all he had. It was certainly better than the indiscriminate information he'd been getting from his sources lately.

He folded up the map. He now had something to look forward to. It wasn't quite New Year's yet, but he made a two-part resolution. The first part was that he'd ring in the New Year at Venice Beach. The second part was that he'd soon be breaking his red marker in half.

# 29

Where was CARL? Was he on vacation? Had he been overthrown by a more benevolent acronym like FRAN (Foreigners Rarely Attract Negativity)? Or had he just grown weary of playing the same old games and winning them all the time? Kael couldn't believe his nemesis hadn't yet made some sort of appearance. No phone calls. No "Thinking of You" Hallmark card. Nothing. It was disturbing, but Kael wasn't complaining. He wasn't celebrating, either. With just ten hours to go until the premiere of his much-anticipated slide show, he knew that CARL still had ample time to set up an ambush.

Except for his continuing nightmares of Molly, the last few weeks had gone about as smoothly as one could expect in CARL's backyard. Paige's film had been entrusted to a group of French tourists returning to Bangui. Several days later, a Peace Corps truck from Bangui just happened to be leaving for Bayanga. It brought out the developed slides along with a projector courtesy of Stan Pulaski, the Economics Officer at the American embassy.

In an accompanying note, Stan had relayed that the Ambassador's laundry boy had been eliminated as a potential suspect in the rash of thefts, but during questioning, he had admitted to buying an inferior laundry detergent and pocketing the difference in price. As per Kael's advice, Stan was trying to smile as much as he suspected CARL was.

For the slide show's theatrical venue, Mayor Likéké had volunteered the use of his bar and his electricity. All he asked in return was that he be allowed to sell beer to the audience before and after the show. Kael, who couldn't remember ever vetoing beer, had said, "Why not?" He had even offered to buy the first round for The Three Stooges, who had all promised to attend.

It was all coming together. Only CARL could ruin it. Kael saw his slide show as the *Titanic*, cruising along in calm waters and CARL as the iceberg, lying in wait. He was out there bobbing around somewhere between Kael's house and the mayor's bar.

Kael was stretched out on his condom-cloth sofa, contemplating his tenuous hold on the events leading up to the slide show that evening when Assan walked in through the front door carrying two stuffed sacks. Kael could see a ripe orange papaya and the prickly end of a pineapple poking out of the top of one of the cloth bags.

"Looks like it was a good day at the market," said Kael.

"*Oui, monsieur*. I found fruit, mushrooms, avocados, and eggplant."

"All my favorites."

"*Oui, monsieur*. I also got some information."

Kael sat up. "What kind of information?"

Assan moved closer and lowered his voice. "Some of my Muslim brothers have heard rumors of a dead elephant discovered in the forest."

Kael's first thought was that CARL had something to do with it. This was simply the first phase of his diabolical plan to destroy the slide show. He was a cunning adversary. "Do you know where it is?"

"*Oui, monsieur*. It's not far."

"Not far, huh?" There was that phrase again.

"*Oui, monsieur*. If we take the truck, we could be there in a half hour."

Kael stood up. "What are we waiting for, then? Let's mount up."

"*Oui, monsieur*."

While Assan put away the groceries in the kitchen, Kael left a short note for Josie, who'd be home from school at noon. They should be back before then unless CARL had something else up his sleeve, like a flat tire, or an overheated engine, or a crocodile man in search of human flesh. Josie was to stick around the house and to stay away from the river. He could play with the toilet as long as he didn't flush anything that didn't belong in there. That included the papaya, pineapple, mushrooms, avocados, and eggplant in the kitchen. They had to be consumed first.

Kael and Assan headed south out of town. After about ten kilometers, they turned east onto an old logging road. It was almost identical to the one heading out to Zenith's camp. It, too, was being overrun by the forest's advancing armies of vines, branches, and root systems. Driving the truck through such a tangled mess was a bit like steering a comb through a child's snarled hair. Kael could almost hear the forest's screams of protest.

They bounced around in their seats for roughly fifteen minutes before Assan announced, "*E si awé*."

Kael parked the truck. He then followed Assan down a claustrophobic footpath. At times like this, being short had its advantages.

Assan stopped to sniff the air. "We're close. Do you smell it?"

Kael inhaled through his nose. "Either Dexatrim II is cooking or there's rotting meat out there."

Assan pointed off the trail. "It's that way."

As they pushed through the thick underbrush, the odor of decomposition became more pungent. Kael heard the flies buzzing before he saw what was left of the elephant's carcass. It was mostly hidden behind the massive flange-like roots of a kapoc tree. Up close, the remains didn't much resemble an elephant. It looked like someone had draped a thin, dingy sheet over a few piles of rocks. The shroud of skin was torn in places, revealing bits of bone and moving masses of maggots. Kael thought he might never be able to eat macaroni again.

The tusks were missing. They had been ripped from the elephant's face, which no longer looked anything like a face. It was hard to believe that this maggot motel was once five tons of living, breathing pachyderm.

Assan said, "It's been here a while, maybe two or three months."

"Let me guess," said Kael. "It didn't die of natural causes."

Assan crouched down to examine the head. He picked up a stick and began poking around the partially exposed skull. At one point, the stick plunged into an opening.

"A gunshot wound," said Assan. "Very large caliber. Maybe a .375 or .458."

Kael knew all about .375s and .458s. They were the calibers of choice for big-game safari hunters in Africa, as well as bear hunters in Alaska. It was just one more similarity between the two places to pass on to Tallin. A bullet that big could stop a train, and the exit wound would be tunnel-like through which one could drive another train.

"Are you sure? That's pretty heavy artillery."

"*Oui, monsieur*. Most of the local poachers use old *mas* .36 French military rifles. They leave much smaller holes than this one."

"So," said Kael stroking his beard, "we're talking about an expensive rifle. Who around here could afford something like that?" He knew the answer even before he finished asking.

Assan responded in a whisper anyway, "The *sous-préfet*, the police commissioner and the mayor."

"The Three Stooges," said Kael in a normal voice, "and I'm buying them beers this evening."

There wasn't much more they could do with the putrefying elephant. Soon the forest would reclaim everything but the bones. Eventually, those too would disintegrate into the soil, providing nutrients for new plant life. A thousand years from now, a one-hundred-foot-tall red mahogany might grow in this very spot. That thought comforted

Kael for a few seconds until he realized that a futuristic logger would probably come and cut it down with his laser chainsaw to make thousands of carved wooden elephants, miniature replicas of a species gone extinct hundreds of years earlier.

During the drive back home, Kael asked Assan to quietly check into the poaching activities of Moe, Larry, and Curly. He said, "We probably can't get them for this particular elephant, but we might be able to nab them on something."

"*Inshallah*," said Assan.

* * * * * * * * * * * * * * * * * * * *

By the time Kael arrived one half hour early for the eight o'clock p.m. slide show, the mayor's Chainsaw Bar was filled to capacity. The whole village had turned out. Several panels from one wall of the bar had been removed to allow those who couldn't push in the opportunity to view the proceedings from a swept plot of dirt out front.

At first, Kael hoped that this architectural modification was the mayor's idea and not that of a surging, unruly crowd. Then he remembered the dead elephant and his initial feelings of compassion for Mayor Likéké's legitimate business seemed inappropriate. This was puzzling to Kael, because it was the first time in his memory that he was not in complete support of a drinking establishment.

He made his way through the throng of humanity, many of whom were more concerned with trying to make a buck rather than finding a good seat. Small-time entrepreneurs were hawking cigarettes, candy, peanuts, palm wine, corn whiskey, sugar-coated balls of sesame seeds, *beignets*, and fried plantains. Kael politely refused all offers. At the bar's entrance, he was greeted by a bouncer who could have played the entire left side of the Dallas Cowboys' offensive line. Kael introduced himself as the show's producer and was allowed to pass. Once inside, he found Paige setting up the projector. She was wearing a loose-fitting jumper of African material. The pattern looked like bugs, but they could have been microscopic parasites magnified thousands of times.

"Quite the crowd, huh?"

Paige looked up. "I just hope none of them have anything contagious like T.B. or typhoid. The whole village will be infected in one night."

"Nothing happens that fast in Africa," said Kael. "Are you ready?"

"Just about. *Monsieur le Maire* even patched in a microphone, so everyone outside can hear, too."

"That sounds awfully generous." He spotted the mayor in full cowboy regalia, minus the boots. He was working the room, strutting from table to table to shake everyone's hand. "Call me cynical, but I have a feeling he'll want to use that microphone for some political campaigning before the night is through. I now know why he was so enthusiastic about this whole thing and it wasn't just for the beer sales."

"So what?" said Paige. "He wins, but so do we, right?"

"In theory," said Kael.

Bermuda and Zenith showed up with Assan and Josie a little before eight. They all joined Kael at a table set up at the front for the mayor and his distinguished guests. Even Assan was welcomed. The mayor really was reaching out for votes.

There were still two empty seats—those reserved for the *sous-préfet* and the police commissioner. They would arrive only at their convenience, immune from the eight o'clock invitation. Being timeless was a perk that came with their positions of power. Kael hypothesized that Central Africa probably wouldn't join the twentieth century until roughly the twenty-first or twenty-second centuries. By then, its leaders would have decided that they were ready for a fashionably late entrance into the modern era.

Waiting around in a bar was anything but torture for Kael. He bought a round for the table and had one sent over to Paige, who was dutifully standing guard by the slide projector.

More than halfway through his beer, the din of laughter and chatter subsided. Kael turned around to see the *sous-préfet* and the police commissioner entering the bar. They were dressed in similarly tailored leisure suits. The police commissioner's was a conservative business gray. The *sous-préfet's* was another flavor from his fruit-bowl collection. This one was Granny Smith green.

They both seemed to bask in the attention lavished upon them. Everyone wanted to shake their hands, and they were more than happy to reciprocate. There was a lot of, "You've arrived?" with the "you" in the plural or more respectful form. Kael secretly yearned to hear some smart aleck shout out, "You've arrived... forty minutes late." But no one did.

When they finally made it to their seats, they still had plenty of handshakes and smiles left over, even for Assan, who politely offered up one of his hands like everyone else. Allah must have instructed him to leave his wrist-grabbing greeting of respect at home this evening. It was a bold statement for Assan, at least in Kael's mind, and he wondered if anyone else had noticed.

After everyone was strategically seated—Assan was placed at one end while the police commissioner was at the other—Kael asked *Messieurs* Wabunda and Yakonomingui for their drink requests. Not surprisingly, they both ordered Guiness Stouts, the most expensive item on the menu and the official beverage of choice for pretentious *fonctionnaires*.

The mayor walked over to Paige's projection table. He lifted the microphone to his mouth. "Is it on?" His voice exploded through the speakers. "Good. Welcome, citizens of Bayanga. Tonight, our American neighbors will entertain us with a slide show. But before that, I have a few announcements. First, if your glasses are empty, order your drinks now because the bar will be closed during the actual presentation, which I'm told will take approximately thirty minutes." Over the grumbles that didn't require a microphone to be heard, he continued. "Don't worry. When the show is finished, we'll open up the bar again, and you can drink until your money runs out." He laughed at his own joke. "My second announcement concerns the sawmill. Another logging company has assured me that they are extremely interested in coming to Bayanga soon to put everyone back to work, and they've promised that they will pay even higher wages than before."

The police commissioner and the *sous-préfet* started the applause. It quickly spread throughout the bar until the only ones not clapping were "the American neighbors" and Assan, who was guilty by association.

Kael caught Paige's glance. He shrugged his shoulders and mouthed the word, "politics."

She responded by mouthing the word, "sucks."

When the room was almost quiet again, the mayor said, "*Merci. Merci bien.*" He pulled a folded piece of paper from the breast pocket of his Western-style shirt. "I have a final announcement."

Kael applauded. Josie followed his father's lead and joined in.

The mayor said, "*Merci. Merci bien.* The document I hold in my hands is a list of names. It was compiled by myself, *Monsieur le Sous-Préfet et Monsieur le Commissaire de la Police*." He ceremoniously unfolded the paper.

Kael leaned close to Bermuda's ear and whispered, "I don't know about you, but I'm pulling for Miss California to win. I really liked her talent of applying suntan lotion evenly over her entire body." Bermuda elbowed him in the ribs.

The mayor held the paper high over his head and waved it at the crowd. "There are six names on the list. Each one is a known crocodile man living within our jurisdiction. We know who you are. We know where you live."

Kael shifted his gaze to Assan, who seemed unaffected by the mayor's threats. *Allah akbar*, no doubt. Assan's only visible reaction occurred just after Josie draped a reassuring arm across his friend's shoulders: he patted the boy's bare knee. Kael couldn't have been more proud of either one of them.

The mayor stared in the general direction of Assan. "Let this serve as a warning. If there are any incidents of sorcery occurring near the river, we will find you and lock you up for many years, no matter who you know." After pausing several seconds to let his words sink in, he smiled. "Now sit back and enjoy the show."

Kael watched the mayor walk back to his table, the same one where less than an hour earlier he had welcomed Assan with a vigorous handshake. This was the behavior of an individual high on mood-altering drugs, or just one of CARL's soldiers doing his job. Nick had been right. When it came to lying, backstabbing, and being two-faced, few could compete with Bayanga's ruling triumvirate.

While The Three Stooges congratulated one another with pumping handshakes and mirrored looks of superiority, Kael joined Josie, Zenith, Bermuda and Paige, who had gathered around Assan to lend him their support.

Kael spoke to Assan. "It's still not too late for Hawaii."

Zenith said, "I'm there."

Bermuda said, "Can I get on that list, too?"

"No fair," grumbled Paige. "I've still got a year and a half left on my Peace Corps contract here."

"We'll save you a spot on the beach," said Bermuda.

Assan remained silent throughout, so Kael asked him, "What does *Allah* want you to do?"

Assan smiled. "He wants me to stay with you, *monsieur*. We have much work to do."

Kael looked past Assan to where The Three Stooges were huddled together. "We certainly do."

The slide show would be almost anti-climactic since the mayor had already provided the entertainment for the evening with his tales of crocodile men and generous logging companies. As the project director, it was Kael's job to rally the troops.

"All right, kids. Let's not forget what they say in the theater: 'The show must go on.'"

"They also say, 'Break the mayor's legs,'" said Zenith.

"I believe that's, 'Break *a* leg,'" said Kael.

"I like Zenith's version better," said Bermuda.

"Me, too," said Paige. "A femoral fracture would lay him up for months."

"As tempting as that sounds," said Kael, "I think TRAP, Peace Corps and Yale University all frown on assault and battery."

"Not if we're talking about a Harvard grad," said Bermuda.

"Fair enough," said Kael. "Raise your hand if you think the mayor went to Harvard?" When no one's arm moved, he said, "Raise your hand if you think the mayor can even spell Harvard?" There were lots of smiles, but not one hand budged. "I say we just bore him to death with Paige's slide show."

"Let's get it on," said Paige puffing up her chest. She swaggered over to her spot next to the slide projector and microphone.

Zenith shook her head. "Anybody here think Paige can spell Harvard?"

The slide show went well. It told the story of a little girl who dreams one night that a giant butterfly wakes her and offers to teach her about the magic of the rain forest. She climbs on his back and, along with the viewing audience, discovers a hidden treasure of beauty, splendor, and goodness that is important to her family, her village, her country and her own uncertain future.

Paige's original idea had the little girl hitching a ride on a disease-spreading tsetse fly. The kinder, gentler butterfly was Kael's suggestion.

Using the mayor's microphone for good instead of evil, Paige narrated in the Sango language. She stuck to the script, except during one of Zenith's slides depicting the rotting carcass of a poached elephant. Instead of saying, "Poachers are destroying our forest," and moving on to the next slide, she ad-libbed by inserting the mayor's own words heard earlier that evening: "We know who you are. We know where you live."

Kael thought it a bit out of character. A friendly butterfly or a little girl would never utter a phrase such as that. He looked at The Three Stooges. There were no visible reactions from any of them. The mayor seemed to be daydreaming. He was probably busy adding up the night's bar receipts in his head. Maybe that was why he wore sandals instead of cowboy boots: his toes were more accessible for counting purposes.

The *sous-préfet* and the police commissioner hadn't been paying attention, either. They were still engaged in a hushed conversation that had started several slides earlier. In Kael's mind, they were greedily discussing just how big their cut should be.

When the slide show ended, the audience clapped enthusiastically. The mayor quickly took over the microphone. He even assumed credit for the raucous applause.

"*Merci. Merci bien. Oui, mesdames et messieurs,* the bar is now open for your drink orders. Don't go home thirsty. Stay. Dance. Drink."

As if on cue, one of the mayor's flunkies started playing a scratchy record of African *soucous* music. Guitars, horns, drums and harmonized Zairian voices boomed through the strained speakers at a volume several notches above comfortable. Within seconds, two dozen couples had already packed the cement dance floor.

Kael enjoyed watching Central Africans dance. Their movements, unlike his own, looked effortless. It was all in the hips. The upper body just went along for the ride. Why, in a country rife with disease, high infant mortality rates, and low average life spans, was no Central African child cursed with the most common American birth defect: two left feet?

Kael suddenly had the beginnings of a new theory. He made his way over to Paige, who had just finished packing up the projector.

"Do you have your copy of *The Encyclopedia of Infectious Tropical Diseases* handy?"

"Right here in my backpack."

"Great. Could you check and see if dancing is listed?"

"Dancing?"

"Yeah, I think it may be caused by a parasite with rhythm and I want to know how to get it."

She pointed toward the dance floor. "My suggestion would be to kiss the mayor. If dancing is a disease, he's got it."

Kael saw why she had directed his attention to the dance floor. *Monsieur le Maire* was up, shuffling his feet and grinding his hips with his partner, *Monsieur le Sous-Préfet.* This was not unusual behavior in Central Africa. Men often danced with other men. They weren't homosexuals. They were just full of parasites, if Kael's theory was valid.

"Excellent idea," he said. "I've been informed that you know who he is and where he lives."

Paige cringed. "I'm sorry. Maybe I have a parasite that makes me blurt out things like that."

"Don't worry about it. All they heard tonight was the applause and the constant ka-chinging sound of their cash register."

The mayor and the *sous-préfet* were joined on the dance floor by the police commissioner. He approached his fellow Stooges as if to cut in, but neither one sat down. They just made a space for him. For such a big man, he was feather light on his feet. He definitely had the parasite, and it had probably laid eggs.

"Just look at them," said Paige. "They make me sick."

"What doesn't?" said Kael with a grin.

Paige stuck her tongue out at him. "Dancing, for one."

Kael stood up. "We'll just see about that. During my first attempt at the samba, I nearly dislocated a hip."

"Were you in much pain?"

"Not at all. The hip in question belonged to my dance partner."

\* \* \* \* \* \* \* \* \* \* \* \* \* \* \* \* \* \*

Thirty-six hours after the slide show, Kael was summoned to the office of the *sous-préfet*. Finding him at his desk at the scheduled appointment time was a bit of a surprise. That he was accompanied by the mayor and the police commissioner was not. Stooges tended to travel in packs of three. Kael suspected that CARL was hiding in a nearby closet, listening and plotting out his next bizarre scheme.

After the prerequisite handshakes, Kael took his reserved seat between the mayor and the police commissioner. The *sous-préfet* didn't waste any time with small talk about the shade of his nail polish boldly matching the orange of his leisure suit.

"We've called you here because of some serious allegations."

Kael asked, "Does it have anything to do with my dancing?"

"No," said the *sous-préfet*. "It concerns your organization's involvement in poaching activities."

Kael wondered if they knew that Assan had begun looking into their operation. "That's part of our job. TRAP is following the directive of your own government to arrest and prosecute poachers caught within the Doli-Ngili Reserve."

The police commissioner asked, "Does that include your own employees?"

Kael smiled at the inference. "I can say without a doubt that no one working for TRAP is poaching." He almost added that such a scenario would be tantamount to a policeman stealing, but decided that wasn't such a good example.

The police commissioner asked, "Does one of your researchers, a *Mademoiselle* Zenith Rocco, own a tranquilizer gun?"

"It's not a tranquilizer gun," said Kael. "It shoots darts for taking elephant skin samples.

The dart falls to the ground with a tiny core of skin that can be analyzed to find out who is related to whom. The elephant is not tranquilized. It walks away unharmed."

"*Très interessant*," said the police commissioner. "Does *Mademoiselle* Rocco own a chainsaw?"

"She might," said Kael. "I do. I keep it in my truck for clearing fallen trees blocking the road."

"We know," said the mayor.

Kael figured that Jacques, the *sous-préfet*'s guardian/spy had probably poked his big nose around the truck, sniffing out anything that might get some coins thrown his way.

"What is the significance of a chainsaw?" he asked.

The police commissioner leaned in closer. "When you combine it with a tranquilizer gun, isn't it obvious?"

"No," said Kael calmly staring back into the police commissioner's bloodshot eyes.

"Did the C.I.A. teach you to lie so well?" asked the *sous-préfet*.

"I'm not lying about anything," said Kael.

The *sous-préfet* said, "You're very good. The C.I.A. must have excellent instructors." The mayor and the police commissioner nodded in agreement.

Kael took a deep, fortifying breath through his nose. Even though it reeked of body odor, he held it in his lungs for a few seconds before exhaling slowly through his mouth. "*Messieurs*, why don't you make like ink and get to the point?"

"Very well," said the police commissioner. "We believe your organization is tranquilizing elephants, and while said elephants are asleep, you cut off their tusks with a chainsaw."

"What?" said Kael not knowing whether to laugh or scream. "And I thought my theories were out there. You're kidding, right?"

"Not at all," said the mayor. "We have proof."

"A chainsaw in the back of my truck doesn't prove anything," said Kael.

"We saw your slides," said the mayor.

"I know," said Kael. "I was there."

"Then you saw the elephants without tusks," said the *sous-préfet*.

"The only elephant without tusks was the rotting carcass of one that had been poached, and I can assure you that it was not killed by TRAP," said Kael.

The police commissioner said, "We're talking about the elephants still able to walk around."

"So," said Kael, "let me see if I've got this right. Once TRAP cuts off the tusks with a chainsaw, the elephant wakes up from his drug-induced sleep to go about his business as usual, just minus his two front teeth?"

"*Exactement*," said the mayor.

"This theory of yours just keeps getting better all the time," said Kael struggling to keep a straight face. It suddenly occurred to him that there was more. "Are you also saying that after we perform these illegal harvests, we take pictures of the elephants and then flash them around at village slide shows for everyone to see?"

"*Exactement*," said the mayor.

Kael laughed. He couldn't help it any more than he could stop his knee from jerking if some doctor tapped it with a little tomahawk-shaped hammer. "There's just one small problem with your theory, guys: every elephant in the slide show, except the dead one, had two normal tusks."

"Your C.I.A. should be very proud," said the *sous-préfet*.

"I know I'm impressed," said the mayor.

"I applaud your training," said the police commissioner. "If it weren't for the photographic evidence, you'd be very convincing. You see, *monsieur*, we saw the slides. The whole village did. I counted at least six elephants with no tusks or only one."

Kael was flabbergasted, but it somehow seemed appropriate that the number of mutilated elephants observed by the police commissioner was also the number of alleged crocodile men operating within the region. Rather than get upset, he remained rational. Someone in the room had to be the voice of reason.

"I don't recall seeing any elephants like you've described in the slide show," he said, "but I have in the past seen healthy elephants that have lost a tusk due to an injury of some sort. Also, some tusks are simply not as well-developed as others." He almost added, "like your brains, for example," but held back. Nick would have been proud of his restraint. "Maybe you just saw tusks that weren't as long as you thought they should be. We can blame that trend on poachers. They prefer elephants with long tusks because they're worth more. That means that the only elephants left to breed are the ones with short tusks, and when short-tusked elephants reproduce, their offspring will more than likely have short tusks as well."

The police commissioner clapped his hands. "You tell a good story. This one was just as entertaining and just as believable as a giant talking butterfly."

"I knew I should have included a crocodile man in there somewhere," said Kael sarcastically.

"No need," said the police commissioner. "We know that Assan is involved, too."

"Here's an even crazier idea," said Kael. "Why don't we go over to my house right now and review the slides together? With a little luck, we can clear things up and get back to arguing over more mundane subjects like the connection between the C.I.A. and TRAP."

"That's not necessary," said the police commissioner. "We've already seen your slides."

The mayor added, "And we have no doubt that you have doctored them by now to fit your outrageous story."

"If that's the case," said Kael, "why wait until after the slide show to doctor them? Wouldn't it have been smarter to do so before, or simply not use them in the first place?"

The police commissioner punched the *sous-préfet*'s desktop. "You Americans think you can get away with anything. This time, however, you underestimated our detection abilities."

"I won't dispute that." Kael felt like he had been committed to an insane asylum where the patients were in charge. He wished some secretary had been taking minutes of this meeting of the mindless. A word-for-word transcription would be funnier than any joke he could possibly tell Nick.

The police commissioner asked, "Do you find this humorous, *Monsieur* Husker?"

Kael suddenly realized that he'd been smiling. "I'd say no, but I'd be lying."

"What's one more tree in a forest?" asked the police commissioner.

Kael wanted to strangle the man with his own penis. Then, the mayor. Then, the *sous-préfet*. Tomorrow's fantasy headline would read, *DICK DICKED; PRICK PRICKED; SOUS-PREFET SAVED BY SHORTCOMINGS; CLAIMS HE WAS INCHES FROM DEATH.*

Kael felt much better. The only revenge he ever truly needed took place in his own fertile mind—that and a snide comment. He smiled at the police commissioner. "Is the sky blue in your world, *monsieur*?"

He watched the police commissioner's hands begin to tremble. The fingers twitched as they splayed out, attempting to span the *sous-préfet*'s vast desktop acreage. Before they reached up to wrap around Kael's vulnerable throat, Kael stood up. Putting distance between himself and the epicenter of seismic activity seemed like the smart thing to do.

"I should be going," he said.

"Quickly," suggested the mayor.

"I'll walk you out," said the *sous-préfet*, obviously anxious to vacate the room as well. Once outside, he whispered, "*Monsieur* Yakonomingui doesn't like you very much."

Kael said, "I think you can speak up. It's no secret."

The *sous-préfet* didn't adjust his volume. This proved to Kael what any Stooges fan knew with certainty: Curly was afraid of Moe.

"He knows you paid Assan's fine. He wants you both out of Bayanga."

"Tell him if he'd never arrested Assan, I probably never would have come."

"I'm not going to tell him something upsetting like that," said the *sous-préfet*, "unless, of course, it's a direct C.I.A. order to test my potential as a field agent. Is it?"

"No," said Kael smiling.

"Good. That would be a tough one. Have you gotten me an application, yet?"

"I'm sure it's coming."

"Excellent. I just wanted to make sure you hadn't forgotten me."

"No chance of that," said Kael.

He returned home and immediately dug out the slides. Since he had no electricity, he couldn't use the projector. Plan B worked just as well, maybe better. He sat out on the deck with the day's first beer in one hand and individual slides held up to the sunlight in the other.

As expected, he couldn't find any elephants with one or no tusks. He heard Assan in the kitchen, having just completed his morning market run. Kael called him out and picked an elephant slide at random. "Look at this and tell me how many elephants without tusks you see."

"*Oui, monsieur.*" Assan examined the slide. "None, *monsieur.*"

"OK. Try this one." Kael handed him another.

Assan concentrated on the second slide. "Two, *monsieur.*"

"Two! Where?"

"The two on the right, *monsieur.* I don't see any tusks on either one of them."

"Let me see that." Kael grabbed for the slide. He held it up. "That's because one is facing away from the camera, and the other, from the shoulders forward, is out of the frame."

"*Oui, monsieur*, but you asked me how many elephants without tusks I saw. I saw the elephants, but I didn't see their tusks."

Kael stood so that his back was to Assan. "Do I have a nose, Assan?"

"Of course, *monsieur*."

Kael turned back around, satisfied that he had proven his point. "It's just like with the elephants. We can't see their tusks because of the way the elephants are positioned in the photo, but we can logically assume that they're there."

Assan nervously shifted his weight from one foot to the other and then back again. "It's not the same, *monsieur*."

"Why not?"

"Because I saw your nose before you turned around. I didn't see the elephants in your slide before they turned around or stepped partially out of the picture. They may have tusks. They may not. I can't say for certain."

"Have you been chatting with CARL?"

"Who, *monsieur*?"

"Never mind. What's for lunch?"

"Fish balls."

Kael expected the occasional culinary surprise. After all, this was Africa, a place where people snacked on live termites. But fish balls? He'd never heard of such a thing, but if fish eggs could be considered a delicacy, why not? They probably tasted just like chicken.

He said, "I'm sure they'll be delicious, but in the future, if you ever feel the need to neuter something, do both of us a big favor and start with the police commissioner. OK?"

Assan smiled. "I beg your pardon, *monsieur*, but we're still not seeing the same picture. My fish balls are flakes of boneless fish filet rolled-up, breaded and deep-fried. They were *Mademoiselle* Molly's favorite."

Kael pointed to his own mid-section. "My stomach, which I can't see, but I know it's there, thanks you." His pointing finger dropped about six inches, where it feigned a slashing motion. "And my original request concerning the police commissioner... it still stands."

"*Oui, monsieur*."

# 30

Kael awoke to the incessant chattering of a Greater Honey Guide darting back and forth outside his open window. They were peculiar little birds. They guided people and other large mammals to bees' nests by attracting attention with their distinctive call and then flying towards a source of honey in short bursts, stopping frequently to call and, apparently, to check the progress of the followers. After the honey-craving villagers opened up the nest to feast on the honeycomb, they would often leave some behind for the bird. Many African tribes believed that if they did not, the bird would lead them to a dangerous animal the next time.

Kael wasn't in the mood to chase after a silly little bird. He hadn't even had his first morning cup of coffee yet. So, he just lay there in bed underneath his mosquito net wondering why Molly kept chattering at him while he slept.

He'd had another Molly dream last night. It was the fourth one in five days. Sadly, the dream had become his one and only sleeping partner and it was the first monogamous relationship he'd had in years. He had to admit, though, that he was getting used to its company. This familiarity made it less frightening, but more disturbing, because it refused to go away. It had become the proverbial clingy lover who overstays their welcome.

Kael had assumed Assan's release from prison would have kicked the dream out into the street. No such luck. The dream was now receiving its mail in Kael's bed. Next, it would be rearranging the furniture and ordering him to pick up his dirty socks and put them in the clothes hamper where they belonged.

Last night's dream had a new wrinkle: the crocodile man was now armed with more than just powerful claws. In one armor-plated reptilian hand, he held the barrel of a .375 caliber rifle. He used the butt end to keep Molly's head underwater. At least he didn't use a tranquilizer gun and a chainsaw.

What did it all mean? The sudden appearance of the .375 made sense. It had been on Kael's mind a lot lately, especially since Assan had recently discovered two more elephants lying dead in a remote streambed. Both were young females and both had been killed with .375 bullets drilled right through their brains. Their tusks, probably not yet fully grown, had been removed. Size didn't seem to matter anymore.

The crocodile man in Kael's dream continued to wear a cowboy hat just like the mayor. Did Mayor Likéké also own a .375? Was he somehow involved in Molly's death? Was Molly pointing out her killer? If it was the mayor, the *sous-préfet* and the police commissioner had to be in on it, too. Kael wasn't ready to theorize just yet, but he began to wonder if his dreams would stop when he brought down The Three Stooges, not that he needed any additional incentive.

So far, Assan hadn't found out much more than what the two of them already knew: The Three Stooges were damaged goods. Their mutual mission in life was to rid Bayanga of TRAP. Their claim of tranquilizer guns and chainsaws was just an elaborate smokescreen to protect the region's real poachers: themselves.

In the two weeks since the slide show, they had used every opportunity to chastise TRAP in public. Official town meetings couldn't start without at least one of the Stooges mentioning something about tranquilizer guns and chainsaws. Around the TRAP watercooler in Bayanga it became known as the "TGC Obsession." Zenith thought TGC should stand for "Three Goddamned Crooks." Bermuda liked "The Grand Conspiracy." Kael preferred "There Goes CARL."

The honey guide was back. He chattered noisily as he impolitely peeked into Kael's open window for assistance. He was annoyingly persistent.

"I don't want any honey," said Kael, who suddenly realized he'd never uttered that particular phrase in bed before, "but go find me a .375 and we'll talk."

The honey guide zoomed off again. Kael couldn't tell in which direction the bird was headed this time, but the obvious guess was towards the mayor's house.

Kael wished it were that easy. Maybe it was. He just needed someone who would act like a Greater Honey Guide, someone with a powerful craving who would sing to get it. One indigenous species came to mind: the Bird-Brained Leisure-Suited *Sous-Préfet*. He was perfect and Kael had just what he wanted, or at least could make one up: a C.I.A. application.

He reached under the mosquito net for the pen and paper sitting on the table next to the bed. Three essay-type questions immediately came to mind: 1) As an agent of the C.I.A., you must be able to carry out missions of extreme secrecy. Do you have any prior experience with covert and/or illegal operations? Give examples, and please be specific; 2) As an agent of the C.I.A., you must have an extensive knowledge of firearms.

List all guns and calibers with which you are familiar, keeping in mind that the .375 has recently been named the official C.I.A. weapon of choice; 3) Agents of the C.I.A. are often asked to kill. Do you have any prior experience with murder?

Kael was having fun. He'd be sure to include a statement to the effect, "Failure to completely answer any of the questions will result in your disqualification as a potential agent for the C.I.A." His final instructions would be, "When you have completed all the questions, seal the application in a plain white business envelope and deliver it with the code words, 'Honey guides love Honey Nut Cheerios' to the person who gave you the application. Tell no one of your official candidacy with the C.I.A. You will be contacted at a later date. Have a nice day."

He'd fool around with it for a day or two. It had to be convincing. He'd get some ideas from the women. Paige would probably want to know the *sous-préfet*'s medical history. Zenith could type up the application on her computer. Maybe she could come up with a fake C.I.A. letterhead to give it an official look, not that the *sous-préfet* would doubt the document's authenticity. Kael was only giving him what he wanted, sort of.

There was a "*Ko ko ko*" at Kael's bedroom door.

"*Oui?*"

From behind the door, Assan said, "The coffee is ready, *monsieur*. I also made *beignets*, but I must run quickly to the market. We're out of honey."

Kael smiled. The honey guide had been right to drop by this morning. "*Merci*, Assan. As long as you're there, pick up some bread, too."

"*Oui, monsieur.*"

Kael stretched. What a big-dot day. He hadn't even crawled out of bed yet and he'd already accomplished two things: buying bread and bamboozling the *sous-préfet*. *Père* Norbert would be proud.

Kael slipped into some clothes and found Josie sitting at the breakfast table. He was playing with a *beignet* on his plate as if it were a soccer ball. The index and middle fingers of his left hand "kicked" the ball of fried dough to his opponent, the fingers of his right hand.

"*Bonjour, Papa*. The score is tied, three to three."

Kael's hand ran on to the field of play and snatched up the ball, which he then popped into his mouth. "Goal! USA wins!"

"But the game was between *Centrafrique* and the Congo."

"USA wins, anyway. We're not very good at soccer, but when it comes to eating, we're number one."

Kael was already on his second cup of coffee when Assan returned with the honey. He placed it on the table between Kael and Josie. Josie grabbed it first.

"*Centrafrique* wins!" he announced to the crowd of three.

Assan ignored the brief pandemonium. "I bought more than honey, *monsieur*."

"Great," said Kael. "No sense wasting a trip to the market for just one item. Did you get the bread?"

"*Oui, monsieur*. I also paid for some information about four poached elephants."

This woke Kael up better than his two cups of coffee. "Where?"

Assan hesitated. "Are you asking where I got the information or where the elephants are?"

"Both."

"Some Pygmies in the market told me. I gave them five hundred francs. They said the four elephants are on the *Legué ti Crépuscule*."

*Legué ti Crépuscule* was a combination of Sango and French. Loosely translated, it meant, "the path of dusk." Kael had never heard of it. "Do you know where to find this *Legué ti Crépuscule*?"

"*Oui, monsieur*. It is a trail several kilometers past *Mademoiselle* Zenith's camp."

"Excellent," said Kael. "We can stop and pick her up. She may be interested in this."

"Can I come, too?" asked Josie, honey dripping from his mouth and fingers.

"Sure," said Kael, "but only if you admit that soccer is a sport for weenies."

"What's a weenie?" asked Josie.

"A soccer player," said Kael.

Josie smiled. "Then I admit that soccer is a sport for soccer players."

"You really are my son," said Kael. "Last one to the truck is a soccer player."

\* \* \* \* \* \* \* \* \* \* \* \* \* \* \* \* \* \* \*

They found Zenith replacing the batteries in one of her pound puppies. She looked up only when Kael started to bark.

She yelled down the path. "Come closer and I'll shove a battery up your ass, too."

Kael stopped baying. "You don't have to tell me twice."

"Good. What brings you out here?"

Kael had made his way up the footpath and was now standing next to a kneeling Zenith. "We're on our way to look at four poached elephants. Want to come along? You could bring your fancy computer program and try to identify them by their tail and ear features. Sorry. There won't be any tusks to examine."

Zenith summed up her feelings in one word, "Shit."

"Nicely put," said Kael.

"Figuring out who they are could help my research," Zenith admitted. "I try to keep track of events like that, especially if these four elephants were part of my study group."

"That's what I thought," said Kael.

Zenith closed up her dog's battery case and stood up. "Do you think The Three Stooges had something to do with this?"

Kael sighed. "If we find a cowboy hat or a fruity leisure suit at the murder scene, I'd bet the police commissioner's life on it."

Zenith said, "I'll take a piece of that action. Let me go grab my laptop and I'll meet you back at your truck."

When Zenith jogged up to Kael's idling Toyota, he was waiting behind the steering wheel. Assan and Josie were standing in the bed, leaning on the pick-up's roof.

"Do I get to ride shotgun?" she asked.

"You're lucky," said Kael. "Those two don't know anything about first dibs."

Zenith climbed into the cab. She set her backpack on her lap. "That's one way to look at it. The other is that I had to come all the way to Africa to find not one, but two gentlemen."

Kael shifted the truck into first gear and eased out the clutch. "Lord knows that species died out in New York many years ago. I heard one was spotted in Connecticut, though." He found second gear.

"I can tell you he wasn't from Yale," said Zenith. "So, where are we going?"

"Assan's going to bang on the roof when we get there. It's some place called *Legué ti Crépuscule*, which I guess means 'path of dusk.'"

Zenith chuckled. "I suppose *Legué ti Crépuscule*, in its simplest translation, could mean 'path of dusk,' but it doesn't. And I should know because I helped name it. It's supposed to mean 'Sunset Boulevard.' It's an elephant trail that intersects with another trail the Africans like to call '*Legué ti* Cowboy.'"

"Cowboy Boulevard?" asked Kael.

"Rodeo Drive," said Zenith. "That one's a little tougher to translate into local lingo."

"Why did you get to name them?" asked Kael.

"They're just elephant trails. The forest is full of them. The names aren't official or anything. For research purposes, Bermuda and I came up with the idea of naming the larger trails rather than saying, 'You know that trail about five kilometers past your camp that runs east-west?' Now, we just say Sunset Boulevard and we both know exactly where we're talking about. The Africans have even picked up on them."

"The mayor probably thinks *Legué ti* Cowboy was named after him." Kael down-shifted to negotiate several water-filled potholes in the road. "Why Sunset Boulevard and Rodeo Drive?"

"We were homesick, so we named them after famous roads in our hometowns of New York and L.A. In addition to Sunset Boulevard and Rodeo Drive, there's the Ventura Freeway, the San Diego Freeway, Broadway, Forty-Second Street, Fifth Avenue, the Coast Highway and the New York Thruway."

After about twenty minutes of bouncing around on their seats, Zenith informed Kael that Sunset Boulevard was around the next bend. She had no sooner finished her pronouncement when there was a banging on the roof above them.

Kael slowed to a stop. His peripheral vision caught someone peeking into his open driver's-side window. Turning his head, he gazed into the big, brown face of Assan, who was leaning forward from the bed of the pick-up.

"*E si awé, monsieur.*"

Kael nodded. "*Merci*, Assan."

"*Oui, monsieur.*"

All four exited the truck. They gathered by the front bumper where Sunset Boulevard started. It was a wide, well-worn path that ran perpendicular to the road and deep into the dense forest. Assan took the lead. As usual, Kael brought up the rear. He heard Josie tell Zenith that the last one there was a weenie.

Elephant trails weren't just for elephants. Other animals like bongo and duikers also used them. So did poachers. Along the way, Kael looked for torn pieces of brightly colored polyester snagged on low branches. He didn't find any.

After thirty minutes of steady hiking, Kael was beginning to think that they had been duped out of five hundred francs by some slick Pygmy con men. He asked Assan, "So, where are these poached elephants of yours?"

"Not far," he responded.

Kael looked right at Zenith, who was smiling. "I asked for that, didn't I?"

She nodded in the affirmative. "Rookie mistake."

Kael sighed. "Lead on, Assan. I won't ask any more dumb questions."

"*Oui, monsieur.*"

Ten more minutes and they reached the edge of a large grassy clearing. It was not nearly as bustling with activity as the last one Kael and Josie had visited near Zenith's camp. There they'd witnessed a cocktail party of elephants, bongo, buffalo and bush pigs. Here, a female sitatunga was the only visible mammal. She momentarily looked up from her grazing to check out the approach of Kael and the rest of his troupe. After several seconds of open-mouthed gawking, she went back to her meal with indifference.

"Do you smell it?" asked Assan.

Kael sniffed the air. Something ahead was rancid.

By himself, Assan walked farther up the path. One hundred feet away from the group, he stopped. He turned back and in a loud but calm voice, informed everyone, "*E si awé.*"

The sitatunga, still chewing, sprinted into the cover of the trees.

Kael followed Josie and Zenith to a spot next to Assan, who was now crouched down inspecting what appeared to have been a massive, three-headed, twelve-legged creature. It was covered with flies, maggots and whitewashed bird droppings.

Josie uttered the Sango equivalent of "yuck."

Zenith said, "It looks like an adult and two adolescents."

"That only makes three," said Kael. "I thought there were supposed to be four."

Assan stood up. Kael watched him plod farther up the path. His mannerisms suggested an elephant man more than a crocodile man. His nose rose into the air to search out peculiar odors. With each stride, his head bobbed from left to right and back again. If his ears began to flap, Kael was going to scream.

Fifty feet away, Assan paused. Kael hoped it wasn't to defecate on the path. The elephant man turned around. Thankfully, he didn't trumpet through his nose. His words, however, were just as attention getting.

"I found number four."

The fourth elephant was large, probably a bull. His state of decomposition was comparable to those of the other three, roughly one or two months according to Zenith. This, along with their massive head wounds, suggested that all four were killed at the same time and with the same weapon. To Kael, that meant a .375, and three very greedy Stooges.

Assan said he wanted to explore the clearing a bit. Josie, holding his nose, asked for and received permission to tag along with him.

Kael turned to face Zenith. Something in her stance—a slump of dejection in her shoulders along with a frown on her face that was more severe than the one she displayed when Paige said something non-Ivy Leaguish—made Kael theorize that she was angered by what they had found. This didn't surprise him. Four of her elephants had been slaughtered. Animal researchers often became personally attached to their subjects. The best example was Dian Fossey with her mountain gorillas.

Kael asked, "Can you identify the elephants?"

After a few seconds, Zenith seemed to rediscover her professional manner and answered, "I can't, but my computer should be able to." She opened up her laptop and began the booting-up process. "If these four have been catalogued sometime in the past as part of my database of three thousand individuals, the computer only needs me to enter a few key features like notches on the ears, or old scars, or something as small as missing tufts of hair on the tips of their tails. It shouldn't take more than a few minutes."

Kael asked, "Can it identify their killer, too?"

"Sorry," said Zenith, "but The Three Stooges aren't part of my database."

"They're in mine." Kael waited for Zenith to perform her magic. He understood very little about computers, but he knew that they were no more intelligent than his blender. By pushing a few buttons, a computer sifted through volumes of information in a matter of seconds. A blender functioned just as impressively by making one hell of a margarita. Could a computer serve up a tropical drink? He didn't think so.

Zenith was standing next to the lone bull when she called Kael over. She looked up from her computer screen with the same look of anger she'd displayed earlier. She said, "I'm pretty sure I know who they are."

"All four?"

Zenith nodded. "This one here is Prince Charles. The other three are Lady Diana, William and Harry." She closed her eyes and pinched the skin at the bridge of her nose.

"This sucks. It's enough to make me quit."

"That's what they want," said Kael. Zenith didn't respond, so he said, "I didn't realize you'd given your elephants real names. I thought you'd just use numbers or something."

"Names are easier for me to remember. I called this one Charles because of his big ears. They're huge, even for an elephant. Diana got her name because she often bickered with this one over food and water, not unlike the real-life feuding couple. According to my mitochondrial DNA studies, William and Harry were Diana's offspring. I can't say if Charles was their father or not."

"Have you named all your elephants after famous dysfunctional families?"

"No, some are named after my own dysfunctional family, like my rebellious cousins

Isabelle and Sophie. Others are named for my favorite artists: Pablo Picasso and Vincent Van Gogh. Do you remember that new bull we saw at the edge of the clearing that day with Josie? I named him Kael."

"I'm flattered."

"Don't be. You just happened to be there when I first observed him. And besides, all the good names were already taken."

"Well," said Kael, "it looks like Charles, Diana, William and Harry are available again."

"Yeah. I just don't understand why he killed William and Harry. It makes no sense. Their tusks were years from maturity."

"What a coincidence. So are The Three Stooges." He got her to crack a smile. "We'll get them."

"I doubt it, but everybody's got to have a dream."

"Actually," said Kael, "I'm trying to get rid of one." Glancing over at the highlighted names of Charles, Diana, William and Harry on Zenith's computer screen, he got an idea. "Can you do a quick search for another elephant?"

"Sure. All I need is an accurate description."

"Male. Old. Large, inwardly curving, creamy yellow tusks. Two big notches on his left ear. On his left flank he's got a ragged scar that looks like a backward question mark."

Zenith typed in the data. "Not bad for a rookie. Where did you see this guy?"

"Josie, Assan, and I saw him on the main road between Nola and Bayanga when we first arrived. It was Josie's first encounter with a live elephant."

Zenith looked at her screen. "Hmm... you can tell him that he saw a former President."

"Which one?"

"Ronald Reagan."

"Wow," said Kael. "Not everyone can say that they saw Ronald Reagan shit on the road. How did he earn that name?"

"He's old and he's got a scar on his stomach. The human Ron has one courtesy of John Hinkley's assassination attempt. I don't know how elephant Ron got his." She closed up her computer.

"Thanks. Josie will get a kick out of that. Now, where did he and Assan get to?"

Zenith motioned toward the clearing. "I saw them earlier heading over towards Rodeo Drive, on the other side of *Le Bistro*."

"*Le Bistro*? Don't tell me there's a French cafe way out here."

"Sort of," said Zenith. "This clearing is a favorite watering hole for elephants and other forest animals passing through. They all stop here to eat and drink, just like they do in the clearing near my camp. That one I call Grand Central Station because it's busy all the time. Some other clearings are called The Big Apple, The Hollywood Bowl, Central Park, and Venice Beach."

Kael's geography lesson of American names in very African places was interrupted by Josie who raced down the path and kept repeating, "Guess what I found? Guess what I found?"

Assan plodded behind. He never seemed to do anything in a rush.

Josie finally reached his father's side. For effect, he exaggerated his huffing and puffing, but Kael could see that he wasn't even sweating.

"Guess what I found?"

"Not another dead elephant, I hope," said Kael.

"Smaller."

"A dead baby elephant?"

"Smaller."

"The *sous-préfet*'s brain?"

"Smaller."

"The *sous-préfet*'s penis?"

Josie giggled. "Smaller."

Kael looked at Zenith, but she just shrugged her shoulders. "There is nothing smaller," he said, "except maybe the mayor's conscience or the police commissioner's sense of humor."

"I can hold it in my closed hand," Josie hinted.

"I give up."

"Show him, Assan."

By this time, Assan had caught up. He held out one fist. His fingers blossomed open to reveal a tarnished brass cartridge. "It's from a .375," he said.

"I found it," said Josie.

"It was high in the crook of a tree," said Assan.

Josie said, "I saw something shining in the sunlight, so I asked Assan to boost me up. Can I keep it?"

Kael felt inspired to utter a phrase heard in every cop show: "As soon as the boys in the lab are done with it."

"What boys?" asked Josie.

"Oh, I forgot. We don't have boys in the lab. Come to think of it, we don't have a lab, either. I guess it's yours, then."

Assan handed it over to Josie, who responded with a polite, "*Merci.*" He then ran down the path, holding the cartridge high in the air as if it were a bullet seeking out its next innocent victim.

Assan said, "I climbed up into the tree, too. Several meters above where Josie found the cartridge, I discovered a perch strong enough to support a man. I think it's where our killer sat, *monsieur*. It gives an unobstructed line of sight to where all four elephants fell."

"So, our poaching Stooge isn't afraid of heights." Kael made a mental note to pose a question about acrophobia in the *sous-préfet's* C.I.A. application. He said, "If either of you had the opportunity to ask the *sous-préfet* any question whatsoever, and you were guaranteed of an honest response, what would you want to know? Assan?"

"Does he truly believe I killed *Mademoiselle* Molly?"

"Good. What about you, Zenith?"

"Does he own any clothing in earth tones?"

"Highly doubtful," said Kael.

"What's this all about?" asked Zenith.

"Come on," said Kael. "I'll explain on our way back to the truck. You're going to want to smother me in kisses."

"Highly doubtful," said Zenith.

# 31

In the dream, he was the one being chased through the forest. He was the hunted, not the hunter. He was the frightened victim with nowhere to hide.

In the dream, he tried to run, but couldn't. The vegetation was too thick. It clawed at him like a wild animal tearing at his clothes and scratching his face, arms, and legs. It held on, stubbornly refusing to let go. Where was his machete when he needed it?

In the dream, he used his bruised and bloodied forearms like a battering ram to punch through the tight weave of vines, brambles and woody branches. Progress was slow, but he had to keep moving forward. To stop was to die. Something was behind him. He could hear it crashing through the brush and getting closer. The time for silence and stealth was over. Raw, noisy power was his only chance of escape.

In the dream, he stumbled into a clearing. It appeared from nowhere. One second he was tangled like a fly in a spider's web. The next, he wasn't. So he ran.

In the dream, he was fast. Nothing could catch him. He started to feel better about his predicament. He thought he might get away. Then, he tripped on something unseen. Just before his knees and elbows hit the ground, the dirt beneath him changed into water. He splashed in like a flat stone, and started to sink. He struggled to keep his head above the surface. He wasn't much of a swimmer. His musculature was all wrong. It was too thick, too dense, too compact. Luckily, his strength made up for what he lacked in form, enabling him to awkwardly tread water. He looked back to see what had tripped him up. There, on the bank, was a shiny brass cartridge. Was it the one he had lost? He wanted to go back and pick it up, but he knew he didn't have time. Whatever was pursuing him hadn't given up. It was still coming. He couldn't see it yet, but he could feel its presence. It was angry. It was obsessed. It was hungry.

In the dream, he kicked and flailed until he reached the other side. He didn't look back. He was too busy just trying to stay afloat. As soon as he crawled up on the opposite sandy shore, a light misty rain began to fall. He didn't care. He was already soaked, so a little more couldn't hurt. He wanted to rest, but there was no time. He had to keep running.

In the dream, he followed a muddy trail up the side of a steep hill. At first the rain felt soothing on his face, but the higher he climbed, the harder it poured from the blackening sky. By the time he reached the summit, each drop had the size and sting of a bee. He searched for shelter from the swarm. He found a temporary haven under a small grove of mango trees. Their thick canopy of leaves formed a kind of leaky umbrella. The raindrops that made it through were more like butterflies than bees.

In the dream, he spied a small white cross stuck in the ground at the far end of his arboreal sanctuary. As he walked over for a closer inspection, hundreds of other crosses came into view. They were spread out across the valley and up the side of an adjoining hill. Some had writing on them. Some didn't. One was inscribed with the name Pablo. Others said Vincent, Sophie, Isabelle, Charles, Diana, William, and Harry. There were many more names. Some he recognized. Some he didn't. He looked for, but couldn't find, one marked Ron. For some strange reason, that was discouraging.

In the dream, he stopped checking for names on crosses when he came upon a large rectangular hole in the ground. He stepped closer to the muddy edge and peered into the abyss. He expected it to be black, but it was as white as the crosses. He couldn't distinguish where the sides ended and the bottom began. He craned his neck for a better view. That was when the waterlogged earth beneath him gave way. There was nothing he could do to keep from sliding in.

In the dream, he floated more than fell. It took a long time to reach the bottom. He didn't panic on the way down. He stretched out all four limbs. He wasn't a man out of control. He was a flying squirrel, gliding from an upper branch to a lower one. His landing was cushioned by a humped island of money rising up out of the mucky bottom. He hit the pile of wet bills just off center and slid all the way down on his stomach, feet-first. When he finally skidded to a stop, his first thought was that he was rich. As he giddily stuffed his pockets with fistfuls of money, it dawned on him that for the time being, he was safe, too. Whatever had been following him surely wouldn't hurl itself into the hole. Or would it? His next thought was that he had to get out. He could always come back later to retrieve his fortune.

In the dream, he struggled to climb back up the pile of money, but it was like trying to swim up a waterfall. He gave up after numerous attempts left him exhausted and no closer to his destination. He next tried to scale the sheer, slippery sides of the pit. That didn't work, either. There was nothing for a finger or toe to grab onto. He couldn't yell for help. The thing that was chasing him might hear. There was nothing he could do. He was trapped.

In the dream, it continued to rain. Muddy rivulets cascaded down the sides of his earthen prison, filling the bottom with warm brown water. It rose up past his ankles, his calves and his knees. He tried to scramble higher up the money pile, but each step triggered an avalanche of twenty-thousand-franc notes that swept him down the mountainside and back into the rapidly rising water. When it reached his waist, he got an idea: he could float out. He'd ascend with the water. It was all so simple.

In the dream, he looked skyward. This time he took pleasure in the sting of each raindrop as it collided with his face. He shut his eyes to the liquid darts, but opened his mouth to drink in some of the life-saving pain. It was delicious. It tasted like cigarettes.

In the dream, a trumpet sounded from above. High piercing notes rained down on him. Through squinted eyes, he found the source of the noise: peering over the edge of the pit loomed the large gray head of an elephant. But there was something terribly wrong about it. Its tusks didn't originate from the upper jaw and swoop down. They sprang out of the top of its massive head and flared off to either side like some sort of weird mutation of an elephant and a long-horned steer. No matter where those two tusks/horns popped out of, they were undoubtedly worth a lot of money. Where was his gun when he needed it?

In the dream, both tusks/horns suddenly broke away from the elephant's head. They plummeted down with the rain, aiming right for him. He had nowhere to run, nowhere to hide. In a knee-jerk reaction, he held his hands up as if to miraculously fend off the two approaching projectiles. He might as well have spit at them. Just before they impaled his chest, he screamed, "Why, why, why?"

In the middle of the night, Bolo awoke to the sound of a gentle rain. Water leaked through his thatched roof and plopped down on to his left cheek. He positioned his mouth directly underneath the constant drip. Just water. It didn't taste anything like cigarettes. He rolled over and went back to sleep.

# 32

'Twas the night before Christmas,
And all the while,
Kael was still stirring,
Bothered by a creature, half-man, half-crocodile.
Josie and Assan were nestled,
All snug in their beds,
While visions of murder danced through Kael's head.
Molly in her tie-dye,
And the crocodile man in a cap,
Kept Kael from settling down for a long winter's nap.

That, and the ninety-nine percent humidity. Cold beers and colder bucket showers helped battle the greenhouse-like conditions, but only for a little while. Within minutes of toweling off, he was perspiring again. It was almost as if his skin had sprung thousands of tiny leaks. Why couldn't dreams bubble to the surface and evacuate as easily?

There was a barely audible "*Ko ko ko*" at his door. Did Santa Claus do that in Africa, since there were few chimneys to climb down? He asked who was there.

"Me," came the muffled reply.

"Santa?" asked Kael, hopeful that this would be the year he'd finally get his pony.

"No."

Kael was crushed. "Then who is it?"

"Me."

This exchange could go on ad infinitum. Kael got up off the couch and pushed open the door. No one was on the other side, but someone was standing back in the shadows of the bamboo grove.

In non-native English, but much more decipherable than a Texas drawl, the stranger said, "Honey guides love Honey Nut Cheerios." One arm clad in a plum polyester fabric was thrust into the dim light. A hand with a long red pinky fingernail held a thick white business envelope.

Kael reached out and accepted the offering. "This is all very C.I.A.-like," he said.

"That's good, isn't it?" asked the stranger in the shadows.

"Of course. It will reflect favorably on your application as long as you've answered every question truthfully and completely."

"I have," said the stranger. "I even gave answers to questions you didn't ask."

"That's very commendable," said Kael. "At this initial stage of the application process, being honest and thorough are a candidate's best chance for acceptance. Once you're a C.I.A. operative, you'll have plenty of opportunities to lie and withhold information."

"I'm already very good at that, too," said the stranger.

"So I've heard. On behalf of the C.I.A., we thank you for your enthusiasm."

The stranger stepped out of the shadows to shake Kael's hand. The light spilling out from the open doorway hit the *sous-préfet*'s face like a spotlight. He didn't seem to mind that his cover was blown.

"*Merci*. I'm counting on you to make certain that my application goes immediately to the director of the C.I.A. in Washington."

With his free hand, Kael held up the thick envelope. It took all of his self-control to keep from ripping it open like that first present on Christmas morning. "I promise that this will go to the proper authority as soon as possible."

"*Merci. Merci beaucoup.*"

"Merry Christmas," said Kael. Turning to re-enter his house, he slapped the envelope against his bare, damp thigh. There really was a Santa Claus, after all, and he wore polyester.

Kael showed uncommon restraint, but like Christmas, this was an event worth celebrating. Before opening the envelope, he went to the refrigerator and removed a cold Mocaf. He even poured it into a clean, non-chipped glass. It didn't get more special than that. Accompanied by the bottle, the full glass and the envelope, he retired to the comfort of his living room.

He sat on the couch next to the Christmas tree: a six-foot-high section of bamboo decorated with shiny stones and serrated shells. A dried-up skin, which had been shed by some adolescent snake going through a growth spurt, was suspended like a garland between several branches. And dangling by a piece of string from a limb near the top was the .375 cartridge discovered out at *Le Bistro*. That was what caught Kael's eye as he tore into the envelope.

The first page of the application summarized the *sous-préfet*'s medical history. Paige would be pleased, as would her alma mater's medical school if she ever convinced him to donate his corpse for scientific research. He was a polyester petri dish of malaria, amoebic dysentery, filaria, scabies, ringworm, chiggoe infestation and shistosomiasis. He'd also had gonorrhea thirteen times. He probably refused to wear condoms since they didn't come in polyester.

Kael flipped the page, anxious to check out the *sous-préfet*'s responses to the essay questions. For the most part, he didn't disappoint. He was just as candid, bragging about his nefarious activities like someone overdosing on truth serum. Some of his claims were mind-boggling, even for Africa, where lies grew faster and taller than bamboo.

He freely admitted to his involvement in numerous covert or illegal enterprises such as embezzling of public funds, tax scams, poaching, and the trafficking of bush meat. He named his partners-in-crime as Police Commissioner Yakonomingui and Mayor Likéké.

It came as no surprise that the meat trafficking was connected to the mayor's Cameroon beer runs. What stunned Kael were the details of The Three Stooges' poaching operation.

According to the *sous-préfet*, two cousins of the mayor had been surreptitiously placed close to TRAP to gather information about the organization, as well as the whereabouts of elephants. The first cousin was Jacques, the ancient sawmill guardian. Kael already knew about him. He was harmless, except to Kael's beer supply. The mayor's other cousin was someone called Mangala. That name didn't ring any immediate bells, so Kael read on hoping to unmask the mole. He soon discovered that he *did* know *Monsieur* Mangala, but by his aliases of Dexatrim II and The Appetite Assassin. He was Zenith's incompetent cook.

If Zenith ever found out, the man's spying days were over. So were his days of walking, eating solid foods, and breathing without the aid of a respirator. There had to be a way of handling this delicate situation. Kael didn't want to end up with a dead cook and an American researcher in prison. Assan was sure to have some less-violent suggestions. Kael would ask him in the morning after they'd opened up their Christmas presents.

Another question he needed to pose to Assan was, "Who is Bolo?" The *sous-préfet* had fingered him as their poacher-for-hire. He was the one who did the actual killing. Kael figured that The Three Stooges were able to tell Bolo where the elephants were because of information supplied to them via Dexatrim II. It was an ingenious operation, far more sophisticated than a typical Three Stooges slapstick routine like the one about tranquilizer guns and chainsaws.

The next two essay questions elicited rather vague responses from the *sous-préfet*. He would sooner accept his poor fashion sense than admit to a lack of knowledge about anything, and that included firearms. He explained that his role in the poaching operation was not that of a shooter, but more as a planner or organizer. He wrote, "My brain is much stronger than my trigger finger. And doesn't the I in C.I.A. stand for intelligence?"

Kael wondered if it was the *sous-préfet*'s massive cerebral cortex that came up with the brilliant idea to shoot William and Harry along with Charles and Diana. The man was a double-knit nitwit.

When asked if he'd ever murdered anyone, the *sous-préfet* had responded, "No, but one of my partners has."

Kael suspected the police commissioner, but wondered if his dreams were telling him otherwise: Was it the man in the cowboy hat—the mayor? And was Molly their victim?

The rest of the application was more bravado than anything else. It was certainly entertaining. The *sous-préfet* was not exactly acrophobic, but he did have an irrational fear that he wouldn't be able to reach heights of passion. He was deathly afraid of becoming impotent. His solution seemed to be to keep his penis in a state of perpetual erection.

He claimed to sleep with an average of ten women per week. That was over five hundred per year. His proudest conquests were married women, including three of his sisters-in-law and the wife of his boss, Nola's *préfet*. He went so far as to compare himself to Agent 007, James Bond, although he admitted that his trysts had little effect on world peace.

Kael suspected that the *sous-préfet*'s assertions were just as fictional as Ian Fleming's promiscuous protagonist. If they were true, however, Kael had a new theory: he no longer needed money to make the *préfet* his ally.

Kael put the application in his underwear drawer for safe keeping. If underwear did one thing well, it was protecting valuables. He then placed a few presents under the tree before falling into bed alone. He hoped Molly and her crocodile man wouldn't climb in later.

They didn't. They'd decided to take Christmas Eve off, which meant that his nightmares observed Christian holidays or they were simply as exhausted as he was. Whichever it was didn't really matter. Kael was just grateful to be included in another Christmas miracle.

The next morning was as atypical as the night before had been. Since Josie and Assan were unfamiliar with American Christmas traditions, the usually chaotic opening of presents did not occur. There was no ripping, no tearing, and no extra points awarded for speed. Their methods more closely resembled veteran bomb squad personnel inspecting suspicious ticking packages. It took them longer to open their gifts than it had taken Kael to wrap them.

Assan kept insisting, "This is not necessary, *monsieur*. You already gave me my freedom."

"I got that on sale," Kael responded.

Assan's presents were all purchased from local Muslim merchants. Their tiny wooden stalls located near the village's open-air market were treasure chests of overpriced junk, but Kael did manage to find some cooking utensils, clear plastic sandals in Assan's size of forty-two, and an exquisitely embroidered, white, knee-length shirt called a *bubu*, and matching light cotton pants that had no special name except pants. According to the merchants, it was the official uniform of relaxation for Muslims.

When Assan removed it from the wrapping, he uttered some non-traditional words of Christmas praise that somehow seemed appropriate, what with a large-caliber brass shell casing hanging as an ornament in their bamboo tree.

He said, "*Allah akbar.*"

Kael nodded as he held up his empty mug. "More coffee would be *akbar*, too." Assan, who was closest to the coffeepot, volunteered to pour.

Josie received a new pair of shoes: French knock-offs of Nike cross-trainers that were more expensive than the real thing. He immediately put them on as if to verify that they truly were his. They were a little big, but at his current pace of eating and growing, Kael figured they'd fit perfectly by noon and would be too tight by dinnertime.

Josie's excitement level peaked just after opening what looked to be a gift-wrapped, six-foot section of bamboo. Kael said he hoped it was a stick for spanking. It turned out to be something much more enjoyable. It was a graphite fishing rod and spinning reel that Kael had purchased from a German tourist who spoke English better than he did.

Kael showed his son how to work the reel without tangling the line, just as his father had shown him. He added one more bit of advice that his own father had neglected to tell him: "Never hook a dog in the nose."

Josie nodded solemnly before asking, "Can I hook a fish in the mouth?"

"I don't know. Why don't you go down to the river and find out." Kael tossed him a small tin of hooks, sinkers and lures that the German had generously included in the deal. "Everything you'll need is in there, except the fish stories. Those you'll have to make up yourself."

Josie sprinted out the front door with his Christmas haul. He was a mere blur in his new French sneakers. He'd probably shave off several seconds from his previous best time down to the riverbank.

Just about the time Kael was thinking a world record might fall on this day, Josie popped back into the living room. He walked over to where Kael was still sitting on the couch and hugged him around the neck with his free arm.

"*Merci, Papa.*"

Kael squeezed back with both of his arms. So what if the record didn't tumble today.

Before breaking the clutch, Josie whispered, "I like Christmas."

"And I like fish," said Kael, "so go catch me some."

Josie bolted from the house a second time. The record, Kael theorized, was still in jeopardy.

While Kael sipped his coffee, Assan meticulously picked up all the neat little piles of folded wrapping paper in front of the tree. When Assan had completed his task, Kael topped off his cup of coffee and poured one more. He offered it to Assan and asked him to sit for a few minutes. Assan obliged, leaving his tidy stack of gift wrap next to his presents.

Kael asked, "Do you know anyone named Bolo?"

Assan held his coffee cup in his lap with both hands. "I know many, *monsieur*. Bolo is a very common name throughout Central Africa. It is probably like Kael in America."

Kael smiled. "How about a local poacher named Bolo who may be working for the *sous-préfet* and his two friends?"

Assan took a long noisy slurp of his coffee before responding. "I have heard stories of him, but they are confusing. Some say he is Central African. Others say he is Congolese. Still others say he is a Pygmy. One story even says that he is white. He may be a combination of any of these, or none at all."

"Do some digging and see what you can find out. He could be the one with the .375."

"*Oui, monsieur.*"

"Another thing," said Kael. "Do you know Mangala?"

"*Mademoiselle* Zenith's cook?"

"The same. Did you know that he is also the mayor's cousin?"

"*Non, monsieur.* They are of different tribes. The mayor is Gbaya from Nola, and Mangala is Yakoma from out East, somewhere near Bangassou."

"I guess that would make them distant cousins, then."

"*Oui, monsieur.*"

"I'd like them to be distant again. Mangala's been spying for the mayor. He gathers information about *Mademoiselle* Zenith's elephants and then passes it on, probably through the mayor, to this Bolo character."

"So Bolo knew that those four elephants would be at *Le Bistro*?"

"Sort of," said Kael. "He was probably told that they were frequently observed there and if he waited around long enough, he'd be successful."

Assan took another static-sounding sip from his coffee. He peered over the rim of his cup and said, "Would you like me to speak with Mangala?"

"*Inshallah*," said Kael. "No violence, but you can threaten him with it."

"That is understood, *monsieur*, when confronted by a convicted crocodile man."

Kael smiled. "I'd forgotten about your reputation in this town. My suggestion would be to encourage Mangala to go back East, far away from you, me, the mayor, and *Mademoiselle* Zenith, who, by the way, can't find out about this. If she knew what Mangala has been up to, she'd make him prepare and then eat his own testicles. You may want to mention that to him."

"*Oui, monsieur.* Is there anything else?"

"Just to wish you a Merry Christmas, Assan."

"*Merci, monsieur. Allah akbar.*"

Why didn't people heed the Postmaster General's advice to mail early? It was three days after Christmas, and Kael continued to receive presents. There was still no pony under his tree, but Assan informed him that Bolo had been found. At least, a Bolo had been found. Whether it was the *sous-préfet*'s Bolo or not wasn't yet determined, but this Bolo wanted to sell some poached ivory and leopard skins to Assan's Uncle Moussa. It would happen in two days at Moussa's house in the village of Lidjombo, about thirty kilometers south. Uncle Moussa had agreed to help his favorite nephew as long as he, Moussa, would be immune from prosecution.

That was just fine by Kael. He wanted Bolo. And he wanted The Three Stooges.

The day of the sting was cool by Central African standards: in the eighties instead of the nineties, so Kael couldn't understand why he was sweating. Assan, who was sitting next to him on the truck's passenger seat, looked comfortable enough. He was even wearing jeans and a long-sleeved sweatshirt, which seemed to support Kael's theory that Central African men never perspired. He suspected that their sweat glands were surgically removed at the same time they were circumcised in some sort of buy-one-get-one-free deal offered during tribal initiation rites for adolescent boys. Of course, Assan would deny everything. Total secrecy was an integral part of the ceremony, as was screaming uncontrollably as soon as that dull rusty blade got to within six inches of one's foreskin.

From their parked truck, Kael and Assan had an adequate, though sometimes obstructed view of the door leading into Uncle Moussa's fenced-in compound. It was roughly two hundred feet away, but with Kael's binoculars, it seemed to be just inches past the pick-up's hood. The truck, with its recognizable TRAP logo stickers on both doors, was camouflaged by wedging it into the middle of a small bamboo grove. The breezes coming off the nearby river blew the thick bamboo stalks to and fro. They occasionally swayed across Kael's field of vision like retired chorus-line dancers: synchronized for the most part, but creaking nonetheless.

This was Kael's first-ever official stakeout. He asked Assan, "Do you think Bolo will show up on time?"

Assan kept his eyes glued to his uncle's front door. "*Inshallah.*"

"Do you think he'll show up late?"

"*Inshallah.*"

"Do you think he'll show up at all?"

"*Inshallah.*"

"Do you think he'll see us?"

Assan turned to face his inquisitor. "*Non, monsieur*, but he might hear us."

Kael smiled. "Then keep your voice down."

Assan whispered, "*Oui, monsieur.*" He then turned his attention back to his uncle's compound.

In the ensuing silence, Kael formulated a new theory: Central African men made the best stakeout partners. They spent most of their lives sitting around waiting for something to happen anyway.

Assan took his surveillance duties more seriously than did Kael, who thought it superfluous to have four good eyes watching the same boring door. One functioning, far-sighted eyeball seemed sufficient for the job and Assan had two.

Kael found something more entertaining to while away the time. Just outside his driver's side window, a Walking Stick slowly tight-roped its way across a split and rotting bamboo pole. Walking Sticks, Kael theorized, were the super models of the insect world. This one, at fifteen inches, was way above average in bug-length, was more twig-like than Twiggy herself, and its only concern was its own survival among the shorter, fatter, uglier masses of its society. That was why it looked more like a stick than a scrumptious bug, which was an amazing adaptation until it encountered a creature that preferred the taste of sticks to bugs.

Kael estimated the Walking Stick's speed at less than one inch per minute, which was only slightly better than that of a real stick. After observing three feet of progress, Kael felt a gentle touch on his forearm. He flinched. His initial thought was that another Walking Stick had snuck up from behind. It was Assan's hand. His other hand held the binoculars up to his eyes.

"Bolo *a si awé, monsieur.*"

Kael looked straight ahead toward Moussa's compound. Uncle Moussa, clad in a flowing white *bubu* and a white skullcap, was standing in the now open doorway. He was talking with a shorter, stockier man. The stranger was dressed in tattered dark shorts and a matching sleeveless shirt that revealed biceps the size of Kael's thighs. Kael didn't even want to see what those pythons looked like through the binoculars. A military-style duffle bag was slung over what Kael hoped were the man's football shoulder pads. That couldn't possibly be just flesh and bone under his shirt. Kael suddenly wished he'd chosen kung fu lessons in the sixth grade instead of guitar.

Before ushering his guest through the doorway, Uncle Moussa leaned forward to blow his nose without the aid of a handkerchief or Kleenex. He simply pinched off the end of his nose between thumb and forefinger and flung the effluent to the ground.

"That was the signal we agreed upon," announced Assan. "It's definitely Bolo."

"A short tug on an earlobe would have worked just as well," said Kael.

"*Oui, monsieur.*"

After Uncle Moussa and Bolo had disappeared on the other side of the closed compound door, Assan and Kael waited another five minutes before exiting the truck. Kael asked, "Do you think Bolo has his .375 in that duffle bag?"

"*Inshallah.*"

"Do you think CARL's in there?"

"I don't know this CARL you speak of, *monsieur.*"

Kael smiled. "I should be so lucky."

When they reached Moussa's door, Assan clapped his hands three times in unison with the words, "*Ko ko ko.*" The door swung open and they were warmly greeted by Uncle Moussa holding a tray of four teacups and a steaming teapot.

"*Salaam aleikum.*"

Kael and Assan both responded, "*Wa aleikum as-salaam.*"

Moussa switched from Arabic to Sango. "Come in. Come in. I was just about to pour."

They were led across the freshly swept dirt of the compound. If not for the fact that it was dirt, it would have been clean enough to eat off of. The pattern of the broom strokes reminded Kael of a maroon paisley shirt he'd worn for his seventh-grade school picture. It definitely looked better on dirt.

Moussa's large house loomed to their right. A tin roof over real bricks, not of sun-baked mud, made Kael wonder if Uncle Moussa did more than dabble in the lucrative business of poached animals. There were even screened-in windows with colorful curtains and women's laughter behind them.

The three men remained outside and walked along the length of the house. When they reached the far corner, they turned right. There, in the shade of an avocado tree, Bolo's bulk tested the leg-strength of a straight-backed chair. Before him were three less-stressed chairs around a knee-high table. His duffle bag lay innocently at his feet like a big green sleeping dog.

Moussa set the tray down on the table. He said, "Bolo, these gentlemen would like to ask you a few questions. It's best if you cooperate."

Bolo gave no verbal response, but his dark eyes bounced from Moussa to Kael to Assan to his duffle bag to the general direction of the front door of the compound.

Kael didn't want any fight-or-flight response, especially from a man as ripped as his shorts. Up close, there was no doubt in Kael's mind that he, Assan, and Moussa had less muscle mass combined than Bolo. If push came to shove, Kael pictured hot tea flying everywhere, a possible gun pulled from the duffle bag, and his own blood spilled all over the pretty paisley pattern of the dirt. It was a scenario he wanted to avoid.

As calmly as he knew how, he said, "We just want to know about your relationship with Mayor Likéké, *Sous-Préfet* Wabunda and Police Commissioner Yakonomingui."

Bolo snaked two muscular fingers into the front pocket of his shorts. He fished out a paper folded up as many times as humanly possible. He opened it up and handed it to Kael.

The original Declaration of Independence was in far better condition than Bolo's abused document. The numerous creases were only a few folds away from wearing completely through and it almost seemed to be dissolving between Kael's sweaty fingertips. Despite these frailties, the typed lines were still legible.

> To Whom It May Concern:
> This letter is to certify that *Monsieur* Ndinga Bolo is immune from arrest and prosecution for any crime committed within the jurisdiction of the Bayanga *Sous-Prefecture*. He is to be released immediately. Any authority not adhering to the above instructions will be punished to the fullest extent of the law.

Bolo's own Declaration of Independence was signed and stamped by each of The Three Stooges.

"This is impressive," said Kael, "but unfortunately for you, it only works on people who are afraid of the *sous-préfet,* the mayor and the police commissioner. I'm not. How about you, Assan?"

"*Non, monsieur.*"

"And you, Moussa?"

"*Oui, monsieur.*"

"Wrong answer," said Kael with a sideways glance, "but it's still two to one." He folded the letter up half as many times as Bolo had and stuck it in his own shirt pocket.

Bolo finally broke his silence. "Will I have to go to prison?"

Kael said, "That depends on what you tell us about..." He patted the letter in his pocket. "...your friends."

"They are not my friends," Bolo said.

"All right," said Kael. "What would *you* call them?"

"Thieves."

"I'd agree with that," said Kael. "How about you, Assan?"

"*Oui, monsieur.*"

"And you, Moussa?"

"*Non, monsieur.*"

Kael shook his head. CARL had come disguised in a *bubu*. "The two votes that count are already on your side, Bolo. We want to help you. Right, Assan?"

"*Oui, monsieur.*"

Kael decided to give it one more try. "And you, Moussa?"

"*Oui, monsieur.*"

Kael smiled. With the right questions, even CARL could come around to his point of view.

While Moussa went ahead and poured four cups of tea, Kael pulled an empty chair up close to Bolo. He made sure to position one of the chair's legs so that the duffle bag's shoulder strap was looped around it. He sat down. Now the bag was trapped. It didn't move unless Kael's chair did, too.

Bolo chugged his cup of hot tea the way Kael imagined fraternity brothers would during teatime drinking games at some English university like Oxford or Cambridge. Sipping slowly from his own cup, he asked, "Do you want another, or would you first like to go to the local hospital's burn treatment unit to swallow some salve?"

Bolo set his cup next to the teapot. "Another."

Moussa obeyed and poured. Bolo downed his second cup as quickly as the first. Moussa, whose fingers hadn't yet let go of the teapot's handle, filled Bolo's cup a third time.

Kael said, "Next time, we'll remember to bring bigger cups."

Bolo just nodded. Speaking would have slowed him down. He didn't stop until after his fifth rapid-fire cup and that was only because the teapot was empty. Moussa left to brew a second pot.

Kael said, "Good tea, huh? While we're waiting for more, maybe you could clear up some rumors Assan and I have heard."

Bolo shrugged his mountainous shoulders, which Kael interpreted as a positive sign. "Are you Central African, Pygmy, Congolese or white?"

Bolo said, "My father was Central African—a Sangha-Sangha fisherman. He's dead. My mother was Pygmy. She's also dead. I spend a lot of time in the Congo, but I'm not Congolese. You can see for yourself that I'm not white."

"That was just one of the stories," said Kael, who thought that as long as the guy was talking, why waste time? "When did you start working for the *sous-préfet*, the mayor, and the police commissioner?"

"If I answer your questions, will I still have to go to prison?"

Assan leaned forward in his chair on the other side of Bolo. "Like *Monsieur* Kael said before, it depends on what you tell us. But I will add this: if you *don't* answer our questions, you *will* go to prison."

While Bolo took several seconds to digest Assan's cautionary promise, Kael said, "Come on. Who would you rather see in prison? Those three thieves or you?"

Put that way, Bolo quickly decided that it was in his own best interest to respond.

"I met the police commissioner first. He arrested me for not paying taxes. When I told him I didn't have any money, he said I would go to prison unless I started working for him. He took me to meet with the mayor and the *sous-préfet*. They said they wanted me to kill elephants." He pointed to Kael's shirt pocket. "They gave me that letter for protection. I had no choice. They were going to put me in prison."

Kael asked, "Did they tell you where to find the elephants?"

"Sometimes. The mayor has a cousin who thinks he knows where the big ones are."

"We know," said Kael. "His name is Mangala."

"I know more about elephants than he does," bragged Bolo. "I've lived my whole life in the forest."

Assan said, "That's why the police commissioner hired you. He wanted the best."

Kael winked at Assan. Building up Bolo might tear down The Three Stooges.

Bolo nodded in agreement with Assan's praise. "Then why doesn't he pay me like the best? For every ivory tusk I give them, I only receive one thousand francs. I'm certain they sell it for much more than that."

Kael looked down at Bolo's duffle bag. "Is that why you came to Moussa? So you could get more money?"

Bolo nodded. "It isn't fair. Why should they make all the money when I do all the work?"

"The simple answer," said Kael, "is because you didn't want to go to prison for not paying your taxes."

Moussa returned with the second pot of tea. Like any good waiter in search of a greater-than-fifteen-percent tip, he filled everyone's empty cup to the brim while apologizing profusely for taking so long.

Bolo said, "I have to pee."

Kael said, "After five cups of tea, a camel would have to pee."

Moussa pointed behind the house. "There's an outhouse in the back."

When Kael suggested that Assan go with him, Bolo said, "I can do it myself."

"I'm sure you can," said Kael, "and probably much better than Mangala. I just don't want you to get lost before we discuss what's in your duffle bag." He kicked it gently and his foot hit something hard. A piece of ivory worth one thousand francs? A .375 worth considerably more? Or was it Bolo's Thigh Master, a bargain at just $39.95?

Moussa said, "Don't worry, *monsieur*. He can't escape. The entire compound is fenced in and the rear door is locked tight with the biggest, strongest padlock one can buy. The only way for him to get out is through the front door and he'd have to walk right past us to get to it."

Kael decided to let Bolo go without a chaperon. "OK, but don't be long or your tea will cool down to magma-like temperatures."

Bolo stood up, probably wondering what magma was, and walked behind the house. He left big footprints in the dirt.

Kael waited until he was out of earshot before saying, "I'll bet his pee is only slightly cooler than that tea he drank, which means as painful as it looked going in, it's got to be worse coming out."

Assan and Moussa both agreed that Bolo was tougher than woodpecker lips. They had never before heard of anyone, not even Allah, able to drink hot tea like that.

While Kael's eyes stayed peeled for Bolo's return, he slipped a hand into the unattended duffle bag for a quick feel. His sweaty fingers spider-walked through the interior of the bag until they bumped into what he had both feared and hoped to find: the cool metallic barrel of a rifle. A chill shot all the way up his arm. He pulled his hand out of the green dog's mouth.

He said, "If Bolo's still able to talk when he gets back, I want to ask him about the .375."

Assan said, "We should also find out if he knows anything about Mademoiselle Molly's death."

"I thought *you* killed her," said Moussa to his favorite nephew.

"No, Uncle. I was imprisoned for it, but I didn't do it."

"So you *can't* change into a crocodile like everyone says?"

"No, Uncle."

"Then who killed her?" asked Moussa.

"We don't know," said Kael. "Perhaps she just drowned accidently."

Moussa shook his head vehemently. "Take it from an old man, *monsieur*. There are no accidents."

"You've obviously never ridden in a bush taxi," said Kael.

Assan eased out of his chair. "I think I'll go check on Bolo."

"Good idea. Don't let him pee on you. You could wind up with third-degree burns."

"*Oui, monsieur.*"

After Assan left, Kael checked the duffle bag once more to make certain that it looked just as it had before he'd tampered with it. He made a slight adjustment of one of the folds. Bolo wouldn't suspect a thing. Kael leaned back in his chair and confidently sipped his tea.

Suddenly, Assan was back. "He's gone!"

Kael jumped to his feet, spilling half of his tea all over Bolo's duffle bag. "What do you mean he's gone?"

"He broke through the fence, *monsieur*."

Followed by Assan and Moussa, Kael sprinted to the back of the compound. There, behind the outhouse, he found that several planks from the fence had been torn away and thrown off to the side. Bent, rusty nails stuck out of the discarded boards. Bolo's big footprints disappeared on the other side of the fence where the dirt hadn't been swept clean. Kael couldn't believe it.

Just two feet to the right of the new opening in the fence, the rear door and its big strong padlock, the best one money could buy, were left undisturbed. This fact didn't escape Moussa, who said, "See. I told you he couldn't break through that door."

All Kael could do was shake his weary head and say, "Very nice work, CARL." Then, he remembered the duffle bag left abandoned at the foot of the table. He pictured Bolo doubling back through the compound's front door, waiting for everyone to vacate the area to inspect the damage to the fence, and calmly slipping in to retrieve his belongings during the ensuing chaos. Was the guy that diabolical? Kael headed back for the duffle bag.

Almost there, he got another vision of Bolo. In this one, he was waiting by the table with his loaded .375 resting on one hip. He was prepared to shoot anyone who tried to stop him.

Kael stomped on the brakes just before turning the corner of the house. Assan and Moussa, who had been tailgating, bumped into him, nudging him forward into the wide-open killing zone. Through eyes the size of Thanksgiving dinner platters, he saw only the green duffle bag right where he had left it. The fold, which he had fixed, was unchanged. Bolo was probably halfway to the Congo by now.

Relieved, Kael untangled the duffle bag from his chair's leg. He opened the top flap, and tipped the bag upside-down. Out tumbled one rifle, two ivory tusks about the same length as Kael's lower arm from elbow to fingertip, and one stiff, rolled-up leopard skin.

"At least we got his gun," he said reaching for something positive.

Assan bent down next to the weapon lying in the dirt. "It's not a .375, *monsieur*. It's a *mas* .36."

"What?" Kael was convinced that CARL was toying with them, now. "Let me see that." Assan handed it over. It was an old military-issue *mas* .36 that looked as if it hadn't seen lubricating oil since World War II. Kael wondered when it had last been fired. The inside of the barrel was filthy.

He asked Moussa, "Did Bolo want to sell this to you along with the ivory and leopard skin?"

"Of course not, *monsieur*. What would an old man like me do with such a thing?"

"Oh, I don't know," said Kael. "There are a lot of Bolos for hire out there." He worked the rusted action of the rifle. "I find it curious that this gun isn't loaded and no ammunition fell out of the duffle bag. Why else would he bring it here, if not to sell it?"

Always the diplomat and the good nephew, Assan said, "There is another possibility, *monsieur*. Perhaps Bolo was going to buy bullets with the money he made from the sale of the ivory and the skin."

"Maybe," said Kael, "but if what you say is true, this gun was his livelihood. Would he risk bringing it into the village?"

"He might, *monsieur*, if he had another one out there, say a .375."

Kael nodded. Assan had made a decent argument, but it made more sense to Kael, and probably to Assan as well, that Bolo had intended on selling the *mas* .36 to Moussa. Either way, their conclusions were the same: Bolo still had a .375.

# 34

Three days after the Bolo fiasco, Kael and Josie enthusiastically hopped into the cab of their trusty Toyota truck. Assan had promised to make them a morning *gateau*, a papaya crisp, if "someone" would run to the market for more sugar. Even if Assan hadn't been looking directly at Josie when he said it, everyone knew who the generic "someone" was meant for. It was the sort of errand kids in Africa performed without question, especially when their reward was something sweet to eat.

Kael would have been content to leisurely sip his first cup of coffee, but the mere mention of papaya crisp made the deprived taste buds of his mouth rejoice. They somehow communicated to the brain that sending a boy to the market on foot would take entirely too long. He'd probably stop along the way to chat with a school chum, pat a dog's tick-laden head, or watch someone repair a flat tire. All were unacceptable behaviors when a man's sugar content was dangerously low. He decided to hurry things along by taking Josie in the truck.

The pick-up's bench seat was damp, more on Josie's side than Kael's. Someone had left the passenger-side window partially open overnight. No big deal. That was the advantage of vinyl over leather.

Kael fired up the diesel engine. On this particular morning, its reverberating low-pitched rumble reminded him of his boat, *The Sourdough*, as it cautiously sliced through shallow water at low rpm's. He and Josie should be headed out for halibut, not sugar. Chako should be asleep out on the aft deck, at least until the fishing rods were brought out. Kael checked his rear-view mirror, hoping to find the Wonder Dog curled up in the bed of the truck. She wasn't there, but something else caught his attention in the mirror.

At first, he thought it was a stick. But then, it moved. It wasn't a Walking Stick like he'd observed during the Bolo stakeout. It was thicker and greener. He suddenly realized what it was, slowly emerging from behind the seat just inches away from Josie's left ear.

While Kael's left hand fumbled for and found the driver's-side door handle, his other hand grabbed Josie by the shirt collar and yanked. They both toppled out of the truck and sprawled into a heap on the ground. Luckily, the idling truck was in neutral, so it didn't budge. Kael jumped quickly to his feet like a robotic Olympic gymnast after a dizzying tumbling run. Since he was still clinging to Josie, who couldn't have opened his eyes any wider if he had tried, he dragged his confused son farther from the truck.

By now Josie was ready to cry. He had the frightened look of a kid being punished for doing something wrong, but exactly what his offense had been, he wasn't quite sure and he was too scared to ask.

Kael hugged him and said, "I'm sorry. Are you all right?"

"I think you ripped my shirt."

"We'll get you another one, OK?"

Josie perked right up. "A red one with a number on it like soccer players wear?"

"Sure, if you want to announce to the world that you're a weenie, be my guest."

"Soccer players aren't weenies!"

"All soccer players say that," said Kael. "Now, go find me a long stick. A sturdy piece of bamboo will do. There's a snake that thinks our truck is the Minerva Hotel."

"A snake? How big? Was that why you grabbed me so hard?"

"Yes, I only saw its green head just before it was about to pierce your ear. Now, hurry up with that stick."

While Josie did what he was told, Kael took a wide berth around the truck to the other side. He opened the passenger-side door by stretching his arm out as far away from his body as possible. He kept one eye on the open window and the other at floor level. Nothing leapt out at him. Backtracking through his fresh footprints, he returned to the driver's side where Josie awaited with a six-foot section of bamboo. Kael would have preferred something in the fifteen- to twenty-foot range, but he'd foolishly accused his son of being a weenie only minutes earlier.

"Stay back. I'm going to push the seat forward with this toothpick and see if we can't convince our guest to check out via the passenger side."

"What if he doesn't leave?"

"Then we'll sell the truck and walk to the market."

When the seat back flopped forward, the snake could be seen loosely coiled up around the jack. It was no harmless field snake that could be shooed away with a rolled-up newspaper and feigned bravado. This was three or four feet of Green Mamba, one of the deadliest reptiles in Central Africa, even more so than crocodile men.

Kael poked at the snake with his stick. The snake looked as confused as Kael. It didn't need much prodding. It instinctively struck out at the intrusive stick, but when its fangs failed to find any soft flesh to sink into, it unwound from the jack like a garden hose and wiggled out the open passenger-side door just as Kael had planned. It escaped into the high grass, leaving Kael feeling somewhat smug at having defeated CARL once again.

Kael yelled after the retreating serpent, "*Au revoir*, CARL."

Josie asked, "How do you know its name is CARL?"

"He just looks like a CARL to me."

Josie nodded his head in agreement, even though he probably knew no one else by that name. "Do I look like a Josie?"

Kael smiled. "You do to me."

When they'd finally climbed back into the snake-free cab of the truck to complete their errand, Josie asked an unusual question: "Do you think the *sous-préfet* knows CARL?"

Kael's immediate response was, "Oh, yeah," but then he realized that Josie was talking about CARL the snake, not CARL the acronym. "What made you ask that?"

Josie shrugged his shoulders. "I heard you tell Assan that the *sous-préfet* was a snake. Is he a Green Mamba, too?"

"Sort of," said Kael with a smile. "Sometimes he's a Granny Smith Green Mamba. Other times he's a Banana Yellow Mamba or a Plum Purple Mamba."

Josie accepted Kael's explanation with a nod, which made Kael contemplate at what age kids stopped believing everything their fathers said. He was already starting to question the theoretical connection between soccer players and weenies. Suddenly, it occurred to Kael that Josie, in his kid-like innocence, may have stumbled onto something—a scenario far more sinister that Kael might have otherwise overlooked. Did the *sous-préfet* know CARL the snake?

With Kael's near-capture of Bolo, were the *sous-préfet*, the mayor, and the police commissioner sending a message? Was CARL the snake purposely placed in Kael's truck? Or, was Bolo himself, behind it all? Was he seeking revenge for the loss of his gun?

As theories went, these were out there, even for Kael. They needed to be pondered over coffee and papaya crisp. The combination of caffeine and sugar had a way of making sense of things, even in Central Africa, where almost nothing made sense.

# 35

For five days and nights, Bolo did almost nothing but sit and wait. He ate very little. He slept even less. He made the ultimate sacrifice by not smoking any cigarettes the entire time. He held them between his lips, of course, but he never lit one up. He thought about it a lot, though.

He was hunkered down at Venice Beach, the historical January vacation spot of Ron and Nancy. He'd found an accommodating tree that had clawed its way out of the sandy soil like a gnarled arthritic hand. Like Ron and Nancy, it was old and dying, but still useful for Bolo's purposes.

He sat in the tree's mostly flat palm, about five meters up. There he had enough space to sit upright with a hard backrest, or to partially stretch out for a bad night's sleep if he so desired. Finger-like branches surrounded him with a curtain of camouflage, but they weren't so thick that they impeded his view of everything stretched out below him. If Ron and Nancy made an appearance at Venice Beach, he'd see them, he'd kill them, and finally, he'd chop off their wrinkled faces.

From his treetop lair, and behind powerful binoculars, he scanned the crowds at Venice Beach every five or ten minutes. So far, though, no Ron and Nancy. Hundreds of others had been observed. They basked in the sunshine or the moonlight unaware that they were being watched. He could have easily shot any of them, but this time he refused to settle. He was there for Ron and Nancy and he wasn't leaving until he got them—both of them—right between their tired eyes.

At dawn of the sixth day, a foamy fog surged into Venice Beach like a high tide. It ebbed and flowed, alternately covering, then uncovering. From Bolo's perch, he could only make out the occasional top of an indistinguishable head swimming through the fog below. His job of finding Ron and Nancy became much more difficult.

He didn't give up. That was what amateurs did. When the conditions weren't perfect, they went home. Professionals, like him, stuck it out. They got the job done regardless. In Bolo's way of thinking, the difference between an amateur and a professional was, more often than not, stubbornness. Bolo was supremely confident that he had a streak longer than anyone.

It was that very trait that gave him the opportunity to glimpse Ron's gray head floating through the early morning fog. It wasn't visible for long, but it was him, all right. The two big notches in his left ear were unmistakable. By the time Bolo got the binoculars in his hands exchanged for the .375, and raised it up to the firing position, there was nothing in the scope to shoot. The fog had swallowed up Ron's head for breakfast. It would pop out again somewhere, so Bolo continued to scan Venice Beach through the rifle's scope. His finger rested on the trigger, eager to do its part in the operation.

He spotted some heads bobbing in the fog. A brain shot would be so easy, but he first needed to see the left ear. He had to be certain that he was firing into Ron's brain and not that of some insignificant bystander. An amateur wouldn't care. The fog covered up the heads before he could tell.

Perspiration from his brow trickled down into his eyes. The salt burned, but not enough to make him pull away from the rifle's scope. A few quick blinks helped flush them out. He remained in the firing position, his concentration fixed on what he saw magnified through the narrow tube.

A head suddenly appeared. He checked out the left ear. Two notches just like Ron. It was him.

Bolo hesitated, wondering if he should shoot or wait until he saw Nancy too. After all, he'd come for the couple. If he shot Ron now, the others, including Nancy, would scatter. He could always wait until the fog burned off, but that could take hours and there was no guarantee that Ron and Nancy would stick around. This might be his only chance, so he convinced himself that Ron was the prize. Nancy was just in keeping with his couples' theme of late. Charles and Diana. Isabelle and Sophie. William and Harry. If he shot Ron, there would be no more Ron and Nancy. That was good enough for Bolo.

By the time he decided to pull the trigger, Ron's head was already dipping back into the enveloping fog. Bolo had to rush his shot, something he was unaccustomed to doing. He fired blindly three more times into the thick haze, right where he assumed Ron's bulk would be if he had been dropped, or at least slowed, with the first shot. He had no idea if any of his four bullets had struck eighty-year-old flesh.

Venice Beach was pandemonium. The ground shook from the exodus of fleeing survivors. Bolo felt the tremors climb his tree. He heard, but couldn't see, the mass hysteria he had wrought. Desperation never sounded so noisy. It was a tumult of screams, shrieks, cries, and wails. Beneath it all, like a droning bass drum, were the crazed footfalls of panic. Bolo took pleasure in the fact that, from the sound of things, he was the only one at Venice Beach keeping his composure. He was, after all, the only professional in the bunch.

His tree shook more violently than before. It was enough to knock him right out of his sitting position. He managed to grab onto a sturdy limb for support, but the .375, which had been balanced across his bare thighs, plummeted to the ground. He couldn't tell if it was damaged or not. It was barely visible through the grayish fog.

The tree shuddered again, almost dropping him like a ripe mango. What was happening? Was it a coincidental earthquake? Or were some of Ron's senile friends bumping into things in the fog as they hastily vacated Venice Beach? Bolo got his answer when he was spun around as a result of yet another jolt.

Just below him, easily within spitting distance, was an enraged Ron banging his stubborn octogenarian head against the tree. Obviously he wasn't dead. The old geezer didn't even appear to be mortally wounded. The only physical damage that Bolo could see was a new bloody notch in his left ear.

Bolo held on tight. He was helpless to do anything else. Where was his gun when he needed it?

After a dozen more violent collisions with the tree, Ron started to push. The snapping sound of roots begrudgingly letting go of the soil seemed to spur him on. He put all of his weight and anger into the effort. It was no contest. The tree toppled over and Bolo had no choice but to go with it.

Something hit him on the side of the head. Everything got foggy after that. He floated more than fell. It took a long time to reach the bottom. He stretched out like a flying squirrel gliding from an upper branch to a lower one. He hit hard on his stomach. A trumpet sounded from above. The coppery taste of blood flooded his mouth. Then, there was nothing but darkness, darkness, dark ...

* * * * * * * * * * * * * * * * * * * *

Bolo awoke to a gentle rain and a less-than-gentle headache. Through swollen eyes, he saw that the fog had finally burned off. He had no idea how long he'd been unconscious.

He tried to push up off his stomach, but something sitting just above his spine wouldn't let him. He couldn't turn his head to see what it was, but he hoped it was part of the tree and not Ron's foot poised to squash him like a bug.

He was trapped among the broken limbs and branches that had crashed down with him at Ron's urging. As far as Bolo could tell, they were only around him, not through him. That was a plus and he suspected that Ron was long gone. That was another plus. Now all he had to do was belly-crawl out of his wooden prison.

Progress was slow. His broad chest made for some tight squeezes. He was weak, but still stronger than most. His stubborn streak hadn't been damaged in the fall.

Eventually he reached a spot where he could stand up. When he did, his head revolted. He felt dizzy. He knew exactly what he needed. He reached into the front pocket of his shorts and fished out a mangled cigarette and a pack of matches. A day's first smoke never tasted so good.

He checked himself for injuries. There were a lot of minor cuts and scrapes. Nothing required stitches. Miraculously, he hadn't broken anything but his nose, which had already been rearranged numerous times in the past. Like before, it was tender to the touch. So was a rather large knot on the side of his head.

What concerned him more than his own well-being was the current state of health of his .375. He had to find it. Without it, he was no longer in business and Ron could claim victory. That was unacceptable.

Bolo climbed over and crawled under what seemed like several cords of wood before finally reaching the outer edge of splintered branches from the downed tree. As he walked along the periphery to where the tree had been uprooted, he realized that except for a few birds, Venice Beach had been abandoned. His gunshots had seen to that. A popular gathering spot that had until recently been alive with activity was now as quiet as a cemetery. Unfortunately, there were no dead bodies to show for it. Bolo vowed to fix that.

Within minutes, he found his missing rifle resting comfortably on a tuft of grass alongside the base of the now horizontal trunk. It was just lying there like someone taking a nap in the cool shade. In a funny sort of way, he was lucky that it had fallen to the ground before the tree had been tipped over. Otherwise it would have been thrown, like him, out into the middle of that mess. He'd have never found it then. He had no idea where his binoculars or his machete had been catapulted. Those could easily be replaced, so he wasn't going to waste precious time searching among the ruins. He had too much to do, too much to plan. Revenge would be sweet. It would be perfect. And it would be oh so bloody.

# 36

Kael was driving home after having spent the better part of the morning sitting in on Paige's inaugural Nature Club for Kids. With the exception of the village slide show, it was her first official effort at non-medical environmental education. She'd done well for a practicing hypochondriac, keeping her disease references to a minimum. Only once did she compare a tree's growth in the forest to that of her own intestinal tapeworm.

When Kael arrived home, Zenith's Toyota Land Cruiser Station Wagon was occupying his parking space. He pulled up next to it after briefly considering boxing it in. He found her relaxing on his couch with his last bottle of cold beer.

"Comfortable? Can I get you anything?"

"Food," said Zenith between sips. "Since Dexatrim II ran off without so much as an explanation or a two-week notice, I'm in a constant state of starvation. I've lost eight pounds, so if I ever find that little piss-ant, I won't know whether to hug him or mug him."

"I think there's some leftover fish and rice in the fridge."

"Not anymore," Zenith admitted. "Assan just went to the market to replenish your food stocks. I'm afraid I've done considerable damage since arriving twenty minutes ago."

"Besides food, or to be more precise, my food, what brings you into town?"

"A couple of things. First, I wanted to let you know that I couldn't determine who was originally attached to those two tusks you confiscated down in Lidjombo. They just weren't distinctive enough to identify. They could have come from hundreds of elephants in my database. Sorry. Second, I hate to devour and run, but I'm off to Bangui. I got a radio message from the embassy that a photographer and a journalist are arriving to do a spread on my elephants. I have to go pick them up. I should be gone for three or four days, but you know Bangui. Do you need anything while I'm there?"

"How about a big padlock for my refrigerator and a 'No Parking' sign?" Kael said it jokingly, but he was in an ornery mood, probably from his lack of quality sleep the past couple of weeks. Molly and her crocodile man had been visiting every night. They were even starting to make an appearance during Kael's afternoon siesta.

Zenith drained Kael's last bottle of beer before jumping off of Kael's couch and hopping into her luxury automobile parked in Kael's spot. She waved as she backed up over Kael's garden. Kael yelled after her, "Stay in Bangui a month or two if you have to."

A few minutes after Zenith's hurried departure, Assan waltzed in with a large sack of groceries. He said, "*Mademoiselle* Zenith was here, monsieur."

"I know. She drank my last beer."

Assan reached deep into his sack and pulled out a bottle of "33" beer. "It's cold, too."

"Will you marry me, Assan? You could do worse."

Assan handed the bottle to Kael. "I'm willing to take that chance, monsieur."

"I demand so little and that's exactly what I get."

"*Oui, monsieur*. I bought the beer at the mayor's bar."

"I forgive you. Sometimes collaboration with the enemy is necessary."

"*Oui, monsieur*. While I was there, I overheard two of the workers arguing over who should get to go to Cameroon tomorrow with the truckload of empty bottles."

"There's a beer run tomorrow?"

"*Oui, monsieur*. Do you think they'll be trying to take poached meat and ivory with them?"

"According to the *sous-préfet*'s confessional, that's how it works."

"Can we stop them?" asked Assan.

"I've got a better idea," said Kael. "They have to go through Nola to get to Cameroon. I wonder if the *préfet* and his police commissioner would like to take credit for busting up The Three Stooges' trafficking operation."

"Why would they want to do that, *monsieur*?"

"Because they aren't part of it and because there's no honor among thieves, especially when one is already stealing from another."

Assan said, "I don't understand, *monsieur*, but how can I help?"

Kael said, "I need a bottle opener and some road food. I'm going to Nola."

Upon arriving in Nola, Kael drove directly to the river's edge. There he was greeted by the same ferry operator who just so happened to be waiting on Kael's side, not CARL's.

"Want to make another two thousand francs?"

The ferry operator smiled. "I could get used to foreigners like you, monsieur."

Kael found the *préfet* loitering in his office, not doing much of anything except sitting at his desk with folded hands. There were no papers in front of him, so he couldn't even pretend to be working. Like most bored desk jockeys, he seemed grateful for the interruption.

"*Monsieur* Kael! Come in. Take a seat. It's so nice to see you again. Have you come to buy another crocodile man?"

Kael shook the offered hand. "No, the one I purchased before is working just fine, thanks." He sat down across from the *préfet*.

"I could give you a good deal on a common thief. Two for the price of one."

"How about three?" asked Kael.

"You want to buy three thieves?"

"No," said Kael, "I want to sell them... to you."

From his backpack he produced Bolo's letter of immunity signed by The Three Stooges, along with the *sous-préfet*'s C.I.A. application, minus the part about him sleeping with the *préfet*'s wife. The woman had suffered enough.

"Read those. You can make copies if you like."

The *préfet* read the evidence. When he was done, he asked, "This is all true?"

"I'm afraid so," said Kael. "I didn't want to believe it either, but everything is signed and stamped and we all know it doesn't get any more official than that."

The *préfet* nodded. "They must be stopped... immediately!"

Kael theorized that the *préfet* wasn't all that concerned about the elephant poaching, per se. He'd probably skimmed over those parts. What disturbed him most were the admitted tax scams, the embezzling of public funds, and any profits generated from the illegal sale of ivory. These were all monies that should have rightly filled his own pockets, not those of his underlings.

Evidence to support Kael's theory was soon vocalized by the *préfet*: "Stealing from the people is one thing, but stealing from me is another."

Kael outlined his plan: If they could intercept one of the mayor's shipments of ivory and meat to Cameroon, they could use that, along with the documents, to pit one Stooge against another and the loudest confessor would get the sweetest deal. Cops on TV did it all the time.

It was highly unlikely that any of The Three Stooges would do jail time. Punishment usually involved separation of the parties involved and reassignments to other posts even farther from Bangui. Kael would be rid of the region's worst poachers, not to mention dressers, and the *préfet* would have less competition, which meant that his own pockets would be fuller come tax collection time.

The *préfet* liked it. He said, "If we only knew when their next shipment was."

252

Kael smiled. "Is tomorrow soon enough?" He suggested that they enlist the help of Nola's cooperative police commissioner since part of his job was to randomly stop and search vehicles headed for the border. They could do whatever they wanted with the meat, but Kael demanded the return of any ivory. That was *his* exclusive jurisdiction.

The *préfet* expressed his discontent: "You get the ivory and we get some rotten meat? That doesn't sound fair."

"I'll be in Bayanga, so you get to take full credit for busting up their crooked little scheme. Who knows? Your heroic efforts might result in new postings in Bangui for the both of you. I'm certain Commissioner Dimassé will hear of it."

"That's true," said the *préfet*. "On rare occasions, money is secondary."

"I'll drink to that." Kael hoped his host would see fit to break out a bottle of celebratory beer.

"Good. You can buy. We need to go to the bar in town. They're the only ones who have a generator and a photocopier. You can pay for the copies, too."

On the way to the bar, they picked up Police Commissioner Gozo. As expected, he was an enthusiastic supporter of any plan designed to get him to Bangui where he belonged. While the *préfet* purged his three bottles of Guinness Stout in the bar's outhouse, Commissioner Gozo made a solemn but somewhat inebriated promise to Kael that everything would go as smoothly as Assan's release, and he trusted that Commissioner Dimassé would, again, be pleased with the results.

Kael had more confidence in the Mexican peso.

After dropping off his two new best friends back at their respective offices, Kael drove out to the only bar in town that served Irish coffee. He found *Père* Norbert sitting in the church's front-row pew. He was reading the Bible aloud to himself, practicing for Sunday's mass. He didn't even notice his visitor approaching up the center aisle.

When Kael got to within ten feet, he interrupted. "Is it as good as Dick Francis?"

*Père* Norbert looked up. "Better. It's the ultimate mystery."

"How does it end?"

*Père* Norbert winked. "It doesn't."

They shook hands. Kael explained that he was just in Nola for a few hours. He'd stopped by to say, "*Bonjour*," and to return the borrowed Dick Francis paperback.

*Père* Norbert asked, "So, were you able to successfully deduce who the killer was?"

"Of course not. I didn't think it could be him because he was supposedly out of the country when the murders occurred."

"Didn't I warn you it's never who you think it is?"

"Since when did I listen to a priest, Father?"

*Père* Norbert laughed. "Would you like something to drink?"

Kael smiled. "I'm listening now."

They retired to the kitchen where *Père* Norbert made two strong Irish coffees. Kael filled him in on Josie, Assan, and the continuing saga of The Three Stooges.

"They're certifiable, Father. One thinks he's James Bond. Another thinks he's Wyatt Earp. And the third one is just plain nuts."

*Père* Norbert added more whiskey to his own coffee cup. "There's nothing I despise more than a weak cup of coffee. Have you decided who, if anyone, had a hand in *Mademoiselle* Molly's death?"

"Dick Francis himself couldn't figure that one out. The more I dig, the more I think she accidentally drowned. What possible reason could The Three Stooges have to kill her?"

*Père* Norbert scratched his head. "One saw her as an agent of S.P.E.C.T.R.E. Another saw her as a member of the Clanton gang. And the third one is just plain nuts."

"Chin chin," said Kael as he touched his cup to the literate Father's. He didn't ask, but he was sure that *Père* Norbert's take on his persistent nightmares of Molly's demise at the hands of a crocodile man in a cowboy hat would be just as entertaining.

\* \* \* \* \* \* \* \* \* \* \* \* \* \* \* \* \* \* \* \*

The mayor's truck didn't pull away from his bar until the evening of the following day. The decision to not stop and search the truck as it left Bayanga still made sense to Kael. He couldn't be certain that the ivory was already on board. It might have been stashed a few kilometers north of town. There it would be loaded only if the driver felt confident that they'd pulled another fast one on TRAP. Surely they wouldn't expect any trouble in Nola. Commissioner Gozo had informed Kael that he and his men had never stopped the mayor's beer trucks heading to Cameroon. "Why would we?" he'd said. "The beer bottles were empties."

The next day, there was no word on what, if anything, had happened with the truck in Nola. With no telephones, Bayanga depended on bush taxis to spread the gossip from one town to the next. That long day, the C.O.W.'s never came home.

When none had arrived by the second day, Kael was tempted to drive to Nola. Had the *préfet* and Commissioner Gozo missed the truck? Had CARL won another big one? It was just like him to tease Kael with insignificant victories like the ferry, only to assert his authority when it really counted.

Kael became convinced of CARL's involvement when, after finally deciding that afternoon to drive up to Nola, his Toyota refused to turn over. Assan quickly diagnosed the problem as a clogged fuel filter, not a vengeful acronym.

By the time they changed the filter and bled the fuel system, Kael needed a beer. Driveway auto mechanics and beer went together like... well, anything and beer. While getting one from the fridge, he heard a vehicle pull up out front. It sounded like a big diesel. He opened his Mocaf and went out to investigate.

It was Zenith's Land Cruiser Station Wagon, but because of the tinted windows, Kael couldn't tell if it was her behind the wheel or not. If it was, she was back early from Bangui. The engine was killed and the driver's side door opened.

Zenith stepped out. "I love it when a man welcomes me home with a cold beer."

"Me, too," said Kael. He looked over at Assan. "Quick, go hide the food."

Zenith laughed. "Be nice. I brought you a surprise."

The passenger's side door opened. At first Kael couldn't identify the person getting out of the car. It might have been because the face was shaded by a baseball cap pulled down low over the eyes, but later he decided it was because one never expected to see the Eiffel Tower while sightseeing in Omaha.

The stranger leaned on the open car door. "Got any theories on this one, Pig-Pen?"

Kael nearly choked on his beer. "Tallin? What are you doing here?"

She shut her car door. "I'm a journalist, and your friend Nick sent me over to write the definitive article on forest elephants." She walked around the front of the car to get to where Kael stood. "That and to see my new boyfriend. Where is Josie, anyway?"

Kael laughed. He could smell her coming before she wrapped her arms around him. He decided then and there that he wanted to be reincarnated as a bar of Ivory soap. Granted, life would be fleeting, but it would be oh so enjoyable, unless someone like Police Commissioner Yakonomingui picked him up off a grocer's shelf.

Zenith said, "I hate to interrupt this little love fest, but I should get going. We dropped off Doug the photographer at the market. He wanted to try to snap some pictures. I didn't think it would be a problem since The Three Stooges have other things to worry about these days."

Kael's attention shifted from Tallin's smell to Zenith's voice. "What happened in Nola?"

"You haven't heard, yet? This will make your day, as if I haven't already done that. The mayor's beer truck was stopped and searched by Nola's police commissioner. Inside, among the cases of empty bottles, he found poached ivory and meat."

Kael hugged Tallin since she was closer. "That's fantastic!"

"You haven't even heard the best part," said Zenith. "Traveling with the truck to Cameroon were the mayor and Bayanga's top cop: Police Commissioner Yakonomingui. They're having one hell of a time explaining themselves. Word is that the *sous-préfet* has been summoned to Nola. I think The Three Stooges' long-running off-Broadway production, which enraptured audiences with over-the-top performances and awe-inspiring costumes, is finally closing."

"Nice review," said Kael.

Zenith winked. "Nice job."

Kael shrugged his shoulders. "Want to celebrate with a cold beer from the fridge? It seems fitting that they were purchased at the mayor's bar."

"Another time," said Zenith. "Maybe when you're not home."

Tallin said, "Let me just grab my backpack, Zenith." She turned to Kael. "I thought I'd stay here if that's OK with you, and if you can give me a lift out to Zenith's camp tomorrow morning."

"Sure," said Kael wondering if CARL had died or something. He theorized that the tide book dot for today had to be bigger than his growing erection.

Steadfastly refusing Assan's assistance, Kael helped Tallin with her backpack, not because he was a gentleman, but because he needed something large, behind which he could hide the bulge in his pants. In addition, he tried concentrating on non-erotic thoughts like dead puppies. That usually did the trick. By the time Zenith had departed and Tallin had been shown into the house, the situation was no longer at DEFCON 2 status. The troops were standing down.

Tallin asked, "Where's Josie? I brought him a few presents."

Kael set the backpack down on the floor next to the couch. "He's playing soccer with some friends. Would you like a beer?"

She flopped down on the couch. "I'd love a beer. How about some chips and salsa to go with that?"

"Sorry," said Kael. "The closest thing I have to a snack around here is boiled peanuts. I haven't seen a chip or salsa since I left the states."

Tallin reached for her backpack. "That's exactly why I brought them." From a side pouch she pulled out a bag of tortilla chips and two hefty jars of salsa. "I figured you liked the really hot stuff."

Kael could feel himself getting excited all over again. "You don't know the half of it, *senorita*."

"That's not all," she teased. She removed a small box from her pack and flashed it at Kael. "Later, for dessert, I brought some Jello No-Bake Cheesecake. You want some?"

Kael swallowed. He'd soon need to dive behind the backpack again. "Oh boy, do I."

"It's ready in just minutes."

"I think it's ready now," he said to himself while exiting to get Tallin's beer.

When he got back to the living room, she had shucked off her shoes and was sitting cross-legged on the couch. She traded him an envelope for the fuller of the two beers.

She said, "It's from Stan Pulaski at the American Embassy in Bangui. He asked me to give it to you."

Kael tore open the envelope and read the hand-written note:

Dear Kael,

Can you hear CARL laughing? Now I truly understand your clever little acronym. FYI, we nabbed the thief who'd been stealing from the ambassador. It wasn't the laundry boy. It wasn't the cook, the housekeeper, or the security guard. Get this: it was the Ambassador's twenty-year-old son. Turns out he wasn't here on a break from college. He'd been expelled for on-campus drug use. Since arriving, he's been ripping off his father to help support his habit. Stealing the photographs, he admitted, was just to make it look like a Central African was the likely culprit.

Ambassador Saxon and his wife are devastated. He's requested a reassignment to a desk job at the State Department in Washington. Probably a good move since he's convinced that his son had Central African accomplices who remain at-large.

Visit when you're in town. I'm sure by then there will be a new embassy scandal to share, and my wife makes the best fried chicken this side of the Nile. If that isn't enough of a temptation, I get cases of Coors beer shipped here through the diplomatic pouch. We'll drink to CARL, to crocodile men, and to other things beyond our understanding.

Sincerely, Stan Pulaski

"Good news or bad?" asked Tallin.

"Both, I guess. The ambassador's son learned more than just calculus while away at college and CARL is vacationing in Bangui. I was wondering where he's been."

"Who's CARL?"

"An old friend. He drives the Central African Welcome Wagon. If you stick around long enough, you'll meet him."

"I'm only here for a week."

Kael said, "That's plenty. CARL's not shy."

Josie blasted through the front door. He stood still just long enough to announce in Sango, "I'm going swimming." He then did an about-face to rocket back outside.

"Hold up a second," Kael said in Sango. "We have a visitor."

Josie politely returned to acknowledge their guest. He shook her hand, smiled broadly, and said, "*Bonjour.*"

Tallin responded with a beginner's pronunciation of *bonjour*. To Kael, she said in native English, "He's so cute."

| | |
|---|---|
| Josie, in Sango: | "She's pretty." |
| Kael, in Sango: | "Keep your hands and your dimples off her. Remember, I saw her first." |
| Tallin, in English: | "What did you two just say?" |
| Kael, in English: | "He said he wants to go swimming, and I was just giving him some fatherly advice about where not to swim." |
| Tallin, in English: | "That's nice." |
| Josie, in Sango: | "Can I go now?" |
| Kael, in Sango: | "Sure. Your presents can wait until later." |
| Josie, in Sango: | "Presents?" |

It was Christmas all over again. This time, however, Josie unleashed his enthusiasm on the plastic bag that was delivered from Tallin's pregnant backpack. Inside the bundle of joy were a real soccer ball, along with a hand pump and needle to inflate it, red soccer shorts, and a matching red-and-white soccer jersey with the number 15 and the name Husker stenciled on the back. Josie didn't know which to do first: to pump up the ball or to put on the uniform. He finally decided on Plan C and threw his arms around Tallin's neck.

Kael shook his head. "Buying my son's affections? That's despicable."

Tallin reluctantly let Josie slip out of her grasp so he could try on his soccer jersey. "What? Yours aren't for sale?"

"Of course they are. I'm a lonely man. You bought mine when you pulled that bag of chips from your pack."

"What do I get for the salsa?" She teasingly wiggled her eyebrows up and down.

Kael smiled. "Nothing quite so hot and spicy I'm afraid, but if you want to exchange one dip for another, I think I can accommodate you."

They all went for a swim after that. Kael thought it would be the next best thing to a cold shower... until he saw Tallin in her swimsuit. All those kid-like freckles sprinkled over womanly curves forced him to ponder dead puppies again.

While he sat in strategic, waist-deep water sipping his beer, Tallin taught the butterfly stroke to a giggling Josie. Later, Kael and Tallin threw Josie high into the air so that he could show off his cannonball splash. The three of them stopped to watch the sun drop like a real cannonball behind the trees on the other side of the river. The sky turned red and orange before fading to black.

Kael held Tallin's hand during the steep climb back up the riverbank. Josie raced to the top ahead of them while announcing, "Last one home is a weenie. First one is a soccer player."

Kael yelled back, "What's the difference?

Assan had dinner waiting for them: thick filets of tiger fish, rice, and avocado halves filled with vinaigrette dressing. After changing into dry clothes—Josie into his new soccer uniform and Kael and Tallin into old gym shorts and t-shirts—they gathered round the lantern-lit table.

Tallin said, "It all looks so good."

Kael, thinking more about Tallin than the food on the table said, "It sure does."

After the feast, Tallin made Kael and Josie do the dishes while she showed Assan how to prepare her well-traveled cheesecake. To circumvent the language barrier, she combined her bad French with charades-style clues. They decided to let the cheesecake sit in the refrigerator for only half the time recommended on the box. It was a little runny, but everyone had two pieces. It was the perfect complement to a record big-dot day.

Josie went to bed first, pleading for permission to sleep in his new soccer uniform. Kael kidded him, "You're already a weenie during the day. Do you want to be one at night, too?"

Josie said, "In my dreams tonight, the C.A.R. will defeat the USA when I kick in the winning goal."

"In your dreams is right," said Kael kissing his son goodnight. He then explained to Tallin what Josie had said.

Her response was, "I don't know about you, but I'm kinda hoping that Josie isn't the only one who scores tonight."

Kael chanted, "USA! USA!"

Assan retired to his room, leaving Kael and Tallin alone on the couch. Kael leaned over and kissed her gently on the lips.

"I've been wanting to do that all day."

"Me, too," she said. "Maybe we should go to bed."

"I've been wanting to hear you utter those words since I first saw you in that man-eating elevator."

"Good things come to those who survive their head getting crushed between elevator doors."

They blew out all the lanterns but one, which accompanied them to Kael's bedroom. They dropped the mosquito net down and together tucked it under the mattress.

While Kael stood at one end of the bed trying to figure out his next move, Tallin, who was at the other end, pulled her t-shirt over her head and let it drop to the floor. She had nothing on underneath. In the faint light thrown off by the lantern, he could see that even her breasts were freckled. He'd wondered about that.

She said, "I hope you like freckles."

"More than chips and salsa. You're beautiful, and I'm not just saying that because you took your shirt off for me."

Tallin smiled. "Let's review, shall we? I'm not rich, I don't own a liquor store, you think I'm beautiful, and what was that fourth quality you were looking for in a woman? I think it begins with an N."

"There are so many," said Kael removing his own t-shirt. "Let's see, there's naughty, naked, non-violent and non-contagious for starters."

Tallin slipped out of her shorts and panties. "Does nymphomaniac ring a bell?"

Kael stepped out of his own shorts and boxers. "I've decided that I prefer the term nympho. Nymphomaniac sounds like you enjoy sex, but afterwards, you'll kill me in some horrible fashion."

She said, "Only if you don't measure up, but I see that won't be a problem."

They stepped forward into each other's arms. For the second time, they kissed on the lips. This one was a little longer, a little harder, and a little more electric than the first.

When their lips parted and they were both catching their breath, Kael said, "You need to choose. We can stay out here and get bitten up by mosquitos, or we can slip underneath the mosquito net, eliminate the middle man, and bite each other."

"That second one sounds more economical. Why should the mosquitos have all the fun?"

"When it comes to fun," said Kael lifting up a corner of the net, "I'm betting that tonight, they come in a distant third place."

Later, an out-of-breath Tallin asked, "Did I scream too loud?"

"I don't know," said Kael panting. "I couldn't hear it above by own. Don't worry. I'll just tell Josie it was a couple of wild animals."

"And you wouldn't be lying."

Much later, Kael awoke from a dreamless sleep. His theory was that the screams had scared Molly and her crocodile man away, at least for one night. Just in case they were close, he spooned up against Tallin's back and began kissing her shoulders and neck.

She wiggled in closer. "Again?"

"My vocal cords have recuperated. How about yours?"

She turned around to face him, threw a slender leg over his waist, and rolled. Straddling him from above, she said, "Let's find out."

# 37

In the morning, everyone converged on the breakfast table for coffee, hot chocolate, *beignets*, and fresh sliced pineapple. Conversation was also on the menu.

| | |
|---|---|
| Kael, in Sango: | "Did anyone else hear the hippos last night? I think they were right outside our windows." |
| Josie, in Sango: | "It sounded like they were right *inside* our windows. Didn't you think so, Assan?" |
| Assan, in Sango: | "They were close, all right." |
| Josie, in Sango: | "Was that why Tallin was screaming? Is she scared of hippos?" |
| Tallin, in English: | "What are you guys talking about?" |
| Kael, in English: | "Just guy stuff... things like sports, cars, sports cars and hippos." |
| Tallin, in English: | "Hippos?" |
| Kael, in English: | "Yeah. Josie wanted to know if you're scared of them." |
| Tallin, in English: | "I don't think so. Can we see some?" |
| Kael, in English: | "Assan says they're close." |
| Tallin, in English: | "Awesome!" |
| Kael, in English: | "I couldn't agree more." |

Josie hurried off to school. Assan had errands to run in town. Kael drove Tallin out to Zenith's camp. About two kilometers short of their destination, they encountered a white man walking along the road.

"That's Doug... the photographer," said Tallin.

As they drew closer, Kael could make out the uniform of every male nature photographer working in Africa: a well-worn khaki photographer's vest with matching military-style cargo pants to complete the ensemble. He accessorized with a pair of Nikon cameras slung over his neck, a red bandana handkerchief rolled up and wrapped around his head for a makeshift sweatband, and a full beard. He stuck out his thumb when Kael's truck pulled up next to him.

He leaned in through the open passenger-side window. "Hey, Tallin. Can I hitch a ride into camp with you guys? I was just out exploring."

"Sure. Hop in." Tallin opened the door for him before sliding over to the middle of the bench seat. She did the introductions: "Doug, Kael. Kael, Doug."

Doug climbed in and shook Kael's offered hand. "Pleasure. If Zenith asks, I was out shooting a few rolls trying to get accustomed to the unique lighting conditions here. But just between you, me and the monkeys, I had to escape her cooking. She tried to pass off cement as oatmeal this morning."

Kael said, "Her cook ran off a couple of weeks ago."

"Did he have to take the recipes with him?"

Kael let out the clutch and they were moving again. To make small talk, he asked, "Did you see any animals while you were, um, checking out the light this morning?"

"Literally tons," said Doug with enthusiasm. "I watched three elephants for about forty-five minutes. They ducked into the trees just before you came down the road. This is an amazing place. How long have you been here?"

"Not long. Since November of last year."

"Do you know Bolo?" asked Doug.

Kael was surprised by the question, but theorized that Zenith must have filled Doug in on some of the other residents of the forest. "Yeah, I know him."

"I hear he's in the Congo now," added Doug.

"He might be."

After a pause, Doug said, "We went to college together."

"Who did?" asked Kael.

"Me and Bolo," said Doug.

Kael braked to a complete stop. "We must be talking about two different Bolos because I'm pretty sure mine never got past the second grade. Who's your Bolo?"

"Bolo Wright. Mitch. Mitchell Wright. I gather he doesn't go by that nickname anymore?"

"No," said Kael, suddenly recalling one of Assan's rumors that Bolo was white. "How did he get the nickname, Bolo?"

"In college he always wore bolo ties, so all the brothers in the frat called him Bolo."

Kael wondered if this was just an amazing coincidence, or was Mitchell Wright the Bolo mentioned in the *sous-préfet*'s CIA application? But the other Bolo, the one they'd nabbed and lost in Lidjombo, had admitted to working with The Three Stooges. And his signed and stamped letter of immunity proved it. If Mitch was involved, how did he fit into all of this? A lot of unflattering adjectives had been used to describe Mitch, but stupid wasn't one of them. It didn't make any sense unless CARL was back and he was pissed about what had happened with the mayor's beer truck.

Kael asked, "What college did you and Bolo attend?"

Doug held up a closed fist, but with his index and pinky fingers sticking straight up. "Hook 'em horns. The University of Texas at Austin."

Kael shook his head. "I should have known a Texan was mixed up in this thing."

"Mixed up in what?" asked Tallin.

"Yeah," said Doug. "What did I say?"

"It's just a theory," said Kael.

Tallin turned to Doug. "No need to worry, then. His theories are as palatable as Zenith's cooking. Here's an example: Alaska and Africa are more alike than different."

"They both begin and end with the letter A," said Doug.

"Aha!" said Kael. "That's exactly how my own theory got started."

Tallin giggled. "Most people would have ended there, too."

"That's what makes me so irresistible," said Kael looking straight at Tallin. "I want more."

She blushed at his intended double meaning. She also elbowed him in the ribs.

He pulled into Zenith's parking lot, his brain still sucking on the idea of Mitch and Bolo being one and the same. It was a lot to swallow.

Doug thanked Kael for the lift. With his hand poised on the door handle, he said, "They both have six letters in their names."

Kael said, "Bolo has only four letters."

"I was talking about Alaska and Africa." Doug opened the door.

"Oh yeah, right," said Kael. "Three consonants and three vowels."

Doug stepped out of the truck. "I'll be thinking about this all day. You coming, Tallin?"

"In a few minutes," she said. "You go ahead. I'll catch up."

After Doug had started down the footpath, Kael bragged, "Another convert."

Tallin shook her head. "The man hasn't eaten a decent meal in twenty-four hours so his powers of deductive reasoning have been incapacitated. Plus, he's a photographer."

"That's the best theory you can come up with?"

"Give me a break," she said. "Remember, I'm operating on just a couple of hours of frequently interrupted sleep."

"Does that mean you want a full eight hours tonight?"

"Not at all. I kind of like being stupid."

"Then I'll do my best to keep you that way."

They kissed. Between their lips and their hands, very few body parts were left untouched.

Kael said, "This is my first time necking in the truck."

"Glad to hear it." She held his face in her hands, and kissed his forehead. "I should go."

"I thought you wanted to be stupid."

"Later." She slid out of the truck. Her swollen lips were the last to leave.

"I'll pick you up tonight," he said.

Tallin shut the door behind her. "I know what I'll be thinking about all day."

"Me, too," he said. "Why did she only bring one box of cheesecake?"

# 38

When Kael got home after dropping Tallin at Zenith's camp, he told Assan about Mitch's nickname. He also reminded him of the rumor that Bolo was white.

"Do you think it's possible that Mitch is involved with The Three Stooges?" he asked.

"*Inshallah, monsieur.*"

"Here's something I never thought I'd say: I'd love to talk to Mitch. Unfortunately, he's all the way down in the Congo."

"He's in the Congo, *monsieur*, but not far."

Kael smiled. There was that phrase again. He asked, "How far is 'not far' this time?"

"About twelve hours down river by dugout canoe. *Monsieur* Mitch has a research camp just over the border that he started when he was still working here."

"I'd like to check out that camp of his. Could you borrow a canoe from someone?"

"*Oui, monsieur.* Would you like one fitted with an outboard engine? We could be there in half the time."

"We?" asked Kael.

"Of course, *monsieur.* The last time I let an American go down river alone, it ended tragically. I won't let that happen again."

It suddenly hit Kael that Molly had died down river and Mitch had a camp down river. The coincidences were beginning to pile up.

While Assan arranged for the motorized canoe, Kael paid a visit to Paige. She answered her front door with a thermometer sticking out of her mouth.

"Are you sick?" he asked.

"No," she mumbled. "I always take my temperature three times per day."

"Why do it if you're not sick?"

"Just to be sure," she said.

Kael explained that he needed her to house-sit with Josie for a day or two. She could use Assan's bed. Her other assigned duty was to drive the truck that evening out to Zenith's camp to pick up Tallin, who was spending the nights in his bed. If Tallin needed the truck to get back and forth from his house to Zenith's each day, she was welcome to use it.

"Tell her I had to check out a theory, one that has nothing to do with Alaska."

Next Kael went to the market to pick up some road food, or in this case, river food. He stuffed a sack with *baguettes* of bread, boiled manioc wrapped in leaves, grilled goat meat with hot pepper seasoning on the side, bananas, avocados, and hard-boiled eggs. By the time he got back home, Assan was already filling red gas tanks belonging to an outboard engine.

Assan looked up from his pouring. "Uncle Douda gave me his canoe for free."

"That's great."

"*Oui, monsieur*. He's renting you the outboard."

"Me? What ever happened to 'we?'"

"*We* agreed to Uncle Douda's terms, *monsieur*."

After throwing a change of clothes in a backpack, Kael wrote a short note and left it on the dining table:

> Dear Tallin,
>
> There's nothing more I'd rather do than stay here tonight noisily whittling points off your I.Q., but something's come up. Unfortunately, it won't be me.
>
> I'll be gone for a day or two. Believe me when I say, "I'm sorry," and that I thought our relationship would be much further along before I'd have to utter those two words.
>
> Make yourself at home. If I were the crude type, I'd tell you to take a good look at the floor because after I return, all you'll see is ceiling. Thank goodness I'm more sophisticated than that.
>
> Yours, in theory, Kael

By eleven o'clock, they pushed their canoe away from the riverbank. Assan let Kael be the skipper first. It was either that, Kael explained, or face a certain mutiny down river.

Kael worked the outboard's throttle, getting used to how its thirty-five horses of power collaborated with an eighteen-foot-long by three-foot-wide vessel. It handled like a motorized pencil. He could easily understand how Molly might have accidently tipped hers over.

It felt good to be on the water again. It wasn't exactly the same as cruising *The Sourdough* up Chatham Strait, but there was wind in his face, water under his feet, and a wake at his back.

Within minutes of their departure, Assan pointed out a pair of hippos far off the starboard bow. The tops of their heads could be seen just above the water's surface. They looked like a couple of partially submerged rocks.

Kael said, "Maybe those are the two we heard last night."

Assan simply responded, "I don't think so, *monsieur*."

After a couple of hours, Kael decided that the river needed a psychiatrist. It was obviously schizophrenic. At times it was swift and clean, but around the next bend, it would suddenly become sluggish and murky. With no warning, it went from deep to shallow, exhilarating to boring, and noisy to silent. One minute it was straight, knowing exactly where it wanted to go. The next, it was meandering. It couldn't seem to make up its mind.

Kael knew how it felt, and not just because he'd once been a temperamental teenager. He couldn't decide if his theoretical connection of Mitch to Bolo—the poacher, not the frat brother—was brilliant or pure drivel. He wavered back and forth, but the farther he got down river, the closer he came to the conclusion that it was more likely the latter.

It was just before sunset when they beached the canoe at Mitch's research camp. It was well hidden behind the trees. From the river it was nearly invisible, even for Kael and Assan who were specifically looking for it. Without Assan, Kael would have kept right on going, scanning the riverbank until he happened upon the Congo's capital of Brazzaville, another thousand kilometers down river. That was probably where Mitch was anyway. He wasn't in camp.

They were greeted by an open fire pit, a simple hut made of palm fronds, and next to it, a thirty-foot fiberglass flagpole similar to the one he'd seen in Zenith's camp. Kael theorized that TRAP must give them out to every one of its researchers in the field. At least there wasn't a University of Texas pennant flapping at the top of it.

The fire pit hadn't been used in a while, but the door of the hut was padlocked shut. This suggested to Kael that Mitch hadn't yet abandoned his camp. It was still being used, but for what purpose?

"We should look around," said Kael.

"What are we looking for?"

"I don't know," said Kael. "Ivory and a .375 would be a good start."

Kael grabbed a sturdy stick. Wedged under the hut's padlock and used as a lever, it ripped the hasp's screws right out of the rotting door jam. It made Kael feel buff.

Inside, he found nothing to link Mitch to The Three Stooges. There was no ivory and no .375. He found a small wooden bed with no mattress, some blackened pots and pans, and two storm lanterns sitting on top of a boxed-up single-side-band radio, probably left over from Mitch's days as a researcher. Ironically, there were also a few rusted tools that might allow him to repair the damage he'd done to Mitch's door and lock.

He went back outside fully prepared to tell Assan that his theory was all foam and no beer. But Assan wasn't there. He wasn't down by the canoe, either. Kael called out his name.

A faint response came from somewhere back in the trees: "*Oui, monsieur.* Over here."

Directed by the sound of Assan's voice, Kael pushed through the understory of face-whipping branches. With the sun only minutes from setting, he hoped Assan was "not far." It was already getting dark under the trees.

He finally found Assan amidst a tangle of vines and thorny brambles. From twenty feet away, he could plainly see that Assan's face was shiny with perspiration. If Assan was sweating, something was wrong.

"Are you lost?" asked Kael.

"*Non, monsieur.*"

"Good, because I am."

"I was searching for a private place to relieve myself, *monsieur.*"

"I'd say you've found it," said Kael, "but you didn't need to show it to me. My only advice would be to watch out for those thorns."

"*Oui, monsieur.* Come look closer."

Kael hoped Assan hadn't called him all the way out there just to show off his bowel movement, even if it did resemble the face of one of The Three Stooges. He approached with trepidation.

Next to Assan's feet was what appeared to be an open grave. It didn't contain a body —only body parts in a wide range of sizes and colors, from foot-long straight yellow ones to five-foot-long curved white ones. Except for his grandmother's baby grand piano, Kael had never seen so much dead ivory in one place. It was neatly arranged according to size, not stacked on their sides, but standing upright. Big ones were at one end of the grave. Little ones were at the other end. In between were the medium-sized ones. It was like looking down on a collection of jumbo pan flutes, something Paul Bunyan might have played.

"There are forty-two tusks, *monsieur*."

Kael felt sick to his stomach. "That's twenty-one elephants," he said incredulously.

"*Oui, monsieur*. They were covered with a thin sheet of plywood camouflaged by leaves, rocks and branches. I nearly fell in with my pants down around my ankles."

Kael noticed the piece of plywood shoved off to one side. "We need to figure out what to do next."

"*Oui, monsieur*, but can I first relieve myself? I never did get around to doing it."

"Of course," said Kael.

While Assan went off in search of another men's room, Kael gingerly climbed down into the ivory pit for a closer look. It was deep enough to place his head at ground level. With a grunt, he picked up one medium-sized tusk. It was heavier than it looked. It had to weigh more than twenty pounds, which meant that he and Assan would have to move over one thousand pounds of ivory. That was a half-ton of teeth that was probably worth close to a half-million dollars on the black market. They couldn't possibly take it all back to Bayanga in one trip. The canoe wasn't big enough to hold it all. What they couldn't take this trip, he decided, they'd have to move to a new hiding place of their own until they could come back for it at a later date.

He put the medium-sized tusk back in its row. He was getting his feet in position to try a clean-and-jerk lift with the largest tusk when he sensed a presence behind him. Leaving the tusk where it was, he turned around wholly expecting to find Assan. He was just about to ask, "Did you remember to flush?" when he realized that it wasn't Assan. It was Mitch.

He was ten feet away, bare-chested, and looking so muscular that he appeared to be armor-plated. Resting on one hip was a rifle. It was a .375. As he came closer, Kael could distinguish numerous cuts and bruises on his face, arms and legs. Mitch didn't say a word. Kael theorized that the situation called for a joke.

"It looks like you either went ten rounds with Mike Tyson, or you've been dating him."

Mitch stopped just shy of the pit. He looked down on Kael. "You always were a royal asshole, Husker. What I look like is none of your fucking business. And that hole you're standing in is none of your fucking business, either."

"I was just looking for the outhouse."

"That's not it, but you did manage to fall into some deep shit."

"How deep?" asked Kael wondering where Assan was.

"Way over your fucking head."

Kael said loudly, "I know you're working with The Three Stooges." He was hoping his voice would carry to wherever Assan was squatting.

Mitch frowned. "Give me a fucking break. Those guys are nothing but small-time dipshits."

"Then answer me this: What's worse? A royal asshole or a small-time dipshit?"

"They are equally revolting."

Kael nodded. "Kind of like Donny and Marie Osmond, huh?"

"Cut the crap, Husker. You don't know shit about what's going on here, do you?"

"That's where you're wrong, Mitch. What I know is shit. For example, I found out your nickname is Bolo."

Mitch shrugged his shoulders. "Since when is that a crime?"

"In and of itself, having a nickname is perfectly legal, but when it's connected to that .375 you're carrying and these forty-two tusks I found near your research camp, you've got some 'splaining to do, Lucy."

Mitch pointed the aforementioned .375 in the direction of Kael's sweating forehead. "My nickname's Bolo, not Lucy, and from where I'm standing on the back side of this cannon, you seem to be the one with a shit load of problems—three hundred and seventy-five to be exact. Now, how did you find out about my nickname?"

Kael needed time, not to mention a bulletproof vest. Looking straight into the barrel of Mitch's .375, which appeared to be bigger than most Manhattan apartments, Kael said, "I ran into one of your old frat brothers."

"Which one?"

"Doug. He's a photographer now."

"Dougie Dornhoffer or Doug Klugman?"

"I didn't catch his last name."

"It doesn't matter. Both were assholes."

"Just plain assholes?" asked Kael. "Not royal assholes like me?"

"I'm sure they're royal assholes now."

"Then can I assume you're not going to the twenty-year reunion?"

"That's right, and you won't be attending either, I'm afraid."

Kael needed to stall a while longer, just until Assan got back to save the day. "As long as you're going to shoot me, there's no harm in enlightening me further, is there? Come on. I hate loose ends as much as you do." He carefully picked up a foot-long tusk, one that he realized might have been hacked away from the adolescent face of William or Harry. "Why, Mitch?"

"The money, of course."

"Forty-two tusks is a lot of money. That's twenty-one elephants."

"I've shot a lot more than twenty-one."

As long as Mitch was talking, he wasn't shooting, so Kael asked, "How do you fit in with The Three Stooges?"

"I don't. They have a poacher named Bolo Ndinga, who couldn't count to twenty-one if he took off his shoes and pulled down his pants. He's a perfect match for those three dipshits in Bayanga and he was something of a revelation to me. When I discovered that their poacher was named Bolo, I began using my old nickname again, at least when it came to shooting elephants. I've been careful, but I have to do business with buyers on the black market and they're not exactly trustworthy boy scouts, if you know what I mean."

Kael nodded in agreement. Even with a gun pointed at his head, it was hard to remain silent. He sorely wanted to wise-crack, "Not like you, huh Mitch?"

Mitch continued. "If any of those rugheads started flapping their big lips, they only knew me as Bolo. It's a fairly common name, and it just so happened to be the name of the only poacher endorsed by the police commissioner, the mayor and the *sous-préfet.* That kind of backing, whether it's real or imagined, couldn't hurt. Sure, I'm white and Ndinga's black, but you know how things work here: facts just get in the way of rumors and lies. Most times, everything is so jumbled, it's hard to tell which is which. I guess I don't have to tell you, though, do I? You're the brainiac who thought I was working for The Three Dipshits. Fucking A, Husker! I'll bet you thought Green Mambas just crawled into pick-ups for warmth, right?"

Kael narrowed his eyes, not quite understanding the implications. "How do you know about that? I didn't tell anyone."

Mitch smiled. "I guess I must have put it there."

Kael's eyes were now wide open. "Why? You nearly killed my son."

"No biggie. I was after you, but I would have settled for one fewer half-breed."

Kael no longer cared that Mitch was attached to a loaded .375. "You're sicker than Paige thinks she is. Why me? What did I ever do to you?"

"You're standing there... in the middle of my secret stash... and you still have to ask that?"

"But that's now. What did I do before?"

"You breathed my oxygen, Husker."

"There's plenty for both of us, especially with twenty-one fewer elephants about."

"True, but you were breathing too close. You were looking for a Bolo with a .375. After you fucked up with the other Bolo, I thought you might blame the snake on him or his three dipshit friends. Then I'd just sit back and watch you fuck up again. That's what you are, Husker. You're not a royal asshole. You're a fuck-up. I don't like fuck-ups. I don't like you. I never have. I think we were enemies in a past life."

"Or married," suggested Kael.

"If that were the case, I'd kill myself."

"Like any good spouse, I'd help you," said Kael.

"Go ahead. Make with the jokes. I've got a good one for you. Maybe you'll get as big a laugh out of it as I did."

"What's that?" asked Kael. "The theory that the size of a man's gun is inversely proportional to the size of his... um... brainpan?"

Mitch's finger briefly abandoned its post at the .375's trigger to pull a crumpled, bent, hand-rolled cigarette from the front right pocket of his shorts. He failed in his attempt to straighten it out and placed the crooked stub between his lips. Talking out of the side of his mouth, he said, "For a second there, I thought you were going to say, 'dick.'" His fingers returned to the pocket where they extracted a matchbook.

"No," said Kael. "You're confusing it with the theory that states that a man's penis is in direct proportion to the cigarette he smokes."

Mitch lit his poor excuse for a cigarette while cradling the .375 in his armpit. It remained pointed at Kael's head the entire time.

"That's a good one Husker. A little juvenile, but then, so are you." Mitch blew an expert smoke ring in Kael's direction. It dissipated before reaching him. "Now, it's my turn. Did you hear the one about the hippie and the crocodile man?"

Kael was secretly wondering if *his* crocodile man had fallen into another hole. "Is that the one that starts out: 'A hippie and a crocodile man go into a bar?'"

Mitch shook his head. "Everybody tells it wrong. They didn't go into a bar. In fact, there wasn't even a fucking crocodile man. Not at first, anyway. Three dipshits just assumed there was. Had to be since the hippie died in the water. That's rughead logic for you. Here's how the joke should be told. This hippie—we'll call her Molly—goes down river in search of a poacher. We'll call him Bolo. She finds him poling his dugout up river. They're alone in their canoes, side by side. She threatens Bolo. She tells him he has to stop or there will be consequences. Bolo responds by striking her on the head with his pole. She falls into the water. She struggles to return to the surface, but Bolo's pole keeps pushing her back under. After numerous fruitless attempts, she tires and she drowns. Bolo then tips over her dugout. Just another unfortunate boating accident until the Three Dipshits introduce the old crocodile-man theory."

Kael had just one burning question: "Was it Ndinga Bolo or was it you carrying the big pole on the river that day?"

"See. It's hard to tell, isn't it?" Mitch paused for a few seconds before adding, "Of course it was me. The other Bolo wouldn't have the balls to kill a white woman."

Kael smiled, not from Mitch's story, but from what he glimpsed just beyond Mitch, who, if he'd had eyes in the back of his head, would have seen it too. It was Assan sneaking closer through the forest. He no longer reminded Kael of a lumbering elephant as he had that time out at *Le Bistro*. This time, he was a panther, a silent stalking cat with a big stick of his own clutched in his black forepaws.

Kael said, "You'll get yours."

"Not by you," said Mitch confidently patting his rifle.

"No," said Kael, "by a crocodile man with a big stick."

Right on cue, Assan pounced the final ten feet. He brought the stick down hard across the top of Mitch's head. The blow, which would have crushed a normal man's skull, barely mussed his hair-do. As Mitch turned to face his attacker, Kael found himself frozen in place, involuntarily devising a theory about the relationship of hard bodies to hard heads.

Assan's second parry was to the barrel of the rifle. Wood hitting steel produced the same dull sound as wood hitting the crown of Mitch's skull. This time, however, the steel did what the skull had stubbornly refused to do: it dropped to the ground in a pronounced state of unconsciousness.

Mitch used his emancipated hands to grab the stick that had assaulted him. He tried to wrench it from Assan, but with Allah's assistance, no doubt, the smaller man held on like a waving flag to a flagpole.

With the .375 no longer pointed at his head, Kael decided that it was a good time for him to jump into the fray. Even with a two men to one advantage, they would still be greatly outnumbered in the muscles department, however.

The situation called for brains over brawn, but the best idea Kael could come up with was to throw the small ivory tusk he was still holding. At least he threw it like a man. It struck Mitch's back, which was so broad, Stevie Wonder could have hit it. Mitch didn't appear to notice that Kael had made the decision to get involved.

Assan and Allah were still holding their own. They had even managed to back Mitch up to the edge of the pit.

Kael deftly sidestepped past the columns of ivory until he was able to reach out and grab hold of Mitch's bare ankle. It was right at mouth level, so Kael sank his teeth into the meaty, undercooked drumstick served up before him. He'd never bitten into human flesh before. It tasted like dirt and hair, not unlike a typical fast-food-restaurant hamburger.

Mitch tried to jerk his leg away, but Kael wasn't ready to be excused from the table just yet. He managed to hook Mitch's flailing foot underneath an armpit for better control. With his meal now sufficiently subdued, it was easy to take a second, more ravenous bite. This time, in addition to the main ingredients of dirt and hair, he picked up a hint, just a soupcon, of copper flavoring. He couldn't tell if he tasted his own blood or Mitch's.

The next thing Kael sensed was Mitch falling backwards. He had successfully wrenched the stick away from Assan and Allah. Clinging to the stick, Mitch seemed to float directly overhead for several seconds. With his ankle still securely attached to Kael's incisors, he was able to pivot his bulk around in mid-fall so that he could face the approaching ground. That twisting motion forced Kael to relinquish his dental death grip.

Mitch never reached the ground. His trajectory dropped him right on top of his neatly arranged stockpile of ivory and those teeth bit into Mitch's flesh much deeper than Kael's had. Some ran all the way through like sharpened swords, their bloody points poking out of his broad back. The stick he'd fought over fell from his hands.

"Is he dead?" asked an out-of-breath Assan.

"That would be my theory," said Kael.

"What do we do now, *monsieur*?"

Looking down on Mitch's ivory-impaled body, Kael said, "We could marvel at the irony."

"The what, *monsieur*?"

"Never mind. We've got work to do. We need to figure out what to do with Mitch and all this ivory."

"I'd leave everything right where it is, *monsieur*. Just throw some dirt on top. We don't need to take the ivory back to Bayanga. It would just bring up a lot of questions we don't want to answer. And Monsieur Mitch needs to be buried anyway."

"But what if Mitch had a partner? I doubt it, but what if there's someone else who knows about this spot? They could dig it all up."

"Then we bury everything in a different spot, *monsieur*."

Kael asked, "Did you bring a shovel?"

"*Non, monsieur.*"

"Then I've got another idea. First, help me out of this hole." With Assan's assistance, Kael scrambled back up to ground level. After standing up, he continued holding on to Assan's right hand. He then clasped his own right wrist with his left hand and said, "Thank you."

"It was nothing, *monsieur*."

"It was more than nothing. We're even, now."

"Even, *monsieur*?"

"You saved my life. Mitch was going to kill me."

"He was going to kill me, too, *monsieur*."

"But he was going to kill me first. Thanks for coming back when you did."

"*Allah akbar, monsieur.*"

Kael smiled. "*Allah akbar*, Assan."

By the light thrown off from Mitch's lanterns, they hauled all forty-two ivory tusks, Mitch's uncooperative body and his .375 down to the river's edge. There Kael found Mitch's dugout pulled up on the beach near where he and Assan had left their own. Inside Mitch's was a long stick used for poling. Its other purpose, he'd learned that evening, was to hit Molly over the head and to keep pushing her underwater until she drowned. Kael picked it up and with one mighty swing broke it in half against a sturdy tree. He flung both pieces far into the middle of the swift river.

Next he grabbed the .375. He held it like a baseball bat. He stepped into the batter's box and after several home-run-like cuts, finally made contact with the sweet spot of that same mature mahogany. The walnut stock of the .375 splintered off like a broken-bat single. Kael's hands stung, but he was safely on base.

His next at-bat put a curve on the barrel any professional baseball pitcher would have been proud to have in his arsenal. He tossed the pieces into the bottom of his own dugout. He and Assan then piled as much ivory on top as was considered prudent for a short boat ride upstream.

When Kael had suggested getting rid of the ivory in the river instead of burying it in the ground, Assan had agreed with the plan. He knew of a perfect spot. It was deep with a very muddy bottom. Anything dropped there would sink through thirty feet of murky water. If that wasn't enough, it would be covered by three feet of mud and muck at the bottom. No one would ever find it.

It took three trips to dump all the ivory along with the pieces of the .375. What to do with Mitch was another matter.

They decided to tow him down river in his own dugout. Assan knew of a spot, "not far, monsieur," on the Congo side of the border. It was, according to Assan, frequented by hungry crocodiles that might digest any evidence. If not, if Mitch's body was ever found, the old crocodile man theory would probably resurface as well. It seemed only fitting.

After they lowered Mitch's body into the water, he initially performed an excellent version of the dead-man's float. Then, he sank out of sight just as the ivory had done only minutes earlier. There was no sign of any crocodiles.

Next they tipped over Mitch's dugout, repeating what he had done after he'd murdered Molly. The partially submerged canoe couldn't seem to decide whether to sink or remain afloat, so it bobbed downstream in the gentle current debating its options. Kael wasn't concerned. If someone found it, they'd claim it as their own. Finders keepers, losers weepers.

The short trip back up to Mitch's research camp was one of quiet contemplation. Kael pondered the correctness of their actions. Now that everything was over and done with, he wasn't sure if they were right or wrong. It was probably a little of both. Yes, they'd killed Mitch, but it had been an accident, an obvious case of self-defense. It was kill or be killed, but would the African authorities see it that way? Never.

Assan had already been thrown into prison for a crime he had never committed. Did a foreigner and a Muslim stand any chance whatsoever of remaining free men if they openly admitted to killing someone, regardless of whether it was an accident or not? Kael didn't think so. The Three Stooges would be brought in as witnesses for the prosecution. He could already hear their illogical arguments: The *sous-préfet* would say,

'It was two against one and the Muslim already has a record of killing whites." The police commissioner would say, "The foreigner obviously hired him to do more than just cook and clean." The mayor would say, "Setting us up as poachers was also part of their devious plan."

The American government might get Kael released after months of high-level, hush-hush, international negotiations, but who would rally behind Assan? No one had before, so there was no reason to think anyone would this time. He'd rot in prison because he'd saved Kael's life. Kael couldn't let that happen. Silence had to be the third partner in this fiasco.

When they beached the canoe back at the research camp, Assan asked, "Do you want to continue on to Bayanga tonight, *monsieur*?"

"No," said Kael. "It's dark, I'm tired, I'm dirty, I'm hungry, I'm thirsty, and I can come up with a dozen more whiny excuses if you need me to."

"*Non, monsieur*. That was more than enough. I'll start a fire."

"I'll be up there to help after I get cleaned up a bit. Did you bring any soap?"

"*Oui, monsieur*. It's in my sack right next to my teapot and the two beers."

"You brought beers?"

"*Oui, monsieur*. I thought you'd like them, even if they weren't cold."

"Good guess. That's the second time today you've saved my life."

"It's getting much easier, *monsieur*."

An hour later, they were lounging by a campfire just smokey enough to keep the mosquitos at bay. Both men had already bathed and feasted on the left-over road food: bananas, boiled manioc, a few pieces of grilled goat meat, a *baguette* of bread, and avocados. Kael's two beers were already splashing around contentedly in his bladder like children in a wading pool on a hot day. Assan had a pot of tea brewing over the hot coals.

In the distance, a tree hyrax did its best imitation of a torture victim no longer able to remain stoic from the pain. Its anguished screams, each one louder and more horrific than the preceding one, could have been originating from Kael's own lungs.

He wanted to yell at someone, but who? Who would be the most qualified candidate for his venting? Was it Mitch for dying? Or how about The Three Stooges for sucking him into their insane little world? Or were Nick, Molly, and Josie to blame for bringing him back there in the first place? He might feel a little better if he just blew up at Assan for only bringing two beers.

Unknowingly, Assan defused the situation by asking, "Would you like some tea, *monsieur*?"

"One cup couldn't hurt." While Assan poured, Kael said, "We can't tell anyone about this."

Assan carefully handed a full cup to Kael. "Your secret of drinking tea is safe with me, *monsieur*."

Kael accepted the tea with a smile. "I mean we can't tell anyone about Mitch and the ivory."

"I know, *monsieur*."

Kael no sooner said, "Absolutely no one," when he realized he was wrong. He had to tell Nick about Mitch. If not, Nick would undoubtedly launch a massive search for his missing employee. He'd call in the U.S. Marines to scour every square inch of the Congo, including the rivers. He wouldn't stop until he found something. Kael couldn't have that, even if it meant breaking his five-second pact of silence with Assan.

Kael theorized that if Nick knew what Mitch had been up to—that he'd been poaching elephants and had murdered Molly because she'd found him out—he would scale down his official investigation. Kael would be sure to point out that if the complete truth ever came out, TRAP would suffer the repercussions. Who in their right mind would give over their hard-earned money to a conservation organization that was implicated in a scandalous elephant-poaching operation? Wasn't Nick's success at TRAP dependent on his ability to round up generous donors? His job would become more difficult than that of an Alaskan politician stumping for a return to prohibition.

Kael shared his thoughts with Assan, who agreed that *Monsieur* Nick, and only *Monsieur* Nick, should be told. He would be on their side, "*Inshallah*," according to Assan.

They remained camped out next to the fire. It provided a modicum of comfort for what Kael anticipated would be a fitful night's sleep. He had no doubt that the nightmares were just waiting for him to close his eyes. Maybe not Molly and her crocodile man this time, but he couldn't rule out a very pissed-off Mitch seeking revenge.

But none of that ever happened. He slept soundly, and the only dream he had was of him back in Alaska. It was one of those spectacular blue-sky days and he was fishing for halibut off the aft deck of *The Sourdough*. Chako was curled up at his feet, unafraid of his fishing pole. That was how he knew it was a dream.

His friends from Hidden Cove were also on board. They were fishing, spread out around the boat so as not to tangle any lines. Hector was up at the bow. C.B.'s station was at the port side, while Sam jigged his line up and down over the starboard side. Everyone was in good spirits, even Sam, who kept saying, "What a big-dot day! Too bad Kael's not here to enjoy it."

Every time he said it, Kael would respond, "But I *am* here."

No one paid any attention to him. They just kept right on fishing even though the fish weren't biting that day. No one was reeling anything in, but no one cared, either, except Kael. When he suggested trying another spot, the others completely ignored him like he wasn't even there on his own boat.

After a long while, much *too* long as far as Kael was concerned, C.B. finally hooked something. It didn't put up much of a fight. In fact, it shot to the surface faster than C.B. could reel in the slack. Since it couldn't levitate in mid-air, it waited for C.B. to catch up enough to yank it out of the water for all to see.

It was a halibut, all right, but it wasn't much of one. If it were ten pounds, somebody's thumb was pressing down on the scale. Everyone except Kael cheered. They were acting like C.B. had just landed a world record.

Sam said, "Nice fish. I'll get my camera."

Hector said, "That's a keeper."

"That's not a fish," yelled Kael. "It's fucking bait."

But no one paid any attention. Sam got his camera and took a picture. C.B. and Hector squeezed in close while collectively holding the fish up in front of them, as if it had taken both men working in shifts to bring it in. Their smiles were bigger than the pumpkin seed dangling from the hook.

When the picture taking and follow-up high fives were over and done with, Sam announced, "That's it, boys. It's been a great day of fishing, but it's time to go home."

There was no grumbling except from Kael, of course. He couldn't believe what he was hearing. "What do you mean it's time to go home? There's still plenty of daylight left, and the limit for halibut is two per person per day. We can still catch seven more. Or, we could throw that little one back and catch eight barn doors really worth celebrating."

Once again, his voice fell upon clogged ears.

C.B. said, "Good idea. Let's head home."

Hector said, "Ready when you are, C.B."

Chako got up from where she'd been napping. It was her first movement all afternoon. She stretched before strolling into the wheelhouse. But instead of flopping down on her rug for some more quality sleep time, she jumped up onto the padded leather helmsman's chair.

To Kael, it appeared as if she was actually checking out the navigational charts spread out before her. She then peered down below the steering wheel to seemingly make sure the battery switch was set in the proper position for starting the powerful Perkins diesel engine. It was, so with one knowledgeable paw, she turned the key and punched the starter button. The engine immediately rumbled to life. She moved her paw to the throttle control and eased it forward. The boat began to move. Both paws then went to the wheel and started a turn to starboard.

Kael finally regained his ability to speak. He stammered, "Chako, what the hell are you doing? I can't even get you to fetch a lousy tennis ball."

But she didn't respond. She was too busy bringing *The Sourdough* about. This was somewhat comforting to Kael. She had made a habit of ignoring him in the past, so at least that hadn't changed. What he witnessed next, though, was surreal.

C.B. entered the wheelhouse with two cans of beer. He handed one to Chako, who accepted it between her two front paws. By herself, she lifted it up to her mouth, chugged the contents, and then crushed the empty can against her forehead.

Kael awoke from his dream with a lot of questions, but the two most troubling ones were: Was it too late to get home, and did the Betty Ford Center accept dogs?

# 39

Sam was right after all. It was time to go home. And Kael knew it. He'd caught his fish. He'd even returned it to the water. There was nothing left to do now, but go home.

He'd solved the mystery of Molly's death, so in theory, his nagging dreams of her were over. They had floated far downstream with Mitch's canoe.

He'd been lucky. He knew that, too. Despite playing on CARL's home field, he'd come out a winner. How many foreigners could make that claim? Not once, but twice, he'd kept Assan from rotting in prison: the first time for something he didn't do and the second for something he did. CARL would be doubly pissed over that, and Kael didn't want to wait around long enough for him to figure it out.

It was time to go home. He had beaten The Three Stooges at their own game despite being decidedly outnumbered and heavily out-polyestered. He had caught them with their dirty hands in the ivory jar. They probably wouldn't do any jail time for that, but their names would be shuffled to the top of the *fonctionnaire* shit list. This guaranteed that their next official assignments would be to other villages far away from Bayanga and even farther from Bangui.

Coincidentally, that was what Kael wanted for himself. His work there was done even though he still had more than nine months to go on his TRAP contract. Nick wouldn't hold him to it. If he tried, Kael would release certain embarrassing photographs taken during Nick's twenty-fifth birthday extravaganza. The theme had been, "Quarter of a Century; Quarter of a Brain Cell Left," and the pictures proved it.

All these thoughts bobbed through Kael's head during the seven-hour return canoe trip from Mitch's camp back up to Bayanga. There was little conversation between him and Assan. Male friendships didn't have to be noisy to be meaningful, especially when the two men shared a thirty-foot-deep secret between them.

They were back at the riverbank just below their house by early afternoon. No one came out of the house to help unload their gear. Josie was probably playing soccer, Tallin would be at Zenith's, and Paige, no doubt, was at the hospital for her daily checkup. Kael volunteered to haul everything up the hill to the house if Assan would return the canoe and outboard right away just in case Uncle Douda was renting by the hour.

The house was closed up, but unlocked. After opening the window shutters for some needed sunlight and cool breezes off the river, Kael noticed a note left on the dining table. It was addressed to him.

> *Dear Kael,*
>
> *There's nothing more I'd rather do today than be here to give you a proper welcome back. On second thought, maybe improper is a better adjective. Unfortunately, my lips, arms, legs, and all the freckled parts you like in-between will be busy out at Zenith's camp.*
>
> *I'll be back tonight around six. Believe me when I say, "I forgive you for abandoning me," and that I thought you would be the first one in this relationship who'd have to utter those words.*
> *I made myself at home during your absence. If I were the crude type, I'd tell you to take a good long nap this afternoon because you'll be up all night showing me every imperfection in your ceiling. Thank goodness I'm as sophisticated as you.*
>
> *Yours, for the rest of the week,*
> *Tallin*

Kael found himself smiling when he finished reading and it wasn't just because of a promised ceiling inspection later that evening. For years he'd been searching for someone without a penis who fully appreciated his aberrant sense of humor. Tallin's note did that and more. She encouraged it. She nurtured it. She got it. The last woman like that in his life had been... Molly.

That night, when Tallin pulled up in his Toyota truck, he was waiting outside for her. He couldn't wrap his arms around her fast enough. He opened her car door and gave her his best bear hug before she could exit.

Squeezing just as hard, she said, "Wow! I missed you, too."

His response probably surprised her more than his attempt to crack her ribs: "Do you believe in do-overs?"

"If we're talking sex, you know I do."

"Believe it or not, I was thinking about something else."

"There goes *my* theory," she said. "Do I get a do-over?"

"Of course."

"Then, do you mean like in a Wiffle ball game?"

"Exactly!"

"I wholeheartedly believe in do-overs. They're an important part of the game, just like striking out and foul balls."

"Are we still talking Wiffle ball, or are we back to sex?" he asked.

"Personally, I'd like to get back to sex."

"You always say just the right thing. Unfortunately, Assan has prepared a meal of groundnut stew. It would be impolite to skip dinner."

In her best sarcastic tone, she said, "That son of a bitch. He's always thinking about himself."

"Not always," said Kael.

When she asked him how his trip had gone, he said, "Not as well as we had planned," and quickly changed the subject.

She must have sensed his reticence. She didn't ask for any details about where he had been and what he had done. All she said was, "You can tell me about it when you want to," and the rest of her time in Bayanga, she never mentioned it again.

The remainder of the week would have been perfect if not for the occasions when Kael's thoughts were hijacked by Mitch. He yanked Molly's ghostly image right out of the driver's seat and threw her callously to the pavement. He then zoomed off at break-neck speeds, careening into Kael's conscience and sideswiping his sense of right and wrong. One good thing about Mitch's visits, however, was that he never came when Kael was sleeping.

Molly stopped bothering him, too, that week. His nightmares of her ended as quickly as they had begun four months earlier. He shared this last bit with Tallin, the part about Molly no longer haunting him while he slept. When Tallin asked him why Molly had chosen now, that week of all weeks to disappear, Kael gave her a theory she could believe: sex so good it was all he could think about. He couldn't tell her the whole truth, not that he was lying about the sex. The real reason why Molly had finally packed up and left was because he'd killed her killer. An eye for an eye, a tooth for a tusk, so to speak.

Kael had a phone call to make, so at the end of the week, he volunteered to take Tallin and Doug the photographer to Bangui. Zenith didn't argue. She hated the long drive to Bangui, being in Bangui, and the long drive home from Bangui. She admitted that the only thing she liked about Bangui were the flaky French pastries, but since she still had a few more pounds to drop, she didn't need the temptation.

Kael could almost see Doug's mouth watering as Zenith spoke of her love-hate relationship with *croissants du beurre* and *pains au chocolat*. After just seven days of Zenith's cooking, Doug was visibly skinnier. Paige even diagnosed him with a tapeworm. To which Doug replied, "Not even a tapeworm could survive on what I've been eating."

Kael, Tallin, and Doug made the long, bumpy trip to Bangui in Kael's truck. There were no downed trees, no flat tires, and sadly for Doug, no French pastry shops along the way.

Upon arriving in Bangui, they checked into two rooms at the Minerva Hotel, one for Doug and the other for Kael and Tallin. While she went downstairs to barter with the old man selling butterfly wing art, Kael phoned Nick at his TRAP office. After three rings, he picked up.

"Nick Cinzano, Central African Projects. Can I help you?"

Kael didn't even say who he was. He just started in on his joke: "This guy finds a magic lamp. When he rubs it, a genie pops out saying that he will grant three wishes. The only catch is that whatever the guy wishes for, his worst enemy will receive twice as much. After thinking it over, the guy agrees to the genie's conditions. His first wish is to have one hundred billion dollars. The genie says, 'Then your worst enemy will receive two hundred billion dollars.' With a wave of the genie's hand, the guy is suddenly surrounded by stacks of money totaling one hundred billion dollars. His second wish is for a harem of five hundred beautiful women. The genie says, 'Then your worst enemy will receive one thousand beautiful women.' With another wave of the genie's hand, the guy finds himself in the middle of five hundred beautiful women smothering him with kisses and caresses. The genie asks, 'What will be your third and final wish, Master?' The guy smiles and says, 'I want you to beat me half to death.'"

Nick laughed hard. When he could talk again, he said, "All right, I've got a good one about a Texan for you."

"So do I," said Kael, "but you go first."

Nick told his joke: "A Texan dressed in cowboy shirt, cowboy hat, jeans, spurs, chaps, and cowboy boots walks into a bar in New York and orders a drink. As he sits there sipping his whiskey, a young lady sits next to him. She asks, 'Are you a real cowboy?' To which he replies, 'Well ma'am, I've spent my whole life on the ranch, herding cows, breaking horses, mending fences, so I guess I am.' To be polite, he asks her what she is. She replies, 'I'm a lesbian. I spend my whole day thinking about women. I get up in the morning thinking of women. When I eat, shower, watch TV, everything makes me think of women.' The woman then gets up and leaves. Another woman soon takes her place next to the Texan and asks, 'Are you a real cowboy?' He answers, 'I always thought I was, ma'am, but I just found out that I'm a lesbian.'"

Kael laughed, not so hard that he cried, but it was still a decent reaction considering what he had weighing heavily on his mind: he had his own story of a Texan yet to tell.

Nick must have sensed that something was amiss because he said, "What's the matter? Are you jealous because mine was funnier than yours? I thought you'd be used to that by now."

Some things were best eased into: hot tubs above one hundred and ten degrees, too small jock straps, condoms past their expiration date, second marriages. Murder wasn't one of them, so Kael used the direct approach.

"Mitch is dead."

"Is this another joke?" asked Nick.

"I wish it were." Kael went on to explain the whole sordid tale. He told of Mitch's poaching, of Molly's discovery of it, and of Mitch's cold-blooded murder of her. He told of his confrontation with Mitch at his old research camp in the Congo, of his buried stash of ivory, and of the fight that accidently led to Mitch belly-flopping into his own pit of pointy tusks. He told of how he and Assan had disposed of the body, the ivory, and the .375 in the river, and why it seemed to be the best solution for everyone concerned, including TRAP.

Throughout Kael's telling of the story, Nick said little except, "I can't believe it," and "Shit!" After he'd heard everything, he agreed that Kael and Assan had done right by TRAP. He said, "The negative publicity from something like this could destroy TRAP. Right now, our biggest concern is does anyone else know about this?"

Just you, me, and Assan."

"Good," said Nick, "but do we know if Mitch worked alone or if he had partners?"

"He didn't say anything to make me think he wasn't alone," admitted Kael, "but we moved the ivory just in case." He told Nick of his original suspicions that Mitch was somehow tied to The Three Stooges, but that Mitch had denied it and Kael had believed him. At that point, Kael brought Nick up-to-date on The Three Stooges: their own little poaching operation, their downfall aboard a beer truck stopped in Nola, and their certain necessity to fill out change-of-address forms at the Bayanga post office.

"You've been busy," said Nick.

"The circumstances sort of forced me to be."

"Well, don't worry about what happens next. I'll handle everything from this end. We'll conduct an exhaustive, yet futile search for Mitch. The Congo's a big place, so we may have to concentrate our efforts in the Brazzaville area and south."

"Sounds good," said Kael.

"To put some sort of positive spin on all this, I'd like to get out a series of press releases about losing one of our brave researchers who died doing what he loved best."

"Poaching?" asked Kael.

"I was thinking more along the lines of fighting poaching. There's nothing that brings in more tax-deductible donations than the loss of a renowned researcher who gave everything, including their life, to the cause of conservation."

Not this time," said Kael. "Granted, I didn't know Mitch as well as you, but I never thought much of him. He was an ass who treated Central Africans like shit. He killed our friend Molly, and only a few days ago, he had a loaded .375 pointed at my chest. That doesn't warrant sainthood status in my book."

"Fair enough."

"One other thing," said Kael. "I want to come home."

"Can't say as I blame you. Can I convince you to hold on for two or three more months? It's just until I find a replacement with a better repertoire of jokes."

"I'll give you one month and Rodney Dangerfield's address."

Nick laughed. "In one short month, you expect me to find your replacement and not find Mitch?"

"Just don't get them mixed up," warned Kael.

"Don't worry. I'll cover your ass as if it were my own."

"It is," said Kael, "but only for one more month."

"OK, but I'm hearing rumors that your ass belongs to someone else these days."

"If we're talking about Tallin," said Kael, "thanks for sending her over."

"You can thank me by telling me which of her body parts have freckles and which ones don't."

"I haven't found any yet that don't."

"Geez!" Nick then asked, "She doesn't know anything about this Mitch business, does she?"

"No," said Kael. "Early in a relationship, it's a good general rule to not share that you killed someone."

"It was self-defense, Kael. You and Assan didn't do anything wrong." Nick waited a couple of seconds before adding, "Still, this might be one of those things we take to our graves."

Kael agreed that silence was their best option. He thanked Nick for his help and said he'd see him in a month. After hanging up the phone, he sprawled across the lumpy hotel bed and let out a loud sigh. He felt better having shared his story with Nick. He had no doubt that Nick would handle everything. It was in his best interest to do so and that was all the motivation Nick ever needed.

Tallin hadn't returned, so Kael went downstairs to find her. She was just closing the deal to buy up everything in the butterfly man's inventory and she hadn't done half-bad in the bartering department, either. They celebrated her shrewd business sense over a beer in the hotel bar. It was there, sitting on their barstools, where he told her that he would be returning to the States in one month. He didn't explain why, just that the job he'd set out to do in the C.A.R. had been completed ahead of schedule.

She said, "You don't have to tell me what happened, but does this have anything to do with that day you and Assan took off in the canoe?"

Kael asked, "Can I plead the Fifth Amendment?"

"I don't think it's valid in a Central African bar, but the court takes pity on such a cute defendant."

"That's good. My next ploy was to try squeezing out a few sympathy tears."

"If it's crying you want, let's go up to the room. I'll give you something to cry about."

He chugged what was left of his beer. "I throw myself on the mercy of the court."

She gathered up her butterfly art. "OK, but I get to throw myself on your mercy first."

He didn't know what she had in store for him upstairs, but if it took his mind off Mitch and Molly, he was all for it.

The next day, Tallin hopped a plane to Paris, but not before handing over some Polaroid photos of Josie that she'd asked Doug to take. She thought they could replace the ancient cracked one Kael kept in his wallet. There was also one of her. He thanked her and made a solemn promise to call her in about a month. She vowed to track him down if he didn't.

By the time she cleared Central African air space, Kael was meeting with Stan Pulaski in his office at the American embassy. They shook hands, exchanged the typical polite banter about how each had been faring in the land of CARL, and sat in black and chrome chairs on opposite sides of Stan's matching desk. Kael was glad to see that the desk was smallish.

Stan asked, "So, what brings you to Bangui?"

"I need a passport."

"Did you lose yours?"

"No. It's not for me. It's for my son."

Kael started his story at the logical beginning: Josie's birth. He skipped over the next ten years of in-between stuff, but ended with the news that he would be returning to the States in one month and wanted to take Josie with him. Since he was one-half American, wasn't he entitled to carry an American passport?

"Sure," said Stan. "All I need is a local birth certificate naming you as the boy's father. We'll then issue him a Consular Report of Birth Abroad to prove U.S. citizenship. After he submits that along with a completed application form, the forty-dollar fee, and a couple of two-by-two head-and-shoulder photographs, he'll receive his American passport in four to six weeks. That's the official policy, but I can speed things up. Actually, it's one of the few things around here I can make happen faster if I want to."

"Do you want to?" asked Kael.

Stan shrugged his shoulders. "Why not? Being the embassy's economics officer in one of the poorest countries in the world is comparable to Darwin observing evolution on a day-to-day basis. Bring me a birth certificate and two photos and I'll see what I can do."

Kael already had the photos courtesy of Tallin. They just had to be cropped to the right size. He still needed to come up with a Central African birth certificate, however. Sapu probably had one, but she was hours away and they hadn't even discussed the possibility of their son accompanying his father all the way to the United States. To Bayanga was one thing. To Alaska was another.

Kael wasn't ready to jump into that debate. Not yet, anyway. He would be in a few weeks after he'd organized all the pro-viewpoint arguments in his head and got Josie on board, but that wasn't going to happen in the next few hours. Like most men embroiled in tough relationship issues, he threw down the procrastination card whenever possible.

His other option for a quick birth certificate, besides asking Sapu, was to ask Nasseef.

He knew how to get anything. Besides, there was something else Kael wanted to ask him.

At Nasseef's garage, Kael was warmly welcomed with a cup of very robust Lebanese coffee. Nasseef was so pleased to see his American friend again that he offered a free oil change while they sat and caught up.

When Kael informed Nasseef of his imminent departure to the States for good, Nasseef's jaw dropped. Kael was touched by his friend's obvious discontent until his droopy jaw started functioning again and asked, "You're not taking your truck with you, are you?"

Kael smiled. "No. That will stay here for my replacement, and I will recommend that they retain you as their mechanic. I'll even go one better. I'm going to convince two TRAP researchers, both lovely women, to bring their vehicles to your garage, too."

"This is wonderful news!"

"I'm just sorry I couldn't leave earlier," Kael said only half-joking. "I do have two small favors to ask of you though."

"Such a bargain for three vehicles."

Kael decided to start with the easier of the two: "I have a friend who will soon need a job." He went on to promote Assan as the best thing to happen to automotive repair since the invention of the padded estimate.

Nasseef asked only one question: "Can I trust him?"

"With your life," said Kael without hesitation.

"Good. I can teach anyone how to fix a truck, even you. The more difficult task, I've discovered, is finding employees who won't steal from me when I turn my back."

Thinking of Mitch, Kael said, "TRAP has the same problem. What I've discovered is that there are a lot more horse's asses than horses in this world, but don't worry. Assan isn't one of them."

"He sounds like potential foreman material at *Garage* Nasseef. Bring him by. And what is your second request?"

"I need a Central African birth certificate."

"For Assan?"

"No. It's for my son, Josie. Why did you think it was for Assan?"

Nasseef explained that many of his better workers at the garage had entered the country illegally. Most were from across the river in Zaire and they needed official papers to stay. They could choose to go through the proper channels, but that could take forever and a lot of palm greasing and there was no guarantee that it would be success-ful. Good help was hard to come by, so Nasseef had done what was best for his business: He began supplying forged documents to his employees. It was part of their compre-hensive benefits package.

He took Kael into his cluttered office and shut the door. From his trousers' pocket, he pulled out a key chain holding at least thirty keys. One of them unlocked a tall cab-inet behind his desk. He opened an upper drawer and finger-walked through the files. Halfway through, he stopped, removed one eight-by-six sheet of paper and held it aloft. "*Voici.* One Central African birth certificate. We just have to fill in the blanks and stamp it." He sat at his desk and slipped the certificate into the carriage of an ancient Smith-Corona typewriter. He smiled up at Kael. "Full name of child?"

Kael was able to answer all the questions: father's full name, mother's full name, their respective professions, child's sex, place of birth, and date of birth.

Nasseef pecked out the responses with his two index fingers. When completed, he manually advanced the birth certificate out of the typewriter and said, "Now, all we need is a rubber stamp to make it official."

Kael said, "There are guys on the street who will carve out any rubber stamp on re-quest."

Nasseef grinned. "I know." He spun around in his desk chair so that he was again facing the tall cabinet. This time, he opened a lower drawer from which he removed a shoebox. He twirled back around, set the box on his desktop, and opened the lid. The box was full of rubber stamps. "I've got the complete set," he said.

He picked one at random and read it aloud: "Office of National Security. There's one that's come in handy more than a few times." He set it down and grabbed a second one. "Office of Immigration and Emigration. Enough said." He read a third one: "Of-fice of the *Préfet.* That one would probably suit your purposes, but I have something better." He searched through his remaining stamps. "Here it is. Office of the Mayor. Most births in small villages like Boda are registered at the local mayor's office." He opened the top drawer of his desk, removed an inkpad, applied the mayor's stamp to the pad, and carefully transferred the blue ink to the bottom of the birth certificate. As a final touch, he scrawled an indecipherable signature inside the circular stamp im-print. "That's as official as it gets," he said.

Kael shook his head. "That's downright scary."

"But convenient, *n'est-ce pas?*"

Kael delivered the birth certificate and the photos of Josie, which Nasseef had cropped at no extra charge, to Stan Pulaski, who said, "That was fast."

To which Kael replied, "Even here, the system works sometimes." He asked for a rain check on Stan's offer of an evening of Norman Rockwell Americana as interpreted by a career diplomat: a home-cooked meat-and-potatoes meal courtesy of his bored wife, beer in cans, Ben and Jerry's ice cream, and a violent video. "Maybe next month," he said. "I really have to get back to Bayanga."

"Any more problems with crocodile men out there?" Stan asked.

"Oh yeah," said Kael, "but I'm still alive."

# 40

Kael's final weeks in Bayanga shared the recipe of ingredients for most romantic break-ups: a full cup of melancholy, a pinch of remorse or guilt depending on individual taste, a heaping teaspoon of relief, and a dash of hope for the future. For a while, he'd ache, he'd mourn, and he'd swear off ever working in Central Africa again. He'd recover eventually. One day, probably in less than a year's time, he'd miss the idiosyncrasies of Zenith, Bermuda and Paige, but not those of the idiotic Three Stooges. He'd just as soon forget some things. Back in Alaska, he'd yearn for warm beers and boiled chickpeas, but would prefer to never see another fruity polyester leisure suit. He'd miss Assan, but not CARL. He'd pine for the monkeys, but not the monkey business.

A party was thrown in his honor. It was held at his house. They drank up his beer supply and they ate up his food, but the idea was all Zenith's, Bermuda's and Paige's.

The Three Stooges couldn't attend. They had all been called to Bangui for some serious ass-chewing. Their careers in Bayanga, legal or otherwise, were over. That alone was worth celebrating until Zenith reminded everyone that the new mayor, police commissioner, and sous-préfet would, in all certainty, be just as despicable. Only Paige and her naivete disagreed, but she was fully convinced that their replacements would be just as diseased. A girl could only hope.

Bermuda presented going-away gifts to Kael, Josie and Assan, who had decided to accept Nasseef's offer of employment in Bangui. Each received matching tailored shirts made from African cloth. Viewed from far away, the pattern was a succession of brightly colored vertical stripes, but up close, each stripe was a column of either elephants or gorillas.

Bermuda said, "We thought it was appropriate attire."

Paige said, "We couldn't find any material with parasites on it, too. That would have been perfect."

"Perfectly revolting," added Zenith. "Personally, I don't even think the gorillas were necessary."

Bermuda said, "Try convincing Charles Darwin of that."

Hoping to avoid an all-out species war, Kael said, "None of this was necessary, but we thank you for your generosity. Every time I wear mine, I'll get sick and think of all three of you."

"Promise?" asked Paige.

"Space Scout's honor," said Kael.

"Let's drink to it," suggested Bermuda.

"Now you're talking." said Kael.

Two days later and one day behind schedule, Kael's hangover had finally subsided to a level upon which aspirin had an effect. He arose from his bed that morning and gently barked out the much-anticipated order to load up.

Josie and Assan did all of the heavy lifting. They did most of the light lifting, too, as Kael had enough trouble just carrying around his own thirty-pound head. He strategically placed himself and his cup of coffee out of the path of his pair of enthusiastic movers, who were able to pack up the truck in less than an hour. Ten minutes later, Bayanga was a blurry Liliputian village in his rear-view mirror.

They hadn't gone twenty bumpy kilometers when they encountered a living, breathing roadblock: an elephant. Fifty feet ahead, it stepped out onto the dirt road without warning and ignorant of the laws against jaywalking and the slower reaction time of hung-over human drivers.

Kael's brakes squealed, but the elephant either didn't notice or didn't care. It refused to be hurried, which was unusual behavior for an animal accustomed to fleeing into the safer confines of the forest for its continued survival.

This one, an old bull, surely knew what it was like to be pursued by poachers. His long, inwardly curving, creamy yellow tusks would be worth a dictator's fortune on the black market. The fact that they were still attached to the elephant's face was something of a tribute to his cunning and wiles.

Assan said, "Look at his scar, *monsieur*."

On the elephant's left flank, Kael spotted the familiar backward question mark. "It's Ronald Reagan, the elephant we saw when we first came to Bayanga. Remember him, Josie?"

Josie nodded slightly, not an easy maneuver with one's face pressed tightly against the windshield. "He looks bigger up close."

"Who doesn't?" asked Kael.

Assan said, "He's been in another fight since we last saw him. Look at his left ear. It has three notches, now. Before, there were just two."

"And they look bigger up close," said Kael, hoping but failing to get a reaction out of Josie. As Ron ambled across the road to the other side, Kael was prompted to ask the age-old riddle with a sizeable twist: "Why did the elephant cross the road?"

Josie quickly answered, "To get away from the boy with binoculars, tweezers, and a jar."

"That's a good guess," said Kael. He grinned with the knowledge that his son was a comedic prodigy.

Assan said, "I think I know, monsieur. He's old. His eyesight isn't very good anymore. He's in love... with a naked man who lives on the other side."

Kael laughed. So did Josie. Assan smiled. For a guy who prayed more times in one day than he smiled, it was an above average punchline.

Ron didn't hang around to hear any more silly suggestions as to why he was crossing the road. Kael theorized that animals whose faces were hacked off just for their two front teeth have long ago dropped their sense of humor like a superfluous appendage that only served to slow them down.

Ron silently slipped into the trees. His wide rump was the last to enter. It lingered there at the edge of the forest just long enough to make Kael think that they were being mooned ever so subtly.

The rest of the way to Nola was clear sailing. Kael's headache didn't even get in the way. By the time they stirred up the dust on the Catholic mission's driveway, he felt good enough to ask *Père* Norbert for one of his Irish coffees.

They found their unsuspecting host sitting at his kitchen table. He had a coffee cup in one hand and his Bible in the other.

Kael entered the room first. "Cramming for finals, Father?"

*Père* Norbert looked up over his reading glasses. "Each day is a test of faith, but as long as you believe, you pass." He patted his Bible. "It's guaranteed."

Kael said, "I once tried that believing strategy on a calculus exam. I got a thirty-seven percent."

*Père* Norbert stood up to greet his visitors. "I'm no mathematician, but I'd hypothesize that you should have studied sixty-three percent more, my son." He warmly shook the hands of Kael, then Josie, then Assan. "*Bienvenus mes amis.* Sit down with me. I just made a fresh pot of coffee and there are Cokes in the refrigerator."

Josie and Assan took him up on his offer of cold Cokes, but Kael passed. Instead, he asked, "Did I already miss the noon flight to Ireland?"

*Père* Norbert winked. "It just taxied out to the runway. I can call it back if you'd like."

"If it's no trouble," said Kael.

"Not at all." *Père* Norbert reached for a bottle of Jameson Irish Whiskey. "The Irish, like me, are very accommodating when it comes to drinking." He poured the whiskey into a coffee cup leaving very little room for coffee. "You can add coffee to it if you want, but as far as I'm concerned, if you drink straight Irish whiskey out of a coffee cup, it's still Irish coffee."

The longer Kael stared at the full cup, the louder his head protested. "Why don't you keep that one, Father," he suggested. "I'm driving, and this is one time I'd be happy with a lousy thirty-seven percent of what you just poured there."

"I'll never understand how you Americans became a world power." *Père* Norbert grabbed another coffee cup into which he slowly poured whiskey from the first cup. "Say when."

"When," said Kael. The disappointed look from *Père* Norbert told Kael that he had spoken too soon. "Sorry, but I'm driving, and I'd prefer this not be my last drink ever."

"Excellent choice. Live to drink another day. That's my motto." *Père* Norbert handed Kael his coffee cup. "So, tell me. Where are the Three Musketeers off to today?"

"To Boda," said Kael, "to ask Josie's mother if he can go to America with me." He poured coffee into his cup. Combining aged whiskey with freshly brewed coffee was a discovery worthy of the Nobel Prize for chemistry.

"You're leaving?" asked a stunned Père Norbert.

Kael nodded. "It's time. Assan is a free man and we already got rid of the region's biggest poachers. My work is done."

"I heard what happened."

Kael, who was in mid-sip, tried to appear calm. After swallowing, he said, "You did?"

"Of course," said *Père* Norbert. "They were caught right here in Nola. It was big news. It's not every day a police commissioner and a mayor are arrested, although most should be."

"We got lucky," said Kael, who was feeling somewhat fortunate again.

*Père* Norbert asked, "Did you ever find out what really happened to *Mademoiselle* Molly?"

Kael's response was evasive, but it contained just enough truth and common sense to get him elected to political office. "I found out Assan didn't do it. Neither did the police commissioner, the mayor, nor the *sous-préfet*. And the old crocodile man theory... that was nothing but a crock."

"*Alors*, she really did fall out of her canoe and drown?"

"Yes," said Kael, but he neglected to add that she'd had help. He wondered how serious a sin he'd committed by telling half-truths to a Catholic priest.

*Père* Norbert held his coffee cup straight out at arm's length. "I wouldn't do this for just anyone," he said as he tilted his cup allowing several precious ounces of his expensive whiskey to dribble to the floor. "To *Mademoiselle* Molly and her loyal friends. May you may all find peace."

Kael poured out an equal amount from his cup, too, causing *Père* Norbert to say, "You just can't resist adding coffee to my good whiskey, can you?"

Kael just smiled back.

They didn't say another word for several minutes, not until Père Norbert said, "It's a good thing you're doing."

"Drinking in silence?" asked Kael.

"That," said *Père* Norbert, "and taking your son to America. He'll never become a world class drinker, but he may amount to something worth writing me about."

"We'll put you on our Christmas card list," said Kael.

"I'd like that," said *Père* Norbert. "More than straight whiskey out of a coffee cup."

When the drinks were finished and no one desired a refill except *Père* Norbert, he escorted his three visitors back out to their truck. He shook hands at least twice with everyone who climbed into the cab until only he was left standing next to the driver's-side door.

Through the open window he said, "I send you off with an appropriate old Irish verse: May the road rise up to meet you. May the wind be always at your back. May the sun shine warm upon your face, and the rains fall soft upon your fields, and until we meet again, may God hold you in the palm of his hand."

"That's a pretty big hand," said Josie.

"And it looks even bigger up close," said Kael as he let out the clutch.

Six dusty draining hours later, they rolled into Boda. Even though it was already well past sunset, darkness was being kept at bay by the campfires burning in front of almost every house in the village, including Sapu's. Kael's headlights found her and her sister, Tara, close enough to their fire to roast marshmallows if they only knew what marshmallows were.

The way the pair was sitting on their woven mats, their legs stretched out flat at perfect right angles to their straight backs, reminded Kael that African women had a knack for making any difficult task appear easy. They could hold that position for hours without shifting, without cramps, without complaints, and without marshmallows. Kael wished he'd brought some.

The two women shielded their eyes from the headlights pointed directly at them. Kael clicked on the high beams just to let them know that a foreigner was in their midst. No Central African in their right mind, or otherwise—poachers, crocodile men, crooked politicians, and obnoxious airport baggage-handling *godobés* included—would ever consider shining a light into someone's eyes. Some rules of society had to be obeyed without question.

Sapu understood. She squinted into the bright light, and said, "Is that you, Kael?"

Kael responded by turning off the offending lights and lightly tapping on the horn. By then, Josie, who had been in the center position of the bench seat, had already crawled over Assan and had catapulted himself out the open passenger-side door. He sprinted into the four open arms of his mother and aunt. Kael and Assan then disembarked in a calmer, more orderly fashion, as if the bench seat weren't on fire.

Kael got a welcoming hug and three kisses from each of the two sisters. Assan got two very sincere handshakes. While greeting her guests, Sapu never let go of Josie's hand. She only did so begrudgingly after Tara asked for his help to grab a couple of chairs from inside the house.

As Sapu stood there watching her sister and her son walk together towards the house, she said, "He's gotten so big. Look. He's almost as tall as Tara already."

"He probably eats more than her," said Kael. "I know he eats more than me." When Sapu didn't respond to his eating theory, Kael asked, "Where are your other sisters, Anisé and Ebène?"

"They've gone to visit relatives in Boganangone, which is lucky for you. That means we have empty beds. Are you going to Bangui?"

"Yes," said Kael telling another half-truth. It was getting much easier, but after withholding facts from a Catholic priest, this one seemed far less sinful.

He still wasn't sure how best to approach Sapu on the idea of taking Josie to the States. Before leaving Bayanga, he'd made his two accomplices, Josie and Assan, swear on dual stacks of Bibles and Korans that they wouldn't mention a thing about their intentions until he did first. Josie had seemed especially intimidated by the old World War II warning, "Loose lips sink ships," and Kael's modern interpretation, "A slip of the tongue and we're hung."

Josie had even made up one himself that rhymed in both French and English: "*Les secrets restent bien si je ne dis rien,*" or, "Secrets stay if I don't say." Josie was so proud of it, Kael was afraid that his multi-lingual son would brag about it in a third language to his mother, thereby sinking the ship by a more circuitous route. Yet another father-son discussion had ensued. Kael hoped there would be many more.

Josie and Tara brought out the two chairs. They were positioned next to the fire and Kael and Assan were directed to sit down in them. In Africa, women gave up their chairs for men. They gave up most everything for men, so a chair was no big deal. Sapu and Tara happily returned to their mats, pulling Josie down with them.

"Tell me," said Sapu hugging Josie. "How did you get so big?"

"I don't know," he said. "It just happened."

Kael said, "Show them your pythons."

Josie broke free of his mother's embrace. With tightly clenched fists and strained concentration, he held up both arms in an attempt to show off his bulging biceps.

There wasn't much to see, but Sapu and Tara did what any supportive family member would: they oohed, aahed, and tried to look impressed. Sapu even squeezed the one closest to her and nodded accordingly.

"Now," said Kael, "show them how much you like your pythons."

Josie turned his head to the left and kissed the muscle poking out of his upper arm. He then did the same to the right one. His mother and aunt roared with delight.

When Sapu regained her composure, she asked, "Did your father teach you that?"

"Yes," said Josie, "but that was a long time ago when my pythons weren't as big as they are now."

"Of course," said Sapu. "What else has he taught you?"

"Lots of things," said Josie, "like how to catch an elephant with binoculars, tweezers, and a jar, and what should and shouldn't be flushed down a toilet, and how to shift gears in his truck, and how to fish and swim in the river, and... how to be a weenie." He giggled at his last example.

"Hey," said Kael. "You already knew how to be a great weenie long before I came along."

"What's a weenie?" asked a confused Tara.

Kael pointed to Josie, who drew his finger just as quickly and aimed it at Kael. They both laughed at their private little joke.

Sapu said to Josie, "Those are all very good, I think. And what did you teach him?"

Before Josie could respond, Kael said, "How to be a father."

Josie nodded. "That's true."

Sapu smiled up at Kael. "I can see that."

Assan broke the silence that followed with a rousing, "*Allah akbar.*" He then asked if he could take Josie and Tara to the bar with him to help carry back beers and sodas for everyone. When Kael reached for his wallet, Assan said, "*Non, monsieur.* I have money."

"In that case," said Kael, "pick up something good to eat, too."

"*Oui, monsieur.*"

"Can we get some grilled goat meat?" asked an excited Tara.

"And boiled eggs sprinkled with hot pepper?" asked Josie.

"Anything you want," said Assan. "Just remember that you two have to carry everything."

"Didn't you see my pythons?" asked Josie, a bit put out.

After Assan had left with his two willing porters, Sapu spoke up first: "Were we left here alone for a reason?"

"To talk," said Kael.

"About Josie?"

"As long as we're on the subject, I'd like to take him to the United States with me."

At first, Sapu didn't say anything. She picked up a stick and began poking the fire's dying embers. Sparks flew skyward like thousands of ascending fireflies. Kael hoped that she was simply stoking the coals for more warmth rather than preparing a red-hot poker.

He couldn't imagine what she was thinking. His best guess was that she was in shock and the searing pain she was feeling in her womb was nothing compared to the discomfort he would realize after she jammed that hot stick up his ass. After what seemed an eternity of Kael picturing himself as a human popsicle, she spoke.

"Does he want to go?" she asked.

Kael kept one eye on the stick. "Yes, but I haven't told him about any of the bad stuff, except that he'd be far away from his mother. He's not too thrilled about that, but he's eager to fly in a plane."

Sapu smiled. "He wants to be a pilot, you know?"

"Is that before or after he becomes a soccer star?"

"While, I think. He used to tell me that he wanted to be a pilot so he could fly a plane to the United States and see his father."

Kael added, "Probably so he could kick my ass in soccer."

"I don't think so. He's a boy and for some strange reason, boys miss their fathers."

"Do they miss their mothers?"

Sapu tossed her stick into the fire. "He'd better."

Kael theorized that he'd just been given the tower's clearance for takeoff, but he still felt the need to give his full complement of rehearsed arguments: "He'll go to a good school. He'll learn English. He'll eat nutritious foods. He'll meet the other half of his family. He'll see the ocean and snow and mountains. He'll really develop those pythons of his. He'll play on a soccer team. He'll become a pilot if he wants. And he'll never become a weenie. I promise."

"I know," she said. "It skips a generation."

He smiled at her jab like any cocky boxer would. "Despite my inherited weenieness, I'll take good care of him."

"You'll take good care of each other," she corrected as only a mother could.

He nodded. "And you'll be OK?"

"It won't be easy, but knowing Josie will have a better life in America helps. And I've still got my sisters and their children to look after. It might help if Josie spent some time here with us before leaving for the United States with you."

Before responding, Kael checked to make certain that Sapu's stick had already been incinerated. It had, so he felt like he could speak frankly.

"My work in Bayanga is done. We're going to Bangui tomorrow. And a few days after that, we'll fly to the United States. We came to say good-bye."

He wasn't sure, but he thought he caught her eyes roaming in the direction of the fire. Mercifully, there was nothing there to grab but hot coals.

"What if I'd gone to Boganangone with my sisters? I almost did, you know."

"We'd have searched for you. You're Josie's mother. He loves you. Why don't you come to Bangui with us?"

"What about Tara?"

"She can come, too."

"What about my sisters in Boganangone?"

"Leave a note," he said.

"What if I say no?"

"To what?" he asked. "To you going to Bangui, to taking Tara with us, or to leaving a note for your sisters?"

"To you taking Josie away," she said.

Kael couldn't tell if her question was hypothetical or if she was exercising her right as a woman to change her mind. "I'd say you've been a great mother and after you agreed with me, I'd ask you to give me a do-over to be a great father." When she didn't say anything right away, he cautiously asked, "Any other questions?" He briefly considered adding on some sort of endearment like "my little cabbage," but thought better of it.

"Just one more," she said. "What time do we leave tomorrow?"

"Early," he said. "I'm tired of being late."

Assan, Josie and Tara returned soon after that. They were loaded down with beers, Cokes, orange sodas, and an assortment of night-market munchies: shelled peanuts, hard-boiled eggs, grilled goat meat, fried plantains, and boiled chickpeas. All they needed now, according to Kael, was a Super Bowl with a big Roman numeral after it. No one else got it, but Kael was content with the knowledge that in the not-so-distant future, Josie would.

During their impromptu party, Kael learned from Sapu that Dimassé was in town, so after finishing his two beers and more than his fair share of the chickpeas, he asked Assan to accompany him to Dimassé's house. Josie stayed behind with the women and food, not necessarily in that order.

On the way over, Kael explained what Dimassé's role had been in the plot to get Assan released from prison. "Without his help," said Kael, "I don't know if I'd have been successful."

"You'd have found another way, *monsieur*. Allah's plan was bigger than yours and *Monsieur* Dimassé's."

They found Dimassé right where Kael had expected him to be: relaxing contentedly in his Adirondack throne next to his fire and his family. Kael wasn't sure which one gave off more warmth.

He announced their arrival by saying, "Don't you *ever* spend time in Bangui?"

While Dimassé's family swarmed to welcome their visitors, he answered above the din, "Only long enough to pick up my paychecks."

The wives passed Kael around like three winos sharing a bottle of Ripple. They were more genteel with Assan, who was, after all, just a first-timer. If he ever visited a second time, though, he would be guzzled down with drunken abandon.

Two empty chairs magically appeared next to Dimassé. Before sitting down, Kael introduced two men who had never before met, but whose lives had connected to save his own.

"Assan, this is Police Commissioner Dimassé, a bad fish farmer, but a good letter writer. Dimassé, this is Assan Séléman, quite possibly the worst Christmas present unwrapper ever, but the best thing to come out of Nola since my friend Molly."

"I'm not a bad fish farmer," Dimassé said in his own defense. He held out his hand. "I just had bad advice from our American friend here."

Assan gave Dimassé the traditional handshake of respect. "And I keep telling *Monsieur* Kael that I'm not really a bad gift unwrapper. I just need more practice."

Dimassé nodded emphatically. "It appears that our only mistake was in choosing with whom we associated."

"That's it, exactly," said Assan.

Kael just smiled. He let the two of them have their fun at his expense. He was glad that they had clicked. It seemed only right, as if Allah's plan was bigger than Kael had envisioned. Fate, he'd once heard, led the willing and dragged along the unwilling. He and Assan sat down.

Assan leaned forward in his chair. "I wanted to thank you, *monsieur*, for your letters of support to the *préfet* and the police commissioner in Nola."

"No need for that," said Dimassé. "If you helped catch Bayanga's police commissioner up to his neck in illegal ivory, we're even. That man has been my enemy for many years."

"Commissioner Yakonomingui and I were just beginning to have that kind of meaningful relationship," said Kael. As an afterthought, he asked, "What will happen to him?"

Dimassé shifted in his chair. "That very question is being negotiated in Bangui. He's telling all to save his own skin. I think it's safe to say that his days as a policeman are over."

"Not unlike you," said Kael sarcastically.

"Watch it," said Dimassé. "I can still have you arrested and thrown out of my country."

"On what charge?" asked Kael. "Sanity? No one would believe you. Besides, I'm leaving voluntarily anyway."

"You're leaving?" asked Dimassé.

Kael nodded. "Assan's free. Commissioner Yakonomingui isn't. So unless you have other prisoner exchanges you'd like me to perform, my work is done here."

"You can't leave," said Dimassé. "My wives won't allow it."

Kael laughed. "A few seconds ago, the big bad Bangui police commissioner was threatening to throw me out of his country."

Dimassé shrugged his shoulders. "My wives wouldn't allow that, either."

Kael shook his head in mock disgust. It was the pitied look every guy gave another when he learned who really wore the pants in the family. "Would your bosses let me go if I took Josie with me? To live in the States, I mean."

"Really?" asked Dimassé. "Because I think I could sell that one." After Kael nodded in the affirmative, Dimassé cried out, "Antoinette! Bernadette! Collette! Kael is taking Josie to the United States, and to celebrate this wonderful news, he wants to buy you all beers tonight."

While the women screamed their approval, Kael leaned in toward Dimassé. "I didn't realize that I was the one buying what you were selling."

Dimassé smiled before climbing back up on his soapbox. "He says two a piece!"

Amid the ensuing pandemonium, Kael closed his mouth and opened his wallet. Despite rumors to the contrary, CARL was alive and well and partying in Boda with Dimassé's wives.

Early the next morning, after a continental breakfast of coffee, *beignets* and aspirins, Kael pointed the truck in the general direction of Bangui. With Josie, Sapu, and Tara sitting atop the stacked suitcases in the back and all three waving enthusiastically to the passersby, they slowly rolled through Boda like a float in a parade. They reached Bangui four hours later.

Kael and his dust-covered passengers drove through *Cinq-Kilo*, the *quartier* striving to be the Times Square of Bangui, but without the electricity-dependent neon. It was a collage of market stalls, bars, cars, trucks, mopeds, pushcarts, prostitutes, pickpockets, and plain ordinary folks who were either walking, talking, or doing both.

Sapu and Tara were dropped off to stay with an uncle. They took Josie with them. Kael didn't protest. This was Sapu's chance to say good-bye to her son. And Kael knew that in a day or two, Josie would yearn for a flush toilet, if not his father.

Assan disembarked a little farther down the road. He had family there, too. Every Central African had at least one relative living somewhere near *Cinq-Kilo*. Most had come looking for a better life. Few had found it.

Kael checked into a room at the Minerva Hotel. He cranked up the air conditioning and then went back downstairs to the bar to wait until the temperature in his room dropped into the double digits. He drank his beer while chatting with a prostitute who could have posed on the cover of *Vogue* magazine. He politely declined her offer to accompany him back up to his room.

After a short siesta alone, he would begin to attack his list of errands. He had to pick up Josie's passport, he had to purchase their plane tickets, he had to exchange money, he had to acquire exit papers, and he probably had to do things he hadn't yet thought of. In Bangui, a list that big could take weeks, maybe months. Kael was determined to make it all happen in less than seven days. Others might have scoffed at such a fanciful idea, but Kael had a secret weapon: *Garage* Nasseef, the one-stop shopping place.

Throughout the next five days, Nasseef was able to catch whatever curve ball Kael threw at him. He had connections with the airlines, for a small administrative fee, of course. Kael didn't complain. In just three days, he had two confirmed one-way tickets, window and aisle seats with an empty one in-between, from Bangui to Paris to New York to Washington, D.C. Nasseef had even asked if Kael and Josie had any special meal requests.

"Anything but sardines," Kael had answered.

Two days later, after an additional administrative fee, Nasseef delivered to Kael all the paperwork necessary for a foreigner and his son to exit the country. Kael didn't know if they were the actual documents or expertly crafted forgeries fabricated in the dark of Nasseef's cluttered office. Kael thought the indecipherable signatures inside the ink stamps looked suspiciously like the one at the bottom of Josie's fake birth certificate, but he didn't ask. It would have been impolite.

For one more administrative fee, Kael exchanged his money at Bank Nasseef. He received mostly American dollars, but accepted a few French francs for their short layover in Paris. None of it looked confederate. Out of curiosity, Kael compared the signatures of the Secretary of the U.S. Treasury with those on his exit papers. There were no similarities.

Stan Pulaski had come through, too. He presented to Josie a true blue American passport. Kael was pretty sure that it was the real thing, especially when Stan said that there was no extra administrative fee to pay.

Exactly one week from the day Kael and Josie arrived in Bangui, they found themselves at the airport shoving past the *godobés* to get to the Holy Grail: the one overwhelmed ticket agent on the other side of the check-in counter. Kael led the way while Josie followed in his wake. As instructed, Josie sometimes pushed when his father's progress slowed. When Kael saw an opening, he filled it. They completed the first, but most difficult leg of their journey in less than twelve minutes. Kael told Josie that it was because of teamwork and big pythons.

They checked their bags, showed their passports, and were told that their exit papers were all in order. After hearing that, Kael began to breathe normally again.

Sapu and Tara waited off to the side. They tried to put up a unified brave front and as long as one was stoic, so was the other. But whenever one sister got just a little bit weepy, the other soon followed. Either both were fine or both were sobbing. They were like mirror images of one another, and the one playing the role of the reflection had no choice but to copy exactly what her twin did.

Now bag-less except for their carry-ons, Kael hustled everyone upstairs to the bar to await the announcement to board the airplane. He ordered beers and sodas while Sapu and Tara held Josie between them. The mother and the aunt each claimed an ear into which they whispered final instructions. Like a dutiful son/nephew, Josie just kept nodding yes.

Nasseef showed up with Assan, who would drive Kael's truck back to the garage to await his replacement. Assan had already completed five full days at the garage. Both he and Nasseef seemed happy with the arrangement. Nasseef even announced in front of his newest employee and everyone else in the bar, "I don't know how I ever survived without him."

Kael said, "I know exactly what you mean." He gave the truck keys to Assan.

Assan pocketed them and then presented a going-away gift to Kael. It was even wrapped in shiny silver paper and tied with a red ribbon.

"Should I open this now?" asked Kael.

"*Oui, monsieur.*"

Kael handed the gift back to Assan. "You do it. You said you needed the practice."

Assan accepted the challenge. With one mighty tear, the gift burst forth: a lavishly embroidered Muslim *bubu* with matching drawstring pants. The white linen material with rich ivory-colored embroidery was a far more elegant ensemble than the cheap cotton imitation Kael had given Assan for Christmas.

"It's from the holy city of Mecca," said Assan. "I asked one of my uncles to bring it back from his pilgrimage for me."

"Then you should keep it," insisted Kael.

"*Non, monsieur. Allah akbar.*"

Kael raised his eyebrows the way stunned parents did when their angelic children back-talked to them for the first time. He had heard Assan praise Allah many times before, but he couldn't recall ever hearing Assan respond negatively to one of his bossy suggestions. They grew up so fast these days.

"What's Nasseef teaching you at that garage of his?"

"Many things, *monsieur.*"

"Are any of them legal?" Kael winked in Nasseef's direction.

"*Oui, monsieur.*" Assan pushed his gift back into Kael's hands. "This is yours, *monsieur.* I've never worn it. I only asked for it because I didn't think I would ever have the opportunity to make my own holy pilgrimage to Mecca. But now, thanks to you, I know that one day I will. *Monsieur* Nasseef has even offered to help."

"As long as it doesn't interfere with his work schedule at the garage," joked Nasseef.

This time Kael accepted the generous offering. "*Merci*, Assan."

"*De rien, monsieur.*"

"No," said Kael finding a place for it in his carry-on backpack. "It's more than nothing. It's something very special."

An out-of-breath Stan Pulaski showed up. "I really need to start an exercise program. That run from the parking lot to the bar seems to be getting longer. Sorry I wasn't here earlier. Do you need any embassy assistance checking in? I'm here to serve."

Kael held out his glass. "Then fill it up. We're all set."

Stan picked up one of the open bottles of beer on the table and poured. "My day job should be so easy. By the way, you got a last-minute message from Dr. Cinzano. I hope it makes more sense to you than it did to me. He says that there's no replacement for you yet. He's been too busy searching in all the wrong places. He wishes you a bon voyage and he'll see you in D.C."

Kael knew exactly what Nick meant: Mitch's body hadn't been found. He thanked Stan and invited him to sit. There were plenty of extra chipped glasses to go around.

Ten minutes later, the party reluctantly broke up to allow Kael and Josie to board their flight to Paris. But first, all pitched in to chug what beer and soda was left. Next, everyone's bloated stomachs sloshed their way back downstairs to the one and only gate.

When they reached the point where only ticketed passengers could proceed farther, Kael and Josie stopped for handshakes, hugs, and three-cheek kisses. Kael got so caught up in the frenzy that he found himself hugging a complete stranger. He apologized and then told a teary-eyed Sapu, "She didn't mean anything to me."

Sapu didn't get it. She'd left her sense of humor back in Boda, right where she was probably wishing she'd left her son.

Kael held her, letting his shirt double as a handkerchief. "I'll take good care of him."

"I know," she sobbed. Just don't let him forget me."

Kael pulled her face close to his so that her nose was touching his. He looked straight into her wet eyes and said, "Of course not, Agnes."

She managed a smile before pinching him on the soft skin just above the elbow. He was sure he'd have a bruise.

Before he could retaliate, she dived back into the crowd, probably to find Josie for one last embrace, not to mention a pinch if he got mouthy with her. Kael was looking around at all the unfamiliar faces when he spied one that wasn't: that of Dimassé.

"It must be payday," Kael said above the roar of the rabble.

"Probably not for another three or four months," joked Dimassé, who was all too familiar with his country's inability to make payroll on a regular monthly basis.

"What are you doing here?" asked Kael. He reached out to shake a hand he assumed he'd already shaken for the last time.

Dimassé grabbed the offered hand and used it to help wedge himself past the last two people blocking his way. "I brought you a surprise."

Dimassé stepped aside, allowing another man to take his place. The stranger didn't move on. He just stood there... smiling.

It took Kael's synapses a few seconds to connect. The man before him had aged ten years. He was no longer a skinny kid who weighed one-hundred-and-thirty pounds, one hundred of which was attitude. He was a man now.

"Bart?" Kael asked tentatively.

The man's smile got bigger. "*Oui, monsieur.*"

Forsaking the traditional handshake, Kael grabbed Bart by his broad shoulders and yanked him in like a bear mauling its hapless victim. Bart didn't struggle. He chose instead to squeeze his attacker just as hard, maybe even harder. The guy had some pythons.

When they separated, Kael glanced over at Dimassé, who was beaming with pride. Bart had gotten his father's smile, which took up the entire lower half of their faces, but Dimassé had gotten back much more from his son.

"Nice surprise," said Kael, who thought he saw the beginnings of a tear forming in one of Dimassé's eyes. He couldn't tell for sure because Dimassé turned away. Kael doubted that the criminal element of Bangui knew that they had such a sensitive police commissioner.

To Bart, Kael said, "I hear you've become very successful."

"*Oui, monsieur.* I'm a fisheries expert with the Food and Agriculture Organization. I'm making enough money to pay back my father for all those fines he had to pay for me when I was younger."

"I'd say he got his money's worth," said Kael.

Assan politely interrupted them to say that it was time for Kael and Josie to board their plane. Kael and Bart vowed to write. Dimassé promised to take Sapu and Tara back to Boda.

Assan ran interference to reunite Kael with Josie. When Kael found him, he asked, "Are you ready for this, kiddo?"

Josie wiped away the tears from his eyes with his bare forearm and said, "Last one to the plane is a weenie."

And with that they passed through airport security, were deemed safe to other passengers, gave their tickets to the agent standing in front of the door, and exited the terminal building to walk across the tarmac to their waiting plane.

Once outside, Kael peered up towards the observation deck where everyone who was staying behind, gathered to watch the plane take off. He found their group of well-wishers front and center, which made him theorize that Dimassé had flashed his police badge to get them there. He pointed them out to Josie. Everyone was up there—Sapu, Tara, Assan, Nasseef, Stan, Dimassé, and Bart—arms waving like they were all fending off voracious mosquitos. Kael and Josie cooly waved back.

Above the noise of the rowdy crowd on the observation deck and the jet engines warming up in the distance, Kael could still hear Assan yelling, "*Salaam aleikum! Salaam aleikum, monsieur!*"

It was the Arab equivalent of *Aloha*, in that it could mean both hello and good-bye. *Salaam aleikum.* Peace be with you.

On board the plane, Josie was enamored with his adjustable seat, the pop-down tray, his reading light, his call button and his personal air blower, but they all paled in comparison when he found out that the plane had a flush toilet. He used it seventeen times between Bangui and Paris. Not even the movie could keep him in his assigned seat. Kael thought they might have to make an emergency unscheduled stop in Tripoli, Libya, to pick up some extra blue-colored toilet water. When the flight attendant asked

Josie if he'd like to visit with the pilots in the cockpit, he asked if he could use their toilet. Kael theorized that his son would become a plumber, not a pilot.

In Paris, they had a few hours to kill, so they took a bus into the city. Josie was more impressed with the variety of cars than with the typical tourist attractions of museums and monuments. It was uncanny to Kael that Josie, who had never been exposed to the Madison Avenue definition of what was supposed to be sexy and attractive, picked as his favorite cars the most expensive ones: Porsches and Ferraris. He'd have to be one successful plumber.

On the flight from Paris to New York, Kael was exhausted. He conned Josie into staying in his seat to play a newly invented version of the license plate game. His job was to look out the window searching for other planes. If he saw one, he was to look at its license plate to find out which state it was from. Kael reminded him that the plates from his new state of Alaska were blue and gold. When he found one, he could wake Kael up.

One hour into his nap, Kael was jolted awake, not by Josie, who had also fallen asleep, but by the resurrection of his dream. Molly and her crocodile man were back. After a month-long hiatus, his head was again filled with an orange and green tie-dyed t-shirt, red sneakers, a violent struggle in calm water, and Molly's melodic screaming before she sank below the surface. Why was it back? He'd freed Assan. He'd killed Mitch. He'd done the right thing this time with Josie. So why was she back? Had CARL stowed away for some last-minute hijinks before they reached American air space? Or, Kael pondered, was there something he still needed to do?

He ruminated over that possibility for a good fifteen minutes, but came up with as many ideas as Josie had Alaskan license plates. He flagged down a passing flight attendant and asked her for a beer—her choice—hoping it would help him to think better. Some of his best theories came when he had a buzz on.

Suzi—spelled with an "I"—brought him the beer, a can of St. Pauli Girl, and asked for three dollars, exact change if he had it. Kael wondered if her hair color was found anywhere in the natural world.

He fished through his wallet for some singles. He found three ones and he also discovered what he thought might be his little bit of unattended business: the letter from Molly's parents to her that he'd found in the post office box in Bangui. He'd never forwarded it. He'd stuck it in his wallet with good intentions, but a bad memory.

He unfolded it and looked at the return address in the corner: 5029 First Avenue

South, Minneapolis, Minnesota. He could always mail it when they arrived in New York. That would be easy enough. Those overpriced airport boutiques sold envelopes and stamps. He just had to drop it in one of the mail slots at JFK before they boarded their flight for Washington.

Deciding that that would be his new plan of action, he reached for a congratulatory plastic glass of beer that was sitting on his tray. The half-full can was there, too. He'd always liked the St. Pauli Girl label of a buxom blond beer maiden. St. Pauli. Wasn't that the city right next to Minneapolis, but spelled with and "I" just like Suzi? Close enough.

Kael's mind, like those of all great theorists, started to make connections that seemed farfetched to those of a more common sense. St. Pauli Girl beer, a letter that needed to go to Minneapolis, which just so happened to be the Twin City of St. Paul, and a recurring dream about a blond Minneapolis girl. It was more than a weird coincidence. He'd based past theories on a lot less.

Right then and right there, he came to a nutty decision: he and Josie were going to Minnesota. He'd hand deliver the letter to Molly's parents and he'd visit her gravesite. He'd tie up all the loose ends once and for all. This time, he'd do with the letter what Molly had told him to do with Josie ten years earlier: he'd go all the way. Maybe that would put an end to this crocodile man nonsense still rattling around in his head.

Just then, Suzi came back. She placed two small packets on Kael's tray.

"Nuts," she said.

"I certainly am," said Kael.

# 41

Kael was afraid that changing the airline tickets he'd acquired through Nasseef would be like Suzi letting her hair grow out to its original color: it could be done, but it would take some time. After being in Africa, he'd forgotten how helpful the people on the other side of the counter could be. The ticket agent in New York patiently searched for and found a flight to Minneapolis leaving in an hour. She also booked Kael and Josie on a flight the following morning from Minneapolis to Washington, D.C. She credited their New York to Washington fares towards the increased cost. She reserved them a rental car in Minneapolis, though she couldn't fulfill Josie's request of either a Porsche or a Ferrari. She accepted Kael's credit card and in less time than it took to get ripped off in Bangui, handed him two boarding passes to Minneapolis. Not one rubber stamp was required throughout the entire process. God bless America.

Josie didn't mind the detour. He got an extra flight out of it and was told that there were flush toilets throughout the Twin Cities metropolitan area.

With a new travel itinerary in hand, Kael tried calling Nick at the office only to get his voice mail. He left a short message telling him about the change in plans and that he'd see him in less than twenty-four hours. After hanging up the phone, Kael and Josie boarded their flying toilet bound for Minneapolis.

Minnesota was known as "the Land of Ten Thousand Lakes," but to Kael and Josie, who had just come from Africa, it was "the Land of the Wind-Chill Factor." When they landed, it was three degrees with a wind chill of minus thirty-four. The ground was already covered by a half-foot of snow, and according to their pilot/weatherman, more was on the way.

Kael and Josie retrieved their bags from the carousel, and right there in the middle of the terminal, began layering on as many cotton garments as they could. When they were done, their luggage was considerably lighter.

At the rental car desk, they got a Chevy Cavalier. Kael explained to Josie that they were lucky since it handled much better in the snow than a Porsche or a Ferrari. The agent agreed. She gave Kael a street map, and circled in red pen where to find 5029 First Avenue South.

"It's right near Washburn High School," she said. "That's a good landmark to ask for if you get lost, but that won't happen here. All the streets in Minneapolis run east-west, and are numbered sequentially. All the avenues run north-south and are either numbered sequentially or are in alphabetical order. If you know your ABC's and how to count, you'll be fine. Everything makes sense."

"What if I just came from a place where nothing made sense?" asked Kael.

"Wisconsin?" she asked.

"No," said Kael wondering what she meant. "How about hotels near Washburn High?"

"There's a nice bed and breakfast just a few blocks away at Fifty-first and Nicollet." She circled it on Kael's map. "It's called Elmwood House."

They found 5029 First Avenue South right where the map showed it would be. It was a nice white stucco with blue trim in an upper-middle-class neighborhood. Kael wondered if this was where Molly had grown up.

When they knocked on the door of the enclosed front porch, a woman the right age to be Molly's mother came out of the house. Clad in jeans and a bulky sweater, she was comfortably dressed for sitting in front of a roaring fire. She briskly walked across the porch in sheepskin-lined slippers and pushed the porch door wide open. Seemingly fearless of the two strangers on her stoop, she stood there with arms wrapped around her torso more for warmth than protection.

She said, "Come on to the porch, boys. It's too cold to talk with that door open."

Kael and Josie did as they were told. She closed the door behind them.

"Do you want to shovel my walk for money?" she asked.

"No," said Kael, who suddenly realized that with no winter coats and with socks on their frozen hands instead of mittens, they probably looked homeless. In a weird way, they were. He removed one of his four socks, reached for his wallet, and extracted the letter. He gave it over to the woman without saying a word.

"Special delivery?" she asked.

"You could say that," he said.

After unfolding it to reveal the addressee and the sender, she gasped ever so slightly.

"Oh my God. I sent this to my daughter." She clutched it with both hands against her chest. "Do you work for the post office?"

"No," said Kael. I was a friend of Molly's."

"Then why are we standing out here freezing? Let's go inside and sit by the fire. You boys can take your... um... shirts and socks off."

The inside of the house was tastefully decorated in a rustic northwoods cabin motif. Antique duck decoys were everywhere and for some strange reason, Kael got the distinct impression that they had all been carved by someone in the family and lovingly kept up to be passed on to future generations.

They were led to the back of the house where the smell of wood smoke was stronger. The room where they finally settled was three walls of floor-to-ceiling book shelves and a fourth wall that was taken up by a massive stone fireplace, which was the focal point for all the furniture. The mantel was big enough to sleep on, but one would have to first remove the twenty-plus framed family photos sitting up there in order to stretch out.

Kael recognized many of them to be Molly in various stages of development. Her hair had been even blonder as a kid. In one, she was probably younger than Josie, maybe eight or so, she was cuddling on a couch with a stuffed animal. The animal was a crocodile.

The woman introduced herself as Ann McGinley, Molly's mother, and before Kael could say who they were, she asked her guests if they would like some coffee or cocoa.

Kael said, "A coffee for me, Kael Husker, and a cocoa for my son, Josie."

"I know those names." Without further explanation, she left to fulfill her promise of hot beverages.

Kael and Josie peeled off a few layers of clothing. Then they sat on the distressed-leather couch facing the fireplace. Josie was confused that the McGinleys could have a fire inside their house and that it wasn't even used for cooking.

Kael said, "If you think that's strange, just look at what's coming into the room." He pointed toward the doorway.

Josie followed his father's finger. "What is it, a rat with curly hair?"

Kael laughed. "It's a dog called a toy poodle."

The poodle, not much bigger than a softball and about as heavy, hopped up on the couch between Kael and Josie. It decided Josie was the more comfortable of the two, so it curled up contentedly on his lap. Josie didn't know what to do. He tentatively touched the bouffant hair sitting on top of the poodle's head like a fez. When the dog didn't growl or snap back, he gently stroked his new companion's tiny body. The dog licked Josie's magic fingers.

"I think he likes me," he said.

"Yeah," said Kael. "There's nothing like the relationship between a boy and his rodent."

Mrs. McGinley returned with a tray holding three steaming mugs, a sugar bowl, and a creamer. She set it down on a nearby ottoman. "I see you've already met Tiger. He's our watch dog, meaning he watches people come and go through this house."

Kael wondered if Tiger watched because he was waiting for Molly to return. Dogs remembered, even ones that looked like another species.

After everyone got their mug and Josie swore that he wouldn't spill his all over Tiger, Kael told Mrs. McGinley how he had come upon the letter in Bangui. He expressed his sympathies over Molly's death without revealing how she had actually died. He didn't think her parents needed to know that part, especially since that would mean confessing to his role in Mitch's demise. Their daughter was dead. Would their pain be diminished knowing she'd been murdered? He didn't think so.

When he informed Mrs. McGinley that he and Molly had been Peace Corps volunteers together, she said, "I know. Unlike some mothers and daughters, like my mother and me for instance, Molly and I talked. It wasn't always like that, mind you, but since she moved back here to get her doctorate at the University of Minnesota, we became best friends. That's what I miss most. No one else wants to share their secrets with me."

Kael certainly didn't. "How about Mr. McGinley?" he asked.

"Thank goodness he doesn't have any. He simply doesn't have the time. He teaches biology at the U, which he's been doing for over thirty-five years. And when he's home, he carves those darn ducks of his, which he's been doing since he was a teenager. His only secret is how he managed to bag me. I'm still trying to figure that one out. More coffee?"

"No, thanks," said Kael, "but you could give me directions to the Elmwood House B&B and the cemetery where Molly is buried. Josie and I would like to pay our respects before we leave tomorrow morning."

"That's sweet," she said. "The Elmwood House is nice, but I have a better idea. Why don't you and Josie stay here tonight? We have plenty of room and Mr. McGinley would love to hear about your work in Africa. He'll be home for supper in about a half-hour. I always make extra. Tonight it's lasagna. Do you like Italian food?"

"I like it. Josie wants to marry it. Are you sure you made enough?"

"There's plenty. I've got garlic bread and I'll toss a salad, too. What time do you fly out in the morning?"

"Eleven," he said.

"That's perfect. You can stop by the cemetery tomorrow. It's so pretty in the morning."

Kael couldn't refuse her Midwestern hospitality. She probably wouldn't accept no for an answer, anyway. If she could no longer talk to Molly, she'd do the next best thing: talk to Molly's friends, whether they wanted to or not.

Shortly thereafter, Mr. McGinley arrived home wearing a rumpled trench coat and carrying a well-worn brief case big enough to hold a week's worth of clothes. He didn't seem surprised to find two strangers in his house and two extra places set at his dinner table. He was tall and robust for what Kael guessed to be fifty-something, but was probably closer to sixty-something. Spending the bulk of his days surrounded by twenty-somethings probably slowed the aging process, according to Kael's latest theory.

Mr. McGinley introduced himself as Mike. When informed that Kael was an old friend of Molly's from Africa, he asked, "Were you there when she died?"

"No, sir, I wasn't." Kael didn't add that she'd been with him ever since.

Mr. McGinley seemed to deflate. It was obviously not the response he'd hoped for. Mothers wanted their daughters back. So did fathers, but next on their list, they wanted answers.

In a matter of seconds, he switched roles from grieving father to perfect host. He asked, "Would you like some wine with dinner? Molly liked to have Chianti with her mother's lasagna."

"That would be nice," said Kael.

The meal that followed was delicious. So was the Chianti. Like Molly, it was bold and full of flavor. The talk around the table was mostly about her. The subjects of Africa and Alaska came up, too, so Kael threw out his theory that the two places were more alike than different. Mrs. McGinley enthusiastically jumped on board. Mr. McGinley, on the other hand, would only say that it was "an interesting hypothesis."

Mrs. McGinley asked, "Does Alaska have music similar to what Molly was studying in Central Africa?"

"Not exactly," said Kael, "but my theory isn't exact, either. There are traditional songs by Native Alaskans, and they're as culturally significant to Alaska as Molly's Pygmy music is to Central Africa."

Mrs. McGinley turned to her husband. "Isn't that amazing, Mike?"

"Very interesting, dear."

"After dinner, we should let Kael listen to some of Molly's recordings."

Mr. McGinley said, "Don't torture our guests, dear. I loved my daughter very much, but I didn't love her taste in music. That stuff of hers is weird."

"I think it's beautiful," she said. "Besides, I thought Kael could listen to that talking on the one tape and tell us what Molly and her Pygmies are saying. He understands their language."

"I could try," interjected Kael.

"OK," said Mr. McGinley, "but believe me. Molly's stuff is much more palatable with alcohol. The Chianti's finished, but I can get us some beer. There's a six-pack in the fridge."

Kael said, "With a beer, I could listen to a life insurance salesman's pitch."

"That might be preferable," said Mr. McGinley.

While Josie scarfed down the last piece of lasagna, his fourth, the McGinleys ran their errands: Mrs. McGinley went upstairs to fetch the tape and a portable cassette player and Mr. McGinley went to the kitchen to get the refreshments he'd promised. He came back first with two frosted mugs and two bottles of beer.

Kael suddenly felt queasy and it wasn't from the wine he'd consumed. Rather, it was from the beer he hadn't yet tasted. He said, "St. Pauli Girl, huh?"

Mr. McGinley poured. "It was Molly's favorite."

"Her favorite, huh?"

"Despite what her mother says, Molly's taste in beer and wine was much more refined than her taste in music."

Mrs. McGinley bounded in with a portable cassette player, which she placed on the dining room table in front of Kael. "I think the batteries are still good in here." Next, she removed a cassette from its clear plastic case, and inserted it into the machine. Before pushing the play button, she said, "We got a box full of these tapes sent to us. They were recovered from Molly's research camp. Each tape is dated in Molly's handwriting. I'd know her numbers anywhere. The one I'm going to play for you is from September 9th."

Mr. McGinley spoke to Kael: "In case you didn't know, Molly drowned on the 10th, at least that's the best estimate anyone could give us."

"I think that's why I like this tape so much," said Mrs. McGinley. "It was her last one. We know that for sure."

Mr. McGinley said, "I don't listen to them as much as my wife, but I'll admit that it's nice having them here in our house. They're not Molly, but they were her passion and that's what we were missing most around here."

Mrs. McGinley lovingly touched her husband's hand before pushing the play button. The music that came out of the single speaker was a sound like no other. The high piercing harmonies of feminine voices bordered on screaming. To Kael, it was the sound modern art might make if it could sing. For all of its foreignness, there was, however, a hauntingly familiar quality. Kael recognized it as the anguished sound made by Molly in his dream, just before the crocodile man pushed her under the water.

Mrs. McGinley asked, "How do they make their voices do that?"

"I'm guessing torture," said Mr. McGinley.

Kael didn't say anything. He was completely mesmerized by the music. When the singing stopped, there followed several seconds of silence. Then, there was a loud click as if the recorder had been turned off, or on. Kael couldn't tell which. The tape kept rolling. After a few more seconds of dead air, Molly's voice came on. Of that, Kael was certain. She was speaking in Sango with a Minnesota accent. The other voices on the tape, as many as four or five, were those of Pygmy men. They, too, spoke in Sango. What they said was incredible. What they said later was something even Kael couldn't have theorized, not in a million years, not after a million beers.

Over coffee the next morning, Mrs. McGinley told Kael that the cemetery where Molly was buried was just ten minutes away and was one of the prettiest spots in the entire city. "It overlooks Lake Calhoun," she said almost as if bragging about her vacation cabin.

"Prime real estate," said Mr. McGinley. He waited until his wife got up from the table to tend to the toast. Then, he whispered in Kael's direction, "People are just dying to get in."

Mrs. McGinley returned with a plate of unbuttered toast. "That joke is almost as old as you are, Mike."

He reached for a piece of toast. "Yes, dear. Do we still have any homemade jam?"

Kael didn't pay much attention to what was said after that. He hadn't gotten much sleep. He hadn't dreamt about Molly, but he'd thought about her while he lay awake in her bed most of the night. He was still hung over from what he'd heard on the tape the night before. He'd given a false translation to the McGinleys. Molly and the Pygmies weren't really discussing the origin of the song and the meaning of the lyrics, as he'd said. He didn't tell what he'd heard because he wasn't sure what it all meant. He did have a theory, though.

After breakfast, Mrs. McGinley gave them some winter clothes from a box. Each got a hat and a pair of gloves. In Molly's closet, she found an old sweater for Kael and a nice down ski jacket for Josie.

When Kael offered to send them back, she said, "Don't be silly. We'd just give them away to strangers, eventually." On the porch, she gave big hugs to her departing visitors.

318

"Lakewood Cemetery is a big place. It's easy to get lost in there. If you do, just look for Hubert Humphrey in the northeast corner. He and Molly are practically neighbors."

Lakewood Cemetery was surrounded by a sturdy wrought iron fence any maximum-security prison would have been proud to own. Kael and Josie followed it around until they found an entrance. They drove past marble monuments of varying sizes and symbolism. Obelisks, some resembling a shorter Washington Monument, soared toward the heavens pointing out the departed one's new location. Statues of children stood around as if waiting for a school bus to pick them up. There was a life-sized bronze elk standing on a boulder overlooking a small frozen lake. Private mausoleums were constructed to look like miniature versions of the Parthenon or an Egyptian pyramid. Molly's marker was much simpler. It was flush with the ground, but someone had recently shoveled off the snow. The inscription read:

MOLLY MARIN McGINLEY

MARCH 17, 1955 – SEPTEMBER 10, 1990

"WHOM THE GODS LOVE DIES YOUNG."

Kael had never known her middle name. From underneath his sweater, he pulled out two bottles of St. Pauli Girl beer that he'd taken from the McGinley's refrigerator earlier that morning. He'd left a ten-dollar bill in their place. When he'd snatched the beers, he'd noticed on the kitchen counter the envelope he'd delivered to Molly's mother. It was still unopened. He'd wondered if it ever would be.

Josie, well trained in his duties, pulled out his Swiss army knife even before being asked. He opened the first bottle, which Kael took. He told Josie to open the second one, too. Josie did as instructed. After opening the second bottle, he held it out for his father.

Kael said, "Keep it. That one's for you."

Josie beamed. He started to put it to his lips when his father's voice stopped him.

"It's not for drinking," he said. "It's for pouring." With that, Kael slowly dumped out the contents of his bottle all over Molly's grave. Josie did the same.

Kael said, "Chin chin." He wanted to say something more meaningful, but it was too damn cold and he had too many questions icing up his mind. The puddles of beer were already beginning to freeze up and he wanted to know if Molly's thirst was finally quenched and if what had happened in Central Africa was similar to what had happened at Hidden Cove. That was his theory, anyway

# 42

Kael hadn't called ahead, so when he and Josie arrived in D.C., no one was waiting to greet them at the airport except milder temperatures. They were fifty degrees above those in Minneapolis, so they more than made up for the lack of familiar faces. Kael and Josie took a cab straight from National Airport to TRAP headquarters.

They decided to check in with Nick first. Actually, Josie made the decision based on the simple fact that the elevator ride to the sixth floor was longer than the one to the fourth floor where Tallin's office was. Kael hoped Tallin would understand that this was one of the few times when length mattered.

After exiting on the sixth floor, they walked down the long hallway to where Delia sat behind her reception desk. Her caftan-of-the-day was blue and she was as big as the sky. Her smile was unchanged. It was as wide and warm as the Grand Canyon in July.

"Mr. Husker," she said. "It's so nice to see you again. We've been expecting you."

It took a second or two for Kael to remember that African-Americans spoke English and not Sango. "It's great to see you, too, Delia." He shook her hand. Her fingers were as plump as boiled hot dogs.

One bun-less frankfurter with a manicured blue fingernail pointed in Josie's direction. "And who is *that* fine looking young man? Please tell me it's Harry Belafonte finally coming around to ask me to marry him."

"Unfortunately," said Kael, "it's just my son, Josie, but he's single."

Josie stepped forward. He shook Delia's hand and said, "*Bonjour.*"

Delia clapped her meaty hands together. It sounded like thunder up close.

"He speaks French?" she asked. "Harry, move over. Delia's found someone else."

"I'm afraid he doesn't speak much English," said Kael.

"That's even better," she said. "A man who can't speak can't lie."

"We'd find a way," said Kael.

"Don't I know it?" she said.

As much as Kael wanted to hear about Delia's man problems, he had other, more important matters, so he changed the direction of the conversation. "We're here to see Nick. Is he in his office?"

"You missed him by a day," she said reaching for a note on her desk. "He had to go up to Yale yesterday afternoon to guest lecture for one of his old professors." Reading from the note, she said, "He's very sorry that he missed you, but he'll be back in two more days. He said to tell you that his office is open and you should make yourself at home. He suspected that you already had a place to stay in Washington, but if you didn't, you should call his wife. His final instruction was that you should have a good pun for him when he comes back. He said that jokes and riddles wouldn't count. It has to be a pun."

Kael said, "Then I guess we'll go down to the fourth floor."

"To call on Ms. Korne?" Delia said winking.

"That's a yes," said Kael, "especially if you said 'to crawl on Ms. Korne.'"

Delia laughed. "Tell me, Mr. Husker. What's she got that I don't have more of?"

"Me," said Kael. He and Josie returned to the elevator.

\* \* \* \* \* \* \* \* \* \* \* \* \* \* \* \* \* \* \*

Two days later, with Tallin's help, Kael knew everything. It was ingenious, but still illegal, not to mention immoral and unethical. His Hidden Cove theory, which coincidentally supported his other theory that Alaska and Africa were alike, turned out to be true. He even had the hard evidence to prove it.

What he *didn't* have anymore were the disturbing dreams of Molly popping up in his head like rude, uninvited guests. They'd found somewhere else to crash these days. The one on the plane between Paris and New York had been the last one. Then he'd heard her tape. He was concentrating on a new theory to connect the two incidents when he got off the elevator at the sixth floor and bumped right into Delia, who was getting on. His daypack, which he was holding by a shoulder strap in his hand, nearly fell to the floor. He said he was sorry, but she just laughed.

"A little thing like you isn't going to hurt me," she said. She informed him that Dr. Cinzano and his pun were in and that both were in fine form. Holding the elevator doors, she said, "I once entered a pun contest, myself. I sent in ten different puns in the hope that at least one of them would win. Unfortunately, no pun in ten did."

He smiled. "Not bad, Delia."

She let go of the elevator doors. "Feel free to use it with Dr. Cinzano. I haven't told it to him, yet."

Kael walked through the maze of hallways to where Nick's office was. The first time he'd been escorted there by Delia, he'd felt like a lost child. He still felt that way, but at least he knew where he was going this time.

Nick was waiting for him like a mugger in the open doorway. He said, "Pig-Pen!" and hugged Kael so tight that he was lifted right off the ground.

Kael hugged back, but it was more of a survival reaction than a heartfelt embrace. He simply didn't want to be dropped from such a dizzying height.

Nick set him gently back to Earth. "You've lost some weight, buddy."

Kael pinched one of Nick's love handles. "I think I just found it."

"Office work," said Nick. "Where's Josie? You brought him, didn't you?"

"He's downstairs with Tallin."

"He's coming up though, right?"

"In a little while," said Kael.

"Excellent. I can't wait to see the little guy." Nick pulled Kael into the office and closed the door behind them. "You should know that nothing turned up in the search for Mitch's body. I think he's crocodile turds by now."

"He was that when I met him ten years ago."

"If we were all as lovable as you, the world would be a pretty boring place. So let's hear your pun."

"You go first," said Kael.

"All right. A woman has twins and gives them up for adoption. One of them goes to a family in Egypt and is named Amal. The other one goes to a family in Spain and they name him Juan. Years later, Juan sends a picture of himself to his biological mother. Upon receiving the photograph, she tells her husband that she wishes she also had a picture of Amal. Her husband says, 'But they're twins. If you've seen Juan, you've seen Amal.'"

"Not bad," said Kael, "for an amateur. Some friars were behind in their monastery payments, so they opened up a small florist shop to raise the necessary funds. Since everyone liked to buy flowers from the men of God, the rival florist across town thought the competition was unfair. He asked the good fathers to close down, but they refused his request. The money was just too good. So the rival florist had no other alternative but to hire Hugh MacTaggart, the roughest and most vicious thug in town, to 'persuade' them to close. Hugh beat up the friars and trashed their store saying he'd be back if they didn't close up shop. Terrified, the friars did as they were told, proving that Hugh, and only Hugh, can prevent florist friars."

Nick tried not to, but he couldn't help from laughing. "Not bad, but mine was definitely better."

"Then why did you laugh harder at mine than I did at yours?" asked Kael.

"I don't know," said Nick, "but I'll bet you asked that same question in the locker room when you were in junior high school."

"Now that's funny," said Kael.

"Like most comedic geniuses, my best stuff is impromptu." Nick motioned for Kael to sit in the guest chair. "We have a lot of catching up to do." He then plopped down in his own chair on the other side of his desk. "So, you went to Minnesota to see Molly's parents, huh?"

"Yeah," said Kael. "They're nice people."

"You didn't tell them how Molly really died, did you?"

"No. I didn't think it would help."

"That's good," said Nick. "The last thing we need is a lawsuit. Mitch was working for us and I have no doubt that some sleazy lawyer out there could hear that and say that as his employer, we were somehow responsible for his actions. The publicity alone would kill us."

"The McGinleys didn't seem like litigious people to me."

"These days, you never know."

"I guess," said Kael. "How's your Sango?"

"Like my car," said Nick. "A little rusty, but still functioning. Why?"

Kael reached into his daypack and took out the cassette tape. "This is a copy of one of Molly's Pygmy music tapes. Mrs. McGinley made it for me."

"I sent her a box of those things."

"I know. She told me. She was very grateful. I think you should listen to this one." Next, Kael pulled from his daypack a portable battery-operated cassette player he'd borrowed from Tallin. He set it on the desk, inserted the tape, and pressed the play button. It was the last ten seconds of the Pygmy screaming song.

"Weird stuff, isn't it?"

"It gets weirder," said Kael.

When the music ended, there were several seconds of silence, followed by a loud click, and then a few more seconds of dead air before Molly's voice came on.

| Molly: | "Tell me again about the poaching." |
|---|---|
| Pygmy #1: | "*Monsieur* Mitch poaches elephants." |
| Molly: | "How do you know?" |
| Pygmy #2: | "It's our forest. We know." |
| Molly: | "How many elephants has he killed?" |
| Pygmy #3: | "Many." |
| Molly: | "*How* many?" |
| Pygmy #4: | "Many many." |

Kael stopped the tape there. "This recording was made the day before Molly died. I think after she heard this, she went down river to confront Mitch about what she'd learned."

"That sounds like Molly."

"There's more," said Kael. He depressed the play button a second time.

| Pygmy #1: | "And he isn't alone. He has help from others." |
|---|---|
| Molly: | "Who?" |
| Pygmy #2: | "*Les Mademoiselles.*" |
| Molly: | "Which *Mademoiselles*?" |
| Pygmy #1: | "*Mademoiselle* Zenith." |
| Pygmy #2: | "And *Mademoiselle* Bermuda." |
| Molly: | "How do you know?" |
| Pygmy #2: | "It's our forest. We know." |

Kael stopped the tape again. He looked across the desk at Nick. "After Zenith and I discovered some poached elephants, two of which were adolescents with their faces hacked off, she said, 'It's enough to make me quit.' At the time, I thought she meant quitting working in Africa, but after hearing this tape, I think she meant quitting her work with Mitch."

All Nick could do was shake his head and say, "This is unbelievable."

Kael said, "I don't think Zenith and Bermuda did the actual poaching. I do think they were telling Mitch where to find the elephants, though. That certainly would have been easy enough for Zenith. Her research was to identify individual elephants and track their movements through the forest."

"Unbelievable," said Nick.

"I think I know how they did it, too. I saw flagpoles in all of their camps."

"Don't tell me," said Nick. "They climbed to the top of their flagpoles and yelled across the forest to each other."

"No," said Kael. "They weren't flagpoles. They flew their school pennants from them, but that wasn't why they were there. They were radio antennas. Zenith and Bermuda both had single-side-band radios and I found one boxed up in Mitch's camp. I never put the two together until I heard this tape."

"Why would they help Mitch?"

"That's what I had to ask myself. Why? When I found Mitch's stash of ivory, I thought he was killing elephants for himself. But after I found out that Zenith and Bermuda were in on it, too, I figured there had to be more there than simple greed. I came up with a theory."

Nick rolled his eyes. "Not another theory."

"I can't help it. It's like breathing for me or telling lousy jokes for you."

"Cute. So what was your theory this time?"

"The Hidden Cove theory," said Kael.

"The what?"

"Let me explain. First, I accessed TRAP's computer network while you were lecturing up at Yale."

"From where?" asked Nick.

"From the chair you're sitting in right now. You said to make myself at home in your office, so I did."

"You'd need my password to do that."

"I know. It was kind of fun trying to figure it out. What I know about computers could be written on the pinhead of the *sous-préfet*, but Tallin is very user-friendly."

"So you've told me."

Kael said, "We tried your kids' names, Darcy, your birth date, the Latin name for gorilla, *Doli-Ngili* and its English translation of Elephant-Gorilla, Yale, their motto, which we discovered is *lux et veritas*, or Latin for 'truth and light.' I'm guessing you didn't know that."

Nick shook his head no. "I thought it meant 'stodgy and overpriced.'"

Kael continued. "I mean, we tried everything. Finally, I had another idea: your old nickname. *Puru ti kondo*. And it worked."

"Clever," said Nick. "What were you looking for?"

"I wanted to access the Doli-Ngili financial records. I wasn't exactly sure what I was searching for until I found a lot of anonymous donations."

Nick said, "I could have told you that. Some of our more generous contributors wish to remain anonymous and we respect their right to privacy."

"I don't doubt that, but I found something very peculiar. A large percentage of the anonymous donations to the Doli-Ngili project were cashier's checks written from the same bank in Geneva, Switzerland: *Union de Banques Suisses.*"

"The Swiss are a very generous people," said Nick.

"Agreed," said Kael, "but according to TRAP records, those checks were all collected in other cities like Chicago, New York, and Columbus, to name a few. How did they get there?"

"I'm sure you have a theory," said Nick.

"I do now. I didn't until I remembered my first meeting with your boss, Joseph. He mentioned that he had just returned from Europe and he would soon be leaving to speak about primate conservation at the Columbus Zoo. He was hoping to get another plaque to hang on his wall. Do you remember that?"

"Vaguely. Joseph travels a lot."

"And he always brings home a lot of money," said Kael. "I cross-referenced the list of anonymous checks with the dates of Joseph's speaking tours. Tallin found his itinerary in the computer, too. The two lists matched. So, either some rich person from Geneva was following Joseph around the country like a benevolent stalker, which is highly unlikely, or Joseph was writing the checks himself and contributing them to his own projects. We're talking about millions of dollars, far too much money to be explained away as Joseph's philanthropic donations. I know for a fact that TRAP doesn't pay that well, so I think Joseph was involved in the poaching scheme with Mitchell, Zenith, and Bermuda. That's my Hidden Cove theory."

"I still don't get the Hidden Cove part?"

"It's simple," said Kael. "My old hatchery, Hidden Cove, was sold off to a private, non-profit group called the Northern Aquaculture Project, or NAP. Hey, that's pretty close to TRAP, isn't it? Anyway, as a private non-profit, they're allowed to harvest enough salmon to pay their operating costs. That's what Joseph, Mitch, Zenith and Bermuda were doing. They were harvesting elephants to support their own projects."

"I can't believe it," said Nick.

"I can," said Kael. "Where is Joseph this week?" He asked the question even though he already knew the answer thanks to Delia.

"Geneva," said Nick.

"According to his itinerary, he goes there quite often."

"TRAP's European headquarters are located there."

"How convenient," said Kael.

"This is all mind-boggling,"

"I know," said Kael. He reached over and hit the play button of the tape player.

| | |
|---|---|
| Molly: | "Why didn't you say anything before about the poaching?" |
| Pygmy #1: | "No one asked us." |
| Molly: | "How long has it been going on?" |
| Pygmy #2: | "A long time." |
| Molly: | "How long?" |
| Pygmy #2: | "Since the time of *Monsieur* Nick." |
| Molly: | "Did *Monsieur* Nick poach elephants, too?" |
| Pygmy #3: | "Yes, many." |
| Molly: | "How many?" |
| Pygmy #4: | "Many many." |

Kael stopped the tape. He couldn't look directly at Nick, so he stared at the window to Nick's right. "Kinda blows your socks off, doesn't it? I know it did mine."

Nick massaged his temples with his fingertips. "I can't believe it. You and your stupid theories finally got one right."

"You throw enough of them out there, one of them is bound to hit something."

Nick leaned forward. "You've got to believe that I knew absolutely nothing about Mitch killing Molly."

"I believe you," said Kael, now staring farther out at the buildings on the other side of the window.

"He went off the deep end. He wasn't following protocol anymore. He was killing elephants left and right and they didn't even have to have large tusks. I hoped that by moving him down to the Congo, he might cool his jets. Obviously, he didn't."

Kael was finally able to look directly at Nick's face. It was still a nice face, but not the one Kael remembered. "Why Nick? Why'd you do it?"

"I'm guessing you mean the poaching." After Kael nodded, Nick said, "We preferred to call it 'culling the herd.' That's what they call it in southern Africa where they manage their elephants like deer. Culling seemed less despicable than poaching. Basically, there were too many elephants and we needed money. The elephant population in the Doli-

327

Ngili was out of control. They were wandering into town. They were scaring people. They were destroying property. They were wreaking havoc on my gorilla research. There were so many elephants in the forest, they were chasing out the gorillas. The Doli-Ngili elephants had, in effect, become pests that were worth a lot of money, and that was what we were short of. Good research isn't cheap."

"But the lives of elephants are, huh?"

"No," said Nick. "I didn't mean that. I just meant that our research was important, not just in determining best management practices in the Doli-Ngili, but in other parks and reserves throughout Africa. Believe it or not, too many elephants is just as bad as too many poachers. Either extreme will destroy the dynamics of the forest."

"So will too many researchers," said Kael. "Explain to me how you could convince an elephant researcher like Zenith to buy into a plan that involved killing the very species she was studying. It doesn't make sense."

"Sure it does," said Nick. "It supported her research. You've heard me joke hundreds of times about how competitive researchers are. I was one, so I should know. We're cut-throat when it comes to getting grants and press. I could offer both to Zenith. I recruited her and Bermuda both out of Yale and I promised them top-of-the-line equipment and impressive resumes when their research was completed. A few less elephants in Zenith's study group wasn't going to change that."

"It was more than a few," said Kael. "It was 'many many,' if I recall."

"Like I said, Mitch got carried away. The plan was to only cull enough elephants to control the population and to financially support the Doli-Ngili's needs. Our jobs here depend on how much money we bring in to support our work. You have to believe me when I tell you that I never took any money for personal use. No one did. It all went back into the project."

"I'm curious," said Kael. "Did you ever think you'd get me on board this train?"

Nick flashed a sheepish grin. "I don't know. I never would have thought I'd be up in the engine room stoking the fire and tooting the frigging horn." He ran his fingers through his thick hair. "So, what happens next?"

"Good question. I didn't like Mitch. Joseph didn't make a good first impression. I liked Zenith and Bermuda. And for some strange reason—I'm theorizing it's your attachment to Darcy and the kids—I still like you. That makes it three to two in favor of leniency, but it has to end now. No more poaching."

"It ended when Mitch died."

"And TRAP doesn't touch another franc of the money left in the Swiss account. It all gets donated anonymously to some *other* elephant conservation organization. I think Molly would approve of that."

"Joseph wouldn't."

"Then you can tell Joseph that the next plaque he gets will look nice hung on the wall of his prison cell."

"Good point," said Nick.

Kael didn't know what to say next, so he didn't say anything. Neither did Nick. For an awkward thirty seconds, no one spoke a word.

Nick broke the silence when he asked, "Are we OK?"

"I don't know. I was thinking about subjecting you to ten years of the old silent treatment, but I haven't had too much success with that strategy in the past."

"Besides, you'd miss my jokes too much."

"You'd miss mine more," said Kael.

Nick said, "Maybe. Would it help if I said, 'I'm sorry?'"

"It couldn't hurt."

"Then I'm sorry."

"And it'll never happen again?"

"Never."

"Ever?"

"Never ever."

"Swear it on the names of your children."

"I swear on the names of my children, Savannah and Forrest, that it will never ever happen again."

"Good," said Kael, "because I *hate* puns."

Nick smiled. "Can I buy you a cup of coffee?" He got up from his chair. "I'm not talking about the TRAP coffee room. I'm talking about a nice little coffee shop around the corner."

Kael stood up and said, "If we pick up Josie on the way, you can buy him his first cup of over-priced American coffee."

"Anything his little heart desires."

"You'd better hope we don't pass by a Porsche dealership or a toilet store on the way."

# 43

After Tallin was all buckled in, she said, "I think you should write a book."

Kael was busy trying to twist his personal blower open to a level greater than what was available to passengers flying coach. He said, "It's hard enough reading one." He had no success with the blower, so he leaned back to try another daunting task: to get comfortable in the dreaded middle seat on an airplane about to fly across the continent. Josie, in the window seat to his left, and Tallin in the aisle seat to his right, had already claimed his two armrests. What made it all bearable was the fact that soon the beverage cart would be coming up the aisle and later that day, he would be back on soggy Alaskan soil. Seven straight days in Washington had been enough to make Kael think that maybe Texas wasn't such a bad place after all.

Tallin said, "No, really. It's quite a story."

Kael grabbed her left hand with his and brought it to his lips. He gently kissed her fingers and she never realized that he'd slyly reclaimed his armrest by slipping his free right forearm underneath. "No one would believe it," he said, all the while wondering if the same ploy would work on Josie.

"Then write it as a novel."

"Could I be taller?" he asked.

"Sure. You're the one writing it."

"Could I have a normal name like Jim or Bob?"

"Why not?"

"Could I have a harem of super models?"

She smiled. "This would be your only way."

He gave her the evil eye. "Could I have a freckled blonde without an attitude?"

"I'm afraid not."

The flight attendant briefly interrupted to offer a daily newspaper. Kael took a *Washington Post*, though he had no idea how he was going to read it in such cramped quarters. This past week he'd been amazed by the talents of the businessmen he'd seen commuting into work each morning on the D.C. metro. They could read a newspaper folded up to the size of a dollar bill so as not to disturb the personal space of their fellow travelers. That sort of thing was probably one of the elective courses taught at business schools. That was his theory, at least.

Tallin said, "I could help you write it."

"I'm sure you could," said Kael scanning the headlines of his newspaper. "I've always had trouble making good loops on my letters, but you're on vacation."

"Only for the next three weeks."

The plane started to back away from the terminal. Josie abandoned his armrest to concentrate on what was happening outside his small window.

Kael reclaimed his rightful territory, allowing him to open up the newspaper. A small article at the bottom of page three grabbed his attention, which certainly wasn't riveted to Tallin and her literary fantasies. He wanted to forget a lot of what had happened, not write it down for posterity, even if he were taller with a regular name and a harem full of super models. He just wanted it to end, and the dozen or so lines he found in the *Post* helped.

### OESWI REPORTS RECORD REVENUE
By Blair Flax, Post Staff Writer

OESWI, Only Elephants Should Wear Ivory, a small Washington-based conservation group, has reported a record individual donation of 2.3 million dollars. A spokesperson for the organization, Ms. Felicity Feeley, said, "We're in a state of euphoria. Our yearly budget is just under $300,000. To whomever did this, we thank you." The money was donated anonymously, but with one stipulation: that it be used for elephant conservation in Africa.

In a recent Washington Post investigation of D.C.-based nonprofits, OESWI was the top-ranked conservation organization for having the smallest percentage of its budget going towards administrative costs. Anything less than 30% is considered acceptable for charitable organizations. OESWI uses a mere 9%, meaning 91% of its revenues go directly into its conservation programs, which include education and anti-poaching campaigns.

Tallin nudged his arm off her armrest. "So, what do you think?"

"About what?" he asked.

"Earth to Kael. The book, of course."

"I'd rather go fishing."

"What if Ernest Hemingway had said that?"

"He probably did."

# Acknowledgements

Coffee shops have been very good to me. This story was written in coffee shops all around Southwest Minneapolis. And when I met with my old friend and soon-to-be publisher, Chip, to talk about my novel, it was in a coffee shop in Brainerd, Minnesota. So, thank you to whomever started the whole coffee shop craze. They made me a published novelist.

To Chip and Jean Borkenhagen and their publishing company, River Place Press. Thank you for having a cup of coffee with me, for agreeing to take me on, for designing a kick-ass cover, and for guiding me through the publishing maze. You both beat cancer so I can only assume that working with me was not your worst experience.

To my editors, Angela Foster and my brother-in-law who was conveniently an English teacher, Steve Stromme. You both helped me chop out so much stuff that I may have enough unused material for a second novel. Chip, are you game?

This is a story about someone who died way too young. Most of us have people like that who we keep alive in our memories. For me, it is my mom, Joyce; my sister, Judy; my brother, Walt; and my friends Jim, Baba, Ted, Russ, Assan, Kevin, Karen and Raj. They never got to write their stories, but they did inspire mine.

Finally, to my wife and son, Denise and Josh. Thank you for always being there when I returned. Every day, I got to play in a make-believe world, but what was even better was that every day, I got to step back into the real world to be with you two. Ernest Hemingway said: "There is nothing to writing. All you do is sit down at a typewriter and bleed." I hope I didn't get any blood on you.

## About the Author

Phil is a writer, musician, and radical environmentalist—the three things his pragmatic high school guidance counselor specifically told him not to pursue. Phil's writing, whether in a novel, a song, a poem, a children's book, an article, an opinion piece, or even a professional work product, includes varying degrees of his sense of humor, which he thinks is as important to his survival as coffee spiked with Irish Cream, John Prine songs, a good boat, and his vintage Martin D-28 guitar.

At the age of three months, Phil flew to Japan (with some assistance from his mother), and that trip, according to his father, is when Phil caught the travel bug. This desire to see what was over the next hill led to stints as a student of marine biology in Florida, a Peace Corps volunteer in Central Africa, a fishery biologist in Alaska, a grad student in Vermont, a game park director for the World Wildlife Fund in the African rain forest, a ghost writer for Minnesota Public Radio, and more recently, a part-time bluegrass musician and full-time expert on aquatic invasive species (AIS) in Minnesota.

Phil and his wife, Denise, live on a quiet lake in Minnesota where he continues to write, play music with his band—Hans Blix and the Weapons Inspectors—and fight the good fight to preserve the natural world. And yes, he still enjoys doing what others tell him he shouldn't.

philiphunsicker.com